I0658824

# TELLS OF CUTEZAR

## A *UNIVERSAL SCIENCE SHIP*
## *M. CURIE* DISCOVERY

By Jo Bower

## TEN TALENTS PUBLISHING

Ten Talents Publishing,
An
Imprint of Jo Bower
http://jobowerwrites.wordpress.com

Without the following people, this series would not exist:
Troy A. Bower
Jan Mills
David and Charla Martin
Angie and Tom Durrance
Elza Boldman
Jerry Randall
Many friends who read the manuscript and gave suggestions.
My husband, Monty, who tolerated the whole process without needing to read or judge its contents.

## Presuppositions of the
## *USS M. Curie* Discoveries Series

We believe God created the entire universe and all that is in it. Believing that, we must also consider the creation to include all Beings as well as matter.

And, because He creates out of love, God creates a way to communicate with those beings, according to their unique nature.

The *USS M. Curie* discoveries are stories of God's creations and how they communicate with the Universal Creator.

## CHAPTER ONE

"Craig, I'd hold on if I were you," Captain Alan Brodsky counseled with a quiet grin. He motioned to the helmsperson.

Craig reached for the back of the captain's chair as the ship's sudden forward thrust caused exploding stars to threaten an invasion of the very space he occupied.

"Got a problem, Chaplain?" the Captain asked innocently over his shoulder. Forcing himself to let go of the chair, Chaplain Craig Lea slipped his hands into his pockets and bluffed. "No. No problem, Captain." With a smile, he added, "But I gotta admit seminary certainly didn't prepare me for this!"

At the captain's request, Chaplain Craig Lea stood on the bridge of the Universal Science Ship M. Curie. The viewing screen that encompassed the entire front of the bridge afforded a panoramic view of the star system they were approaching as it narrowed from a wide-slung band of stars to individual dots and planets.

Enchanted by the silent gliding points of light appearing even in his peripheral vision, Craig felt pulled into the timeless beauty of space.

"Understand now why I invite our new officers to the bridge on their first year anniversary?" The captain brought him back to the present.

Reluctantly the Chaplain dragged his gaze from screen. "Ummm, yes. Good view!"

Captain Brodsky suddenly leaned forward. "There!" He pointed to a spot on the viewing screen. "There it is!"

Craig's excitement surfaced again as he watched the planet change from a dot to a round ball with distinguishing features as the ship swiftly advanced.

Chaplain Lea's first post out of seminary was Crytis III, a planet on the trade route from which the military shipped equipment and troops all over the southern quadrant. After seven years of ground assignment, he was delighted to discover Captain Brodsky's posting for a chaplain; such requests came only when the spiritual community grew large enough to warrant a full-time position.

A mixture of military and civilian crew manned the Universal Science Ship M. Curie. While military personnel handled operations, civilians took responsibility for scientific and medical functions. The Chaplain, though military, served both communities.

Craig had chosen space travel as his second option in basic, and the fun of using that training still lingered after a year aboard the Curie.

"Standard orbit," the Captain ordered.

"Standard Orbit, sir."

Craig was vaguely aware of the tactical officer's response. The movement of the ship as it responded to the helm and matched its velocity to the gravitational pull of the planet's atmosphere held his attention.

"Security team to shuttle bay," directed the Captain. They silently watched until the shuttle appeared on screen and set course toward the surface of the planet. Captain Brodsky turned to his second in command. "Houng, you have the conn. I'll be in my quarters." Commander Houng nodded and the Captain addressed Craig. "Chaplain, join me?"

No response.

"Craig?"

"What? Yes, Captain?" Craig tore his attention from the planet's blue-green haze.

"My quarters?" the captain repeated.

"Of course, sir."

Over coffee, the Captain got down to business. "I think we'll be here a while. The scientists requested a temporary chapel on the surface after it's cleared by security."

"Okay." Craig hesitated. "Will I be allowed to participate?"

"In the excavation?"

"It is a routine exploration of a deserted planet, isn't it? A training mission for the students?" Craig inquired hopefully.

"I'll see if the scientists will allow an amateur to indulge a hobby and join the dig," Captain Brodsky promised.

For a second Craig tried masking his excitement but gave up. "Thanks, Alan!" The Captain's first name sounded surprisingly gleeful. "I'll get my gear together, Captain," he added more sedately.

"Craig." The Captain stopped him as he started out the door. "That's not a guarantee. We have some real purists aboard."

Craig grinned. "In my profession one needs a certain amount of faith." And the door closed behind him.

Craig found the Chief Science Officer waiting in his outer office.

"I hear you've been on the bridge," Dr. LaShonya Reed remarked she followed him into his office.

Craig grinned. "The Captain was testing the stability of my inner ear.

"He's celebrated anniversaries that way as long as I've been aboard," Dr. Reed replied. "Says it gives non-bridge officers a sense of the adventure and belonging."

"Well, it gave me a sense of disorientation," Craig laughed. "But that's not to say I didn't like it."

She smiled. "I'm sorry I missed it."

Perching on the edge of the modular workspace, Craig put his hands in his pockets and spoke as casually as possible. "What are the chances of me seeing some action when you're cleared to start the dig?"

"Dorinda told me about your hobby. I got curious and looked up your record of finds." Dr. Reed took a seat. "Put your request into the Captain, and I'll see what I can do."

"I've already done that," Craig answered.

The doctor's comm button beeped. She tapped it and answered. "Dr. Reed."

"Dr. Keal here. I need to know what you require for my medical team on the planet."

"On my way," she answered. She paused at the door. "Oh. Craig, you might get your gear together."

"All right!"

On his way to the chapel the next day, Craig heard his name.

"What's going on?" LaShonya hailed him.

"It's Tuesday, group day. I'm due at 1550," he reminded her.

Each Tuesday small groups gathered at the end of each watch for study, teaching sessions, and fellowship.

She nodded. "I missed this morning. The exec committee met." She grinned. "You're approved. But you'll have to dig on your free time. They want a full time chaplain down there."

"The Captain told me that." He shook his head. "The exec committee's a tough test to pass. Thanks for the good words."

"Anytime. But your record of finds didn't hurt." She put her finger against his chest. "Listen close. If this were anything but a routine dig, they would have denied you in a second."

"Okay, message received." He grinned. "How long before work starts?"

"'Bout a week." Smiling at his impatient expression, she explained. "We're all anxious. But security has to complete a physical evaluation. Meanwhile we'll do atmospheric studies and below the surface scans for possible sites. By the time we get down there, we'll know where to set up the station, where to dig, and how deep the ruins are buried. And the students can get their hands on the scanning equipment as well as the surface tools." She started down the corridor.

"Do we have both sizes of lasers on board?" Craig called after her.

"Yes, Craig, you can use a hand laser." LaShonya waved over her shoulder.

"Good!" Craig celebrated, "A hand laser."

Archaeologists used two sizes of lasers in the early stages of the excavation. The ground laser sliced layers of land for sifting or removed layers of dirt covering specific ruins. Hand lasers did close work and cut small blocks of earth. On the lower, diffused settings, they proved perfect for clearing fine particles of dirt from artifacts and faces of buildings.

Craig stepped into the conference room and greeted the assembled crewmembers. Discipline overruled excitement as he began the session.

Two days later, he received a summons to the bridge. He hesitated as the turbo lift doors opened. "Permission to enter the bridge?" he queried.

Captain Brodsky swiveled his chair and beckoned to him. "You can relax the protocol a bit. I just need to know who's on the bridge. All you need to do is announce yourself."

Craig looked around the bridge. "Chaplain on the bridge."

The crew grinned and Captain Brodsky nodded. "That's fine. Welcome. LaShonya has something she thought you'd like."

"'Shonya," Craig greeted her. "What is it?"

Dr. Reed looked up from her science station and greeted him. "We finished the survey of the surface. I thought you'd like to look at this before I go on to something else." She addressed the computer: "Computer repeat display with model."

Walking around the three dimensional planet suspended at eye level, Craig studied the topographical configuration of the planet. The display highlighted mounds that were different from the rest of the terrain.

"These are the sites?" he stated more than asked, pointing out the highlighted areas.

LaShonya nodded. "Are you through with that one?"

Craig walked around it again then nodded.

"Computer, MRI display of tells number two and six." Dr. Reed commanded.

Although the technology had long since been replaced, the initials MRI, magnetic resonance imaging, had become a generic term applied to any three dimensional image of an object's inner parts.

"Impressive," Craig commented as rooms and outlines of artifacts appeared inside the two mounds.

"It's not enough to identify all the layers of the structures, or get a good look at individual artifacts." LaShonya took up her commentary. "But it's enough info to let us limit our actual hands-on sites to one or two and

10

put together the culture and language. Then it's sufficient to generate printouts of the rest."

"The MRI identifies the tells most likely to contain the most info?" Craig asked.

"Exactly." She smiled, pleased at his understanding. "Because we're training, we'll initiate two digs. A lot of the time one's enough, and the rest are left intact."

"There are some weird beliefs out here about disturbing the past," Craig commented.

"And some not so strange," LaShonya agreed. "This way we can satisfy our need to know the past without unnecessarily disturbing other sites." She spoke to the computer. "Laser directional display." She smiled up at Craig. "This is the fine-tuned scan to show the laser techs where the clusters of artifacts lie so they won't destroy anything when they slice the earth for sifting."

"Not much room for error, is there?" he observed, watching the computer draw lines across the model of the two tells.

"True," she agreed. "But the ground laser's guidance system is very precise." After letting him study the image a minute, she spoke to the computer: "Stop display." She turned to him as it disappeared. "We're automatically linking all relevant work done on personal computers to the ship's system so it'll be available to everyone as well as entered into the ship's permanent record. Remember that if you do any personal work."

"Yes ma'am." Craig grinned, doing his best Forest Cabrailes imitation. "Thanks for thinking of me. When does work begin?"

"Security has cleared this area." The captain had come to look over their shoulders. "Monday morning we'll take equipment down. You can set up chapel then. Security will continue their exploration of the planet while we set up shop."

"I'll try to keep busy meanwhile." Craig grinned and headed for the lift.

"Dr. Reed?" Lt. Reecer, the communications officer, looked up from his station. "Private communication for you."

Frowning, she wondered where to take it.

"Important?" Captain Brodsky asked.

"I don't know," she puzzled. "I'm not expecting anything."

"Reecer, put it in the bridge conference room," the captain instructed.

"Thanks." LaShonya quickly entered the adjoining room and touched her comm button. "Ready."

"LaShonya!" The deep voice that filled the room radiated delight.

"Art!" For a second his name was all she could get out. "Ah..." She stuttered, "Where are you?"

"On my way to Sicto Broadcasting Station. I'm presenting a paper at graduation this year." Hurrying through the explanation, he approached the real reason for the communication. "You've been thinking about my offer?"

"Every day," she said softly. "When can we be together?"

"I'll make connections on my way back. You're staying at Thakos six a while, right?" He consulted his computer. "How long you going to be there?"

"At least three months. It's a teaching exercise."

"You have some good students?" He was stalling and they both knew it.

She nodded briefly and got to the point. "Art, can I give you my answer when I see you?"

He grinned. "If it's the right one."

"I haven't said no," she replied. "It'll be good to see you."

"You too." He gave a farewell gesture. "Captain Norman, out. I love you, LaShonya Reed."

He signed off before she was forced to reply. Wandering around the room, she tried to work out her feelings for the fiftieth time since her last leave.

Captain Arthur Norman's ship belonged to a class of "leading edge military exploration ships," as he described it.

They first met two years ago, on the edge of a cliff while hiking the same trail of Mount Szar on Crytis IV, and had been seeing each other as often as schedules allowed. During their first meal together, he had teased, "When the Curie's sent to a planet, we've already been there twice."

With a twinge of humor, LaShonya remembered she'd forgotten to ask Art how many times his "leading edge" ship had been to the uninhabited planet of Thakos Six.
During their last leave together, his offer of a job and proposal about their relationship had resulted in many hours of serious thought.

Art delighted, confused and frightened her. His unusual mixture of flamboyance, logical thinking, flippant humor and sound judgment made him unlike anyone she'd ever met. He exhibited the same basic soundness as her parents who believed in the goodness of man but ignored the existence of the spiritual dimension. Art was solid.
She loved being with him, but became uncertain how she felt when they were apart. Uncertainty was something she didn't often feel, and never liked.

"Why don't I just relax, say yes, and enjoy the challenge of the job and Art's company?" she asked herself. She wasn't afraid of risk, yet something bound her to the Curie. "On a military ship they don't have the luxury of vespers, and perhaps not even an organized spiritual community," she mused as her thoughts rambled.

It didn't bother her that Art lacked a spiritual dimension. She knew he, like her parents, was undemanding in his tolerance and belief in human goodness. He would allow her to live the way she felt was best. She wouldn't admit it to herself, but her lack of concern over their basic difference left her with a disquieting, vague, undefined sense of guilt.

"I could take care of the lack of an organized community, perhaps even teach Art about human spiritual needs," her thoughts continued, "but Chaplains aren't posted to ships until spiritual communities already exist. And of all captains, Art wouldn't request a chaplain. There would be no Craig." The thought startled her. "Why did I think of Craig?" she demanded of herself.

With an impatient gesture, she dismissed the thought and returned to the bridge.

## CHAPTER TWO

"Here, Andez, fasten this to the frame."

Craig unfolded the shutter-like photo responsive panel that turned dark in strong light and clear in the absence of light. He hooked it to the rail driven into the ground and heaved it over a set of ultra-light metal ribs, also attached to the ground rail, making sure the panel slid into the proper grooves on the rib.

"Got it!" Andez Ronger, Craig's Chaplain's Assistant, called from the other side, and fastened it to the rail on his side.

A series of twelve interconnected panel-covered ribs made up the building. Panel number seven contained the opening for the door.

In a short time, Craig and Andez had erected the temporary structure. With a satisfied smile, Andez unfolded the molded plastic doorframe and they snapped in into place.

"There you go, Rev. One instant, ready to occupy chapel and Chaplain's quarters."

A product of the ancient blend of early Spanish missionary teaching and spiritualism of the ancient South American Indians, Andez had problems deciding on an appropriate title for Craig. He'd confessed "Father" didn't seem right, nor did "Chaplain." In the end, they agreed on "Craig" or simply "Rev."

Craig paused and looked around, reflecting on Andez's dedication to the chaplain's work, and his refreshing attitudes and expression of faith.

The open space around Craig was quickly becoming a camp as scientists and security teams together completed the rest of the buildings.

15

By nightfall, all the buildings were in place and calculations of coordinates for the first ground laser cut were in progress.

Before going to his quarters, Craig finished setting up the chapel furniture. Stepping back, he surveyed the finished room.

"Almost like home," he mused.

With living quarters located in the back third of these portable buildings, each scientist or couple lived behind the lab where they worked. Heavy, luxurious, soft-textured curtains acted as sound mufflers and privacy partitions.

Quarters consisted of two rooms, living and bath. The furnishings were "instant beds" (a folding frame with a rigid fabric inset), table and dining room-style chairs, portable climate control devices, and solar lamps. Meals were beamed down from the ship.

As evening came, many of the crewmembers, including Captain Brodsky, joined the scientists as they gathered for vespers following the evening meal.

"As we have often observed," Craig paused and met the gaze of different people around the room. "We can worship in all sorts of places. And we have come to worship in yet another place. I don't know about you, but this may be the most unusual place in which I have worshiped."

Evening vespers consisted of a short lesson followed by discussion, or "dissection" as the scientists called their analysis of it, then prayer and fellowship.

Usually vespers were brief, but tonight the community lingered, drawn together by the strangeness of the place and need for companionship, on the planet known only as the sixth planet from the star Thasos.

Finally Captain Brodsky took the floor and announced, "If anyone has duty, now's the time to go." He waited until

16

the exodus ended and addressed the dozen remaining people. "Several of us must admit this is their first expedition into deep space. There's a military tradition initiating such travelers. Everyone except the storyteller uses virtual-reality headpieces and the first-timer describes their first experience of warp speed while standing at a viewing port. The computer creates the scene as everyone experiences the speaker's description.

"Have you entered the raw material into the computer?" He asked the new crewmembers.

The storytellers nodded as the small headpieces were produced and passed out. Craig listened without any gear, recreating his own feelings on the bridge.

Quantro Smith, a PhD student in documentation under Dr. Oliver Zamwashi, spoke first. "I was standing at the viewing screen in the fifth level conference room, waiting for Oliver to continue orientation."

Looking around the room, Craig could tell by their posture everyone was transported to the conference room. Intrigued, he watched them experience Quantro's wonder.

". . .When blue, red, and yellow explosions came toward me. I wasn't aware we were going to warp speed so, for a minute, I didn't realize what I was seeing. I was slightly light headed and reached out to lean against the window."

Amazed at the listeners' complete absorption in the experience, Craig watched as hands groped for the support of the window.

"When I realized what I was seeing, I got as close to the window as possible to block everything else out. I was propelled through space without a vehicle." He finished and waited for the computer to finish the recreation.

Captain Brodsky removed his headpiece and handed it to Quantro. "Use this while the chaplain describes his experience." He grinned at Craig. "I was there."

17

Quantro adjusted the earpiece, flipped the eye panel into place, and switched the voice module on. He motioned Craig to begin.

"The captain requested my presence on the bridge to celebrate the anniversary of my first year aboard," Craig began. "I was standing directly behind the conn, amazed by the breath of vision the viewing screen provides. The bridge was silent. The peacefulness of the stars gently gliding in front of and around me as far as my peripheral vision could see blotted out everything else. In the background, I heard the Captain's voice but didn't pay attention to the order. Suddenly a bright flash of light disoriented me with a display of fireworks that would rival the New Year Eve's celebration on Tauras V: brilliant blues, yellows, reds and oranges leapt away from me, and then seemed to implode into the very space I occupied.

"I guess it lasted only a few seconds. Seemed more like a lifetime. I, ah… I was completely unprepared for the sudden burst of speed. I reached for the back of the Captain's chair and he grinned at me over his shoulder. 'Got a problem, Chaplain?' he asked innocently, knowing exactly how I felt. I wasn't about to give him the satisfaction of knowing he'd surprised me. I shook my head to clear it, let go of the chair, put my hands in my pockets and bluffed. 'No problem.' When I looked up again, I wondered if I'd imagined it. All I saw was the silent passage of stars."

To better visualize the experience and filter out distractions, Craig had closed his eyes as he talked. When he opened them, it surprised him that several people had pushed their eye panels back, regarding him with amazement.

LaShonya broke the silence. "That was one of the better descriptions we've heard."

Craig looked around with a self-conscious grin. "Words are the tools of my trade."

Captain Brodsky smiled. "I wasn't going to take the ritual to its fullest, but that deserves the highest honor."

"What?" Craig asked LaShonya.

"It means the Captain relates his first experience," she replied. "Put it on." She removed her computer controlled head- piece. "I've seen this before."

Adjusting the headgear, Craig met Captain Brodsky's gaze.

"Ready?" he asked.

Craig nodded and flipped the eye panel into place.

"My first assignment as a young lieutenant was on one of the last of the warships, the USS Eisenhower. Despite the absence of conflict, we maintained strategic defensive patrols of the outer perimeters. I was weapons specialist for the defensive systems, so I was considered bridge crew.

"The viewing screen was half as large as they are now, but they were adequate. One day I was on my back, changing a decaying gel pack when the captain barged onto the bridge. 'Everyone stay where you are,' he ordered. I stayed on my back and looked out the viewing screen just as he ordered warp speed,"

From the upside down world Captain Brodsky created, Craig again felt lightheaded at the sudden speed. He saw the blue, yellow, and red bursts of color, but they were going the wrong direction.

". . . But they were going the wrong direction," the captain was saying. "'What?' I asked myself. I lifted my head and hit it on the bottom of the weapons panel."

Craig saw the panel and felt the pain.

"Then I realized I was still on my back. I arched my neck back so far it made me dizzy, but I watched the whole process upside down. The stars jumped away from me instead of toward me." He paused, and then finished with a boyish grin. "Every once in a while I still get the urge to lay on my back and look out the screen when I know I'm about to order warp speed."

Craig pulled the headpiece off. "These make plain story telling kind of dull, don't they?"

"Yes, but until the perfection of the virtual-reality recreation, storytelling had nearly died out. VR recovered a lost art," the Captain reminded him.

"What's the rest of the story?" Roger Lavera, a graduate student asked.

"We had to break up a minor skirmish on the rim. A couple of traders threatened to take a planet with them in their fight over territory." The Captain's tone dismissed any serious discussion of the mission. "Things like that happen a lot the farther away from a base you get."

Roger accepted the Captain's explanation, but had another question. "Are there any other first-time deep space travelers' rituals?"

"Yes, but most them are not worthy the dignity of perpetuation," Dr. Zamwashi, the tall, dignified director of documentation from The Republic of New South Africa replied in his deep, distinctively accented voice.

"Well put, Oliver," the Captain approved. "But we could have a couple more stories before we call it a night."

It was late by the time Craig pushed aside the heavy curtain and sat down to study the MRI displays. When the computer screen blurred, he requested a printout so he could stretch out in bed and study. The computer synthesized paper and printed the requested documents in one operation.

Part of the printout remained on his chest when he woke up, and the rest lay scattered on the floor. He

20

touched his communicator button. "Computer, time please."

"Good morning, Chaplain. The time is 0650," the computer's voice replied.

Craig ran his hand over his face. "Lea out," he grumbled and grudgingly left his bed.

Freshly showered and shaved, he stepped into what he considered the planet's morning hours. There was a distinct dark time on the planet, but no dawn. It was dark one minute and light the next.

He found a rock and sat down to survey his surroundings.

Everything was flat — the tops of the hills, the sides of the hills, the floors of the valleys — like hand carved sculptures. No rolling hills. No rounded peaks. Everything stood at rigid attention. Straight up and down. The hills were tall enough to change the scenery, with great mesas as tops, long and wide enough to hold entire cities.

Rock.

Everything proclaimed ROCK!

Craig knew that probably wasn't the case because of the different colors brightening the landscape. Layers of crimson, blue, and green twinkled in contrast to the brown sides of the hills and valleys.

"Mineral deposits," Craig mused aloud. "Not exactly hospitable to humans, but not hostile."

He saw no evidence of animal or insect life. Calm appeared to prevail, except for an almost visual presence of static electricity.

Taking the computer from his pocket, he unfolded it to its eight by eleven-inch size and chose the voice module. Aloud he worked on different endings for the evening's lesson. Immediately he became engrossed in the study, and Dr. Cabrailes, the site director, startled him when he called across the compound. "Chaplain, the ground laser's in position. You might as well be part of this." Craig looked up and waved. "Be right there."

"Bring your computer. We're linked into the system," the doctor instructed.

Craig arrived at the tell just as the lecture started. He joined the group of young scientists standing around the portable lectern on which Dr. Cabrailes leaned.

"Consult your computer link on the tell." There was a rustle of movement as they followed instructions. "The top five feet of this tell are debris and soil. Then you begin to see the remains of a structure." He held up his screen and pointed to an area that showed up darker than the debris. "Trace the outline. Looks like we have a triangular structure in the foreground." Heads went down throughout the group as scientists consulted their screens. "Today, we'll cut five one foot deep layers off the top. We'll stop at the peak of the first structure. We'll use the hand lasers to clear the top. Should be a good day's work."

"Forest, why don't we just slice the whole five feet off at once?" Roger asked.

"Three reasons," Dr. Cabrailes answered. "First, the ground laser's tractor beam's not made for big, heavy loads. Transportation is working on that, but it's not quite ready. Second, Daniel wants dirt in all five pits. Everyone can sift at once. Third, Oliver can determine how fast to proceed by the time periods represented in the age span of the artifacts." He looked up with a grin. "His words, not mine. Any more questions?" Everyone appeared satisfied. "Okay, get to it."

Craig joined the group of people around the ground laser.

"Craig." Dr. Cabrailes singled him out. "We could use an extra pair of hands at the sifting pits."

I'll report to Dr. Kobee whenever he's ready." Craig knew he had to prove himself and this tedious job always needed the most helpers.

"Here we go, people. Everyone stand clear." The tech took a final citing on the top of the mound and repeated the co-ordinates to the computer. "All clear," he called again, then spoke to the computer: "Computer, engage laser."

A thin shaft of red safety-light appeared at the top of the tell and moved slowly across the top of the mound. A few stones and rocks tumbling down the mound's sloping sides were the only indication of anything happening.

"Disengage laser," the tech instructed the computer when the light cleared the tell. "Engage tractor beam," came the next command.

Magically, a foot of earth separated from the rest of the mound.

Dr. Daniel Kobee, the artifacts director, appeared at the tech's elbow and pointed to the spot where the earth was to be deposited, apologizing. "I'm sorry I didn't have the coordinates ready for you ahead of time. I'll get them for the rest of the pits, will the tractor beam hold while you do the calculations?" he finished hopefully.

"It should." The tech nodded. He reached for the measuring scope and took a quick look. "I know techs who can take the citing without these," he explained as he laid the scope down. But I'm not that good yet." He gave the computer the coordinates.

The earth floated to the sifting pit where workers were already waiting and hovered a few inches above the ground.

"Computer, release tractor beam," the tech ordered and, with a dull thud followed by soft billows of dust, the earth plopped into the boxed-in sifting pit.

Craig observed the operation a couple more times before reporting to Dr. Kobee.

The artifacts director, a medium built man, mid-thirties, always leaned forward slightly as if pushing time out of the way to make room for his work. Things not related to his work simply didn't register. But an inner fire that fueled enthusiasm and passion for his work made up for his preoccupation.

"Chaplain, I hear you want in on the action," was his greeting. Craig nodded. "You willing to start at the bottom?"

Craig chuckled. "As long as I don't get stuck there."

"Well, when this is done, we'll all move on," Dr. Kobee assured him.

Craig grinned, catching the excitement of the first hands-on day at the site of a new dig. "Give me my equipment, Doctor."

A large sieve and a container of instant silicone that protected the artifacts from oils on human fingers were delivered along with the instructions on how to record any artifacts.

Dr. Kobee assigned him to pit number two.

As soon as Craig sat on the ground, his ability to block out everything around him took over and he instantly became absorbed in sifting.

As expected, the sifters from pit number one found very little. They quickly disposed of the task and moved to pit five. It was the reward for taking the thankless job of sifting the top layer. Craig and the second pit crew proceeded more slowly, expecting to find some artifacts. Perhaps they'd find coin shaped objects or discarded dishes and toys.

"Were there children here? What did they eat? Did they worship something or someone?" Questions. These same questions always invaded Craig's thoughts when he attended a dig.

Rocks. Thoughtfully he filtered a handful of pebbles through his fingers. They all seemed to be the same size. He repeated the action, and then picked up one of the stones.

"It's round." Pulling out his pocket magnifier given to him as a going away gift when he transferred off Crytis III, Craig slipped the rock into the slot and peered into the tiny scope.

"A bead," he said aloud in surprise. A tiny hole pierced the top and a carved line wove its way around it. Although the stone was brown, the carved line revealed a bright blue core.

"Something interesting, Craig?" Roger Lavera, Dr. Kobee's PhD student, asked.

Craig handed him the pocket microscope and asked, "A bead?"

"Yes indeed, a stone bead." He took it out of the scope and fingered it. "Anymore where these came from?"

Craig sorted through a hand full of sediment from the sieve and came up with a half dozen more. Slipping one into the scope, he brought it into focus.

"Look, this one's square with the same carving on it." He held out the scope.

Roger studied it briefly then handed the scope back. "See how many of these you have and we'll make a display."

"Roger!" Another sifter called the team leader, and Craig went back to picking through the silt in his sieve.

Roger returned in a moment. "Craig?"

No answer.

Roger touched him on the shoulder. "Craig?"

Craig looked up. "Yes?"

"Can I borrow your scope?"

"Of course." Craig absently handed over the instrument.

"You really get into things don't you?" It was more of a statement than a question. But Craig was already concentrating. Roger grinned and went to examine the small artifact discovered in pit four.

By the end of the session, Craig counted eighty small stone beads. Their shapes varied: round, square, octagon, and pyramid. Each revealed a single carved line that revealed a shiny blue core. An eerie glow peeped from under the lid of the container as carried his find to the lab.

"After vespers tonight we're having an open house of sorts in the lab," Dr. Kobee said, taking the beads and arranging them on an imaginary string.

Craig found a pile other sifters brought in and copied his action. Soon they had rows of beads emanating streaks of blue light.

"Impressive," they said, and chuckled together at their unison response.

Craig glanced at his watch. "I've got some work to finish for tonight. It's been fun, but gotta run." He quoted Dr. Kobee's five-year-old son's favorite parting.

"You're supposed to influence my son, not imitate him," Dr. Kobee scolded.

Craig laughed. "Oh! I knew something was wrong."

"Out!" the Doctor ordered.

"Yes, sir!" Craig said as the door closed behind him. He was pleased, not only with his find, but also with the good humor between them. He knew Daniel Kobee was probably one of the Captain's "purists on board". Craig felt they'd crossed both personal and professional barriers.

Dr. Kobee had always seemed stern and somewhat remote in most of Craig's contacts with him. Even after vespers with his son, Nathan, perched on his shoulders and clutching at his straight black hair, it was "Chaplain, good thought," or merely a nod and a handshake. Although on a first name basis with most of the scientists, he always thought of Daniel Kobee as Dr. Kobee.

"Maybe we're seeing beyond the other's professions and discovering each other as people," Craig mused as he went to his quarters.

In preparation for vespers, Craig habitually retired to his quarters or office as the scientists and crew ate their evening meal. The second day on the surface he followed this routine, shifting gears from amateur archeologist to chaplain. Craig was grateful he'd followed it that night.

In their excitement, the scientists consumed the evening meal quickly and arrived, ready for vespers, earlier than usual.

Several of the crew had beamed down, but Captain Brodsky sent his regrets as engineering was engrossed in a perplexing problem.

Dr. Zamwashi, filling in for Andez, finished the greetings while Craig saved his closing thought, and they were ready for him to speak. Asking for an outline, he entered the chapel while the computer compiled it.

Craig began with a series of questions. "What is the origin of this place? We have enough evidence to assume intelligent beings dwelt here. Did they worship something? Or Someone? How did they conduct their lives? How did they express their needs? What needs did they see in themselves? And did their worship system meet their perceived needs? How did they express their beliefs?

"These are the questions we ask when we examine the artifacts from a tell. But how often do we ask them of ourselves?"

The audience was in a thoughtful mood and the "dissection" of the devotion ranged from the Deity's place in the universe to how human's perception of their spirituality and Divine actions effected culture through the centuries. It was a good session, but in anticipation of the artifacts showing, the hour was still early when discussion faded.

"Craig, you coming over to the artifacts lab?" Roger Lavera greeted him on the way out.

"Dr. Kobee invited me." Craig nodded. "I'll shut things down here and be over in a few minutes."

"Good, we wanted to make sure you knew. You'll be surprised at some of the other things we found," Roger promised.

By the time Craig got to the display, people were already everywhere, laughing, talking, spraying silicone on their hands and handling the artifacts. Before turning his attention to the displays, he wandered around, greeting people. As he approached the tables, Dr. Kobee stood on a chair and whistled.

"Can I have your attention?" He waited for silence. "Touch the displays as you like. This is your last chance to get close to what we find without the tedious process of documentation, photography, and in-situ preservation. You'll be interested to know we've done some testing and the computer dates these artifacts are at least six-thousand of our years old," his voice trailed off.

"And if the top layers are six thousand years old," Roger took up the thought.

"We have a major find here." Dr. Kobee finished.

"All right!"

"Wow!"

"Terrific."

"Absolutely marvelous."

The younger scientists and Ph.D. candidates were vocal in their elation, but it seemed to Craig even the more seasoned scientists were caught up in the possibilities.

"Look around, read the notes and think about the culture," Dr. Kobee instructed, and the gathering again broke into small clusters of people.

Craig started at the table marked level five, intending to work his way down to one. As Roger predicted, he was pleased and surprised. He examined objects that resembled garment fasteners and coin shaped objects with wavy lines carved on them. Showing through the brown stone were the same bright blue lines as the beads. At level four he found stone statues with large angular heads and round, but humanoid, bodies. Among level three's artifacts he found woven metal ropes resembling belts, some very long and some very short. At level two, he found Roger contemplating the eerie glow produced by the collective effect of the beads.

"What do you suppose makes them do that?" he wondered out loud.

"They look electrically charged." Dorinda Brodsky joined them.

"Dorinda!" Craig hugged her. "I didn't know you were here."

"Alan didn't want to leave the ship again until they solve the engineering problem, so he sent me to take notes. He'll be down later."

Dorinda Brodsky matched her six-foot husband in height, and Craig stood a full inch shorter than she did. Their friendships' roots reached back to early childhood and the relationship had long ago deepened into a familial bond. They took turns fulfilling the role of big brother or big sister according to the other's need.

Dorinda shared Craig's passion for archeology, but since she was six months pregnant, the Captain had begged her to refrain from fieldwork on the strange planet.

Although she reluctantly agreed, she demanded a daily report from Craig.

They stood arm in arm looking at the beads.

"They do have a haunting quality about them don't they?" Dorinda touched them. "Like they have an inner life of their own."

"Is that intuition or archeology speaking?" Craig teased.

She fingered the beads then compared them to the coin shaped stones of level five. "A little of both, I think," she mused.

## CHAPTER THREE

Craig emerged early from his temporary quarters, refreshed by sleep and a shower. The personal shower, adapted from the technology for instantaneous removal of chemicals in case of accidental exposure, always amused him. It took some getting used to, but he enjoyed the slowly revolving base and Omni-directional water.

With the intention of finding a quiet place to study, he walked toward the tell, but the results of the work done after his departure the day before changed his mind. Climbing the mound, he examined the stone peak, which now poked five feet above the rest of the mound.

Thoughtfully he ran his hand over it, feeling the crevices between the close fitting stones.

"What do you think, Chaplain?" He didn't answer. LaShonya tried again. "Craig, what do you think is under there?"

"'Shonya," he answered looking up, startled. "Good morning!" He crouched by the peak, looking down the mound. "If this is the top of a building, it's quite a structure."

She climbed the mound and they sat together. "It could be the top of a shrine built over a smaller structure, and the artifacts are in the lower building." She smiled and added, "You're up early."

"I came out to study in the outdoor air and got sidetracked," Craig confessed.

LaShonya smiled and looked around. "There's something about the atmosphere. Kind of charged. Like it is at home right before a thunderstorm."

"New Mexico has thunderstorms? I thought it was all desert," Craig teased.

She wrinkled her nose at him. "Where did you grow up?"

"My father was a computer linguistics officer in the Combined Forces. We were stationed on Mars most of my early years. Dad's work was highly classified, so even when we were on earth we lived in a military base climate dome."

"You've been atmospherically deprived," She laughed.

"I liked the domes," he defended his childhood. "It was a fun way to grow up. I'm just not intimately acquainted with electric air."

"You two gonna sit up there and talk all day?" Dr. Cabrailes was on his way to breakfast.

They looked up in surprise and scrambled down the mound.

"I went up to inspect what was uncovered after I left yesterday. 'Shonya came along and we started talking," Craig explained as they joined him.

"Uh-huh." Forest wasn't convinced.

"I came out to study," Craig finished lamely.

"And I came out for an early walk," LaShonya insisted.

"Explanation accepted." The site director grinned as he held open the door of the temporary mess hall.

**

Craig finished the last thought of his lesson and, coming out of his disciplined concentration, heard the hum of the ground laser shut down. A minute passed before he realized it meant something was wrong.

Forest's plans for the morning had included clearing another five feet from the front structure, slicing vertically to track the history of the occupants. The calculation of coordinates, readying the computer, and cutting the earth should have taken much longer than a few minutes. Craig consulted his watch.

"Ten-thirty." He cocked his head to listen again.

Silence.

"Surely the laser didn't fail," he said to himself as he put down the computer and went to the door. Another five feet was exposed on two sides of the structure. But the scientists' attention focused on the sifting pits.

"What?" Craig said aloud, unable to resist finding out what was happening.

Roger stepped back from the group as Craig approached. "In this five feet of earth there are no new artifacts." He anticipated Craig's question. "The same coin shapes, belts, and utensils we already have keep turning up. Hundreds of your beads." He shook his head. "Daniel stopped work to run date tests. We're waiting for the report before they decide what to do next."

The group milled around the shifting pit, speculating among themselves.

"Is it possible this is not a multiple level site?"

Craig heard the question asked as he walked among the scientists. Some asked it in wonder, some in disappointment, some in disbelief, and some in excitement. But they all knew the report would confirm their collective conclusion.

After what seemed hours, Dr. Kobee emerged from his lab. "These samples vary from five to ten years from the first artifacts we found," he announced.

It surprised no one.

"Okay people," LaShonya called for quiet. "All teams to strategy meetings in their labs. We'll have lunch sent to each lab and meet in the," She looked at Craig, the question unasked.

He nodded. "Sure."

"In the chapel at two o'clock for final planning. Go." The group broke into teams. "Daniel," she called as the

33

doctor walked away. "I have a message from the Captain to call in at the earliest convenience. Will you join me?"

As they started toward her quarters, LaShonya turned back and touched Craig's arm. "Thanks, Craig."

"Anytime."

His easy, straightforward response reminded her Craig possessed a depth Art didn't. Art would have agreed by either flirting or tossing a flippant remark. Impatiently she brushed the thought aside. "How do you know what Art would do?" she disciplined herself.

**

Captain Brodsky's face appeared on the comm screen in response to Dr. Reed's summons.

"LaShonya, are you alone?"

"No, I brought Daniel along for a witness," she replied. "Your message sounded serious."

"Fine," he responded. "Serious, but not an emergency. What's the latest there?"

"We've decided it's not a multilevel site. Teams are meeting now," Dr. Kobee spoke up.

"Doesn't that change things?" the Captain asked cautiously.

"It just raises a new set of questions," Dr. Kobee answered.

Captain Brodsky nodded.

"What's the message, Captain?" LaShonya interrupted.

"Okay, LaShonya." He grinned at her impatient question. "Security reports they found signs of habitation."

"Someone lives on this planet?" LaShonya demanded.

"But all the studies show this planet is deserted." Dr. Kobee echoed her disbelief.

"Just as a precaution, I'm sending a security team back down. Post a guard at night. I don't think we need to make a general announcement yet. Just stay around the compound." The captain sounded cautious but not alarmed.

"No one's wandered away yet, or requested a field trip," LaShonya replied. "And if they do, we'll quietly say no."

"Good." Captain Brodsky closed the subject. "Brodsky out."

"What do you think, Daniel?" LaShonya consulted.

"Let's follow the Captain's lead. and keep a low profile," Dr. Kobee counseled.

"You're right," she agreed, "I'll make the rounds of the teams and find out what direction they want to take."

## CHAPTER FOUR

Craig couldn't do anything but wait. With grim determination, he reviewed the lesson for vespers, put out extra chairs, and then made himself study.

His discipline kicked in, but periodically he glanced out the window to see LaShonya moving from lab to lab. However, he was deep in study when the first scientist opened the door promptly at fourteen hundred hours.

The discussion of whether or not to continue at the present site or move to another turned into a fierce debate. The last person expressed her strong opinion, and a tense silence settled.

Forest Cabrailes broke it. "I say we compromise. Test our students' computer research projects. Link them to the ship's system. Use them to study the tells. Two things get done. We test the programs before publication. And we gather enough data to see if the site will hold our interest."

No one objected.

With a nod, LaShonya gave directions. "Return to your labs, make any last minute changes you want, and link everything to the ship's system. Tomorrow we'll go over the programs as a group and after that, run more tests." She looked around the group. "That's all."

**

Vespers felt subdued. Although the dissection didn't lack depth, it remained reserved and the group broke up early. Craig spoke to each person as they left.

"'Shonya, can you stay a minute?" Craig took her arm as she started out the door.

"Sure."

They settled in his quarters over a hot drink. "What now?" he asked.

"About what?"

"The tell."

"Oh. Well. We'll do studies that are more intensive. I think we've got one structure, built and abandoned by the same beings. Our aim — should they decide to stay — becomes to reconstruct the society and find out why they abandoned it."

Craig nodded. "Someone found evidence that the planet is or recently has been inhabited didn't they?"

The abrupt change of subject startled her, but she confirmed his suspicions. "The security teams reported it to Captain Brodsky this morning. What made you ask?"

"The guards taking positions outside. Don't worry, the scientists won't be alarmed." He grinned. "Military routine requires guards to be posted at the slightest possibility of danger to civilians, and that's all I could think of."

LaShonya relaxed. "Let's hope none of my people studied military strategy."

"Did the Captain say what kind of signs they found?"

She shook her head. "He just said he was posting guards at night, and that we should discourage trips outside the compound."

"Um-kay." Craig didn't push. "Can I come to the unveiling of the reports tomorrow?" he asked as she left.

"Actually, I was hoping you'd let us meet here again. It seems to be the neutral corner of the compound." She said tentatively, prepared for a negative response.

Craig nodded without hesitation. "Anytime. And thanks for letting me in on all this."

She tossed a grin over her shoulder as she went out the door and repeated his response. "Anytime."

**✳✳**

They stood in clumps, comparing notes, waiting for LaShonya's arrival.

"There'll be two groups here tonight," Roger was telling Craig.

Craig nodded. "Those who want to put together a picture of these beings."

"And those who want to find a multi-level site," Roger finished. "And I can just about tell you who will be on which side."

"Do it," Craig challenged.

But LaShonya hurried in, apologizing for her lateness. "I had to go back to the ship for some information, and just couldn't get back," she explained. "Okay, let's report. We'll start with artifacts."

Dr. Kobee rose, holding up his computer. "Initially, our reaction was to ask to find another site since the second set of artifacts appeared to be from the same civilization as the first. However..." He paused.

Roger's surprised raised eyebrows amused Craig.

"...However, from working with the experimental simulations we talked about yesterday, we've found additional evidence that suggests there are numerous articles of interest and even possible humanoid remains. The mystery intrigues us. We vote to stay."

Dr. Reed didn't comment. "Oliver, what's your team's vote?"

The tall, African Director of Documentation stood, and in his deep cultured voice reported. "We are in agreement that our process," His articulation produced the word with a long "o" and accent on the first syllable. "Would essentially remain the same. A multi-level site would perhaps be more exciting, but the teaching method is valid." He paused then added with a smile. "We also are intrigued by the initial findings."

Roger was nodding. They all appreciated the contradiction Oliver Zamwashi presented: a perfectionist and a quiet calm spirit existing in harmony and evidenced by a precise vocabulary, dry humor, and mesmerizing speech patterns.

"Your answer is both yes and no then?" LaShonya smiled.

"Precisely, Doctor," Dr. Zamwashi proclaimed.

The chuckles broke the formality of the meeting.

"Forest, what did the site team decide?" LaShonya still held control, even in the meeting's relaxed state.

"It surprised us. We ran scans through all sides of the tell, and from top down through the tell. We used Roger's new projection software. It's one structure all right. Full of chambers and ramps. But we can't dismantle it without ruining it. We've got to uncover it." He stopped and added a personal note. "I like its shape. You don't find it in space everywhere. Let's be happy with what we've got."

Craig noted Roger's eyebrows were again raised in surprise.

"Do we actually have a unanimous decision from this group?" LaShonya conjectured.

Laughter served as common consent.

LaShonya continued, "I'm glad we agree. I was late because of some research I conducted just in case you wanted to move. Preliminary tests on the tells in this area reveal every tell in this sector is exactly like this one."

"That'll stop ya' short." Forest echoed everyone's surprise.

Shonya grinned. "Shall we continue removing five feet of earth at a time, sifting and cleaning each foot of the structure as we go?"

"Sounds like a good plan." Forest again spoke for the group.

"My team will conduct the scans to determine how the artifacts lie and get coordinates to the laser techs," Dr. Zamwashi elaborated.

"And I assume you'll want to intensify in-situ infrared photos of the soil before it's removed from each level. Then you'll document each level's artifacts after they're extracted?" LaShonya asked and ordered at the same time.

"That was our intention." Oliver replied gravely.

"Roger, you'll have charge of the sifting operation." She shifted her attention and smiled at his delighted expression. "Take all artifacts to Dr. Kobee's lab. And finally, we'll issue hand lasers to everyone not otherwise engaged. Use only the lowest diffused setting to clean the dust from the crevices." She grinned at Craig. "Forest, if we have an extra hand laser, I promised the Chaplain he could play with his favorite toy."

When the laughter died, and Craig's blush faded she added, "Now, we have some calculations to do. In the morning we'll put this into action."

## CHAPTER FIVE

Craig slept in the next morning after working most of the night completing the evening's lesson and catching up on his "paper work."

The number of reports required of the military chaplain was the defense Craig used when the rest of the crew gave him a hard time about his flexible hours.

The hum of the ground laser finally woke him and he lay reviewing the recurring conversation between himself and the crewmembers.

"But think of the time I spend with the computer," he would groan. "When you do something, the computer records you doing your job. I do mine, then have to record the number of counseling sessions I conduct since most of what I do, except vespers, is confidential."

"But you don't have to find things to do to fill your shift," the crewmember would grumble, and the argument would go on.

With a smile, Craig prepared for the day and arrived at the tell as Forest issued the hand lasers.

"Morning, Craig," the Doctor greeted him. "We thought the sound of the laser might bring you out."

"You worked kind of late didn't you?" LaShonya joined the conversation.

"Um-hum," Craig acknowledged. "I did today's work last night so I could sleep in this morning and still indulge in my hobby. What were you doing up so late?"

"Indulging in my own hobby," she answered as she walked away. She didn't tell them Art's last communication said he was arriving in three days, and she had paced the floor, trying to come up with answers to the questions he brought with him.

"What's her hobby?" Craig asked.

"Being alone, as far as I can tell." Forest grinned, handed him a laser, and gave a quick situational report. "The structure's cleared ten feet on all sides, and fifteen feet on two sides. The laser's working on the other side right now and the sifting pits are ready. While the pit crews get caught up Oliver will decide where to cut next."

"Right," Craig nodded. "Shall I just pick a spot?"

"We saved you a spot. South face, next to Carol Madjer. Work slow. If you find anything unusual yell for Oliver."

Craig eagerly climbed the tell and went to work, the laser gently humming in his hand. He re-discovered the quickest way to clear the crevices was to move the laser from right to left, almost as if he were drawing with it.

Just before the noon break, he thought he felt a stone move as he rested his hand on the upper right hand corner.

"No," he told himself, "I'm imagining it." He pushed again, and the stone swung inward. "What?" he breathed. Powering down his laser, he spoke to the young scientist working the next space.

"Carol, look at this."

Carol powered down her laser and slid over to him. Craig pushed on the left corner of the stone and it swung back into place. Then he pushed the upper right hand corner. It opened.

"A way in? Or a vent?" Carol responded with excitement. She looked around for Dr. Zamwashi and found him moving equipment toward the back of the structure. "Oliver," she called.

He looked up. "Carol?"

"Please come up here. The Chaplain found a stone that moves."

"A what?" the doctor said to himself. However, he handed his armload of equipment to a team member and climbed the tell.

"Watch." Craig handed him the laser and repeated the demonstration.

Oliver nodded solemnly. "All work stop please," he called to the workers on the structure. "Some investigation is required before we allow you to continue. Here, Craig, time for you to rest." He handed the laser back as he gently issued the order.

Dr. Zamwashi called in his team and measured the precise location of the stone from each corner and the top of the structure. He then used the co-ordinates to locate that same stone on all other sides of the structure. Sending a team member to the designated stone, he ordered repetition of Craig's action.

Each stone in that position swung inward, creating a set of windows.

"Close them quickly," Dr. Zamwashi instructed. "Until we take samples we do not want to further contaminate the inside air."

The site, artifacts, and documentation teams held a brief meeting, which broke up in laughter.

"What's so funny?" Craig asked Roger.

"With all this technology they can't figure out a way to get an air sample other than the old fashioned way of letting a vacuum tube down. Someone'll have to return to the ship and rig something up. They goofed when they didn't anticipate finding an intact structure that needed air samples extracted." Craig frowned. "Archaeologists' humor."

"OK. Why not let the computer do it?"

Roger shook his head. "Archeologists still like to do some things the old fashioned way. Sometimes strange particles are floating in the air that our computer isn't calibrated to look for."

Dr. Kobee stepped out of the artifacts lab and looked around. Roger gave him a wave of acknowledgment. "See ya' later, Daniel beckons."

At lunch break a spirit of adventure replaced subtle disillusionment. The speculative conversation centered on what the mysterious structure contained.

After lunch, Dr. Zamwashi studied the next section before Okaying the cut, and cleaning of the structure's face resumed.

Time passed quickly. The hand laser's efficiency enabled the team to clean all exposed surfaces in less than two hours and preparations for the next cut began.

Roger took the artifacts from the last cuts to Dr. Kobee's lab as the team beamed back from the ship with their invention—a long, clear tube attached to a hose that connected to a tiny hand-held pump. Normally the pump created vacuums in injection rod tubes in preparation for medication.

"Very inventive," Dr. Zamwashi commented dryly. "Run preliminary tests of the sample. As soon as we have results, trigger the stones again." He sent one of his team to open one of the stones just enough to insert the newly created device.

Craig left the site to prepare for the evening's vespers. He settled down to study, but the lack of sleep caught up with him. Before he was done, he fell asleep at his computer.

He became aware of a strange humming at his ear. Waking up slowly, he stretched. The humming grew louder. He looked around.

"The laser!" His hand laser, still on the table where he'd absently laid it, glowed and blinked through its clear case. Puzzled, he regarded it for a moment thinking, "That's strange." Suddenly he understood.

"It's overloading!"

Carefully getting up, he gave it one last look and ran for the door.

He breathed a sigh of relief when he crashed out the door and almost ran down the guard taking up his post.

"Tim!" Craig hailed him. "My hand laser's overloading."

"It's what?" Although he didn't understand, the lieutenant led the way back inside.

A dangerous red-orange light now came from the hand laser.

"It's discharging internally," Lt. Gram corrected Craig's diagnosis.

Gingerly he turned it so he could see the power switch. *"It's still switched off,"* he thought. He fished the small rod used to open the case of his weapon out of his pocket and carefully reached for the laser. "Weapons overload, lasers discharge internally," he quietly lectured, inserting the rod into the case of the laser. "Let's hope the same company that makes our weapons makes the hand laser." With a twist of his wrist, the case came apart. "They come apart for cleaning," he continued his calm commentary while his hands were busy. "I think I can remove the power unit." He gently pried at the small round power disc. It didn't budge. In desperation, he dug harder. Suddenly the unit popped out and flew across the room.

Craig caught it as it came his way. In surprise, he looked at the guard.

Lt. Gram grinned, and the laser lay silent. Craig fingered the unit in silence for a long minute while Lt. Gram examined the laser's interior.

"I didn't accidentally turn it on, did I?" It was a statement more than a question.

Lt. Gram shook his head. He held it out for Craig's inspection. "See the black marks? It looks like a computer circuit that's been zapped."

"Zapped?" Craig repeated.

"Struck by lightning or intentionally subjected to a power surge. They do it in testing labs. Sometimes a power surge will cause a weapon to spontaneously power up."

"A surge!" Craig became aware of the lieutenant implication. "My work!" The computer was off. He ordered the computer to power up and checked his file. Complete.

"Even if you were still working when it happened, computers have built in protectors," the lieutenant reminded him. "Hand lasers aren't supposed to need then."

"So something external activated it?" Craig double-checked; not quite believing it was possible.

"I'd say so, sir. I'd report it if I were you." Lt. Gram turned to leave.

"How did you know what to do?" Craig stopped him.

"I do double duty. When I'm not filling in as a guard, I'm the weapons specialist, Chaplain," he grinned.

"Well, I'm thankful for weapons specialists," Craig shook his hand. "Thank you."

"Thank you, sir. I'm glad we got it in time."

Craig stood for a long time looking at the laser, remembering the ship's engineering glitch.

The scientists came to vespers puzzled and discussing a strange phenomenon among themselves. It took all the discipline Craig had to keep his mind on the lesson.

He stopped LaShonya after the discussion. "What's all the excitement?" he asked as casually as possible.

Hesitantly she told him. "Early this evening there was an unexplained power surge. Computers shut themselves down all over camp. Even one or two hand lasers powered up by themselves."

"Anybody hurt?"

"No. You just switch the laser on then off again."

"Come here." Craig led the way to his quarters and handed her the two parts of the laser. "Only I was asleep, and didn't hear it come on. We nearly had a problem."

When she understood the implication, she felt a sudden uncharacteristic twinge of fright. "I'm glad you're alright." The emotion in her voice surprised them both. Resisting a sudden urge to hug him, she settled for patting his arm.

He blinked a couple of times, feeling her confusion and stuttered, "Ah, me too."

# CHAPTER SIX

"If it weren't for a weapons specialist, I wouldn't be here right now."

Captain Brodsky grew concerned as he listened to Craig's explanation of laser's destruction.

"For some reason I remembered what Dorinda said about the engineering glitch. Did they figure it out?"

"Yes and no," the Captain said, thoughtfully. "They decided it was a power surge. But no one has encountered anything like it before, so protection wasn't built in. So far, we haven't figured out where it came from. LaShonya thinks it and the power burst yesterday are related. She and her directors are on board now running more atmospheric studies."

"Captain Brodsky to the bridge," the Captain's comm button summoned him. "I've gotta go. Check back with me before you return to the surface."

They went toward the turbo lift.

"Chaplain?" Craig's comm button spoke and they stopped.

"Lea here," he answered.

"Craig, Oliver here. You'll be pleased to know we found another set of moving stones. They are located five meters below the first set. They are located to the right of the others and open by pushing the upper left hand corner."

"It's a strange puzzle." Craig answered. "Thanks for letting me know. I'll make sure I check them out when I return."

"You're really enjoying this, aren't you?" The Captain observed, amused.

"Uh-huh, and the scientists are humoring me," Craig smiled.

"Well, you've helped most of them through some sort of difficulty in the last year. And they like you." The Captain entered the turbo lift. "Check back before you leave," he repeated his order.

The crew came to attention as Captain Brodsky stepped onto the bridge. "As you were," he murmured.

"LaShonya, did you find anything new?" he asked.

"Craig and I were sitting on the tell yesterday morning, and I thought the air felt charged. Kind of like before a storm," LaShonya told him. Being raised in rural southwestern New Mexico, the Captain nodded in understanding. "So I'm running tests on the electrical charges in the air."

"Anything interesting?"

She nodded. "For one thing, the charge grows stronger, and then subsides. For another, something strange happens with the negatives and positives. It's like they change places periodically. It's not something that happens in Earth's atmosphere."

"Could this explain the engineering glitch and hand lasers spontaneously powering up?"

"Maybe. The switching releases a lot of energy."

"Any danger to the people on the surface?" The Captain wondered.

"It could cause an energy build up, but I don't think it's dangerous," she replied.

"Captain?" Lt. Phil Reecer interrupted, "Message coming through from security team three."

"On screen."

The picture flickered once then became clear.

"Captain Brodsky?"

"Brodsky here. What is it, Nuilla?"

49

"Sir, you'll never believe what I'm looking at." The security commander's voice matched his incredulous expression.

"Reecer, scan the area and put it on screen."

"Yes sir," Reecer replied then spoke to the computer.

The bridge crew gasped as the picture materialized.

"Any sign of life?" Captain Brodsky's voice sounded strangled.

"No, sir," Commander Nuilla replied. "But there seems to be some sort of force field around it. I can't get close enough to touch it."

"What is it?" Commander Houng, second in command, asked.

Captain Brodsky suddenly came to life. Swiveling his chair around, he started issuing orders. "LaShonya, get every scientist on board up here, and tell surface personnel to view this with us."

"Yes, sir!" She went to the communication station.

"Captain, Lea here."

The captain touched his comm button, "Craig?"

"I'm checking in. I'm on my way to transporter room one. You wanted to talk to me?"

"You're not going anywhere. Report to the bridge immediately. Brodsky out."

"What happened?" Craig asked the air.

He started to announce himself as he stepped out of the turbo lift, but words refused to form. All he could do was stare at the viewing screen.

Pyramid-shaped buildings, clustered in groups of three's, filled the screen. Their peaks protruded from clear dome-shaped awnings fastened to the buildings approximately three meters above the ground. Between the buildings, the awnings extended to the ground, creating a plaza in the center of each cluster of buildings. Enclosed walkways connected the clusters.

Returning to reality, Craig became aware of the turbo lift doors swishing behind him as more people joined the scientists already crowding the bridge. Voices from the surface jammed communications frequencies, echoing the same questions people on the bridge expressed.

"Is it inhabited?"

"Any signs of life?"

"Why didn't it show up on our scans?"

"Isn't this planet supposed to be uninhabited?"

The Captain broke into the curious chatter. "Get the co-ordinates of the team and lock on in case we have to remove them quickly," he ordered.

"Yes, sir," the tactical officer acknowledged. "Locked on."

"Where are they in relation to the tell?" The Captain asked without taking his eyes from the screen.

"One hundred degrees due east, sir," the TAC officer replied.

"Sir," Commander Nuilla broke in. "The force field is down. I'm touching the dome."

Another round of speculation began on the bridge and the planet's surface.

Suddenly the picture broke up.

"Reecer, get it back!" the Captain barked. "Commander Nuilla, are you there?" he asked the security team leader.

"Yes, sir. Anything wrong?" The commander's voice came through clearly.

"We're losing the viewing screen. Stand by. And be ready to beam aboard."

"Standing by, sir," the Commander acknowledged.

The visual static cleared. But instead of the city filling the viewing screen, two beings appeared.

Deafening silence reflected the mute astonishment of everyone on the bridge.

They were small beings, dressed in white robes, with angular heads, seemingly too large for the size of their bodies. Their features were also large: low foreheads, large eyes and mouth, and straight, protruding noses. They had no hair.

Between the two beings stood a black box about the size of a small chair, and the beings rested their small hands on the top of it.

One of the beings spoke. The lips moved and humans heard high clicking sounds and guttural syllables. After a short delay, an electronic voice spoke English.

"We monitored your communication and obtained enough samples to program this translating unit to speak your language."

"Like a video out of sync with its sound." Craig thought.

"We concluded you have not come to harm us. Yet you act strangely according to our customs. When your people found our city we knew we must establish communication."

"We could not find any trace of civilization when we studied the planet. We hope we have not offended your civil laws in any way," the Captain responded.

Silence.

The box spoke the being's language. The second beings lips moved, and presently the box translated.

"We developed ways to avoid discovery. We are a very private society, wishing to keep to ourselves. What is your purpose in uncovering the old structures?"

"We are a scientific expedition. Some of our people train others to learn about ancient cultures by studying that which they left behind," the Captain carefully explained.

Silence. Translation.

The first being spoke. Slowly words issued from the box. "Our device does not yet have adequate data to translate all your concepts. It cannot tell us much about certain subjects. There is much we need to know. At the next period of light, we will speak again. You are welcome here. Beware of the disruption. We must now put our protection in place."

The communication ended abruptly.

Conversation suddenly returned at full volume.

"All the studies stated with certainty this planet is deserted."

"Where have they been all this time?"

"What kind of device do they use to avoid detection?"

"What relation are they to the beings who dwelt at the dig site?"

"They built the same shaped buildings."

"They have concept translation devices!"

"Obviously highly evolved beings."

"They've been watching us."

"Why did they wait until now to contact us?"

"We found them. Maybe they hoped we would just go away."

Craig got tired of the conversations swirling around him and sought out LaShonya as Captain Brodsky ordered the security team aboard.

"'Shonya, what now?"

She looked up from her station with a smile. "Negotiations, I suppose. We'll need permission to continue the dig. It may be helpful to come to our conclusions, and then compare them with any records the culture kept. That is, if they have a recorded history."

Her excitement was under control as she kept busy plotting co-ordinates, scanning the location of the beings' city, and pushing sensor pads. But her eyes were sparkling green lights. She touched his arm. "Vespers better be short this evening. We have a lot of new data to analyze."

That brought him back to reality. "Vespers!" He checked his watch. "I've got a lesson to finish." He turned then returned. "Can you get away?"

"I'll be there, and I'll keep you posted." She saw the pleasure on his face and experienced a confused urge to touch him.

Joining some of the scientists, he beamed back to the planet's surface. Speculation was suspended long enough for the transfer but resumed immediately as they materialized on the surface.

"It's fun to see these calm, sober intellectuals shocked into excited chatter," Craig thought with a smile as he headed for the chapel.

The spirited discussion following vespers focused on the Cutezarians as part of the universal creation. Few of the scientists retained the human tendency to think God existed for humans only. Yet many of them had not thought much beyond God as the creator of the universe and everything in it. Everyone left more thoughtful than they came.

As his congregation filtered out into the night, Craig briefly wondered about the content of the evening's discussion under Andez Ronger's leadership on the ship.

LaShonya interrupted his thoughts. "Craig, can we use the chapel in about an hour for a general discussion time?"

All Craig wanted after the emotionally charged day was an early bedtime, but he capitulated and gestured around the room. "The neutral corner's all yours."

## CHAPTER SEVEN

The scientists returned bringing computers, cups of coffee and snacks, prepared for a marathon discussion. Craig watched in amusement as chairs became desks, tables, and footstools.

He heard their expressions of despair that the dig might not continue mixed with the hope of enlisting the beings to help. And he considered their speculations about the city, the beings, and their plans to get into the structure. Watching them gesture, discuss and drink, Craig leaned against the doorframe, feeling a sense of history.

LaShonya walked by and paused. "You look tired. Whatcha thinking?"

"About the historical implications of this occasion," Craig replied to her puzzlement. "The thousands of times people like these have gathered like this to brainstorm," he explained.

"Romanticism?" Puzzled, she frowned.

Craig grinned and shook his head. "Um, no. More a sense of continuing community." He stopped. "Sorry, maybe there's touch of romanticism in me." Smiling he added, "I wouldn't admit that to just anybody. And I'm tired."

She laid a hand on his arm. "Never mind. It's okay."

"Hey, in the excitement, I forgot to ask about the air sample," Craig suddenly remembered.

"So did I." Snapping her fingers, LaShonya turned around. "Oliver, what did the air samples turn up?"

He nodded and consulted the computer in front of him. "The composition closely resembles present air, except it approaches a state that can only be described as supercharged. There is no measurable pollution," he reported. "Nor does present day air contain more pollutants than the structure's air."

Routine, even in Oliver's expansive language. Everyone nodded.

"If it gets too late, I'll close the chapel." LaShonya volunteered. "With operations temporarily suspended we can sleep in tomorrow, and you have your regular duties."

"Okay," Craig nodded. "I'll drift away if it gets too technical. For now, I'll listen to their theories."

She laid her hand on his folded arms. "Get some sleep, I'll brief you later."

"Yes ma'am," he grinned, trying to deny he liked her attention. However, he did admit his combined activities as chaplain and amateur scientist were getting the best of him.

Although he fell asleep as soon as he crawled into bed, strange, unsettling dreams made him restless. Great electrical storms popped, crackled, and disturbed the air around him. The dream bewildered and frightened Craig, but he was drawn to the beautiful streaks the electricity left in the air.

Little by little, he became more afraid than fascinated. All at once, he couldn't breathe. His skin burned and itched. Tossing and twisting, he tried to get away from the storm's irritation. In anger, he threw his pillows and bedclothes off the cot.

Someone touched him. And he felt warm and comfortable.

"Craig!" Her voice came through the fog.

\*\*

LaShonya was engrossed in discussion with Quantro Smith, Oliver Zamwashi's PhD student, and was about to ask his ideas on the best way to obtain viewing privileges of the historical records when the lights flickered off and the computers suddenly powered down.

Silence.

After some minutes, Daniel Kobee expressed their thoughts. "There's something eerie about the atmosphere."

"It felt like a mild electrical current going through me," Quantro added.

Silence.

They drew a collective breath of relief when power returned.

"I think we'd better call it an evening," LaShonya took charge. "Anyone lose anything?"

"I wasn't working," Oliver said.

"Me neither," Daniel affirmed.

"I'm out," Forest spoke up.

"Good. Let's put Craig's chapel back into order. I'll tell him we're leaving."

"Craig?" 'Shonya called, pushing back the curtain. In a sudden rush of panic, she noted his shallow breathing. "He looks like a kid having a nightmare. Or he's ill," she said as she retrieved the blanket and pillow. She covered him and touched his moist forehead.

"Craig?"

As she checked his pulse, first at his wrist, then his neck, he tried to wake up. All he wanted was to tell her he was tingly all over but okay. It just wouldn't work. The switch from his brain to the rest of his body seemed stuck in the off position.

"God, no, please no," LaShonya silently cried as childhood memories flooded her memory. Angrily she shook them away, knowing Craig wasn't going to die. "He's just ill," she said aloud to re-assure herself.

Tearing her gaze from his face, she crossed the room and pushed the curtain aside. "The Chaplain's ill. Someone help me get him back to the ship."

The scientists scrambled to the back of the building. LaShonya knelt and checked Craig's pulse again.

Her touch ended his mental drifting. Fighting for strength, he managed to take her hand.

LaShonya grasped his fingers. "That's an improvement. When I first came in, he wasn't moving at all," she told Oliver as he knelt beside her.

Craig tried to open his eyes, but the effort was fruitless. Giving up, he drifted back into the comfortable grayness as it settled over him. His grasp loosened, and his hand slipped out of LaShonya's.

"We've lost him again," she sighed.

Oliver stood and tapped his comm button. "Transporter."

"Lt. Commander Cooper," the answer was short and terse.

"Dr. Zamwashi here. Three to beam up. Get a transport and medical team. Notify the Captain the Chaplain is ill."

"Yes, sir."

Oliver bent down and, because of his height, easily lifted Craig from the cot. "Ready, now," he said

"Transporting."

Craig felt the jolt as they laid him on the freestanding transport and couldn't stop a small sound from escaping.

"Careful, Oliver," LaShonya said. *"At least he can feel it,"* she thought.

Dr. Jeffery Keal, chief of medical staff, hurried into the room and ran the small life signs reader over Craig's body. "His breathing's shallow, heart rhythm irregular, and he's in shock. Let's get him to sick bay."

Far away, Craig could hear them talking above him as he floated along.

"How long has he been like this?" Jeff questioned LaShonya.

"Can't have been that long," she replied. "It wasn't more than an hour and a half after he went to his quarters that the lights and computers went off. And I heard him moving around for a while, so forty-five minutes." She thought a minute. "Probably less than that. When I touched his forehead, his hair was still moist." She reached down, brushed Craig's hair back, and touched his face. "See the moisture from the pain of moving him is already gone. On the planet his forehead was still moist."

Craig felt the touch and moved his head toward her to prolong the contact.

The doors of sickbay swished open and the med tech took charge of the transport.

"Do a full set of scans," Jeff instructed the med tech. "I'll be right in."

"How did he look when you found him?" The doctor continued questioning LaShonya.

"He'd tossed his pillows and thermal sheet half way across the room. He was quiet, but sweating like he'd been tossing and turning," she answered.

Jeff nodded. "I'll let you know as soon as his condition changes or I know something," he said, and disappeared after the transport.

Dorinda Brodsky hurried down the hall toward sickbay, but LaShonya intercepted her, leading her away from the door.

"'Shonya, how's Craig?" she asked as she grasped LaShonya's hands.

"We're not sure."

"What happened?"

"We don't know."

"Has he been conscious at all?"

"On the planet he took my hand while I was checking his pulse. He made a sound when Oliver put him on the transport, and responded to my touch, but nothing coherent."

Jeff ran every test he could think of. He checked the computer's conclusions and then did another examination.

Some movement returned. Craig's breathing became less labored. His muscles relaxed and the heartbeat became less erratic. But he showed no signs of regaining consciousness. As the doctor checked his readings one more time, Craig turned his head and sighed.

It sounded like "'Shon."

"Craig," Jeff called.

No response.

"Brodsky to sick bay," the comm button broke in.

"Dr. Keal here."

"What's the Chaplain's condition, Jeff?"

"Stable, Captain. Some movement has returned, but he's not yet awake." The doctor hesitated. "Can you come down?"

"Be right there." The Captain replied. He turned to his first officer. "Houng, you have the conn. I'll be in sick bay."

"Alan?" Commander Houng stopped him. "You'll let us know?"

"As soon as I know something."

The captain greeted the two women in the corridor before entering sickbay. "'Shonya, any news?"

She shook her head. He put his hand on her shoulder and leaned over to kiss Dorinda. "Hi."

"Hi," she smiled softly.

"You ok?" he asked.

"Yeah." She smiled at his concern.

"Dorinda had a couple of twinges earlier this evening," he explained.

"Did Ruth check you out?" LaShonya asked.

Dorinda nodded. "That's how I knew about Craig. We'd finished the exam and were just chatting when the call came through. I'm fine."

"Jeff asked me to come down," the Captain changed the subject.

"You can come in now." The med tech summoned from the door.

Craig moved restlessly on the monitoring table. Every so often, a small sound escaped as he moved his head.

"He's trying to regain consciousness," Jeff said, watching the fluctuating graphs above Craig's head.

LaShonya reached toward Craig, but drew back.

"It's okay," Jeff assured her. "He responds to touch."

With a small nod, she put her hand on his chest. "Craig, wake up and tell us what happened."

At her touch, he became quiet and his breathing deepened.

Jeff looked down from the panel. "I didn't have that effect on him."

Captain Brodsky slipped his arm around his wife and quietly asked, "Is there something going on here I don't know about?"

"'Shonya and I aren't sure. They've been getting closer lately," she smiled back.

"Alan," Jeff spoke, shaking his head. "I've checked and re-checked the data, and I'd swear Craig was struck by bolt of lightning. Under these conditions, I don't know where he got that kind of charge. As far as..."

Movement caught his attention. Slowly Craig turned his hand over and closed his fingers around 'Shonya's hand.

"As far as I can tell," the doctor continued with a smile. "He should recover."

"Glad to hear that, Jeff." The Captain turned to go. "I'll be on the bridge."

"Wait." LaShonya spoke absently. "Jeff, could this have anything to do with the power surges? Dorinda, what time did you feel the twinges?"

"About ten fifteen," She said, suddenly anxious. "Why?"

"That was about the time the power went off."

"But if the atmosphere effected Craig, why not the rest of you?" the Captain wanted to know.

"Wait a minute." LaShonya thought back through the incident. "Both Daniel and Quantro remarked on how charged the air felt."

"But why Craig?" Captain Brodsky repeated.

"Maybe his system was already shut down. So he couldn't resist the electrical current," Jeff speculated.

"I assume he was sleeping soundly," LaShonya added. "He was exhausted."

"And Dorinda, being pregnant, is more aware of her muscular reactions than the rest of us. If we felt anything, we probably ignored it." That brought another thought to mind. "Dorinda, are you the only pregnant person aboard?"

"No, Lt. Reecer's wife is much farther along than I am, and there are a couple of others."

"Bill, call Dr. Canady and have her check with her other pregnant patients," Jeff addressed the med tech.

"No need to do that, Jeff." Dr. Ruth Canady came in looking as if she had been aroused from a deep sleep. "Gina Reecer's on her way in. We're going to have a baby tonight."

"Is she due?" Dorinda asked.

"A week early, but it's okay." She noted Craig's fingers still clenched around LaShonya's hand. "Some improvement, I see." She nodded toward Craig.

"He's moving and responding to touch," Jeff affirmed.

"Good. I'll be in OB." With a yawn, she crossed the room to the surgery suite.

"I need to get back." The Captain stood at the door. "Call me when he wakes up." He paused in the open door. "I'm moving the ship to a higher orbit just for precaution. Then we all need some rest, don't you think?"

## CHAPTER EIGHT

Sickbay was deserted.

The Reecers had a new baby girl. Gina was sleeping and Phil was sitting quietly in her room, watching his girls.

Several hours ago, Jeff had left orders and finally went to his quarters to get some sleep.

LaShonya alone remained, unwilling to pry her hand from Craig's hold. She alternately prayed, napped, and talked to him.

Slowly the grayness in Craig's head separated from the light, like a dimmer switch bringing lights up in a theater.

Gradually he became aware of the hand he held and a pressure on his right arm. Painfully he turned his head and willed himself awake. He touched 'Shonya's head with his free hand, not knowing why she slept there.

"'Shonya?"

A voice was repeating Craig's shortened version of her name.

"'Shonya?"

She assumed the doctor or the med tech had returned. Opening her eyes, she prepared to explain Craig wouldn't let go of her hand.

But no one was there.

It was Craig's hand on her head. Suddenly she sat up and found herself looking into his puzzled eyes.

"'Shonya? What are you doing here?" he asked slowly. "Where is here?" He added, looking up at the fluctuating graphs on the monitoring panel.

"You wouldn't let go of my hand." She held up their interlaced hands with a smile.

Suddenly flustered, he apologized, "Sorry."

Although his grip loosened, he didn't let go. Instead, he drew her hand to his chest, held it in both of his, and closed his eyes. Wonder filled his voice when he spoke again.

"It was. No, seemed important. Couldn't lose contact. Not with you." He frowned. "What happened? Sickbay. How long?"

Before LaShonya could answer, the med tech came hurrying in. "Dr. Reed, the Chaplain's readings are going wild!" He stopped and let out a long breath. "You're awake, Chaplain!" he exclaimed. "The way the readings looked, I expected convulsions." He touched his comm button. "Dr. Keal?"

"Keal here," came the doctor's sleepy voice.

"The Chaplain's awake, Doctor."

"I'll be there in five minutes. Keal out." Jeff checked the computer screen. It blinked six-thirty am. "Seven hours." He marked Craig's period of unconsciousness and touched his comm button.

"Captain Brodsky, Keal here."

The Captain, wearily climbing out of bed in response to his wake-up alert, responded, "Brodsky here, yes Doctor?"

"Sorry it's so early, but Craig's awake."

"I was just headed for the shower. What's his condition?"

"I'm not sure yet, I'm leaving my quarters now."

"I'll be down as soon as I get the watch started." He kissed Dorinda as she stirred. "Craig's conscious. Will you go back to sleep and rest? Jeff will want to run tests before he allows visitors anyway."

She nodded, and soon fell asleep.

"How is he?" Jeff asked as he entered the med tech's station, noting LaShonya's hand in Craig's.

"He's asleep again, Doctor," the med tech replied. "He woke up, talked with Dr. Reed briefly then announced he needed a nap. But he hasn't once let go of her hand."

"That's understandable," the doctor smiled. "She's his link to reality." He stepped into the bed area. "Have you been here all night?" he asked LaShonya.

With a nod, she touched Craig's shoulder. "Craig, Jeff's here, and probably wants to talk to you."

Craig turned his head toward her and opened his eyes. He looked puzzled for a moment, and then smiled. "Hi."

"Jeff is here," she repeated.

"Could he tell you what happened?" Jeff asked.

She shook her head.

"Ah, Craig, do you suppose you could let go of "Shonya's hand so I can examine you?" Jeff asked casually, consulting the monitoring panel.

"Maybe." A tiny trace of humor came through. Reluctantly he let go of her hand, but she didn't withdraw it immediately. Finally, she patted his hand and turned to leave.

"'Shonya," Craig stopped her. "Thanks."

She lifted a hand. "Anytime."

"I'll be right back, Craig," Jeff said and escorted LaShonya to the door. "He'll be disoriented a few hours. Stop back by after you've rested."

LaShonya nodded. "Call me if there's any change."

Although he was dozing when Jeff returned, Craig responded to touch. He woke, again, not quite sure where he was. The doctor didn't like the dazed, puzzled look in his patient's eyes.

After a few seconds, Craig acknowledged the doctor. "What's wrong?" he asked.

"How do you feel, Craig? Do you hurt anywhere?" he answered with another question.

"Exhausted. Stiff. Hurt all over. My skin's irritated."

"Any tingling?" the Doctor asked.

"Um-hum," Craig murmured, drifting back toward sleep. "Hands and legs."

Captain Brodsky entered and Jeff motioned him to the table. He touched Craig's shoulder again.

"Craig, stay with us. Captain Brodsky came down to see you."

Craig lifted his head and greeted the Captain drowsily. "Alan. Hello."

The Captain smiled at Craig's use of his first name. Craig didn't usually use it except when they were alone or with Dorinda. He laid his hand on his friend's shoulder.

"We were afraid you wouldn't wake up. Lots of people are praying."

"Tell them thanks." Craig closed his eyes.

"Craig," Jeff prompted. "One more question. Then you can sleep." Craig opened his eyes and nodded. "How much of last night do you remember?"

"Last night?" he asked. "How long have I been here?"

"It's seven in the morning," Jeff told him. "You've been out approximately eight hours. Now, how much do you remember?"

Craig thought back. "Tired. 'Shonya ordered me to bed. I did some things, showered, and went to sleep. I remember hearing 'Shonya's voice and touch. I wanted to talk. Couldn't. After that, confused voices. Gray. Floating. 'Shonya's voice. She touched me." He paused, considering. "I have this lingering feeling, holding on to someone, for dear life." Closing his eyes, he reflected, suddenly embarrassed.

"Shonya."

The doctor nodded. "She stayed all night."

67

"A lot to ask of a friend," Craig observed drowsily. He closed his eyes and remained quiet so long Jeff motioned the Captain away from the table.

As they moved away Craig said, "The dream."

"The what?" Captain Brodsky returned to the table.

"The dream." Craig's brain worked better with his eyes closed.

"What was it about, Craig?" Captain Brodsky prompted.

"Electric storms. The air popped and crackled. Frightening and beautiful. More frightening than beautiful." He sighed. "'Shon, ah, 'Shonya and I talked about the air feeling like before it rains." He drifted a minute. "I was hot, prickly all over, and uncomfortable. Then calm. 'Shonya touched me. I couldn't talk to her." He sighed again and murmured sleepily, "It's. Confused."

They let him sleep.

"He seems so tired and," Captain Brodsky searched for the right word.

"Disoriented?" Jeff supplied. The captain nodded. "He'll get over it. The scans don't show any further deterioration in his EEG since last night. He absorbed just enough to scramble his system, but not enough to permanently damage it." He paused before deciding to express his theory. "Captain, I don't think it was just a dream. I think his subconscious interpreted what really happened. But I can't explain it."

"Captain?" the comm button startled them both.

"Brodsky here."

"The negotiation team's assembled in transporter room one," Commander Houng reported.

"I'll be right up," he answered, then turned back to Jeff. "Dorinda will be down. Use your judgment about letting her see Craig. His disorientation will worry her. We don't want her going into early labor."

"He'll be sleeping anyway."

∗∗

The dream returned. Craig was again on the planet. The air, popping and crackling around him, made him twist and turn seeking an escape from the irritation.

"Craig!" He heard his name and calmness settled over him. 'Shonya checked his pulse, but it seemed different.

Rested, LaShonya stopped by to check on Craig before resuming her station. Alarmed to see him fighting in his sleep, she ran across the room and touched his face.

He took a deep, ragged breath and became still.

Hoping to trigger a response, she laid her hand in his and fought the tenderness that overtook her. "Craig, take my hand." "He's just bringing out the compassion in me," she lectured herself as his fingers slowly closed around her hand.Craig's nightmare ended.

"'Shonya?"

His eyes held the same puzzled look as before while he struggled to remember. After a while, they cleared and he was fully awake.

"Well," he said wearily between a sigh and a smile. "Here we are again. Me holding on and you patiently enduring it." He held up their hands. "It's a nice fit, come to think of it." He closed his eyes. "Can I borrow it a minute?"

Dr. Keal barged into the room. "The readings just went wild. What happened?"

"I suppose there was a recurrence of the dream. He was thrashing around when I came in. I touched his face; he took my hand and calmed down."

The doctor looked down and smiled at Craig's firm grip on LaShonya's hand. "Again? Don't stay all night," he admonished.

He turned to go, but changed his mind and went to the med cabinet. "I think I'll give him something to stop the dreams so he can really rest."

Soon after he administered the drug Craig's hold relaxed.

Flexing her hand, LaShonya remarked, "He's got quite a grip even while he's asleep."

"Electric shock is a strange thing," Jeff told her.

"You're certain that's it?"

He nodded. "His complaints and symptoms confirm it. But there are no burns, no entry or exit points. I don't know how it happened. Did Alan tell you about the dream?"

She nodded and looked at the doctor earnestly. "Will Craig recover completely?"

"He should. I'm going to get him up when he wakes up and check his balance. I'm worried because he's made no effort to get up or expressed hunger or thirst. He's just drifting."

Simultaneously they became aware of someone else in the room.

"Dorinda!" Jeff broke the huddle.

"Is Craig alright? You looked so solemn." She asked anxiously.

"We were just talking," LaShonya assured her.

"Can I see him?"

"Yes, but I gave him an injection to help him rest," Jeff answered.

"Why?" Dorinda wondered aloud. "Alan said he's sleeping most of the time anyway."

Jeff led her to the table. "He's been restless. I'm hoping to give his muscles some rest too."

She nodded, reassured. Crossing the room, she touched Craig's shoulder.

"'Shon," he sighed.

"It's Dorinda, Craig."

"Ummm," he acknowledged her.

Dorinda searched the doctor's face for reassurance.

"He needs to rest right now," Jeff responded. "It's okay. He's stabilized. But it'll be several days before he has much strength."

Jeff took LaShonya aside. "I'm glad he's sleeping. Alan thought Craig's disorientation would worry her." Pausing in puzzlement, he added, "I didn't know they were that close."

"They've known each other most of their lives. Even went to school together before Craig went to the academy," she replied. "They're like family. Neither one had any brothers or sisters. They adopted each other, as Dorinda tells it. There was quite a celebration when he came aboard."

Jeff still looked puzzled. "I never thought about it before, but is Dorinda younger than the Captain? She's not my patient."

"Almost ten years." LaShonya smiled. "Craig wasn't sure about it when they got married. But he's accepted it. It's a good marriage from his point of view. They've established a spiritually centered marriage. Since Craig's been aboard, he and the Captain have become good friends. I don't know who of the three is most excited about the baby."

"One more thing I need to warn you about," he stopped her as she turned to go. "For a couple of days to a week he's going to be frustrated. His ability to concentrate simply won't be there. He'll be jumpy. I don't think the symptoms should last long. But he should be encouraged to just relax for a while."

"Okay. I'll take him to the dig."

"That should do it." The doctor paused, thinking aloud. "I saw a couple of conventional electrical shock patients when I was a resident: both complicated by burns. It's hard to predict how Craig's going to react. Still, the less stress for a while the better. He'll need all our prayers to help him deal with the frustration."

"Thanks, Jeff. I'll pass the word along."

Dorinda joined them and took LaShonya's arm. "How about lunch?"

"Lunch? Already?" Jeff checked the time, surprised. He made sure Craig was resting, left orders, and joined them.

# CHAPTER NINE

The negotiating team had spent the morning learning what they could about the beings, and in turn attempting to communicate the purpose of the mission.

"We are the Cutezarians," had been the starting point. From that very basic statement, they began branching out.

At first, the translators worked slowly, making communications laborious. But as the exchange continued the expanded database allowed faster translation. By lunch, break communications were progressing at an acceptable rate.

Captain Brodsky kissed his wife, greeted Jeff and LaShonya, and wearily slid into a chair next to her in the ship's public mess hall.

"How are negotiations going?" LaShonya asked.

He chuckled. "They aren't yet. We spent the entire morning learning the basics about each other." He took a bite of his sandwich. "How's Craig?"

"Sleeping," Jeff told him.

"Tell us about the Cutezarians. Craig will want to know when he's ready to talk," Dorinda prompted.

"They're fascinating beings. They've become secretive over the years, but wouldn't disclose what caused it. They allude to the time of the ancient shame. They're highly evolved beings with conceptual, spatial, and moral abilities. Their buildings float above the ground on a cushion of air. I've got to find out how they do it."

"Dr. Keal, sick bay. You'd better get down here," the comm button interrupted.

Jeff pressed the button. "On my way." He looked at LaShonya. "I assume it's about Craig. You'd better come."

Dorinda started to get up, but the Captain eased her back into her chair. "It's okay."

"I'll call if there's a problem," LaShonya promised as they hurried away.

They found Craig moving restlessly, resisting whatever was going on in his head.

"I can't wake him, nor can I get him to calm down," the med tech reported.

"I probably shouldn't have given him anything." Jeff bent over and touched Craig's skin. "Hot and clammy." He checked the panel and seemed satisfied with the readings. "Not any worse. Let's wake him and see what we get."

LaShonya touched Craig's face, and then stroked his chest. Craig relaxed a little. "Come on Craig, wake up. It's only a dream."

Jeff administered a counteragent to the earlier injection.

Craig gradually woke up, fighting his way through the electrical storm. "'Shonya, where are you? Where are you? Are you alright?" He called and called.

"Craig, I'm right here. I'm okay. Here take my hand."

Slowly Craig reached out and slid his hand into hers. The tension ebbed from his body. He opened his eyes, again puzzled, struggling to remember, and then becoming aware of his surroundings.

"Hi." He regarded his hand interlaced with LaShonya's and shook his head. "Getting to be a habit. Sorry."

"I'm starting to like it, I think," she confessed. "What was the dream about?"

He frowned. "The storm. Only you got lost in it. It scared me." He stopped abruptly and shifted his attention. "Jeff, can I sit up?"

"That's what I've been waiting to hear." The doctor held out his arm. "Take hold of my elbow and pull yourself up."

He did. Slowly and stiffly. LaShonya put her hand in the small of his back and assisted him. Pulling his legs up, he draped his arms over his knees for support and let his head drop forward.

LaShonya rubbed his back. It felt natural.

Gingerly moving his head from side to side, he smiled. "That feels good, 'Shonya."

"Everyone's starting to call me 'Shonya," she complained as she massaged.

"It's a perfectly good nickname," he defended himself without looking up. "I feel awful."

"Thank God you're here to feel awful," 'Shonya answered, suddenly serious. The depth of her feelings startled her.

He lifted his head, sharing her surprise.

Jeff sensed the importance of the moment. "Ah," He cleared his throat. "Craig, could you drink something? We need to keep you from getting dehydrated."
Craig nodded absently without shifting his gaze.

"Yuck. No." He dropped his head again working the tense neck muscles.

"I'll get something with nutrition in it." At the med tech's station, Jeff keyed a formula into the food synthesizer, and called Captain Brodsky.

"Yes, Jeff?" He and Dorinda were on their way out of the public dining hall.

"Craig's okay. I think it was a reaction to the injection. Dorinda can come down. Visitors are welcome."

He returned to find Craig again regarding 'Shonya with wonder in his face.

"Here, drink this," he said, breaking the spell.

Craig obeyed. The milkshake-like drink settled his burning stomach. "Good. Thanks."

"And some water." Jeff handed him another glass. "You'll probably want just liquids for a while. I'll leave orders for the med techs so you can have it anytime you want," he explained.

"I'm going to be here that long?" Craig fought the fear that suddenly jumped at him.

"Umm-hum," was the only answer he got. "Do you want to try standing?"

Craig stretched. "Maybe." He swung his legs over the side of the table and gingerly shrugged into the robe the doctor handed him. Sliding off the table, he stood but immediately leaned back against the table in response to the sudden buzzing in his head.

"What is it?" Jeff steadied him with a hand on each shoulder.

Craig shook his head, trying to clear it.

"Don't do that," the doctor admonished quietly.

"Too late," Craig groaned and closed his eyes to shut out the spinning room.

"Dizzy?"

"Definitely."

Jeff grinned grimly. "Do you feel like you could walk if your head was clear?"

Craig opened his eyes and lifted his head to meet the Doctor's concerned gaze. "Do I have strength in my legs?" he rephrased solemnly.

Jeff nodded, "Do you?"

Craig stood slowly and took a couple of steps. He nodded "yes" and instantly regretted it.

"Don't do that," Jeff repeated.

Retreating to the table, he was still leaning against it when Dorinda and the Captain arrived.

Dorinda hurried across the room.

Craig braced himself for her hug and heard 'Shonya draw a sharp breath when she realized Dorinda's intention. With a small motion, he assured her he could handle it and received Dorinda into his arms. She held him and he rested against her shoulder. For the first time since their childhood, he was grateful she was taller than he was.

"It's okay, Dorinda." His voice was shaky. "I'm tired, but okay." He faked a smile and changed the subject, "How's the kid?"

"Moving all the time." She released him with an affectionate smile and rubbed her stomach in the universal, content, baby-comforting manner of pregnant women.

Gingerly Craig eased back onto the table with 'Shonya's help. He greeted the captain and asked, puzzled, "What's going on?"

"Negotiations with the Cutezarians. I'm on my way back after lunch break." He stopped. "Are you ok?"

"Not yet," 'Shonya answered for him.

Craig gave her a look of gratitude and the Captain got the message. Checking his watch, he took Dorinda's hand.

"Glad you're up," he said. "Don't try to force it. Take it easy." He addressed Dorinda, "See me off, will you?"

Dorinda smiled. "He doesn't want me to tire you," she whispered to Craig as she kissed his cheek. "I'll be back."

Craig grinned and returned her kiss. "Bye."

The door closed behind them. Craig dropped his head and blew out his breath.

"When is someone going to tell me what happened? How long I'm going to be here? And when will the dreams go away?"

"Jeff's at the tech's station. I'll get him for you," 'Shonya answered.

"'Shonya?" He stopped her as she turned to go. "I think I'd better lie down."

She helped him get comfortable, fleetingly wondering what it would be like to have Dorinda's liberty to show her affection for him. She met his eyes and his expression made her wonder if he knew.

But he just smiled and closed his eyes.

"He's right," she thought. "Now's not the time to deal with this." Aloud she said, "I've got some studies running that I need to check on. I'll tell the med tech to send for me if the dream comes back."

He nodded, caught her hand, and held it briefly before letting go.

Stopping by the med tech's station, she relayed his request. "Jeff, he wants to know what happened, how long he's confined and when the dreams will stop. And I promised you'd call me if it comes back."

"He doesn't ask for much does he?" Jeff grinned and went to talk to his patient.

But he was already sleeping- calm and quietly resting.

"I'll tell you the bad news later, Chaplain." The doctor told the peaceful form. Returning to the med tech's station, he reported, "I'm going to my quarters to get some sleep. Call if his readings fluctuate. I'll be back about 1700."

He paused at the door and considered Craig's quiet body. "I'm afraid it's more serious than I thought."

## CHAPTER TEN

The Cutezarians withdrew, discussing the merits of allowing the humans to continue the dig, and Captain Brodsky got up to stretch his legs. With negotiations going well, he relaxed.

As he inspected the walls of the room, the Captain remembered Craig's description: stone, straight up and down, as if carved out of rock.

The room was located on the first level of one of the great pyramids. It resembled an inquiry room, a sedate, quiet, room with low stone walls around boxes of seats. One set of twenty seats stood on each side of the room, and low tables sat in the center between the two sets of boxed in seats. Even the furniture was stone.

The two teams of negotiators sat in the boxes and a panel of ten Cutezarians occupied the tables.

The huddle broke up and the spokes being approached the translation box. "We do not understand your purpose, but grant you permission to uncover the old structure. In time, your people may come and visit our city. Your scientists may view our records of the time you decide the structures were built and compare them with your conclusions. We must, however, have enough time to prepare our population for your activities. And you must always be on your ship before the darkness ritual. Do you agree to the terms?"

The Captain answered carefully. "We agree. We will wait until you notify us before we allow our people to travel beyond the work site. When we are here, we will leave before the darkness ritual. We will conduct our studies, formulate our ideas and compare them to your records at your convenience."

"It is agreed." The beings said.

"It is agreed." The humans affirmed.

It was 1600 hours before the negotiation team beamed back to the ship. The Cutezarians, at first cordial and accepting, suddenly became quite anxious to send them back to the ship.

Captain Brodsky gave the crew a wave that served as the "At Ease" command as he stepped onto the bridge. Wearily easing himself into the conn chair, he pushed the all-ship intercom pad.

"People, this is the Captain. It went well. The dig will continue. The Cutezarians have offered their records so we can compare our conclusions. This is perhaps one of the few instances this opportunity exists. They agreed we could visit after the citizens have been prepared. Brodsky out."

'Shonya communicated the news to the team on the surface, adding, "Full staff will return tomorrow."

Dr. Kobee received the communication. "Acknowledged. We've used the down time to finish analyzing and cataloging all the artifacts we've found. By the way, tell the Chaplain his beads may not be beads at all. Last night after the computers shut down, the bead's glow intensified. When Roger picked one up today, he got a tiny shock. How is the Craig, anyway?"

"He's been awake, but still sleeps most of the time," 'Shonya answered. "Thanks for the information. Goodnight. See you in the morning."

"Good-night, LaShonya. Tell Craig we're praying for him." Dr. Kobee signed off.

**

The Captain's announcement shook Jeff awake from a deep sleep. He took his time as he freshened up prepared for the rest of the day. He prayed for Craig at the same time.

80

"Crisis time." He said to himself as he entered sickbay. "How's the Chaplain?" he inquired.

The med tech looked up, puzzled. "He hasn't moved for hours. I was just about to call you. Take a look at the readings."

Something strange caught his attention. At first glance, they looked normal but, upon close examination, they were uncoordinated. Craig's pulse didn't match the breathing rate. The brain waves didn't match the nerve activity. The peaks and valleys of normal sleep patterns were alarmingly absent.

"He literally hasn't moved." Jeff mused.

Craig was lying on his left side with his knees pulled up slightly.

Touching Craig's shoulder, the doctor called his name. "Craig?" Shaking him slightly, he repeated, "Craig?"

No response.

"Craig!" Louder.

The doctor suddenly bent over and looked at Craig's face. The gray complexion and dark circles under the eyes alarmed him.

Suddenly he straightened and called the med tech. "Bill, get me Dr. Reed stat!"

Bill urgently contacted 'Shonya and she hurried in within minutes. "Jeff, what's wrong?"

"I'm not sure. But I can't wake him. I don't like it."

Craig didn't resist at all as they shifted him onto his back. They watched his hands fall to his sides and his head settle on the pillow, and then looked at each other.

"I prayed the dreams would stop so he could rest, but no one naturally sleeps this soundly." Jeff gestured to the panel. "The readings are all out of sync." He regarded 'Shonya gravely. "He responds to your touch. See what you can do. He's got to wake up."

Nodding slightly, 'Shonya took Craig's hand. "Craig, wake up. I need to talk to you." She opened Craig's robe, stroked his chest and touched his face. "Come on, Craig, come back."

He moved his head slightly. When she brushed his hair back from his forehead, he groaned.

Following an inspiration, she felt for his neck pulse. "Craig." She called, following the pattern, resting her hand near his.

He suddenly began twisting and thrashing.

"Watch out." She warned as Craig threw the pillow off the table, then the thermal sheet.

"He must be reliving what happened on the planet." Jeff said in amazement.

'Shonya watched for a moment. When she couldn't stand it anymore, she reached toward him, but Jeff stopped her.

"I need to know if he actually had convulsions." He put his arm around her. "I know it's hard. He was quiet when you found him, right?"

She could only nod in despair.

The med tech came to see what Jeff required.

"Get the sedative, stimulant and muscle relaxant I prepared. I'm not sure what we'll need," Jeff ordered over his shoulder. The tech nodded silently.

Craig appeared under attack. His hands covered his face and then tried to push whatever it was away.

"Oh God," 'Shonya prayed, "help him."

Gradually Craig's movements slowed, then ceased. But his breathing remained shallow. Sweat beaded on his forehead.

"This is how you found him?" Jeff finally asked. 'Shonya nodded. "Okay, what happened next?"

"I pushed the curtain aside and called to him." She whispered.

"Do it." The doctor pushed her forward. "Exactly like last night."

"Craig?" She called.

Retrieving the pillow and thermal sheet, she covered him. As before, he became calm. She touched his moist forehead.

He moved his head and tried to speak. "Shon?"

"I thought he looked ill or like a kid having a nightmare, she said, omitting her panicked prayer. "Then I went back to the chapel." She walked back a few steps from the table and turned her back to it. "Craig's ill. Someone help me get him to the ship." She repeated her words. "Then Oliver and I knelt by the cot." She whispered to Jeff. They moved back to the table. "I checked his pulse and he took my hand."

"Do it."

"Craig." She reached for his wrist with one hand, and checked his neck pulse with the other.

Craig closed his fingers around hers while his other hand reached up and took her hand from his neck. The readings returned to their previous readings. He took a deep shuddering breath and let it out slowly.

LaShonya Reed and Jeffery Keal did the same.

"Now what?" 'Shonya asked. "He's still not awake."

"After his reaction to the last injection, I'm reluctant to use a stimulant," Jeff responded. "Obviously, I ruled out electrical stimulation since I can't predict how he's going to react. It'll take too much time to recalibrate the computer to his system to get an accurate prediction. Judging from his color when I came in, I think we almost lost him."

"What do you suggest?" She asked him, catching his urgency.

83

He threw up his hands. "I don't know. I called you because you're the person Craig's responded to. I hoped you could wake him so I wouldn't have to resort to medication."

She looked down at Craig. His complexion was ashen. He released her hands and his arms fell to his sides.

She suddenly shook him by the shoulders. "Craig." The panic she fought crept into her voice. "Please, God no!" She prayed, "I can't watch anyone else die!"

In desperation, she sighed. The tenderness she'd felt earlier returned and without knowing why, she touched his face, leaned over, and kissed him. Maybe she felt a response. She kissed him again.

"Ummm," was all she got.

Another kiss.

"Oooooh." The sound came with his breath release.

Nothing more.

In exasperation, she looked up at the doctor.

"Bill, the stimulant." He took a deep breath. "We're going to have to risk it." He spoke softly, almost as if he didn't say it aloud, he wouldn't have to do it.

'Shonya turned away, unable watch. "God, please, not Craig. Help him."

Jeff laid the rod against Craig's neck, making sure he found the elusive vein.

"What's it for?"

Jeff pulled the rod back, startled by Craig's soft fuzzy-voiced question. Looking up, he encountered Craig's unfocused gaze. After a brief hesitation, he silently handed the injection rod back to the med tech.

Shonya spun around, her expression mirroring Jeff's relief. "Craig!"

He took her hand as if it were the natural thing to do and regarded her with a frown, trying to bring back a vague but powerful impression.

"You didn't," His voice drifted away.

"She didn't what?" Jeff asked

"I almost thought," He started again.

"It's okay, Craig." She put her hand on his chest. "Just relax," she said gently, her eyes challenging Jeff to keep quiet.

"We almost lost you," Jeff began.

Suddenly memories flooded Craig. He raised his head as memories overtook him.

"What is it?" 'Shonya prompted.

Letting his head fall back onto the pillow, he breathed a deep sigh. "I remember it all." He closed his eyes.

"Do you feel strong enough to get up and talk about it?" Jeff asked.

No answer. Craig's deep, labored breathing prompted Jeff to raise his voice. "Craig!" He called sharply.

With a small gesture of impatience, he stepped away from the table. "Are we back to square one?" He asked in despair. "God, touch him. Do what I can't," he prayed. Meeting 'Shonya's concerned gaze, he instructed wearily. "Wake him up."

"Can't we just let him sleep?"

Jeff shook his head. "It's been almost twenty-four hours. We nearly lost him. I've got to know if the readings are wrong about the damage and if it's still taking place. If I need to start neuro-muscular treatment. Well, I need to see him move around," he explained in a rush.

She nodded, catching his unexpressed self-doubt and concern.

"Craig?" She shook him slightly and brushed his still damp hair away from his face. "Come on, we need you to concentrate. Craig!" She caressed his face and her voice reflected the sudden urgency she felt. "Wake up! We've got to have your help." She began to realize how very much she wanted him to be all right.

Something reached him.

He took three, deep, ragged breaths. Then, with a sigh, he opened his eyes, his expression reflecting puzzled thoughts as he put things back into order. Unhappily, the doctor noted how long it took before awareness of reality replaced puzzlement.

Craig frowned, attempting to capture the escaping impression of something happening he didn't quite remember. "'Shonya. Hi." He looked around the room.

Jeff stepped back to the table. "Am I going to have to call 'Shonya every time I want you awake?" he scolded with a smile he didn't feel.

Another frown. "What?"

"Never mind." Jeff extended his arm. "Can you sit up?"

Craig pulled himself up, sat with his arms draped over his knees, and moved his head to stretch the neck muscles.

Jeff called the med tech to bring the muscle relaxant, but Craig pulled away when he laid the rod against his neck.

"Believe me, Craig, it's just a mild muscle relaxant so you won't feel so stiff and sore."

Craig capitulated.

Watching closely, Jeff was half-afraid even a simple muscle relaxant wouldn't work right. After a while, Craig sighed in relief.

"Better?"

Craig moved his shoulders and legs. "Much. Thanks." Turning his head, he regarded Jeff with a long sober look. He took a deep breath and asked, "It wasn't just a dream was it? The electrical storm."

With a shake of his head, Jeff handed Craig the glass of formula the med tech brought and talked while his patient drank.

"I think your subconscious interpreted it fairly well. From all indications, you received an electrical shock in some form. I expected a quicker recovery. You must have taken a stronger charge than I originally thought. The strange thing is…" He paused. "There are no burns."

"I felt like the air attacked me," Craig supplied.

'Shonya nodded. "That's consistent with your movements while you were dreaming."

"Will the dream return?" Craig asked.

"I'm not sure."

Craig acknowledged Jeff's honesty with a sober nod.

"I need you to get up and move around. Can you do that?" The doctor asked, raising the table so Craig could lean against it.

Gingerly Craig slid off the table. "The buzzing's still there." He reported cautiously, moving toward 'Shonya a few steps.

"Feel okay?" she asked.

"I don't know." He grinned slightly.

"Why don't you go over to the lounge and sit a while," Jeff suggested.

Craig slowly went to the area that served as the waiting room and perched on the arm of a chair.

"You look pretty good," Jeff observed.

"Light headed, off balance, but almost acceptable," Craig allowed.

"Dr. Reed, Captain Brodsky." Her comm button spoke into the silence. She touched it and responded. "Reed here."

"'Shonya, can you join me on the bridge? The Cutezarians have sent notification they want to talk."

"On my way."

"I assume you're in sick bay?" the Captain stated more than asked.

"Yes."

"How's Craig?"

"I'm standing here looking at him sitting on the arm of a chair." The Captain heard the smile in her voice.

"Progress! Thank God."

We did that already," Craig spoke from across the room. When they were alone he looked up, ready for business. "Jeff, how much electricity did I absorb?"

"I'm not sure. Enough to scramble you, that's for sure." He answered truthfully.

"Scramble?"

"Um-hum. You know the electrical impulses that start your heart, move your muscles? It scrambled those impulses along with others, like your balance, your concentration, communication skills, and ability to think logically. Sometimes the system shuts down indiscriminately—sleeping when you get quiet, or sometimes the reverse."

"How long?"

"I don't know. You need to avoid stress for a while. Look, I've got to check on an OB patient. Dr. Canady's off today. Gina Reecer had her baby last night."

Craig frowned. Something wasn't right, but he couldn't quite remember.

Jeff watched him struggle. "She's a week early." Craig nodded slowly. "Your electrical storm caused computers to power down, Dorinda had twinges and Gina went into labor. All within the same time frame." He turned to go. "Stay up as long as you can. As soon as you lie down your system will shut down again."

He stopped at the med tech's station. "Let the Chaplain do most anything he wants except lie down. That's okay too if he seems extremely exhausted. If he wants something to drink, give him the formula and water."

"Go ahead, I'll keep track of him," Bill Chung promised. Dr. Keal waved as the door closed behind him.

Craig wandered sickbay until he ached. He leaned against the doorframe and got Bill's attention. "Can I take a shower and maybe get dressed?"

"I don't know why not," the tech replied. "I'll send the orderly to your quarters. Uniform or casual?"

"What?"

"Your clothes, Chaplain, uniform or casual?"

"Oh. Casual's fine."

## CHAPTER ELEVEN

Dr. Reed looked up from the science station. "Electrical current's growing stronger. It builds and recedes in waves, but each wave grows stronger than the last."

"Here comes the communication, sir." Lt. Reecer announced.

"On Screen," Brodsky ordered.

"On screen," Reecer replied.

\*\*

Showered and dressed, Craig resumed pacing restlessly around sickbay. He activated the comm screen just as the Captain ordered the message put on screen.

The metallic computer voice was speaking. "Before the darkness ritual we reviewed our agreement, and feel you did not properly understand the requirements. We refer to your answer." The box was quiet as the Cutezarians conferred.

"Here we go." The Captain said to himself. "I should have known. It was too easy."

The box spoke. "Your answer 'when we are here, we will always leave before the darkness ritual' is not acceptable. You said, 'leave the city before the darkness.' We meant..." The pitch of the box rose. "You must always leave the surface before the darkness. Disruption!"

\*\*

Craig bolted, leaving the tech calling after him.

"Dr. Keal, Bill Chung here." The med tech hailed the doctor.

"Keal here."

"Doctor, the Chaplain was listening to the bridge communication and suddenly ran out. I couldn't stop him."

"Thanks, I'll look for him."

Exiting the turbo lift onto the bridge, Craig heard the Captain's explanation about building the compound on the surface and how long they had remained on the surface.

The Cutezarians erupted into speech all at the same time, shaking their large heads and waving their short arms.

Finally the translator box spoke, spitting the words out as it matched the panicked speed of the Cutazarians' words. "But you must not. The disruption is strongest this darkness. You must remove all beings from unprotected structures. We put ourselves in danger by removing our protection device long enough to warn you. The disruption comes with the darkness. Now. We must replace our protection." The screen went blank.

"Captain." Craig leaned on the railing separating the science and navigation areas. "The disruption is the electrical storm. It builds in intensity to a terrible peak then ebbs away. Then builds up again."

One look at Craig's haggard face convinced Captain Brodsky.

Swiveling his chair around, he ordered: "Lt. Reecer, open the frequencies to all personnel on the surface of the planet. Override all communications."

"Done." Reecer replied after the briefest delay.

"All personnel on the surface of the planet, this is Captain Brodsky. Prepare for immediate emergency evacuation. You are in danger. Bring only the most sensitive equipment and most valuable data. Do not waste time. Gather in one place in the middle of the compound. We'll beam you up as fast as we can. I repeat this is an emergency evacuation. Brodsky out."

He turned back to Reecer. "Put it on screen."

"Yes, sir."

The viewer showed the compound as it came alive with running figures.

Craig watched fearfully, knowing what could happen. "God, help them. Keep them from panic."

"Amen." The Captain added.

And Craig realized he had spoken aloud.

**

After an unusually long workday, the evening meal on the planet had been served late. Drs. Cabrailes, Zamwashi and Kobee ate together, discussing the progress.

At the Captain's communication, Dr. Cabrailes, as site director, made instantaneous decisions. Calling for attention, he instructed, "Take only your personal computers, the hand lasers, the ground laser and scanning equipment."

The three men looked at each other, coming to the same conclusion.

"The Chaplain," Dr. Kobee said.

"The computers," Dr. Cabrailes added.

"The lasers, the lights." Dr. Zamwashi was getting up.

Dr. Kobee finished by quoting the Cutezarians' last words of their first communication. "Beware of the disruption. A total disruption of electrical class systems."

"Us," Dr. Zamwashi intoned.

"Let's get out of here." Dr. Cabrailes.

They each hurried to get their team together, and within a few minutes, the first group gathered at the designated place.

**

Captain Brodsky hailed the transporter chief.

"Cooper here." His voice held a sharp edge.

"Commander, commence bringing people aboard and keep on until they're all off the surface."

"Yes, sir. I have a suggestion." Cooper's insolent manner bordered on insubordination.

"What is it?" The Captain encouraged, ignoring the tone.

"Have each team assemble at a different point. The tech in each transporter room will lock on to a different location." The commander replied.

"Do it," Captain Brodsky ordered.

**

Jeff announced himself to the bridge crew and went directly to Craig. By this time was leaning against the rail, supporting himself with both hands behind his back.

"Craig, you shouldn't be here. You can't subject yourself to this kind of stress."

"You wanted me awake and moving around," Craig challenged quietly.

"You know what I meant." Jeff stopped, seeing he wasn't getting anywhere. "How ya' doing?" he asked with a sigh.

"Not good," Craig answered truthfully.

"Dr. Keal, transporter one, stat," Cooper's hard voice ordered.

"On my way," he replied. He pointed at Craig. "You get back to sick bay."

"Ok. But this is an emergency," Craig said.

"You'll be the next emergency if you don't do what I say," the doctor threatened quietly.

"Let me make sure they're all okay."

Jeff gave up and detoured past 'Shonya's station on his way to the lift. "Keep an eye on him. If he shows signs of agitation, drag him back to sick bay."

'Shonya nodded, wondering if she could physically drag Craig anywhere. Conflicting feelings tore at her. With a twinge of guilt, she concluded that, given the same circumstances, Captain Arthur Norman would be right where Craig was. She also knew Art's driving instincts would be duty not pastoral. "You've got to stop this. This is not the time," she disciplined herself.

Dr. Keal hurried below deck and shouldered his way through the crowd in transporter one to reach Roger Lavera, who sat on the edge of the pad stage, gasping for air.

"Sick bay, Keal here. Oxygen, transporter room one, stat." Kneeling on one knee in front of Roger, Jeff held up the life reader.

His pulse was too fast, blood pressure up, heart irregular. "Your system's running away. Calm down if you can," he commanded handing Roger the small oxygen unit a med tech delivered.

Roger closed his eyes, inhaled the oxygen, and slumped to one side, almost losing consciousness.

"Roger!" Jeff said sharply, catching him and pushing him back into sitting position. "What happened?"

Roger sat still for a long time, struggling for composure. When he looked up, his eyes echoed Craig's puzzled expression.

"Oh please, God, no," the doctor prayed.

The look didn't last long. Suddenly Roger grabbed Jeff's arm so hard they both nearly toppled.

"I couldn't find Daniel. The last time I saw him was in the artifacts lab. He said he had to finish a date test before he left. I went back to get my computer and he was gone, but his gear was where he left it. He had said something about retrieving Craig's computer so I took his stuff and ran toward the chapel. But something happened. I couldn't walk. Couldn't breathe. Couldn't talk. One of our team found me and hauled me to the beam up point."

All the words came spilling out at once. Suddenly Roger stopped and gulped for air. Jeff handed the oxygen unit back and he inhaled for a minute. "I don't know if Daniel's on board. I've got to know!" His voice rose in agitation.

Jeff looked up at Commander Cooper. "Contact all transporter rooms and see if anyone's seen Dr. Kobee. If not, ask the Captain to scan the compound."

The commander, an abrasive, anti-authority transporter technology expert, whose language and attitude were tolerated only because of his knowledge and dedication to technology, nodded and swore under his breath. "He'd better not still be down there."

Jeff threw him a sharp look of reproof and returned his attention to Roger. "Is that enough, Roger?" the doctor asked. Roger nodded. "We'll find him," Jeff assured him. "Now, can you stand?"

He nodded again and together they got to their feet. Roger's readings fluctuated suddenly and he swayed slightly, reaching for Jeff's arm.

He steadied himself. "It's okay."

"Dizzy?" Jeff asked remembering Craig's symptoms.

"Lightheaded," came the answer. "It's gone now."

Jeff motioned to the tech. "Take Roger to sickbay. Run the same scans we did on the Chaplain. Prepare a comparison report. I'll be down as soon as I check the other T-rooms." He paused. "And call me if the Chaplain isn't there."

Hurrying people made it nearly impossible for Dr. Keal to get through the halls. He mainly saw people who were lightheaded. But he lost count of the dozens of many bumps, bruises, and skin irritations hi treated. There was even a broken collarbone.

Conducting an informal triage, the doctor sorted out those who needed treatment in sickbay. Tissue regenerators treated the skin irritations and bruises. He was able to send the majority of patients to their quarters. As he went, he recorded orders for each patient, knowing he couldn't remember it all by the time he was done.

At one point, Jeff suddenly stopped and punched his comm button. "Sickbay."

"Chung here."

"Run full scans on anyone who comes in with even one of the same symptoms Chaplain Lea exhibited," he ordered.

"Yes sir. That'll keep us busy. Shall I send you help?"

Jeff looked around with a sigh. "No. I think I've got it."

"We'll take care on anyone you send in," Bill assured him.

"Thanks."

Jeff lost track of time as he examined people and made decisions. Suddenly his comm button startled him.

"Dr. Keal, Chung here."

"Yes, Bill."

"You kept us busy, busy. I just now realized I didn't tell you the Chaplain isn't here."

"Thanks. I'll take care of it." Muttering to himself, Jeff entered transporter room six. "Terrific. I wouldn't be surprised to find him lying in a corridor somewhere."

## CHAPTER TWELVE

"Captain, this is Commander Cooper." The Commander's irritating, sharp-edged voice broke the silence that had settled on the bridge as they watched the hurried evacuation.

"Yes, Commander," the Captain answered.

"We're missing Doctor Kobee."

Craig, now sitting on the rail, took his eyes off the screen, slid to his feet, and looked at the Captain in distress.

Cooper's sharp voice continued. "Roger Lavera was searching for the doctor on the surface when they forced him to return to the ship. We've searched everywhere on board."

"We'll scan the compound. Everyone else here?" the Captain asked.

"And accounted for," came the reply.

"Good work, Commander. Brodsky out." The Captain turned to 'Shonya.

"Already scanning, Captain." In a few minutes, she reported. "Found him."

"Reecer, get us a picture," the Captain ordered.

"Got it."

Craig fought panic as the picture materialized.

Lying in what appeared to be his quarters, Daniel Kobee seemed pinned down by an overturned table across his legs.

"The table's light enough that he could have pushed it off easily." Craig thought to himself. But when the picture grew sharper, he could see the table wasn't holding him down. Something else was wrong. Daniel wasn't lying still.

Drawn to the screen, Craig moved from the rail to lean against the front of the navigational console.

As Daniel's body twisted and turned, he alternately tried to protect his face and push something away.

Only LaShonya Reed and Craig Lea knew what was really happening.

'Shonya watched in dismay, better understanding Craig's trauma. Then, she was suddenly thrust back, reliving a scene from her childhood. Menacing shadows fought over a weapon, the explosions rocked her child image and bodies flew through the air as she frantically searched for her sister. The accident had killed five people, including her sister, but it really hadn't been an accident. 'Shonya shook her head, unwilling to face the deaths.

Craig watched in despair, reliving the suffocation, terror, burning irritation, and frustration.

Neither was aware of the background orders.

"Get him out!" the Captain ordered Commander Cooper.

"I'm trying. Sir," was the terse answer. The "sir" was there, but barely.

"What's wrong?"

"The computer powered down."

"Auxiliary power, Commander."

"Yes, sir."

Craig crossed his arms and leaned back against the console, unable to take his eyes from the screen. On one level, he prayed. On another, he felt Dr. Kobee's struggle. On yet another, he sensed the threatening weariness of his own condition.

Dr. Kobee finally stopped struggling.

"Reecer, open his frequency." Craig heard his own voice, yet had no feeling of having spoken.

Lt. Reecer checked with the Captain and got a nod.

"Ready, Chaplain."

"Dr. Kobee, it's Chaplain Lea. I'm not sure you can respond, but I want you to know you are not alone." Craig suddenly couldn't continue.

The Captain tried again. "Cooper, can you get him out of there?"

"Another minute, Sir." The commander barked.

"As soon as you have power, get him out."

"Craig?" The static threatened to overcome Dr. Kobee's weak reply.

"I'm here, Daniel," Craig answered.

"Craig, it's real." His voice suddenly came through clearly. "It's all real. Don't ever doubt. I see God."

"We can beam him up now." Commander Cooper reported.

"It's too late, Alan. He's dead," 'Shonya said softly, her eyes on Craig. She was afraid he would cut off his own breath as his head went down so far his chin nearly touched his chest. One hand covered his eyes. In that posture, he became motionless.

The world fell in on Craig. Couldn't breathe. Couldn't think. Just feel. Grieve. And pray.

Captain Brodsky ordered the body brought aboard, moved the ship to a higher orbit, and went to the science station. Perching on the console, he looked down at 'Shonya's grief stricken face.

"Are you ok?" he asked, and received a reluctant nod. "You ready to declare your feelings for the Chaplain?"

"I'm not sure what they are." She was suddenly too tired to be anything but truthful.

"If you do what I'm about to ask, the whole crew and all the scientists will be asking," his said gently, his eyes grave.

"Tell them Jeff's theory about me being the last person he talked to before the shock, and the first person he became aware of after. I became his link to reality. Let us work out our feelings later." She spoke without humor or anger. "What do you want?"

"Talk to him. Bring him back to reality. Convince him his work's done for now. Tell him it's my job to deal with the family. Make him go back to sick bay."

"You're risking a very public display of affection," she replied.

"I can set aside the 'no PDA on the bridge' rule if you can," he said softly.

She nodded, aware of the already existing speculation about her and Craig's friendship. The Captain moved aside so she could leave her station.

Craig looked up when she put her hands on his arms. Unshed tears sparkled in his eyes.

She waited until he acknowledged her and then said softly, "Craig, you've done everything you can for now. The Captain will deal with the family."

Craig looked away. "Nathan," he choked out.

"Daniel's son will need you more later," She reasoned.

But he could only feel. "Oh God, what do I do now?" he prayed without awareness of speaking aloud. Tears escaped and fell down his check.

She reached up and brushed them away. "You come with me back to sick bay. Let us take care of you for a change."

He looked at her a long time as if he didn't quite understand. Suddenly he gathered her into his arms and just stood there: not crying, not speaking, seeking comfort, struggling for control.

In comforting Craig, she found release from her own grief.

Finally, he released her and said softly. "Everything's going in circles. I'm exhausted."

She slipped her shoulder under his arm and they slowly moved up the ramp toward the turbo lift.

Oliver Zamwashi appeared as the doors opened. "Jeff asked me to come get the Chaplain," he explained.

With the sudden drop of the turbo lift Craig groaned and slumped against the wall, his head falling against 'Shonya's shoulder.

"Here, let me." Oliver lifted Craig and, when the doors opened, carried him to sickbay.

It seemed not one more person could fit into sickbay. All the monitoring tables were full. Jeff emerged from the tech's station and looked around, "Let's put him in the isolation room. Did he collapse on the bridge?" 'Shonya shook her head. "What happened?"

They followed Oliver into the room as she explained.

"He showed up during the Cutezarian's message, explaining the disruption is an electrical storm. Fortunately for all these people." She gestured around the room. "All the Captain had to do was look at Craig and he understood what a stronger version of the charge would do. He ordered immediate evacuation." She paused a second to regain her composure. "I thought Craig was going to come apart when Cooper reported Daniel missing, but he was under control enough to speak with him before he died."

Oliver laid Craig on the bed and Jeff activated the panel as 'Shonya finished her report. "On the bridge he only said he was dizzy and exhausted, but he didn't tolerate the dropping action of the lift."

"I can understand that." The doctor shook his head as he looked at the readings. "Still out of sync." Turning to 'Shonya he said, "We'll let him alone. I'll call you if anything changes."

"How is he?" Roger Lavera stood in the door.

"The fact that he didn't do what I told him to didn't help," Jeff said grimly.

"OK, I'll go back to bed. But how's the Chaplain?" Roger persisted.

"No worse I guess," Jeff replied. "Go."

"Yes, sir." Roger grinned.

"He'll be fine," Jeff said in response to 'Shonya's unasked question about Roger's condition. "He experienced mild symptoms; didn't even totally lose consciousness."

"Okay." She felt relieved. "I'll talk to Ensign Ronger about planning the memorial service before Craig wakes up. I know he'll want to speak if he can, but we'll get everything else done."

"Good idea," Jeff agreed. "The Ensign will have to take over vespers for a while too."

Shonya nodded. "He's young, but good at organizing." She paused, assuming Andez would be reluctant to take over Craig's role. "I'll tell him it's doctor's orders. That ought to put him at ease." She touched Jeff's arm as she turned to go. "Thanks."

The doctor nodded his answer and turned back to examine Craig. His skin felt hot and damp. "Sleep well. The worst is yet to come," he said. Then he prayed. "God, let him rest. Help me know what to do. We need him."

## CHAPTER THIRTEEN

The Captain sat at the conn with his morning coffee and touched the comm center's button. "Captain Brodsky to the Cutezarian communicator."

He was filled with weariness, and he imagined most of the people aboard the M. Curie shared his feelings. In honor of Dr. Kobee, he had ordered all operations suspended for the next two days. He hoped the scientists and crew would use the time to grieve as well as honor Daniel's memory. He thought of Craig still sleeping in the isolation room, and the part he'd played in saving lives.

"God, be with us," he breathed.

"Captain Brodsky, to whom do you wish to speak?" the metallic voice of the translator box came over the communication system.

"I wish to speak with the chief communicator who spoke with us last darkness." Captain Brodsky requested.

He sipped his coffee and a few minutes later Lt. Reecer spoke. "Communication coming through, sir."

"Ready."

"Leader of the humans, your workers on the planet escaped damage?" the Cutezarian asked.

"All but one escaped," the Captain acknowledged.

"We regret that even one was damaged beyond survival," the Cutezarian said.

"Thank you. We wish to express our gratitude for risking danger to yourselves to warn us. Our spiritual leader was affected in the disruption the darkness before last. His illness and your warning made clear to us the nature of the danger." The Captain finished his coffee. "Were any Cutezarians damaged as the results of your suspending protection to warn us?"

"Not one was damaged." The Cutezarian seemed relaxed and calm, in contrast to the night before.

"I must ask when it is safe for living beings to return to the surface of the planet," Captain Brodsky continued.

"In the daylight there is never danger. There is not always danger in the darkness. But the disruption always follows a time of quiet. Many ancient Cutezarians were damaged beyond survival before we learned to protect ourselves," the metallic voice explained.

"May I ask what the protection is?" the Captain ventured.

"The hard material with which we build our structures, the material which covers the places we walk, and the force that cannot be seen all work together to protect and shield us from detection by your scans as well as from the disruption," the box answered.

"If you come to our ship and stay through the darkness are you in danger?" the Captain asked.

The beings conferred. Finally one spoke.

"Was there any damage on your ship during the disruption?"

"Our ship's transporter computer shut down, but there was no people damage. And there were no effects when we moved to a higher orbit," the Captain reported. "Can we arrange a meeting?"

The box remained quiet longer than normal, then finally translated: "Our negotiators will contact you."

"After our period of remembrance for the one who died, and the recovery of our spiritual leader, we would like to invite you to visit us."

"We will consider the necessary preparations."

The picture faded.

His duty done, the Captain went to sickbay. "How's Craig this morning?" he asked Jeff.

Looking from his computer, the doctor greeted him. "Morning. He's still sleeping. But his readings are more in phase. It's the strangest thing." He shook his head. "I've given him medication, nutrition and liquid by IV. As far as I can tell, the dreams haven't returned. Mostly I'm just letting him rest."

"Will he be able to speak at the memorial service tomorrow night?"

"He should be up and around," the doctor nodded. "I won't tell him he can't."

"Okay," the Captain looked around the nearly empty sick bay. "Everyone else has been dismissed?"

"Roger was the last to go. He went to his quarters this morning."

"Good. When Craig wakes up, tell him LaShonya and Andez took care of the arrangements." The Captain turned to go, but stopped and inquired, "Is he really going to be alright?"

"If we can keep him relaxed and let his body heal, I think so. Can we put him on medical leave a while? 'Shonya suggested inviting him to the dig. I think it's a good idea."

The Captain nodded. "How long?"

"I don't know yet. I'm not sure how Daniel's death and the memorial service will affect him."

"Indefinite then. I'll process the request." He paused then made a request. "Call me when he wakes up. There are a couple of things he needs to know before the service."

"Will do."

The doctor checked Craig's readings once more before going on rounds. Craig sighed, turned over on one side, and drew his knees up.

"Good. Normal sleep movements. Hang in there, Chaplain. Sleep as long as you like."

And he did. He slept all day and all night.

Dorinda came and stayed a long time. 'Shonya came and touched him gently, not to wake him, but in response to the emotions watching him sleep stirred in her. Roger came just to be there, to work through his own trauma and feel reassured Craig was going to be okay.

And Laura and Nathan Kobee came.

In her grief, Laura cried, yet felt comforted. "Craig, if you only knew how much your teaching and life influenced Daniel. You'll never know how much you helped him," she told his sleeping form.

She answered Nathan's questions about why Uncle Craig didn't wake up and talk to him.

They all prayed.

Before breakfast the next day, 'Shonya's comm button alerted her. "Dr. Reed, your visitor has arrived."

In all the activity, she had nearly forgotten Art's visit. Hurrying into transporter room one, she returned Art's enthusiastic hug, trying not to notice the tech's shocked, puzzled expression.

"LaShonya!" Art kissed her playfully.

"Art. It's good to see you." And it was. His cheerfulness lightened her spirits.

Before they sat down to breakfast, he kissed her seriously. 'Shonya couldn't help herself. *"More taking, less giving than Craig's kiss,"* she thought and immediately reproved herself. But she couldn't stop the smile.

Art stepped back. "There. That's the first real smile I've seen."

She was glad to have a concrete excuse for her reserve, but felt guilty for using it. "One of our scientists died last night and our chaplain is ill. Dr. Kobee's funeral is tonight. The doctor asked me to help Craig, that's the chaplain, this afternoon."

Beginning to eat he asked, "What happened?" As she related the story, he became convinced that, for whatever the reason, she wasn't ready to leave.

Conversation drifted from the M. Curie to his own recent missions. As the meal ended, there was a lull in the conversation. They looked at each other in the long pause.

"You can't give me an answer yet can you?" he asked gently.

Relieved, she spoke honestly. "At the very least I would need to get this dig underway even if I were to leave."

"And the other?"

Again, she answered as honestly as she could. "I've got some things to work out yet."

With a nod, he followed her lead. "I came partly to let you know I got new orders. That puts me on hold too. I'll keep the job open as long as I can and wait until you're ready to talk about us."

'Shonya relaxed. She had the time she needed. "Where are they sending you now?"

*×

Mid-morning Sheila Brown glanced at the monitor.

"Look!" She pointed to the screen. "The Chaplain's awake." Noting the time, she called Dr. Keal.

Craig was lying on his back frowning at the ceiling. Jeff stood in the door for a moment and watched him struggle with his thoughts.

"Craig, can I help you?" he asked stepping into the room.

Craig pushed himself into a sitting position, the head of the bed following him into the upright position.

"It's okay," Jeff smiled at his surprised look. "These beds are for patient comfort, not just examination like the monitoring tables. If you lean against it with your head as well as your body for a certain length of time, it assumes you have gone back to sleep and returns to the prone position."

Craig nodded, half listening, his attention drifting. Leaning his head back against the bed, he asked, "Did it really happen?"

"It all happened. It wasn't a dream," Jeff cautiously affirmed, waiting to see how much his patient remembered.

"Daniel's really," Craig stopped and took a deep breath. "He's really dead." He sighed. After a moment, he leaned forward, rested his elbows on his knees, and put his head in his hands. Finally, he sat back and asked, "Laura and Nathan?"

"Grieving, but holding up." Jeff said neutrally. "They came yesterday and stayed a while. Nathan wanted to make sure you didn't go to heaven and leave your body."

Craig smiled sadly. "What about the services?"

"This evening," Jeff answered, giving him time to realize he'd lost a day.

Craig frowned. "But." Something wasn't right.

"You slept thirty-eight hours," Jeff finally told him.

Craig suddenly looked up. "The services! Who's planning? Who's speaking? I need to be there."

"Calm down. 'Shonya and Andez have it under control. They knew you'd probably want to say something if you were able, so they saved you time."

Thoughts and memories flooded Craig and he struggled to put them in order. Jeff mistook it for confusion.

"If you feel you can't, everyone will understand," he said gently.

"I need to do this," Craig said soberly. "I don't know how, but I need to. Can I get up and shower?"

"How do you feel?"

"Tense inside, like I'm going all directions at once. I can't focus. I'm jumpy," he confessed fearfully.

"It's okay," the doctor assured him. "You'll feel that way a while. After the memorial service I've ask the Captain to put you on medical leave until your system gets untangled. I can give you a selective nerve suppressant to help you through the service. But in its present form, it's viciously addictive. I can't keep you on it. Instead, we'll remove you from external stress. 'Shonya suggested you pursue your hobby for a couple of months."

"Months?" Craig repeated.

"Be prepared, but it might not take that long. I had the Captain make the leave indefinite. Go. Shower and shave. The Captain wants to talk to you before the service." Craig's frown stopped him. "What's wrong?"

"There was something I wanted to tell him about Dr. Kobee," Craig said.

"Don't force it. Right before the Captain gets here, I'll give you the larger of two doses. It'll be about a half an hour before you begin to feel its effects." Craig's attention had wandered. The doctor gave him a minute to refocus. When Craig's gaze met his again, he continued. "You'll be awake, but relaxed. I'll send 'Shonya in so you'll have someone to talk to."

Craig's expression remained puzzled so he spelled it out. "Right now your system is either shut down—sleeping—or charged—tense, jumpy, disoriented. I want you uncharged but functional. The first dose will relax you more than you really need to be, but you'll bounce back, maybe even hit normal. The second, smaller dose will be about an hour before the service for maintenance. You'll feel pretty good all afternoon and be able to get your thoughts together for this evening.

"Will 'Shonya bring my log?" Craig asked.

"She'll do anything you want," the doctor grinned and shook his head. "Within reason," he added. The humor was lost on Craig. "I'll call the Captain."

Craig went to shower, feeling shaky and nervous inside, unable to concentrate, and incapable of putting a presentation together.

He began praying, knowing no one could hear. "God, I can't do this alone. I feel worse than the first time I ever spoke in public. I can't think. My emotions overwhelm me. Help me through this. Calm me down. Thank you for Jeff and his help. Give me the ability to follow his orders and courage to fight. Help my frustration. Give me the kind of patience you've taught me to apply to others and help me apply it to myself." He ran out of words. Standing with his face in the stream of water, he let it wash away the tears of grief and frustration.

"I was afraid you'd drowned." Jeff greeted him when he finally emerged.

"The water soothes the prickly feeling," Craig answered guardedly.

"Okay." The doctor motioned him to sit on the bed. "Are you ready?"

Craig nodded reluctantly and Jeff gave him the injection. Within minutes, the Captain walked in.

They shook hands and the Captain immediately got to the point. "I understand we don't have much time. There are a couple of things you need to know. The first is you are the reason we have so many survivors. If you hadn't come to the bridge, I wouldn't have figured out what the disruption does until it was too late. It would have been beyond tragic."

Craig closed his eyes, remembering the horror he felt when he realized what was happening. He nodded, not saying anything.

110

"You okay?" the Captain asked.

Craig looked up and nodded slowly. "I'm still piecing everything together. I was frightened I wouldn't or couldn't get to you in time, and if I did, that I couldn't tell you so you would understand." He frowned. "There was something about Dr. Kobee I wanted to tell you." He faltered and stopped.

"Was it about where he died?" the Captain prompted gently.

After a moment, Craig looked up and said softly, "He was in my quarters wasn't he?"

"Um-hmm." The Captain's tone matched his. "Roger experienced the same symptoms you did while looking for Dr. Kobee. He was headed toward your quarters when it happened. He told Jeff Dr. Kobee said something about retrieving your computer. He must have been overcome in your quarters, fallen against the table and caused it to fall on him. He was dead before we could beam him up." The anguish on Craig's face stopped him.

"Why?" he asked in a strangled voice.

"Craig, you don't know how highly Daniel regarded your abilities as Chaplain and spiritual teacher," the Captain said gently. "I stopped to see Laura on the way here. She wanted you to know Daniel obviously valued your sermon notes as much as he valued his archeological notes. He often told Laura how insightful you are. And he appreciated your relationship with his son." The Captain stopped, seeing Craig's struggle for control. "She wanted me to tell you not to feel responsible." He watched Craig absorb everything. "I'm sorry, I should have waited."

"It's okay. Jeff hopes the medication will help me deal with all this. Right now emotion overrides thinking. Makes me feel like a teenager. Very frustrating."

They went on to speak of Dorinda and the baby, the plans for the completion of the archeological work, and the Cutezarians.

As they talked, Captain Brodsky could see the medication slowly begin to take effect. The expression in Craig's eyes became less haunted and puzzled. His smile was less sad.

He returned to the most pressing subject. "Ensign Ronger will prepare the devotional for the service. What Laura wants from you are your own insights. That's what Daniel found so refreshing."

Craig nodded, less troubled than before, but the sad smile was back. "What time?" he asked.

"Six, instead of vespers."

They sat in silence a few minutes. Presently Craig took a deep breath and let it out with a sigh. It wasn't a sigh of grief, but of relief. He turned his head from side to side, stretching his tense muscles.

The Captain stood to go. "Feel better?"

"Um-hmm. My stomach does anyway."

"Could you eat something?" Jeff entered when he saw the Captain stand.

"No." The thought turned his stomach. "But your formula sounds good. I guess I'm thirsty."

"That's fine. We need to push fluids a couple of days," he answered.

"Captain, thanks for coming," Craig ended the interview. "It helped."

"Good. Remember we're praying."

"Pray for Andez too. He's got a lot of responsibility and not much experience," Craig replied.

"'Shonya said he's doing good work," Jeff assured him. Leading the Captain out of the room, he explained. "The more relaxed he gets, the more he'll want to talk. He hasn't talked much about all this yet, so I'm sending 'Shonya in. He may tell her about it."

"Will he remember enough of the conversation for it to be therapeutic?" the Captain asked.

"Yeah, he'll remember it all. The drug's a selective suppressant not a depressant, although he may sleep some. It provides relief for the patient with wild nerve activity, and intense feelings of well-being for the normal person. That's why it's so psychologically addictive."

In the middle of 'Shonya and Art's tour of the ship, Jeff requested 'Shonya's presence in sickbay. Turning Art over to Roger for the remainder of the tour, she made her way to sickbay.

After conferring with Jeff, she carried the tray of formula and a pitcher of water into the isolation room.

"The doctor says drink," She commanded, putting the tray on the table. As they sat, she in the only chair, and he on the bed, she started. "You've trained Andez well. I've helped a little, but he's got the service ready."

"He thinks he wants to go to seminary when this tour's up. We've been doing some academic preparation." Craig stretched out on the bed.

He was always so casual when he spoke of his accomplishments 'Shonya almost smiled. "How long has this been going on?" she asked and then settled back to listen.

"I first met Andez a month after I came aboard. I was getting ready for vespers and I kept hearing things in the chapel. There he was, sobbing into the upholstery of one of the old red chairs. It took me a long time to get him to talk to me. When he finally did, I almost didn't have time enough left to get ready for vespers. It seems his mother died right after he got here, and he wasn't able to get home. His mother was an important storyteller from his tribe in

South America. One of the last Incas, so Andez says. He loved her in the tribal way some of the ancient peoples have always loved and almost worshiped the old ones. His extent of knowledge about God came from myths and stories that were a mixture of ancient Catholicism and Inca folklore. He started telling me the ancient stories.

"I guess he liked the way I listened. For months, we explored the stories. I showed him where many of the blended beliefs came from, and slowly he came to understand. He showed up in my office one day and wanted to know how to give his very being to God." He paused a long time, looking back on Andez's spiritual journey. He pushed his hair back and smiled. "Enough about my job."

"We have time," she answered cautiously. "How do you feel?"

He considered. "Like I should be worried about something and can't remember what it was," he replied quietly. "But I know what's happening."

"Tell me about the other night," she commented neutrally.

Afraid she had approached the subject too soon, she held her breath as he seemed to withdraw. However, slowly, hesitantly he started, and then the words just kept coming. He told her about the feelings of being attacked: of the hot prickly skin irritation, the frustration of knowing she was there but not being able to respond, and the frustration of knowing things weren't right but not being able to do anything about it. He described all the jumpy feelings, the disorientation and inability to make his intellect override the emotional forces that constantly threatened.

Finally out of words, he fell silent. And they sat quietly.

He changed the subject. "While the Captain was here, I got to thinking about the ifs. What if you hadn't allowed me to take part in the dig? What if I hadn't worn myself out to the point I didn't argue with you about going to bed early? What if you hadn't come to talk to me? What if Jeff hadn't insisted I get up and stay up? What if I hadn't flipped the comm screen on? What if I couldn't have communicated to the Captain what had suddenly become clear to me? God was definitely at work in the situation. I wasn't thinking clearly. God cleared my understanding. If he hadn't, everyone on the planet would have been dead, and we'd been mourning all of them instead of just Daniel." He suddenly fell silent, his grief resurfacing.

They spoke of God's work in their lives, of their childhood, then archeology. 'Shonya merely alluded to her sister's death and resulting family devastation that finally ended in her parents' separation. Craig asked quiet questions and she almost told him the entire story. However, she used restraint, knowing he wasn't ready to deal with her unresolved emotions in addition to his own. Nor did she mention Art. She didn't understand the relationship well enough to discuss it. Instead, she directed the conversation to theology.

As they talked, Craig's movements became almost lazy. The sighs came less often, and the New York accent, inherited from his mother, became more pronounced.

'Shonya realized his censor filters that influenced what he did and said in public were deactivated. He shared his thoughts on archeology, God, and theology freely, without fear of being misunderstood or misquoted.

Suddenly in mid-sentence, he surprised them both with a yawn. A natural, relaxed, late night yawn. Stifling it, he apologized with a grin. "Excuse me."

'Shonya smiled affectionately and stood to go. "I'll see you later."

Jeff returned from rounds and checked in at the med tech's station. "How's it going?" he asked looking at the readings.

"They've been talking for hours. But I think the Chaplain's ready for a nap."

"You had the computer link it to my personal computer like I asked?" he asked softly.

"Every word."

"We'll delete everything but his description of the night he took the charge," he assured Sheila Brown, the tech on duty. "No blackmail, I promise," he grinned.

Just as Jeff approached the door Craig reached up, took 'Shonya's face in his hands and very gently kissed her. Jeff didn't enter, feeling for the second time he was witnessing the deepening of a relationship.

"I'll be back after lunch and bring your log. And we can talk about tonight." 'Shonya touched his hand, her feelings tumbling around and around.

Craig caught her hand as she turned. "Stay?"

She nodded, "Sure."

He sighed. "It's such a relief to just relax."

She was glad for him. Yet, as he settled down to sleep, she worried about the days of frustration ahead. She waited until his grasp relaxed and slipped away.

She almost ran into Jeff. "How's his attitude?"

"I've only seen him that relaxed once," she said with a smile. "It was several nights ago. He was talking to Doctor," She stopped, drawing a sharp breath. She continued after a moment. "He was talking to Daniel at the first showing of the artifacts. Anyway, he's sleeping, but not like before. He decided to go to sleep." She turned to go, then came back. "Jeff, he's so relaxed and feels good today, won't that add to his frustration?"

"It's a risk," the doctor agreed. "But I don't see any other way to get him through the funeral. Nothing short of a miracle could straighten out his electrical system this fast."

"I think God uses doctors too." 'Shonya laid her hand on his arm, her smile returning.

"Thanks, 'Shonya." They both noted he too had fallen into the habit of using Craig's nickname for her. "How about you? You have things to deal with too." He knew about her sister. "You want to talk about it?"

She hesitated. "I guess I've never really dealt with it as an adult. I was so young. This is the first time I've lost someone close since then. Occasionally I've wondered what it would have been like to have a sister. I was so alone. Now I wonder how Nathan will handle being without a father." Her thoughts came out disconnected.

"Do you ever see the bodies?" he asked quietly.

Surprised, she nodded. "I see them fly out of the transport."

"Exactly what happened?" he probed.

"We were traveling. We got on a transport, but I left Charles, my English Butler doll, on the seat outside where we said goodbye to our parents. I wanted it so badly I began to cry. Malena told me to hurry and get it. As I went out the door, a large man almost ran over me as he entered. His bulk covered the whole opening, so I didn't see what he did. But they told me he was trying to hijack the transport, and a man tried to stop him by tackling him. His weapon discharged and triggered the explosion. The next thing I knew bodies were flying everywhere. Well, that's how it seemed to me as a child. The man who tried to stop the terrorist landed at my feet, alive. I guess everyone else died."

She shuddered. "Even after I stopped screaming, I couldn't tell the people who came to help what my name was for a very long time."

She stopped again. "I was only six. I remember mostly feelings and impressions. But I knew Malena was dead forever. I knew it then. I know it now. Still, a weird coldness hangs over my childhood. My parents drifted apart. Mother buried herself in her work, and I guess my father did too. But his attention focused on me. I have many, many memories of my father and very few of Mother. I didn't even know when they finally divorced." She looked up at the doctor. "I know now when tragedy hits it either bonds the family or drives it apart. Of course, as a child I only knew I was there when it happened."

"You got help didn't you?" Jeff asked gently.

She nodded. "And they convinced me I didn't cause it, or couldn't have prevented it. If I hadn't gone back for the doll, I would have died too. But, "

"But what?"

"Watching Craig and Dorinda together, occasionally I want a sister so badly it hurts. I can't help but wonder if I had screamed or something, the weapon might have discharged in another direction, and I would still have sister."

"Does it make it worse that Craig and Dorinda aren't even related?" the doctor probed deeper.

Her response was slow in coming. "Yeah. Jealousy's something I'm not used to feeling."

Jeff brought her back to the present. "You'll have to get over that if your relationship with Craig is going to grow. "

"There is no 'relationship' besides friendship," she protested.

"Oh, is that right? Are you sure?" he teased gently.

The conflict of having to choose between Art and Craig occupied her thoughts. Jeff didn't know about Art. No one knew. People assumed he was an old friend.

Jeff took her silence for consent, but also sensed she was still troubled. "It's okay. You have time to work it out. Craig's not going to be ready for anything for a while."

'Shonya laughed, partly because of the relief of sharing her feelings, and partly because she didn't know how to tell him about Art. "Craig's only half of it."
Jeff grinned. "I wondered about that too."

She didn't take the invitation to tell him. Instead, she gave him a quick hug. "Thanks for listening."

Jeff added. "It's important for you to talk too."

## CHAPTER FOURTEEN


Mourners filled the Chapel, yet they kept coming until the aisles overflowed.

LaShonya, Andez, and Craig entered the chapel from the small office attached to the chapel, casually referred to as the Chaplain's room, and took their places on the slightly raised platform.

It was a large chapel filled with muted colors. Oak pews, saved from a five hundred-year-old crumbling cathedral in old New York City, graced its space. They were a gift from Craig's parents when he received his posting to the Curie.

But the Chaplain wasn't thinking about pews or colors. His attention focused on the people. Moved by their shocked faces, restrained greetings and expressions of comfort to Laura Kobee, he almost panicked.

"God, I can't do this without help!"

No one was in a hurry to start. Craig and Andez let the scientists and crew express their feelings until silence signaled their readiness to begin.

The scripture Ensign Ronger had chosen, "You are not without hope as the world is," sent Craig's thoughts toward God and the hope he felt even in his own difficult condition.

*"Frustration but not despair,"* he thought. Then as he looked at the congregation he added, *"Grief, but not desolation."*

Captain Brodsky and Dr. Keal slipped in the back at the last moment. Noting the detached look in Craig's eyes, Jeff worried about over-medicating him. But moving closer, he saw with relief that Craig's changing expressions indicated he was thinking instead of drifting.

Ensign Andez Ronger's unique way of putting things claimed Craig's attention. "Most of the time," the Ensign said, "I can see why God doesn't do things like I think they should be done. But sometimes I gotta ask 'why?' Dr. Kobee, to my way of thinking, didn't deserve to die.

"And a few years ago, I would have been seething with anger that would have grown into hate. Out there where people don't know God, that's all there is when something like this happens. Frustration, hurt, resentment, then hate and striking out. Where I'm from, that meant hurting someone, or yourself. For most of you, it means silent desperation because having everything you ever wanted doesn't help when things go wrong.

"Either way, there's no place to go, no one to talk to who can comfort you down to your soul. You can only let off steam. But when ya' got God in your life, your soul can be touched. We still hurt, and yell, and feel frustration, but we have someone to go to who can comfort us right down to our souls. God.

"It's not like we don't feel what people without God feel, it's that we have resources they don't,"

Craig's attention wandered as he reviewed the short time he had known Andez Ronger. *"Andez's come a long way from the scared, tough kid from the streets of South America."*

When Andez finished, he invited the congregation to stand for prayer before Craig spoke.

The movement of people standing brought Craig back to the present and he mentally participated in the prayer.

As the congregation settled back into the pews, Ensign Ronger turned and said, "Chaplain."

Without experiencing the awareness of moving, Craig found himself at the podium. He noted the Captain and Dr. Keal were both praying, and from the corner of his eye, he could see 'Shonya's bowed head. He felt a quiet calm settle, first over himself, then the congregation. Standing silently before them a full minute, he composed his words carefully.

"I remember Dr. Kobee best as he greeted me after vespers, Nathan perched on his shoulders." Upon hearing his name, Nathan looked up from the book his mother had given him to keep him busy. Craig smiled at him, before continuing. "Nathan, your father never said much as we shook hands. Just 'Chaplain' or 'Good thought, Chaplain.' He took part in the dissections...." The word slipped out and a ripple of appreciative chuckles quietly swept the room. 'Dissections' was Dr. Kobee's word for the discussions that followed each night's lesson. Craig allowed himself the briefest of smiles. "...And I found him thoughtful and logical.

"We always respected each other professionally. But on the planet, we discovered each other as people. A few nights ago, during the viewing of the first artifacts, Daniel and I found chairs in a corner and stretched out, tired but content. During the course of the discussion, I asked what he thought caused scientists to become the spiritual leaders in the late twenty-second century. I'll never forget his answer.

He said, 'Because we never found the final answer. Every puzzle we solved opened another whole area of questions. While other disciplines leaned toward humans having the power to solve their own problems, we were forced to realize the inevitability of a power beyond ourselves.'"

Craig paused. Heads nodded in agreement as if the scientists had discussed the matter among themselves. He hesitated, struggling for control. After a minute he continued, his voice filled with emotion.

"Many of you know Dr. Kobee died, um, trying to retrieve my computer containing my unlinked sermon notes. I'm awed he could think of me in that time of crisis. But in his last actions, he lived out the standard Believers have held since the time of Christ: thoughtful, considerate actions that benefit others first. It was with this spirit and belief he lived among us. It's unfortunate we have not lived up to the standard as a Human race."

Suddenly Craig stopped again. Jeff and 'Shonya moved forward, both afraid he could not continue. He didn't notice. Looking down at his log containing his notes, Craig struggled momentarily then addressed Laura Kobee.

'Shonya resumed her seat, but Jeff remained at the edge of the platform. Bending over, he addressed the med tech. "Sheila, get a glass of water for the Chaplain." With a nod, she obeyed and Jeff turned his attention back to Craig.

'Shonya let her gaze wander around the room and found Art watching her. Returning his smile, she wondered if her confusion showed in her face. Still smiling slightly, her attention re-focused upon Craig.

"Laura and Nathan," he was saying. "Never forget Daniel's last words. Laura, teach Nathan what they mean. Remember, as I always will." Then he addressed the entire congregation. "Dr. Kobee's last words were, "Chaplain, it's real. It's all real. Never doubt. I see God." He looked up. "It's real, friends."

Suddenly he couldn't continue and abruptly returned to his seat.

As he sat, he caught a glimpse of Commander Cooper's face outside the chapel door. Craig was used to his non-accepting, yet curious presence but the gentleness of Cooper's expression surprised him. Their eyes met for a minute part of a second, before Cooper turned and stalked off.

"God, how do I reach him?" The prayer he often voiced when encountering Cooper flashed through his mind.

Jeff took the last few steps to the platform and sat on the bench. He touched Craig's arm, holding out the glass of water.

Startled, Craig frowned then shook his head as if that would chase away his helpless feelings. With a sigh, he took the glass and gratefully gulped it down in one long drink.

The congregation sat in silence. Tears and sad smiles reflected their mixed feelings about having their faith renewed while grieving the loss of a friend.

Nathan watched his mother's tears a while, and then slipped away from her. He didn't run, but walked quietly across the platform and climbed into Craig's lap.

Craig gathered the small boy into his arms, rested his chin on Nathan's head, and closed his eyes. As the congregation witnessed the child's action, even the least emotional among them could not help but respond.

'Shonya stood at the podium to deliver the eulogy, closing thoughts, and prayer.

As she spoke, Craig gradually got his emotions under control. He felt wetness on his hands and looked down. Nathan's tears were silent, but Craig could feel the tension of sorrow building in the boy's body.

"It's okay to cry, Nathan," he whispered.

Nathan looked up at him and said, "Daddy's not coming back, is he?"

"No he isn't. When people die, they cannot come back," Craig answered.

"Will you go to heaven too?" Nathan asked fearfully.

"Not for a long time yet. And you won't be alone. Your mother will be here," Craig reassured him.

Nathan twisted in his lap, stretched up, and put his arms around Craig's neck. Craig wrapped his arms around the small body and held Nathan tightly, finding comfort in the action. The boy gradually relaxed in Craig's arms and was asleep before 'Shonya said the final prayer.

Jeff was glad Craig carried Nathan while people gathered around Laura and comforted each other. The child acted as a cushion between Craig and all the emotions around him.

As the chapel emptied, Craig spoke briefly with Laura and transferred the still sleeping child to Laura's shoulder. She hugged Craig with her free arm and gently admonished him.

"We'll be alright. You take care of yourself."

Art, 'Shonya, and Craig said goodbye to Andez at the chapel door. 'Shonya and Art took a few steps before she realized Craig hadn't followed. She sent Art on to the R& R deck where they had reservations for dinner and returned to the Chapel.

'Shonya found Craig sitting close to the front, gazing up at the sculpture behind the platform. Exhaustion lined every curve of his face. She tucked one leg under her, sat in the pew ahead of him, and faced him.

"Hi." She was afraid the emotion she felt was more than concern for a friend.

He brought his attention to her face. "Hi."

"You doing okay?"

He shook his head and half grinned. "No."

Comfortable silence settled between them.

Craig shifted his attention back to the sculpture. "I told God when this was over, I'd do whatever Jeff said." Craig broke the silence. "But there's so much to do." He stopped with a small, hurt sound, as if someone unexpectedly hit him.

"Craig, you simply can't. You won't be able to handle it," she insisted.

He surprised her by agreeing. "I know. I can feel it. I just don't know what I can do." The frustration was back.

"We still think it'd be a good idea if you indulged in your hobby at your own pace a while." She ventured, trying to keep from sounding like a conspirator. She needn't have worried.

He was too drained to notice. "Maybe I'll do that." His voice came from far away.

Abruptly he refocused and stood. Putting his hand on 'Shonya's shoulder, he caught her off guard. "'Shonya, when this is over, and I have a better handle on things, we have to talk about us."

And he slowly leaned down to kiss her.

Surprised, she responded.

It was quiet, non-demanding, yet unlike any kiss she had ever experienced.

Considering her face with a small smile, Craig reflected. "I remember that kiss. I didn't imagine it."

Before she could explain about sickbay, he made his way down the aisle and left her sitting alone, more confused than                                    ever.

## CHAPTER FIFTEEN

Three days later the scientists returned to the planet's surface. Operational orders limited the dig to the light hours, living quarters dismantled, and the labs enlarged so more people could work at once. The chapel became a lounge area with refreshments, comfortable chairs, and a couple of cubicles for emergencies or afternoon naps.

'Shonya persuaded Art to give her more time for both decisions. She couldn't bring herself to send him away. Art attracted her, along with his family of five brothers and two sisters who often traveled days to spend just a few hours together.

One of his sisters had come to spend his last day aboard with them. They shared meals and laughter. 'Shonya sent them on their way together with promises to make contact within the next few weeks.

Combing her hair the next morning before she returned to the surface, 'Shonya faced her image in the mirror. "Will I ever work this out?" she asked her reflection. "I have feelings for Art I don't have for Craig." She smiled at herself and admitted, "But I have feelings for Craig I don't have for Art." She looked at the ceiling and prayed, "God, I need wisdom." With a one last sigh, she went to work.

In her first action of the day, 'Shonya appointed Roger Lavera Director of Artifacts.

The crew worked with a renewed sense of mission. Everything had to be done just right so the dig would become a textbook example.

They named the tell Daniel Kobee the First, shortened to Daniel K One.

Jeff reluctantly released his patient from observation.

Craig returned to his quarters with a sense of loss. He couldn't do anything that brought him pleasure, let alone work. He couldn't concentrate long enough. He agreed with Jeff on one thing: no addictive medication.

Yet, at times Craig longed for the relief from frustration, nervous stomach, and uneasiness caused by his emotions pulling in all directions at once.

"There has to be a way to get through this," he repeatedly insisted to himself.

Prayer provided strength and he learned to let the pressure of a set routine go. As long as he remained alone with no demands, he functioned to a small degree. Yet, deep inside he knew he wouldn't recover if he isolated himself.

He wandered around his quarters, drank the formula when he wanted, slept when he felt like it, watched snatches of videos, and read for short periods.

Jeff gave him three days to adjust, then went to his quarters. Craig was casually looking at the printouts of the tells when Jeff announced himself.

"You want to go down tomorrow?" he asked, tapping the printout.

"No," Craig answered slowly, "but I think I need to."

"Craig, you've got to quit all this thinking and trying to work things out," Jeff insisted. "Go to the dig, keep your hands busy, let your mind roam, and don't fight anything." He paused. "Socially acceptable, that is."

Craig merely acknowledged the humor with a nod of his head. "Will I be in the way?" he worried.

"You're still fighting," Jeff scolded gently. "You'll just be an extra pair of hands. 'Shonya's taking care of everything."

"'Shonya?" Craig repeated then nodded. "I remember now. It was her idea wasn't it?" He almost smiled. Jeff nodded. Suddenly Craig relaxed. "Okay. I'll do it. I'll learn to play all over again."

"Don't work at playing, just do it."

\*\*

At first, the only responsibility Craig could handle was in the sifting pits. Sitting for hours, often just feeling the dirt in his hands, he laid aside the small artifacts left in his sieve. He thought about a disastrous experiment of several years ago when someone had tried to introduce automated sifting. Much was broken and much more was simply not recognized as valuable by the automatons. The human brain's ability of discernment was needed, and the little fellows were reprogrammed. Craig felt akin to the discarded automatons, in need of reprogramming.

Roger, after having a taste of Craig's symptoms kept an eye on the Chaplain. Each time he noticed Craig's inattentiveness he touched Craig's shoulder and asked, "You doing okay?"

Craig would stir and nod silently, often unaware his mind had strayed from the work his hands were doing.

Roger also made sure he knew Craig's whereabouts when he left his place in the pit. At first, Roger found him in the lounge looking at the stark landscape or sleeping.

However, by the beginning of the next week he just needed to turn around: he would spot Craig watching as the pyramid emerged from the dirt that had so long covered it.

The artifacts now showing up at the sifting pits were shards of stone statues as well as the familiar beads and coin shaped discs with wavy lines carved on them, sculptures of buildings, beings, furniture, vehicles, and what appeared to be play things made from cloth.

As the days passed, Roger became more preoccupied with cataloging and was less aware of Craig. Once he found

Craig watching the tech set the computer for the next set of slices of earth near the base of the structure. The next day, Roger saw him with Oliver, who was pointing out a third set of stones that swung into the interior of the structure.

These were in a straight line from the first set of windows, so the line from the first set to the second set to the third formed a zigzag.

Roger stopped his activity, intrigued, as Oliver pointed to the same configuration on all four sides of the pyramid. The purpose of the windows remained an unsolved puzzled.

Craig spent evenings alone in his quarters. Toward the end of the second week, Dr. Keal okayed visitors. At first, Craig could only cope with a couple of people dropping by after vespers.

'Shonya and Roger usually came at first, but gradually Oliver and Forest joined them. Then others started joining them. As the days passed, Craig looked forward to the developing pattern: he drank his liquid dinner in his quarters, took a short nap, then a few people stopped by to discuss the day's progress and whatever else came to mind.

Craig's appetite began returning and 'Shonya brought synthesized ice cream, and they fell into the habit of eating together in his quarters.

One evening she asked casually, "Are you up to some excitement?"

He considered with a small grin. "Maybe just a little."

"Tomorrow we finish uncovering the structure."

"Good! What then?"

"We'll scan it again, get proper measurements, map the interior of it, and try to figure out how to get inside," she replied. "If you have any ideas, let me know."

**

Craig joined the crew clearing the remaining dirt from the crevices of the structure's base after the last slice of earth dropped into the sifting pits. He still tired quickly, so he finished clearing his first assigned area, powered down his laser and found a place to sit and observe.

The jobs of sifting the artifacts from the last large chunk of earth and clearing the remaining dirt from the surface of the pyramid were completed at the same time. The crews gathered near the ground laser, waiting for Roger's team to finish preliminary cataloging. When Roger rejoined the group, 'Shonya asked for their attention.

"I know the computer can do this, but let's walk the perimeter and see if anyone can come up with the way in."

She split them into groups. Turning, she looked at Craig as the groups started off. Craig shook his head and waved her on. From his perch on the hill he watched them touch, feel, and push on each stone as they worked their way around the base of the structure. Then, looking up at the top of the pyramid, he followed the line of the building. Suddenly he straightened.

"No," he said aloud. "It couldn't be that easy."

When 'Shonya came around the corner of the building he motioned for her to join him. Then all he could do was smile shyly up at her when she stood before him.

"What is it Craig?" she asked, sensing his excitement.

"What if." He stopped. "It sounds too simple."

"Tell me, Craig," she commanded, sitting beside him.

"What if it's a combination lock of sorts that involves the windows and a ground entrance?"

She laughed, delighted at its simplicity. "It's possible." Seriously she asked, "But where's the ground entrance?"

"I haven't gotten that far," he confessed.

"Let's see if anyone else comes up with an idea." She suggested, and they sat in companionable silence watching the teams.

Finally, looking up at the skies at the beginnings of darkness, she broke the silence. "Are you still confined to quarters in the evenings?"

Craig nodded. "I still need the rest and solitude by the end of the day."

She stood and picked up his hand laser. "How about me putting away your equipment? If you go to the ship now, and we skip dinner, can all of us come by after vespers for discussion?"

"Dinner won't be the same, but I'd like to hear what they have to say," he agreed. "If I'm not up, let yourself in."

**

The dark room and soft music meant Craig was still resting as 'Shonya let herself into his quarters. She listened a few minutes, relaxing herself.

"That's nice," she thought, aware she had no preference in music. She didn't know it was Debussy, but felt closer to Craig as she listened to his choice. Abruptly she thrust the thought aside and, turning on a small light in the corner farthest from the sleeping area, rearranged the chairs to accommodate discussion.

A few minutes later Craig appeared, not yet completely awake. As if by habit, he kissed her, briefly without passion, as he passed.

Smiling to herself, she listened to his splashing noises as he freshened up, and handed him an uneaten half of sandwich when he reappeared.

"It was cold to start with, I hope," she prodded gently. "I know this is the first week Jeff's let you have anything besides his concoction, but eat, or I'll order one of them."

"Actually, I'm hooked on them I think." He grinned.

"Sounds good."

"Eat. I'll be back in a minute."

The group had assembled by the time she got back. Without a word, she handed Craig a glass. Frowning, he took it then held it up in a mock toast when he tasted Jeff's familiar drink.

Smiling, she turned her attention to the group. "You've had a few hours to think about it, let's hear your theories. How do we get in?"

"Perhaps, it's not meant to be entered," was the first comment.

"A monument?" someone else asked.

"Possible," 'Shonya allowed. "But would that be consistent with the structures in which the present day Cutezarians live?"

Silence.

"I wonder if there's a certain place to touch on a certain stone?" came the next question.

"Yes, but how do we find it?" came the counter question.

"Ask the computer to see if there are stones at the base of the structure that swing into the structure like the three sets of stones higher up." Roger suggested.

"We'll do it first thing in the morning," 'Shonya promised. "Speaking of the sets of stones, Craig hatched an interesting idea this afternoon."

All eyes turned his way. "What if the way in is a combination of the windows and a ground entrance?" he asked. "But I haven't figured out where the ground entrance is."

Forest Cabrailes thought for a moment then suddenly went to the quarter's computer. "Computer, image of the tell, Daniel K One."

Everyone gathered around as the computer obeyed.

"Draw a line from window set to window set," he commanded. A less than sign (<) appeared superimposed upon the face of the structure.

"Finish figure using a downward stroke at right angle from the existing angle, ending at the base of the structure," Forest commanded.

The resulting figure resembled a backward Z with a long tail. Forest tapped the stone through which the tail passed.

"This could be the entrance stone. Link to all computers in the system," he added.

"Linked," came the computer's voice.

"Compute all possible combinations of both known and unknown configurations, and link." Forest finished.

The group watched as the configurations appeared on screen only to disappear into memory. They didn't drift away until the computer declared, "Finished, and linked."

"Some interesting designs," Roger declared.

"What if the door's a combination of the windows, and a ground stone, some of them opened, and some closed?" Oliver suggested, remembering Craig's remark about puzzles.

"The computer's figures can still be used," Forest answered. "Any additional ideas?"
Silence.

"Well," Forest finished the discussion. "'Shonya, how about a half-dozen people in turbo packs? Tomorrow we'll work the stones until we find the right combination. Or decide it won't work."

"Fine," 'Shonya agreed.

Suddenly unable to concentrate any longer, Craig felt tired and restless. He got up and wandered around the room.

Forest noticed and addressed the group. "We've made Craig tired. If we don't leave, we'll be in trouble with Jeff."

Roger put a hand on Craig's shoulder as he left. "We have specific orders from Jeff not to wear you out."

"It's okay, Roger," Craig replied. "It's the excitement of getting inside the structure."

Forest came by. "Good work, Craig. We need talented amateurs. Leaps of imagination keep us from getting bogged down."

"Is that a compliment?" Craig asked with a grin.

"Think so," the doctor chuckled.

"Thanks, then, but you all were working. I was just resting and thinking."

"Good work, anyway."

'Shonya, the last to leave, returned Craig's brief kiss from earlier in the evening.

"Good night," he said with a tired grin. He turned out the lights, ordered soft music from the environmental unit, and sat with his feet up until he felt relaxed enough to sleep.

Although he slept late, he arrived on the planet in time to hear the techs in turbo packs receive instructions from Forest about the significance of the graphs they found in their computers.

"Each of the four teams will try graph number one at the same time. If that doesn't trigger one of the openings we'll all go to number two." The group consulted their computers. "Say the window that the line starts on is open, the next closed, the next open. If that doesn't work, we'll start over with it closed. The scan this morning didn't give us a clue." He looked around at their earnest faces.

"Relax. Experiment. Keep track of your progress. And don't forget to push on all four corners of each stone. Think primitive."

Craig watched the activities until he determined the pattern. The people equipped with the turbo packs consulted with the leader of their teams and the computer. Then, accelerating up to the first set of windows, opened the first, left the next closed, opened the third, carefully pushing on all corners until they discovered which activated the stone. After that, they measured from the last set of windows and determined which of the base stones to try.

No results of the first try.

Or the second.

Or the third.

Finally, Craig wandered away and found 'Shonya in her lab. "You're not out watching the fun?" he asked from the door.

She looked up from her computer, catching her breath in surprise. "Morning, Craig. Come in. I'm detail mapping the interior."

He pulled up a stool, perched, and studied the display, glad for an excuse to stay. "Do you think this idea about the combinations will work?"

"It's as good an idea as anyone else had." She patted his arm.

He nodded. "Show me what you've got?"

She spoke to the computer: "Interior of Daniel K One, display one." She turned back to Craig, her face reflecting both puzzlement and excitement. "I've finished two sides. This is the first." She pointed to the display and traced the rooms as she talked. "There's a relatively large room on the ground level. At the back of the room there appears to be an ascending ramp. The next two levels consist of one room, each smaller than the one below it. The ramps connect the levels." She spoke to the computer: "Interior of Daniel K One, display two."

The screen changed, but the display remained the same.

Craig looked, shook his head slightly, and looked again.

"Your eyes are fine," she smiled. "The south side is the same as the north. The strange part of the map is that there are no ramps, doorways, or anything else leading into the interior of the structure. I've got the computer scanning the west side and the results should be ready soon."

She went to her food storage unit. "Something to drink?"

"Some juice maybe."

Before they finished drinking, the computer beeped.

"Display scan results," she commanded and it drew the map.

"Same thing," they said in unison.

"Computer, scan the east side of the structure, then interior of the structure," 'Shonya ordered. "I won't be surprised if it's the same," she told Craig.

"Is it a housing unit?" he asked.

"A multifamily residence?" she answered with another question. Craig shrugged.

Sounds of celebration interrupted them, but her beeper spoke before they could investigate. "Dr. Reed, Oliver here."

"Yes, Oliver?"

"We are in!" His departure from long sentences betrayed his excitement.

"North side. Is Craig with you?"

"Yes." she acknowledged.

"Congratulate him and bring him along."

"Will do. Reed out." She pushed Craig ahead of her. "Go ahead, I'll check the results of the last two scans, and link the whole set to the system. Tell Oliver he can access the maps in five minutes."

A cluster of people hovered around the entrance as the guards coaxed it open. Craig gave Oliver 'Shonya's message. He nodded and went to inspect the entrance stone. Then, accessing the map, he studied it carefully.

"It goes up and not back?" came the surprised question. He checked the time, "Ten thirty," then addressed the group. "Let's take a long lunch break, gather equipment and at one o'clock, send in the first camera crew."

He paused and added with a grin, "Led by me, of course." The group broke up chuckling.

Over lunch, Craig asked, "'Shonya what did the other two scans show?"

"The fourth side's the same as the other three, and the core is solid stone with four shafts running from top to bottom. Air circulation I suppose," she answered.

"The same?" Oliver's fork hovered mid-air. Roger and Forest followed his action. All eyes turned toward 'Shonya. She repeated her analysis of the maps.

"Multi-group dwelling places?" Forest asked immediately.

"We'll know after we've photographed and examined the artifacts," Roger spoke quietly.

Precisely at one o'clock Dr. Oliver Zamwashi dismissed the guard. After fitting the laser recorder with the zero-light scan adapter, he equipped the crew with night vision gear to prevent them from bumping into anything and disturbing the artifacts. Then he sent them into the structure.

"I'll wait for you." He modified his original statement. "I will lead the second team."

They waited impatiently. Occasionally someone spoke, but mostly they stood in silence, watching the entrance, imagining what the team might be recording.

"Here they come," Roger finally announced.

The tech emerged, smiling. "We have a guided tour of the rooms," he assured the doctor. "You're going to like this," he added.

"Thank you very much. I commend your good work." Oliver congratulated the tech. "Now let us discover what it looks like in the light." He held up a chemical filled light stick. "We have consented to test these for the Universal Archeological Institution. They are an improved version of the no-ray emitting sticks. Their light output is constant. Therefore, to shut it off, the casing is rotated."

He demonstrated. "They are made to provide illumination without causing deterioration."

Oliver motioned to the recorder tech to hand him the recorder and removed the zero-light scan attachment. "Computer, link file as Daniel K One Zero Light." He addressed the tech and handed the recorder back.

"Recreate the original recording situation as much as possible. Repeat the commentary as best you can. I would like to use both sets of information for interpretive exercises later."

Oliver stood in the darkness a minute after he entered and felt the silence settle around him. Finally, he held up the light stick. "I wonder how long it's been since this place has seen light," He wondered as he twisted the casing.

The sound vibrated into the darkness. His team members repeated his action and the room sprang into life.

In wonder, they looked around. "Good," Oliver voiced his pleasure. "This is excellent.
Everything is in prime condition. It will be interesting to examine these tables close up." He returned his attention to the structure and addressed the team. "I am going to explore on my own. Take your time and I shall see you outside." He walked around the room several times then went up the ramp to the upper rooms.

An hour and a half later, he emerged and summoned the guard.

"When the recording crew comes out do not let anyone else in." He took Roger by the arm and led him aside. "We have a perfect teaching opportunity available to us. I believe it is best if we limit access. We will link this recording in a separate file and use it as a comparison to the zero-light recording.

"I recommend we return to the ship now, have the teams formulate conclusions from the zero-light vision information and allow time for a rest break. Tonight we will hold a discussion and each team will report. That done, we can compare our first set of conclusions with the information recorded with light."

Roger agreed. They called Forest who consulted with 'Shonya, and the schedule was confirmed.

Before leaving the surface 'Shonya needed to check one more thing. At the structure, she found Craig standing alone, studying the pyramid. Unaware of her, he walked around it then stopped to rest.

"How would you like a private look?" She asked, laying a hand on his shoulder.

He looked around with pleasure. "Are you serious?"

She nodded. "We took a look at the info and there are a couple of things they want me to check before the teaching session." She held up an extra light stick. "We can't touch a thing. We're just going to look. Ok?"

"Anything you say, Doctor," he solemnly promised.

She cleared him with the guard and, slipping inside, they exchanged smiles in the semi-darkness of the entrance. It seemed natural to take his hand. "You ever done anything like this before?" she asked, glad she had issued the invitation.

He shook his head. "I've only worked on multi-level sites. Nothing like this."

"Ready?" she asked.

"Ready."

Opening the light sticks' cases, they viewed the large square room. Carved stone benches stood against the walls, and a massive square stone table, not quite reaching Craig's waist, occupied the center of the room.

"If the inhabitants were ancestors of the present day Cutezarians, they were taller weren't they?" he mused.

'Shonya nodded. "Or sat on very high chairs." They exchanged quiet smiles and went different directions.

"Hey, Craig, come over here," 'Shonya called from the opposite side of the room.

She pointed to a hollowed out shelf carved into the wall. Dozens of small beads filled the indention, each showing its blue core through carved lines.

"These remind me! I forgot to tell you something. Daniel reported Roger picked up one of the beads the day after you became ill, and got a tiny electrical shock."

"Makes you wonder if they're not really beads at all," he replied, reaching toward them.

"That's exactly what Daniel said." She saw the grief on his face and hurried on. "I don't know if Roger's gotten back to them. It might be something for you to pursue."

He nodded absently and wandered away. On each wall he found similar trays filled with the carved beads several places around the room: at least two on each wall, and an extra one in the middle of two walls. He became increasingly intrigued.

'Shonya called him again, and this time he found her examining another shelf carved into the wall. "Look at these jars," she said with wonder in her voice.

Three brown square jars with tight fitting lids decorated the shelf. They were sixty centimeters high with wavy lines carved on all sides.

"But the lines uncover red instead of blue." Craig bent down to get a better look as he spoke.

"I'm dying to know what's in them," 'Shonya agreed.

Craig nodded as he straightened and suddenly felt the room spin. Dropping his light stick, he reached for 'Shonya and leaned against the wall.

She dropped her light and braced him against the wall, her hands on his rib cage.

Suddenly grateful for her presence, he relaxed against the wall, closed his eyes, and waited for it to pass.

"Craig?" she tentatively broke the silence.

Putting his hands on her shoulders, he explained. "It happens if I move certain ways. Jeff doesn't know what causes it, but it's better than it was." Opening his eyes, he pushed away from the wall. "But it still takes me by surprise."

She left her hands on his sides, and they stood looking at each other in the semi-darkness.

Filled with undefined emotion, he slowly leaned back against the wall, pulling her with him. Gently he slid his hands over her shoulders, up her neck and took her face in his hands.

"Craig," was all she could say, knowing the expression on his face mirrored her own feelings.

With a mischievous but gentle smile he murmured, "Sorry about taking advantage of your concern."

He leaned over. The kiss was unhurried, and gentle, yet passionate. They both quit breathing as 'Shonya reached up, put her arms around his neck and returned the lingering kiss.

Finally, Craig closed his eyes and leaned back against the wall. Her head against his chest, 'Shonya tried to decipher her feelings. Presently she felt more than heard his chuckle and looked up.

"I'm not quite ready for this," he said smiling shyly, waiting for his head to clear.

He was quiet so long she wondered if she should call for help. Stepping out of the circle of his arms, she touched his face.

Startled, he moved his head and opened his eyes.

"Shall I call Jeff?"

He shook his head almost in slow motion. "No, I'll be OK." After standing still a few more minutes, he stirred and put his arm around her shoulders. "Shall we go see what the upper levels are like?"

'Shonya retrieved the light sticks and they went up the ramp to the second level. Craig stooped only slightly to fit into the passage. 'Shonya didn't have to stoop at all.

"I bet Oliver crawled through this passage," she laughed, thinking of his tall, lanky frame.

Hand in hand, they wandered through the two upper levels, the curiosity of discovery overcoming awareness of time.

Long platforms carved into the walls provided enough headroom for someone to sit upright. Stone tables of all shapes and sizes were scattered, seemingly without pattern, throughout the two upper levels. And they discovered more ledges carved into the wall at various heights, some seemingly too high for the envisioned beings to reach.

The room on the second level was almost square with the outer wall sloping like the first level, but the third level room looked more like a lopsided triangle.

Blue-tinged beads in carved trays also decorated the walls of the upper two levels. Natural light from windows created by the stones left ajar streamed into them, creating a lighter atmosphere than the lower level.

On the third level, 'Shonya closed the light stick and observed, "The need for artificial light isn't so great."

"And there aren't as many of the trays of beads up here as on the first level," Craig added.

She opened her mouth but Craig stopped her. "Don't say anything. Let me work on some ideas and draw some conclusions."

She nodded. "I'm sure Roger will give you a corner of his lab."

On the way out 'Shonya returned on the second level to measure the different lengths of the carved platforms, and the height of the headroom. "If these are sleeping platforms, it will give us a better idea of how tall and how slender or large they were," she automatically explained.

But Craig wasn't there. She found him back on the third level, looking out the window, totally absorbed in the view. Becoming aware of her, he held out his hand. She crossed the room and took it as he voiced his thoughts. "I wonder. Does God seek contact with these Beings? Are we here to tell them about God? Do they worship something? God created them but what questions do I ask to discover what their concept of God is? Assuming they have one." Sighing, he leaned against the wall. "So many questions."

"And Jeff hasn't cleared you for heavy questions yet," she scolded. Her comm button cut his rebuttal short.

"'Shonya? Roger."

"Roger, what is it?" she answered.

"We're ready to return to the ship. I..." He sounded embarrassed. "I can't find the Chaplain. Does he happen to be with you?"

144

"I think I know where he is," she said as seriously as she could. "I'll bring him when I come. I'm in the structure. Reed out."

"Right." They could almost hear the chuckle in his voice.

'Shonya grinned at Craig. "We've got to go. You know about class tonight?"

Craig nodded. "Roger told me." Taking her hand, he smiled shyly. "'Shonya, I think..."

"You're not allowed to think yet." She patted his arm affectionately. "Just relax. It's okay."

He put his arm around her shoulders and they went down the ramps. "Feeling's what I do best these days," he said wearily. "I'll rest this afternoon. And with your permission, Doctor, I'll sit in on the session."

"Permission granted, Chaplain."

## CHAPTER SIXTEEN

A group of rested scientists gathered in the viewing room after vespers, and 'Shonya took charge. "Three of us in addition to the recorder handlers have been in the structure. We limited access since the opportunity presented to us is highly unusual. We hope to establish a specific method of studying structures without ideal lighting."

Craig slipped in and gave her a small wave. Acknowledging his presence, she smiled and continued.

"We'll have the three teams report. Oliver, describe the method."

He rose to his full height, straight, yet relaxed. He'd spent fifteen years as professor of Ancient African Societies at the Universal Archeological Institution before taking on Galactic Archeology. This role was second nature to him.

"Computer, begin display," he ordered then addressed the assembly. "The significance of our position is unusual. We have the opportunity to move from the unknown, to the observed, to the known. We start, of course, with the unknown. What you are now viewing is representative of no light, computer-enhanced scans. Notice the shapes and forms.

"The room's contents are quite visible: the height of the table and the size of the room. We see indentations, and have a protrusion from the wall. If we turn the picture into a three dimensional model, we see this."

He stopped and considered the room with one sloping wall the computer projected. The color was gray, the furnishings there, but indistinct.

"From this display, I note the lack of indentions in the wall close to the floor, no fire place." Oliver continued his lecture. "How did they heat or cook? Perhaps the answer will reveal itself as we study the next step of display. We will now hear the observations of the site team, then the artifacts team. Following the reports, we will view the lighted archive display. We will then overlay new commentary containing our conclusions on the lighted archive record, and later compare that information with the Cutezarian's recorded history." He paused and relinquished the floor to Forest with an elegant gesture.

Forest walked around the model then spoke to the computer: "Display all levels." The upper levels appeared. "Look at the room's shape. All three sides are the same. Makes us think it's a multi-unit dwelling.

"The bottom floor might be a getting together place. The big table could be for meetings or eating. The other two levels might be private chambers. Are the carved platforms of the upper levels beds? If they are, the inhabitants were taller than our Cutezarians. Everything inside is crafted stone." He stopped. "Roger, artifacts report."

Roger stood silently by the model two or three minutes before speaking, looking at the floor.

"Help him. Give him control," Craig prayed silently, fighting his own emotions.

Finally, Roger looked up. "You and I both wish Dr. Kobee were here. I miss his insight. But the team he put together has done good work. They have supported me while I'm doing my best to put into practice what Daniel taught me."

Clearing his throat, he turned to the model. "On the first level, we find a large table. Along the walls we see..." He pointed to the model. "Benches. We can't see if they're plain or have decorations carved into them, but they are definitely benches. We assume they are movable. That we can't prove."

He stopped to follow the view of the camera as it moved around the room. "There are shelves carved into the wall. On the first level, note the jar-shaped items. I ordered an extra-fine-tuned MRI scan just out of curiosity to see if we could find out what's in the jars." He spoke to the computer: "Computer, add MRI scan to present display."

Roger grinned as little dots appeared inside the jars. "Your guess is as good as mine," he continued after the laughter died. "Actually, we think it's grain. We'll have to sample it before we can tell exactly what variety of grain. But we did have a surprise from the fine-tuned MRI." He again pointed to the model. "Look again at the trays carved into the walls: two half way up on each wall on the first level, one on each wall at the second and third levels. We think the additional shelves are at sitting level. Also notice there are more shelves on the first level than the other two, but all shelves contain the Chaplain's beads."

Craig had to smile. Following the tradition of naming things after the discoverer, the entire community now referred to these objects as "The Chaplain's beads." He hoped the honor included the privilege of studying them. He returned his attention to the speaker.

Roger was finishing. "We are re-thinking the use of these beads. If anyone has any insights, share them with myself, Dr. Reed, or the Chaplain, whose request to study the beads has been granted."

The group approved.

When quiet returned, Roger continued. "Note the smaller tables on the second and third levels. This reinforces the idea of private chambers. Also, notice some of the shelves are so high on the wall beings small enough to sleep on the slabs, or sit at the table couldn't reach them.

They don't have beads in them. Are they for displays? Were they cultured beings who appreciated, for lack of another word, art in some form? The final question is, did they sit in the upper two levels? There are no benches, no chairs." He motioned for 'Shonya to take over.

"Today one of the sifters was moving a pile of dirt and dug into the ground. He uncovered a skull." She had to stop because of the excited chatter. "We're running tests, and by the end of the session we'll have a computer model of what these beings looked like. Now, let's take a break. Then we'll go through it again with the lighted archive and check the accuracy of our conclusions."

A sudden restlessness compounded Craig's growing weariness. He caught 'Shonya's eye, gave her a small wave, and made his way to his quarters. He thought the conclusions were on target and hoped he wouldn't miss any new ideas.

A long shower relaxed him and he stretched out on the bed to read. By the time 'Shonya arrived, he'd fallen asleep.

She watched his restless movements and caught the computer as it slipped from the bed. Glancing at the text, she paged up and found herself reading the third chapter of the Song of Solomon.

"Some people's ideas of light reading are strange." She smiled to herself, remembering Jeff's prescription for relaxation.

On impulse, she tiptoed out and went to sickbay. "The Chaplain didn't eat dinner," she told the med tech. "Can I take him a serving of Jeff's formula?"

"The doctor approved it any time the Chaplain wanted," Sheila answered as she keyed the code into the computer and handed the glass over when it appeared in the synthesizer's receiving tray. "There you go, Doctor."

"Thanks." Returning to Craig's quarters, she almost set the glass down and left, but checked herself. "He'll be upset if I don't show him the computer's image of the skull." She set the glass down, leaned over him and put her hand on his chest. "Craig."

He woke up slowly, becoming aware of the pressure on his chest first, then her voice.

"Craig, wake up," she insisted.

He opened his eyes. "Hi." Pushing himself into an upright position, he ran his hands through his straight reddish blond hair and asked, "What time is it?"

"Nine-thirty," she answered, handing him the drink. "I noticed you didn't eat much dinner, and only half the ice cream."

He nodded. "Uh-huh, lunch didn't sit well today. Thanks." He drank slowly.

"You don't look rested," she commented.

"I think I had too much excitement today," he teased, drawing her down to sit on the bed. "Sorry," she smiled, remembering his kiss.

"I might stay on board tomorrow. What's going on?" He moved over, giving her more room.

"We'll keep looking for the magic window sequence for the other three areas. The sequence that worked on the first side doesn't work on the others. Once we get in, we'll explore them using the same method. Roger can get his samples from the jars and you can get the report from the computer."

"Can you persuade Roger to send me a couple dozen of the beads so I can work in the lab here?" Craig asked.

"Probably, since there are so many of them."

They looked at each other a few silent seconds.

Craig ran his fingers over her hand then rubbed her arm gently, thoughtfully. "'Shonya, I feel so much, I'm afraid to let myself feel without any control. But the effort wears me out. I feel more than gratitude. I can't make promises under these conditions. That doesn't keep me from wanting to say all sorts of things…" His speech was disjointed, hesitant, and finally trailed away.

"Craig," she said, doing her best to ignore her tumbling feelings and make her voice firm. "I've said it once, and I'll say it again. "Let's just relax and enjoy the relationship, whatever it is. If it ups your stress level, Jeff will declare me off limits. And neither of us wants that." With a jolt, she realized she had just used the word "relationship."

Craig grinned and nodded. "Okay, but promise me you'll tell me if things get out of hand."

Although she promised, she was afraid it wouldn't do any good. Things were already out of control, and Craig's concern for her feelings didn't make things easier. He hugged her and held her for a long time. "I don't know what I'd have done without you. I'm glad we were friends before all this mess started, and I'm glad we're still friends."

"Me too." That much she could say with certainty. Mentally she accused him of untactful concern, if there was such a thing. "It would help if he was just a little more selfish," she thought.

Seeking a less emotional subject, she sat up and pulled out her computer. "I almost forgot what I came to show you." She handed him the computer. "This is the skull found today with the computer's simulation of what the being looked like."

Frowning, Craig studied it a long time. "This Cutezarian looks familiar—more familiar since he or she is larger than our Cutezarians," he mused.

"Several people have made similar comments, but no one has come up with any answers." 'Shonya stood. "It's late. You need a lot more rest than you've been getting. And so do I."

He nodded absently, still looking at the computer image. Taking the computer, 'Shonya folded it and commanded, "Here, turn over."

She knew for her own good she shouldn't touch him. But he looked so tired and tense; she resolved to put her emotions aside to help him relax. Craig stretched out on his stomach and she massaged his neck and shoulders. With a sigh, he finally fell asleep.

She failed to keep her emotional detachment, but did manage to resist the overwhelming desire to wake him again for a goodnight kiss.

**

Craig slept late and almost stumbled over a small container in the doorway as he emerged from his quarters. "Beads!" he celebrated.

The attached noted read: "Craig—Roger agreed—lab 12 is yours for as long as you want it. It should have all the equipment you need. Have a quiet day, 'Shonya."

After stopping for a glass of Jeff's prescribed drink, Craig explored the all-purpose, medium sized lab and discovered two techs had been assigned to assist him.

"Dr. Reed thought of everything didn't she?" he remarked to the tech, who introduced herself as Carolyn Graft.

Carolyn smiled. "Orders are: ask no questions, stay out of the way, do whatever he asks, get whatever equipment he wants, and don't be surprised if he doesn't say more than two words all day."

"Are you're just going to sit around here all day waiting for me to say my two words?" His voice carried a smile.

"No. Dr. Lavera, Oh," she stopped and explained in response to his surprised look. "The team bestowed an honorary doctor on him. Anyway, Dr. Lavera left work for us since we're going to be here."

"Good, I won't worry about using up work power." The tech's smile grew. "She said you'd be worried about that."

"Dr. Reed?" Craig asked. The tech nodded. Embarrassed, he looked around. "Well, I guess I'll get started. I'd like to test the substance of the stones first."

Carolyn led him to the back of the lab. "We have the lab set up in stations. Each station specializes in a different area." She pointed around the room. "The one in front of us is composition. The one on the left is temperature. On the right is the mechanical property station and the one in the middle is the interaction station. Any questions?"

Craig shook his head. "Thanks. I'll call if I need anything."

Once alone, he started with temperature instead of composition. His test told him the beads absorbed heat readily and radiated energy.

Then he moved to composition. Putting a handful of beads in the analyzer, he watched the results on screen. He didn't recognize any of the components. "Translate from scientific terms," he commanded.

The computer answered: "Stone formed from inorganic dust bonded to unknown mineral composed of electrically charged particles."

Craig called the tech and asked if that meant anything to her.

After a minute of thought, Carolyn held up her hand with a flash of inspiration and asked the computer "Is it radioactive?"

"Incorrect. The energy is not atomic," the computer answered.

"Photo-electric?" Carolyn asked.

"Correct. Known also as photo-voltaic."

"Is that all, Chaplain?" Carolyn asked.

"Thanks." He then addressed the computer, "Computer, save and link to system."

At the interaction station, he simulated experiments with water, sand, pollution, acid, light, and proteins. The readings varied slightly, but only light indicated any significant interaction.

The pain in his stomach let him know it was overstressed and empty. Massaging it, he remembered the electricity of the storm.

"Hey!" he exclaimed to himself, "What if?" He spoke to the computer. "Computer, run simulation on interaction with electricity."

And he almost laughed aloud as the information was displayed. "It was right in front of my eyes." He said. He looked around and called the tech.

"Carolyn?" She appeared at his elbow. "Can we rig up something to physically give these beads an old fashioned electrical charge? And can we find a way to make the lab totally dark?"

"The second part's easy," she said. "The environmental unit will do whatever you ask. The first part's to so easy." She paused, thinking. "I know! We did some studies a while ago. I have an idea. It'll take a minute."

"I'll wait." Craig reviewed the accumulated data until Carolyn returned. "It's the only logical conclusion," he said aloud, touching his comm button. "Dr. Reed, Chaplain Lea, here."

'Shonya was just putting her equipment away before lunch when her comm button startled her. "Craig, what can I do for you?" she answered.

"Can you take a long lunch and join me in the lab?" he asked.

"When?"

"Give me..." He hesitated, looking at Carolyn.

"A half hour," she mouthed.

"Thirty minutes," he repeated.

"I'll eat, and then be there. Reed out."

Craig signed off and Carolyn brought in a metal box with a lid. "The computer recommended this metal for conductivity." She held up two metal strips and connected them to lead lines, which she connected with a small power source. "We can arrange your beads on the floor of the box, hook the ends of the metal strips onto the sides of the box, put on the lid, and turn on the power. The walls will complete the circuit and create an electrical field inside the box."

Craig gathered two handfuls of beads and laid them in the box. Carolyn sat the box on a heat resistant stand and proceeded.

"Wait," Craig stopped her just before she activated the power source. "One more question. If I want to see the beads without the box, can I do it?"

With a nod, she handed him a pair of non-conductive tongs. "The sides lift out of groves in the bottom. Shut down the power, lift the sides and you have a platform."

"Okay, let's go." They switched the power on, and waited. By the time 'Shonya arrived the entire box was hot and glowing.

"Craig, what'd you find?" she asked.

"Computer, deactivate power," Craig ordered then lifted the sides of the box. "Computer, create darkness," he ordered.

Craig put his arm around 'Shonya's shoulders as the lights went out and said, "Let there be light."

And there was.

The beads lit up the entire room.

## CHAPTER SEVENTEEN

"This explains a lot." 'Shonya finally spoke, caught up in his excitement.

"Especially the trays of beads," Craig added.

"I suppose it means they sat and did something that required light," 'Shonya speculated.

"And the trays higher up provided light for the room." Craig finished her thought, then spoke to the computer: "Computer, maintain darkness and monitor lab twelve until material loses its electrical charge. Link all experiments to system."

As they closed the lab, 'Shonya's comm button activated. "LaShonya, Oliver here."

"What's up?"

"We have entered the remaining chamber. Documentation is proceeding as before. Shall we refrain from entering until you arrive?"

"Please. I'll be down in a few minutes," she answered, sharing a smile with Craig over Oliver's choice of words.

"Pass the word along for everyone to make a trip to lab twelve on breaks and look at the Chaplain's Beads experiment. Reed out."

"An interesting phenomenon," Craig commented, returning to their conversation. "I suppose the mineral in the center absorbs the electrical charge."

"Somewhere in the past some Cutezarian or other inhabitant chipped a stone and discovered the mineral," 'Shonya mused, as much to herself as to him.

"Maybe this is the Cutezarian's basic energy supply," Craig added to her musings.

"It certainly sends us off in another direction." She didn't speculate further.

In the transporter room, she put her hand on his, stopping him from rubbing his stomach, and spoke gently. "You've been rubbing that spot for twenty minutes. You going to take care of it?"

Frowning, Craig explored the painful area with gentle fingers. "Actually, this reminded me of electricity. And that started me thinking. If the beads were a source of light, their energy source could be their ability to absorb the electricity of the storms."

"So you created an electrical field."

"Sort of. With the tech's help," he acknowledged. "You're rubbing your stomach again," she reminded him.

"I'll go by sick bay." His smile was self-conscious. "Will you join me for dinner?"

"If you want." She stepped through the sensor and the door opened.

Craig grinned. "I want."

**

"How's your stomach?" 'Shonya asked immediately as she entered Craig's quarters.

"Jeff's drink and a quiet afternoon took care of it." The words were light, but frustration showed in his face.

"Don't start getting impatient now," she quietly admonished. "You've done pretty well so far."

"I'm constantly praying for patience," he confessed. "I feel better and my head's clear, but I get frustrated easily. And concentration wears me out."

She nodded and took his hand in compassion. As they talked quietly, vespers hour came and went. 'Shonya made no effort to leave. They were comfortable in the conversation with the attraction between them momentarily set aside. And gradually Craig's frustration slipped away.

When the nightly visitors arrived, theories of the stone's use as an energy source dominated their conversation.

"Perhaps the coins provide the energy for something else, comparable to our power discs," someone ventured.

"Could be," Roger allowed. "There are fewer of them than the Chaplain's beads. What kind of machines would they power?"

"We'll have to find out more about the culture before we know," Quantro answered.

"Larger stones could provide enough energy for a central energy unit for a home," another speculated.

"And a collection of larger stones provide energy for an entire city?"

"I wonder what would happen if a structure were made of this stone?"

"Like the tip of the pyramid?"

The last question triggered an idea, and Craig voiced it before thinking. "Can we run scans and see what kind of stone used in both the structures at the site and the present day Cutezarian structures?"

"Good idea." 'Shonya nodded. "I'll put it on the agenda for tomorrow."

Towards the end of the session, Roger turned to Craig and asked, "Craig, what's the decay rate of the stone's energy output?"

"We don't know yet." Craig grinned. "The lab's still lit. The computer's measuring the rate of decay against the amount of charge we gave it. 'Shonya suggested we do studies on the rate of decay if the beads received a charge of the magnitude of the storm." He stopped, becoming aware all other conversation had ceased and everyone was regarding him with amusement. "What?" he asked, shrugging.

"You're sounding more like us every day," Forest finally told him.

"We think you may have missed your calling, Chaplain," Oliver added.

"And you've been discussing this?" Craig was surprised and embarrassed at the same time.

"It's been mentioned," Roger said vaguely.

"Has anyone mentioned this to God?" Craig chuckled.

"We haven't asked God to change your calling yet," 'Shonya assured him.

"That's good of you," Craig laughed. The good humor continued as the scientists prepared to return to their own quarters.

"Don't worry, we won't ask God to change the direction of your life," Oliver chuckled as he left. "Good chaplains are hard to find."

"Thanks," Craig grinned.

"Seriously, take care of yourself. Come back to us as soon as possible." Oliver allowed Craig to see the depth of his emotion. "We miss you at vespers."

Emotion threatened, but Craig choked it back. "I'll do my best," he managed to get out.

He thought they had all gone and sighed as he stretched. Turning around, he met 'Shonya concerned gaze.

"'Shonya!" he exclaimed, dropping his arms mid-stretch.

She smiled. "If you feel up to it, I thought we'd walk down to the lab and see what's going on. We'll stop and get something for your stomach."

He put his arm around her. "Good idea."

But in their pre-occupation with the experiment, they forgot the formula. Opening the door of the dimly lit lab, Craig grinned. "Romantic."

"Too bad we've had dinner," 'Shonya answered lightly.

He took her hand and they went to the computer. "Ask it about decay time." Craig requested as he sat wearily and pulled her into his lap.

She didn't resist, but sat sideways so their attention would be on the computer. "Computer, display the rate of decay of energy output of experimental material."

When the computer answered Craig listened, but didn't understand. "Now, tell me in English, please."

'Shonya made some quick mental calculations. "For each ten-thousand watts applied to the beads, decay to total darkness is ten hours, which gives us two more hours of light."

"Can you have it cross-reference the strength of the electrical storm, apply it to the beads and display the decay time?" Craig asked.

She nodded and rephrased the request. They were fascinated by the calculations and formulas that flashed instantly as the computer displayed its work, and didn't hear the door open.

"Have you two discovered a new scientific method?"

They looked up, startled. 'Shonya moved off Craig's lap, but he pulled her back when he realized who the visitor was.

"Jeff," he greeted the doctor in relief. "The lighting is the last stages of an experiment started this morning."

"The electrically charged Chaplain's beads?" He asked, handing Craig a glass of the formula.

Craig took it with a surprised shake of his head. "How did you know?"

"I went to check on a patient, and Bill said he saw you coming this way. I thought I'd bring your evening snack and see the experiment at the same time," he explained.

"Am I that predictable?"

Jeff nodded. "Almost every night before you go to bed, you request it."

"It settles my stomach so I can sleep," Craig acknowledged, gratefully drinking it.

"It contains a drug that's supposed to do that." Jeff studied the display. "This is really remarkable!" Finally, he nodded and turned toward the door. After a hesitation, he came back and lectured. "Craig, you're too tired. If you keep this up, I'll declare 'Shonya off limits too."

"We'll be done here in just a minute," 'Shonya assured him. "And he'll stay aboard for an extra day of rest before he rejoins the dig."

"I will?" Craig asked.

"You will." She smiled.

"I will," Craig promised.

"Goodnight," Jeff said in resignation.

"'Night," they answered in unison.

With an ironic shake of his head, he activated the exit sensor.

"Computer, repeat results," 'Shonya ordered as they returned their attention to the experiment's data display.

Craig rested his forehead against 'Shonya's shoulder as the computer answered: "Twenty days from charge to darkness."

"So the storms are at their peak every twenty days,'" Craig said wearily.

"Not necessarily," 'Shonya answered, "They may have a period of twilight days before the next storm comes to recharge the stones."

He nodded slowly against her shoulder. "Guess you're right."

His eyes were closed and 'Shonya felt guilty. "Computer, link all data to the system."

"Linked," the computer answered.

"Craig." She moved to face him and his head fell against her collarbone. "Hey!"

"Hmmmmm," he answered.

"Time to get you back to your quarters before I have to carry you," she said.

Craig leaned back in the chair. "I'm so tired I can't move. I think Jeff put something in the drink."

'Shonya slipped out of his arms and tugged him to his feet. "I wouldn't be surprised. You've been a bit too ambitious the last couple of days."

Craig woke up enough to help close the lab, and they made the return journey to his quarters in the twilight-simulated corridors.

"Late date," he smiled tiredly as they entered his quarters. He took her in his arms. In the darkened room they stood quietly, resting in each other's presence.

It surprised 'Shonya that she primarily felt contentment. "Help me know what to do," she prayed.

Presently Craig laid his head on her shoulder, complaining, "I'm falling asleep."

"It's okay," she assured him. "Go to bed. And don't get up early."

He nodded then straightened. Arm in arm they went into the sleeping area. Before sitting on the bed, Craig kissed her: a tired, yet strangely passionate kiss. Its intensity surprised her, but he sighed contently, leaned against her and literally fell asleep on his feet.

She shook him awake and he sat on the bed, allowing his body to fall sideways onto the pillow. With a grin, she lifted his legs onto the bed.

Stretching out he sighed. "'Night." A slight smile played around his mouth. "'Shonya?"

"Yes, Craig?"

"I love you."

'Shonya brushed his straight, reddish blond hair back from his forehead where it always fell. "I won't hold you to that yet, Chaplain."

She let herself out, wondering how things would turn out when Craig was fully recovered. "I guess I'll have to wait and find out," she decided as she reached her own quarters.

**

Dr. LaShonya Reed became teacher and administrator of an informal school, Dr. Forest Cabrailes and Dr. Oliver Zamwashi observers, evaluators, and teachers with Roger Lavera consulting as artifacts director. To help meet the requirements for advanced degrees, the students now became the senior scientists as the second tell was scanned and prepared for excavation.

Jeff examined Craig and declared him off limits for two days to everyone except Dorinda and 'Shonya. Craig stayed in his quarters, knowing his doctor was right; he had pushed too hard.

Mid-afternoon of the first day Dorinda interrupted his study. Laying the computer aside, he greeted her. "Dorinda, come in. I was getting lonely."

She kissed him and got right to the point. "The speculation grows. Are you ready to declare?"

"Declare what?" He faked innocence. "I'm not yet recovered. Jeff hasn't cleared me to declare anything."

"Don't play innocent with me. I know you. Talk to me about 'Shonya," she insisted.

"I've got a lot of feelings for 'Shonya," he started hesitantly. "I don't know what I'd done without her." He faltered. "I'm... I'm better. But I still feel overwhelmed a lot of the time. I'm so tired. It's too much to fight with myself. So, 'Shonya and I agreed not to try to decipher our relationship until I get some balance back."

He stopped, and his smile was shy. "But it's not all tied up in a neat little box, 'cause I like her a lot."

"I knew it!" Dorinda celebrated. "You haven't had that look in your eye since your third year at the academy."

"Calm down. You are not to discuss this with 'Shonya or anyone else. Not even Alan," he warned her. "Don't push us."

"Okay. If you insist." She grinned mischievously.

They sat in comfortable silence. Suddenly Dorinda jumped. "Oh!"

"What's wrong?" Craig cried sitting forward from his relaxed position. Dorinda put her hand on his arm and couldn't answer for a moment.

Craig's voice was strained. "Shall I call Alan?"

She nodded.

He hit his comm button. "Captain Brodsky, Chaplain Lea here."

On the bridge, Captain Brodsky looked up from the results of the tests of the engineering glitch he was reviewing. "Yes, Craig," he answered.

"You'd better come to my quarters. Dorinda's here."

"On my way." Running double time all the way, he arrived just as Dorinda was able to catch her breath.

They were equally pale, and the Captain didn't know who to worry about first. He took his wife's hand but spoke to Craig. "You okay?"

Craig nodded.

Dorinda patted her husband's hand. "I'm okay now too, I think. The contraction didn't last long, and it's the first one I've had in three weeks." She turned back to Craig. "Dr. Canady says I'll probably deliver early. Maybe three weeks early. Somehow, the electrical thing set my body into

165

motion. The baby's fine, but my muscles are changing like they do in the ninth month, getting ready for delivery."

"I'm glad you weren't on the surface," Craig said solemnly.

The Brodskys agreed. "Alan, what made you insist that she stay on board? She always says you never impose your will on her."

The Captain and Dorinda smiled at each other. "It was one of those growing feelings. I prayed to be relieved of the feeling, thinking it was my fears. But the more I prayed, the stronger the feeling got. I didn't tell Dorinda that part, though. She, ah, loves me enough to do what I asked."

Captain Brodsky cleared his throat, and changed the subject. "Have you told him yet?"

"She hasn't told me anything yet," Craig said with a chuckle, the color slowly returning to his face. "She was too busy harassing me about 'Shonya."

"I wasn't harassing," Dorinda argued with an affectionate smile, relaxing after the contraction.

"Told me what?" Craig returned to Alan's question.

"When we're through studying the second structure, a reception in your honor is being planned and the Cutezarians are coming. The scientists will present their conclusions and the Cutezarians will present their historical records," 'Shonya informed him. Then smiling brightly she added, "The next day the recreation officer will lead a tour of the city, and since I'm going to deliver early, and I'm such a wonderful person...." She grinned. "I get to go on the first tour."

Craig couldn't help but laugh. "You deserve that much." He encouraged, but remained puzzled. "What this about a reception? I didn't do..."

The Captain interrupted him. "When the people still on the planet found out you were responsible for the quick evacuation they wanted to express their gratitude. It was their idea. They understand the trauma you went through to go to the bridge."

"But," Craig started.

"They didn't consult you because they knew you'd object," Dorinda broke in.

Craig just shook his head.

"Let them do it, Craig," the Captain urged.

"Okay." Craig gave in. "As long as the Cutezarians are the main attraction."

"They can't help but be. They're fascinating," the Captain promised, then squeezed his wife's hand. "If you're through provoking Craig, I'd feel better if you got some rest."

Dorinda smiled, "Me too."

                                          **

In the middle of Roger Lavera's demonstration of the second tell's cataloging process, 'Shonya's comm button suddenly beeped.

"LaShonya, this is Paji. Would you come to the map lab?"

"On my way, Paji," she replied. She turned to Roger. "You're doing fine." She reached the door and hesitated. "I think you're ready to receive the first artifacts of the second tell," she told him as she left.

Roger looked up and merely nodded.

In what used to be her lab, she looked over Paji's shoulder. "Whatcha got?"

Paji, a small cartographer with glowing black eyes, had always explained her reason for choosing a year aboard the Curie instead of classroom credits as "Mapping something besides a planet in our own system will make me stand out." But 'Shonya suspected her motivation came from fascination with space as well as career marketing.

"I know I'm ahead of myself," Paji was explaining, "But I don't think we have the same configuration inside as the Daniel K One. Look!"

The display showed the structure, but it appeared to be hollow. "There are no ramps, no passage ways." She pointed out, and finished with a question. "Do we have modeling capabilities down here?"

'Shonya shook her head. "We didn't install it since we return to the ship every evening." She planned a minute then instructed. "Do all the fine-tuned scans before the structure's uncovered, then repeat the same set of scans after, and see if there's any difference."

Paji's dark eyes glowed "Good! It'll prove our new software can function as well underground as above."

"Link everything to the main system, and we'll model it tonight." 'Shonya heard her name as she left the lab.

"Good afternoon," Oliver greeted her as he and Forest approached.

"Oliver. How are things progressing?"

"The results of the scans showing the placement of artifacts in the top layers are in, and we have entered the coordinates for the cuts into the computer. The tech verified they are correct." He paused and added with a chuckle. "I think Landers is more nervous at the prospect of a student handling his precious ground laser than we are about turning the whole dig over."

"I always thought the neck extension and the eye of the laser makes it look almost human," she replied with a smile.

Forest appreciated the humor. "I bet Landers thinks it's a friend, not a machine. Anyway," he continued. "Action starts in the morning. We want your OK to quit early and have class onboard tonight.

She checked the time. "Three-thirty. Fine. Do it."

"Good. Inform the Chaplain we will miss discussing our progress tonight. It appears the doctor is disciplining us all in his own way." Although Oliver spoke solemnly, humor twinkled in his eyes.

"I'll deliver the message," 'Shonya promised with a smile.

"See you on board," Forest said as they started away.

"Paji has a project started. I'll stay with her for about an hour, and then be there," she called after them.

Returning to the lab, she told Paji the arrangements and they soon became engrossed in examining the three dimensional parts of the structure as the computer projected them into the room. 'Shonya remembered she hadn't seen the report on the make-up of the stones used in the structure. She pulled out her computer, asked for on screen keyboard to keep from disturbing Paji, linked to the system, and wandered to another desk as she read.

The lab was quiet as they worked. They spoke occasionally, and then silence returned.

'Shonya vaguely heard the door open but didn't pay attention until she heard Paji's gasp.

"Ah, LaShonya."

She barely heard it.

"Dr. Reed!" Her voice rose.

'Shonya looked up. In haste and excitement, she scrambled to her feet.

"We have come to see the ancient structure," the metallic voice of the Cutezarian's translator spoke before either human could think of anything to say.

"Ah, yes, of course." 'Shonya stammered. "I am LaShonya Reed. I am a scientist, and this is my student, Paji Habib." She paused as the boxes worked. "Let me get some light sticks and we can begin." She touched Paji's shoulder to get her attention.

Paji shook her head slightly and dragged her eyes away from the beings. "Ah, yes?"

"Paji, call the Captain. Have him get Dr. Zamwashi and Dr. Cabrailes and meet us at Daniel K One," 'Shonya instructed.

"Yes, Doctor."

'Shonya nodded and turned to the Cutezarians. "I will take you there." She led them across the compound. "The Captain and two other scientists will join us."

By the time they reached the structure, Captain Brodsky had already opened the entrance stone and dismissed the guards.

"We came as soon as we could, Doctor," the Captain greeted her, then he greeted the Cutezarians: "Chief Communicator."

"Captain," the box answered, "we reviewed our records, and find we wish to see for ourselves."

"Those who lived here were your ancestors, you certainly have the right." Captain Brodsky started to lead the procession, but the Chief Communicator spoke.

"Is it acceptable for us to go first?"

In surprise, the Captain stepped back and handed over a light stick. It looked large in the Cutezarian's hand but the Chief Communicator examined it, nodded and, holding it in up, entered the structure. Once inside, the Cutezarians seemed to forget about the humans. Carrying the translator boxes casually, they paid no attention as the devices sporadically spoke English. The humans followed, catching phrases from the boxes.

"The central place," the Cutezarians said to each other, walking around the first level.

"The grain keepers."

"The Spirit shelves."

"Look, the illuminating stones."

Moving from place to place, discovering first hand their history, their rate of speech increased until the boxes translated only an occasional word.

At the ramps, they hesitated and conferred. The Chief Communicator turned to the humans and spoke at a translatable speed.

"It would please us to go into the..." The box paused for a long time searching its data banks for the right concept. "...Meditation Chambers alone."

"Agreed," 'Shonya nodded, a little taken back.

They nodded in return and disappeared up the ramp.

"Meditation chambers?" Forest repeated.

"I wonder what that means to them?" 'Shonya mused aloud.

"I guess intelligent beings need to be alone. Just to think things through if nothing else," Forest replied.

"Yet many beings do not have the need for privacy or being alone that many humans have," Oliver reminded them.

"But the translator box chose the concept of meditation. At the very least, it indicates reflection of some sort," Captain Brodsky countered.

The others nodded. Conversation died.

After a while, Forest and the Captain began exploring what they had only seen in pictures. 'Shonya examined the jars again, remembering the last time she stood there with Craig. Oliver positioned himself in the center of the room by the table and reviewed the arrangement of the room, imagining it lit by the beads. He made mental notes to review the studies on the stones used in the construction of the structure and find out what kind of grain the jars contained.

Presently the Cutezarians came back down the ramp, still talking so rapidly the translation boxes emitted only occasional words. Without another word to their hosts, the Cutezarians walked around the first level room again.

Suddenly they hurried out the exit, their strangely familiar faces glowing with pleasure. The humans exchanged puzzled shrugs and trailed after them.

The Chief Communicator addressed the humans as they emerged. "We have records of this time. We are pleased to find they are correct. We are privileged to be the first Cutezarians to see the inside of an ancient structure."

Captain Brodsky nodded. "We understand. That feeling is part of what drives us to uncover ancient structures. We call it curiosity."

"What is this curiosity?" the box asked.

Oliver answered. "The need to know simply because something is unknown, to prove that which we think we know, and to learn about something simply because it exists."

The Chief Communicator shook his head. "Until you came, it was enough to view the records."

Another Cutezarian spoke. "We found pleasure in viewing the structure. Will you uncover others?" Although the box's voice was stilted, the Cutezarian's excitement came through.

'Shonya nodded. "Yes, we have begun to clear a second structure. If you wish for us to do more, I'm sure we could negotiate to extend our stay."

"Like asking a hungry man if he wants food," Forest muttered to Oliver, smiling at her restraint.

"We will consider that possibility," The Chief Communicator replied.

"There is much we would like to ask you, but what we would learn from you now could change the interpretation of what we see," Forest told the Cutezarians, suddenly sounding very formal for him. "When we meet with you after the study of the second structure is completed, we will be anxious to ask many questions."

"Can we also visit that structure?" the box asked.

"Of course you may," 'Shonya assured them.

Looking into the sky, the Chief Communicator abruptly changed the subject. "We must return to our dwellings and you to your ship." Without further warning, they disappeared around the corner of the structure.

Captain Brodsky turned to follow, but they were gone. "Some sort of transportation device I guess," he mused.

## CHAPTER EIGHTEEN

"Craig!" 'Shonya called his name as she let herself into his quarters. It still felt strange just entering like that, but he insisted.

"'Shonya?" he answered from the closet. "I just finished dressing for dinner. I thought I'd go out."

"Don't hurry. I brought it with me," she called back.

He came out of the huge closet, that also served as the dressing room, in uniform. 'Shonya looked up. "Hmmmm... ." After seeing him in civilian clothes so long, it caught her off guard. It hadn't occurred to her to wonder whether or not he was good looking. But he looked good in the uniform.

"I couldn't decide what I wanted. I thought I'd go to the mess hall and see what everyone else had," he was saying.

"Is quail, cheese, grapes, and hot bread ok?" She shook her thoughts aside.

"As good as anything," he allowed. He leaned against the partition that separated the sleeping area from the lounge and watched her lay out the food.

"I'd forgotten how terrific you look in the uniform," she teased, trying to ignore his pale face and the tired lines around his eyes.

Studying his shiny shoes, he confessed. "I needed a reminder of who I am." He paused. "I'm still a military Chaplain."

"Are you beginning to miss being on duty?" she asked.

He smiled quietly. "I think so."

"That's a good sign." 'Shonya smiled. "But don't get in a hurry."

He nodded, crossed the room and, without otherwise touching her, kissed her. "I know from the last couple of days I'm not ready."

"Okay," she conceded, pleased by his action. "No lectures." She motioned him into the chair.

After a few bites, Craig's stomach began to hurt. "You sounded all excited when you came in and I distracted you. What happened today?" he asked to divert his attention.

Her excitement bubbled back to the surface. "Paji and I stayed in the lab after everyone else had come back to the ship. I was checking the results of Roger's study — I'll tell you those in a minute — when suddenly the door opened. Two Cutezarians came in and announced they wanted to see the structure."

"You talked to them?" He looked up in astonishment, brushing his hair back.

She smiled. "Uh-huh. I sent for the Captain, Oliver, and Forest and we took a tour of one side of the structure."

"What did they say?" he asked, wide-eyed.

'Shonya laughed. "They got excited and talked so fast the translator boxes couldn't keep up."

"Didn't you learn anything new from them?" He demanded, enjoying her enthusiasm.

"Well, yes. They knew about the beads providing light, and they used the concept of meditation to describe the upper chambers."

"Meditation?" he repeated. "Are you sure?"

She nodded, still mystified, "I had this conversation with the Captain and Oliver. Since the box only translates concepts, it could mean several things."

"Anything from just being alone to think, to what I think of as meditation," Craig finished.

"But since the translator's English samples came from us, could it be possible the box used the word to mean the same thing we do?" 'Shonya wondered.

Craig leaned back in his chair with a smile. "Possible, but not probable."

"You're right."

Craig pushed his food around his plate in silence.

After watching a few painful seconds, 'Shonya decided she wasn't hungry either and pushed her plate back.

Seeking a distraction, she pulled out her computer. "I thought you might like to review the results of Roger's test and the scans of the structure's material. Then I've got to go look at Paji's models of the second structure."

She spoke to the computer: "Grain analysis," and handed him the computer. "Here."

"Well, it's edible," he remarked as he read the results.

"Did Roger do any other tests?" She nodded. "The computer indicates when the grain is ground up and mixed with water then fried, baked, or steamed it rises slightly."

"Unleavened bread?" Craig asked.

She smiled at the ancient words. "You got it."

The grain contains what little leavening there is?"

"Seems to be."

"But it takes water to release it?"

"Otherwise it would have spoiled long ago."

"Wonder how it tastes," he mused.

"Bland, according to Roger," she laughed. "We may have to do additional tests."

"Forest is the only cook I know except the people who work on the R&R deck."

"Forest?" She asked surprised, "Hum. I'll talk to him."

"What about the stones in the structure?" He changed the subject, handing the computer back. "Most of the building is the common basic stone found on the planet."

She answered, showing him the screen. "But the last ten rows of the peak are made of the same stone as the Chaplain's beads."

"Maybe they considered the energy-giving stone sacred," he suggested.

"Then we've appropriately named them, haven't we?" She smiled and stood to go. "I've got to meet Paji." She watched him come around the table, not knowing what to expect. "I'll be back after vespers if Paji and I get done."

Craig nodded and took her hands. "Thanks for dinner and the info."

She looked up at him without a word, half-afraid of her own feelings.

"Well, bye," he finally said.

"Bye." She turned to go.

"'Shonya." Stopping her, he put his arms around her from behind and rested his chin on her hair.

She didn't resist and leaned against him, touching his hands. Slowly he turned her around to face him. They stood close, and she slipped her arms around his waist.

Time stopped.

It was a quiet, companionable feeling. For once, 'Shonya forget to analyze her feelings.

Craig gradually became aware of the music in the background, and realized how long they had been still.

'Shonya sensed the change and looked up.

He smiled and shook his head. "You have ah... a..." He searched for words. "A calming effect on me. When you walk in, I relax. I know whatever I say or do will be accepted, and if it's unacceptable, you'll let me know."

"Sounds like a friend to me," she said with a gentle smile.

"Not exactly, but it's a good start," he said lightly then frowned. "There's so much I want to say, but..."

"Craig, its okay," she interrupted him. "I'm not sure what I feel for you, but I like it. Anything more than that, we can deal with when you're well."

Even with that level of non-commitment, he knew the warmth of joy at the acceptance of his deepest emotions by another person.

And it was LaShonya Reed: cartographer, archeologist, leader, administrator, and teacher—creative, thinking, laughing, warm, strong, stubborn, demanding, articulate 'Shonya.

And he fell in love. Strangely, he knew he was falling in love. "Falling is the right word," he thought with ironic humor. The feeling engulfed him and he drifted slowly down through his emotions. "Not altogether unpleasant." Afraid 'Shonya could read every emotion in his eyes, he looked up at the ceiling, striving for some sort of control. "Oh God, what do I do now?" He repeated his earlier prayer.

Watching his changing expressions, she tried to work through her own feelings. "What if I'm not in love, but feel compassion and affection because he turned to me?" 'Shonya wondered.

Aloud she said, "I wish I could read your thoughts like I can your expressions."

He smiled gently. "What do they tell you?"

"You're discovering something, and you're not sure what to do about it," she guessed correctly.

"You'll be the first to know when I get it worked out." He kissed her forehead.

"That's good enough." She couldn't help but kiss him.

His startled reaction surprised her as he gathered her into his arms. And they both knew something had changed between them when he kissed her.

Emotions rocketed around 'Shonya again, sending her back into uncertainty.

They looked at each other a very long time, neither one quite ready to put anything into words.

Finally, 'Shonya touched his face. "See you tomorrow." She activated the door sensor. "But if it's not too late when Paji and I get done, I may stop back by."

"Goodnight, 'Shonya." He watched the door shut and wondered what to do next. Shaken by the overwhelming depth of his feeling, he wandered around the room, rubbing troublesome his stomach.

Suddenly the sharp pain in his stomach demanded attention.

For a couple of days he'd experienced—and ignored—a series of short, sharp, stomach pains. But this one could not be ignored. He leaned against his back a chair, gasping. In the pain he didn't touch his comm button, but gasped, "Computer, emergency, I need to know where Doctor," he gasped. And the pain took over.

Alerted by the strange message, the comm officer activated the comm button for him. "Chaplain?"

"Chris, I need Jeff."

Lt. Chris Standhill, second watch comm officer, didn't take time to answer and contacted the doctor. "Dr. Keal, it's the Chaplain. He sounds in pain."

"Where is he?"

"His quarters, sir," Lt. Standhill answered, opening the connecting frequency. "The link's open."

Dr. Keal hurried out of the recreation area, leaving a half finished Jango game behind. "Craig?" The doctor hailed the chaplain.

"Jeff?"

"What's wrong?"

The suddenness of the sharp pain had subsided, allowing Craig to communicate, but his voice still came in short gasps. "Sharp stomach pain."

"Can you get to sickbay?" Jeff asked.

"Not yet," came the truthful answer.

"Stay where you are. I'm almost there." The doctor called sickbay. "Keal here. I'm bringing the Chaplain in. Prepare his formula with another milligram of milethagran in it."

In Craig's quarters, Jeff found him leaning against the chair; so pale his hazel eyes dominated his face like a large-eyed child.

"Come on, sit down." Jeff helped him around the chair.

Craig sat with a wince and a small grunt of pain.

"Get your feet up," the doctor ordered, touching the keypad to activate the chair. "Recline," he commanded the chair's computer.

The footstool came out and the back extended. Craig laid back and closed his eyes, trying to rub the pain away.

Jeff removed Craig's hand. "I'm afraid rubbing isn't going to help," he said gently, probing Craig's stomach. Craig squirmed, flinched, and clenched the arms of the chair "How long?" the doctor asked.

"A couple of days," Craig managed, opening his eyes.

"This bad?"

Craig shook his head.

"I don't have my life reader, but I'm thinking you've developed an ulcer." He touched the tender spot and Craig moved away from the pain. "I'm afraid you're bleeding."

Craig watched him with growing apprehension. Finally he sighed, laid his head back and closed his eyes.

"Can you make it to sick bay now? Or shall I send for a transport?" Jeff inquired.

Craig opened his eyes and glared at him. "Is that a threat?"

"You're going to sick bay one way or another," the doctor assured him.

Craig deactivated the chair's computer and slowly got up. Standing with a grunt, one hand reached for his stomach, the other for Jeff's shoulder.

The doctor took him by the shoulders. "Dizzy?" he asked.

"Uh-huh." Craig's chin was nearly on his chest.

"Can you walk?"

Craig's head came up. "We've had this conversation before."

Jeff smiled grimly. "Let's not keep repeating it. Can you walk?"

"I think so." Craig moved carefully toward the door. If he concentrated, he could manage. "I'm completely drained. Worse than usual," he commented.

"Loss of blood depletes energy." Jeff took his arm and they stepped out into the corridor.

Craig hoped the corridor was empty, but at the same time wanted to see 'Shonya.

"What are you doing in uniform?" the doctor asked.

Craig had to smile. The tone of voice made sure he understood the real question was "What stupid thing were you doing that required a uniform?"

"Identity crisis," he said shortly. "I was going out to dinner, but 'Shonya," he stopped as they entered the turbo lift. Craig braced himself for the drop. "The lift never bothered me before," he groaned as the turbo dropped.

Jeff steadied Craig with one hand and touched his comm button with the other. "Keal here."

"Yes, doctor?" came the answer.

"Meet me at the lift with a transport," he instructed. He signed off and turned to Craig. "And don't fight me on this."

Craig held up a hand in surrender. "No fight left." As he pushed away from the wall, another spasm of pain hit. "Ummmm,"

Jeff ordered the turbo to hold. The med tech brought the transport into the lift and Craig sat on the edge. "Come on, lie down."

With a sigh, he stretched out, covering his eyes with his forearm. "Give me strength and tolerance for the pain," Craig silently prayed as he felt the gentle drifting of the suspended transport.

Tiredness had all but overcome reality when the med tech touched his shoulder. "Chaplain?"

Craig stirred, but it was too much trouble to open his eyes and move.

"Craig!" The doctor's insistent voice demanded, "I need you to move to the table. It'll hurt worse if we have to move you."

He fought off the tiredness and sat up. The tech adjusted the position of the transport and he moved to the table.

"Are you still dizzy?" Jeff asked.

Craig nodded cautiously.

"Lie down."

Craig obeyed. The doctor let him rest. He ran some tests, checked Craig's blood volume, and did another series of scans.

A spasm of pain woke Craig suddenly. With a moan, he tried to sit up, forgetting he wasn't in his own quarters.

"Easy, Chaplain," the tech said, easing him back.

Craig settled back on the table as Jeff came in from the station.

"Here again," Craig muttered looking up at the panels.

"Here again," the doctor repeated. "Are you ready to talk?"

"Depends on what I hear," Craig said without enthusiasm.

"Try this. Your blood volume is down. You've been bleeding quite a bit. I'm surprised you haven't noticed blood in your urine or stool. My last scan was three days ago, and you weren't bleeding then. But the ulcer's perforated now."

He took a deep breath. "I'm going to try medication first and talk surgery later. The laser makes it a simple procedure, but you're not in shape for it. I'm giving you hemoglobin enhancers to help your body replace what you've lost, and I've put something to seal the ulcer in the formula."

Craig listened, eyes closed, tired and numb. "I can' handle this alone, God," he silently cried.

"We'll try the drug for a couple of weeks. That should take us past the reception and first tour of the city. After that, if you're not healed, we'll talk surgery."

"What are my chances?" Craig asked without opening his eyes.

"Normally, about fifty-fifty," came the reply. "But with your system," Jeff sent the med tech back to the station and laid a hand on Craig's shoulder.

Dr. Jeffery Keal often prayed for his patients, but only in certain circumstances did he pray with them. This was one of those times. Leaving his hand on Craig's shoulder, he prayed, "God, give Craig extra strength. It's difficult to have come this far and have a setback like this. Touch him physically. Make him strong. Renew his spirit. Renew his will to fight. Give me wisdom to choose the best treatment for him." Jeff felt a change in the tension of Craig's body as he spoke.

Craig opened his eyes, allowing the doctor a glimpse into the depth of his feelings. His voice was low, filled with emotion. "Thanks, Jeff." He struggled a minute, then asked. "Can I sleep now?"

"Not yet," he answered and motioned the med tech to bring a tray. "You probably haven't eaten much." He handed Craig the glass of formula and brought the head of the table up.

"It hurt," Craig confessed as he drank.

"Thought so." The doctor nodded. Next came an injection. "This is the hemoglobin enhancer. When you're out of uniform, I'll give you an old fashioned sedative, and you, Chaplain, shall sleep while your body makes blood."

Craig handed back the glass and leaned forward to shrug out of his uniform jacket. The pain came again. He gasped and lay back, waiting for it to pass.

The doctor caught the jacket as it dropped, and then gave Craig the second injection. "Stay where you are." He covered his patient, lowered the head of the table and went back to the station. "We'll move him after he's asleep."

A short time later, he returned to check the panel and found Craig fighting the sedation. "Craig," the doctor said loudly. "Am I going to have to call 'Shonya before you settle down?"

"'Shonya," Craig repeated her name sleepily then fought to open his eyes. "'Shonya," His voice was stronger. "She was coming by after an experiment," his voice trailed off.

"I'll tell her where you are, and that you might live if you follow orders," the doctor promised. "Relax, quit fighting the sedative and sleep or I'll give you a larger dose."

Craig closed his eyes, and raised a hand in resignation. "You win." In a few minutes, he was sleeping.

As they lifted him from the table onto the transport, 'Shonya hurried in. Alarmed by Craig's stillness, she followed but stayed out of the way until the tech left. She brushed his hair back, unable to resist touching him, and looked up to find Jeff watching her, amusement in his eyes.

"What happened?" she asked.

Jeff set his amusement aside, and the serious professional emerged. "He's developed an ulcer and it's perforated. He's been bleeding at least twenty-four hours."

"He complained of being extra tired," she confirmed. "Will he be okay?"

"If he'll give his body a chance. In case the ulcer doesn't heal, we'll do surgery, but he's got to be stronger than he is now," the doctor replied.

"I just left him, I'm surprised he didn't call me," she mused.

Jeff shook his head. "He didn't even touch his comm button. Luckily, the comm officer was running a diagnostic on computer communications. Craig was trying to ask the computer to locate me, but didn't get very far. The computer alerted Lt. Standhill. I was surprised Craig was still conscious when I got to him."

"He's so still," she said.

"I gave him a sedative." Jeff urged her out of the room. "Come back in the morning. But he won't be ready to talk until tomorrow evening."

"I'll check in periodically."

In the twilight of Jeff's light sedation, Craig slept through the night and day, at times vaguely aware of 'Shonya as she came and went, of injections, and Dorinda. But they failed to stir any desire to respond.

At the end of her workday 'Shonya took her computer to the isolation room to finish her daily report, and waited for him to wake up.

In the first minutes of awareness, Craig remembered only that something was wrong. It took a little longer to realize where he was and remember the pain.

"'Shonya," he thought and opened his eyes.

She was there, working. She read a while then input data using the silent on screen keyboard, and then read again. Craig watched, not knowing how much time passed. She finally looked up when her eyes got tired and encountered Craig's sober, steady gaze.

He smiled tiredly, "Hi."

"Craig! How long have you been awake?" She folded the computer and stood.

"I don't know." His eyes closed again.

"Do you remember what happened?" she asked.

"Vividly," came his short answer.

"Still hurt?"

"I know it's there."

They were quiet.

"Want to hear what's happening on the planet?" she finally asked.

He took her hand. "Maybe tomorrow."

# CHAPTER NINETEEN

Dorinda hardly noticed the passing of the next two weeks. Involved with reception plans, she repeatedly studied her husband's notes and watched the recordings of the negotiations. Her anticipation of the scheduled tour grew as it came closer and she became increasingly fascinated by the Cutezarians.

For 'Shonya, the two weeks were equally interesting. The students, in the last stages of uncovering the second structure, spent considerable amounts of time speculating about its use. Further studies confirmed Paji's preliminary projections. The structure consisted of only one large room. Its purpose remained a mystery.

Putting off contacting Art became a daily search for excuses as 'Shonya struggled to define her feelings for Craig. She felt close to him, but still wondered what their relationship would be when Craig recovered and no longer needed her encouragement in the healing process. Would he love her, or grow away from her?

Artifacts occupied Roger's time. Oliver's students photographed the artifacts in situ, lifted them out, photographed again and delivered them to his lab by the dozens. Date, composition and interactive tests filled his days.

However, for Craig, it seemed endless. Scans, exams, injections, inactivity, pain and a special diet occupied his days.

On the second Wednesday, before boredom turned his patient into a caged animal, Jeff extracted a promise from Craig to merely observe and allowed him to return to the dig.

Craig arrived in time to see the techs in packs experiment with the sets of windows to find which combination unlocked the second structure.

"Chaplain!" Forest's large hand engulfed Craig's. A tall, big boned man, Dr. Forest Cabrailes had, in earlier years, spent many hours in Earth's hot southwest sun excavating the last of the that area's North American Indians' sites. Craig often imagined him in an ancient cowboy hat on a horse. His leather-like face broke into a grin as he continued. "Good to see you. We missed you."

Oliver got up from the table the instructors had set up on a rise above the pyramid that allowed unobstructed observation. "Here, sit and watch." He waved Craig into the chair he had just vacated.

"Thanks." Craig sat gratefully and took in the activity below. "How many combinations have they tried?" he asked.

"This is the seventh," Oliver said.

"What else is going on?" Craig asked.

Oliver touched the play pad of the hand-held camera on the table.

Often the old word 'camera' was still applied to the recorder. However, the image archive was radically different from the original picture saving devices. It consisted of three layers. The recording side was a microscopic laser processor. The center, a plasma imager, stored the images. The third layer contained its holographic images at a touch of the keypad.

Craig followed the in-situ pictures of larger Chaplain's beads, gold belts, statues carved from the illuminating stone with wavy lines carved around them, and dishes. Next came a series of pictures of the artifacts by themselves after cleaning.

"The statues from the first structure are somehow different," Craig observed. "Were the statues from the first structure made from this stone? I don't remember."

The two doctors looked at each other. "We'll check with Roger, but we don't think so," Oliver spoke for them both.

"Can't you just see the statues glowing like the beads?" Forest asked.

"Impressive," was Oliver's comment.

"Eerie," Craig added.

A celebration interrupted their conversation and they looked up to see the students slide open the entrance.

"We need to check their method," Forest said. "Join us, Craig?"

Craig nodded, and followed them to the structure. He stayed out of the way as he watched the students attach the zero-light scan scope to the small archive imager.

"Describe your process." Oliver requested, bending slightly toward his student.

"Record first without lights using the zero-light scope," she answered looking up. Oliver reached down and caught the night lenses that fell from her head because she had to look up so far to see his face.

Craig smiled to himself. He liked watching Oliver. He always seemed completely unaware of the aura of elegance everyone else felt in his presence. Craig picked up the conversation again.

"After you make sure your recording is good, what next?"

"Final exam time," Craig heard someone behind him whisper.

The doctor's student repeated the process perfectly and Oliver beamed. "Excellent, Vintera," he congratulated her and then addressed the group. "Let us proceed."

Craig remembered the excitement of his own first major dig, and saw that feeling reflected in the faces around him.

'Shonya laid her hand on his arm. "I heard a rumor Jeff let you out," she said.

Without thinking, he put his arm around her. "And you just had to come find out for yourself," he teased. For a moment they were unaware of the group around them. The students discreetly tried not to disturb them, but 'Shonya cleared her throat as she became aware of their smiles.

"You, ah, you look better." He didn't, but that's all she could think to say. She patted his back and assumed a less intimate posture.

He grinned, suddenly self-conscious. "I tire quickly."

"The pain?"

"Still there."

There wasn't anything else to say.

"You want to look at Paji's maps before you go inside the structure?" she broke the silence.

"Sure. You think they'll let me in?" he asked as they started off.

"I think I can arrange it," she grinned.

To keep from taking her hand, Craig put his hands in his pockets. But seemingly unconcerned, she threaded her arm through his. As she described Paji's talents and work,

Craig listened, watching her in wonder, hearing only part of what she said.

Paji looked up from her station as they entered. "Chaplain, good to see you out," she greeted Craig. "What's the good news outside?" she added, switching her focus to 'Shonya.

"They're in on the eighth try," she replied.

"I'd better get this linked so they can have a map," Paji smiled in reply. She spent a few minutes speaking to the computer, and finally commanded, "Link." Next she contacted Forest.

"Forest, here," his big voice boomed.

"This is Paji. Your maps are ready."

"Good work. We'll take a look before we go in." He signed off.

"Do you want to see them, 'Shonya?" Paji asked.

"Yeah. I showed Craig your earlier maps, so display just the last ones."

Paji spoke to the computer and it displayed one very large, triangular room.

Even in this rough detail, Craig could see stone benches everywhere. At first, he didn't see a pattern.

"Computer enhance artifacts," Paji ordered.

Benches separated from the gray areas. They were arranged in circles. The back row sat against the wall and covered the back perimeter. The next row contained fewer benches, but still formed a circle. The pattern continued until there were four benches in the front row. A circle of about three and a half meters in the very center of the room remained unoccupied.

"A central meeting place?" he mused aloud.

"Looks like it," Paji said.

Suddenly tired, Craig remembered his promise. "I need to get back to the ship. Jeff made me promise I wouldn't stay long. Thanks Paji. Good work," he added. Before he signaled the ship he asked, "Can I come in the morning for my personal tour?"

"I'll put it on my schedule," 'Shonya promised with a smile.

The next morning Craig went straight to the planet as soon as he finished Jeff's morning routine of formula, injections and scans.

"What's the news?" 'Shonya greeted him.

191

"The good Doctor Keal announced my blood level is returning to normal. The medication has controlled the bleeding, but not stopped it completely. He thinks the general hyper-electric state of my body keeps it from healing." Craig didn't mention surgery, but felt convinced it was inevitable.

"I'll get the light sticks," 'Shonya broke the silence.

Standing in the entrance, they looked at each other, both remembering their last tour. Craig took her hand and they smiled at each other in the glow of the light sticks.

"I'll try to behave myself," he promised, leading the way through the maze of benches.

She sat on the front bench and he stood in the center, looking up at the light streaming through the windows created by the open stones.

Finally, he sat across from her. "I feel like. Like I should have prepared something," he told her quietly.

"It does have a cathedral effect, doesn't it?" she agreed.

"Of course that's a human judgment," he said. "But it makes me wonder what they did here."

"There are trays of beads and shelves around the room like the Daniel K One," she observed.

He nodded silently and they sat looking at each other, each knowing the other's thoughts. Suddenly they both smiled, acknowledging the attraction between them.

"Come on. Let's finish our tour." His smile extended to his eyes and voice.

Sometimes holding hands and sometimes separately, they explored the huge room. As she examined the intricate carving on the benches, 'Shonya noted, "Some of these resemble ancient American Indian designs with their straight, angular lines."

Craig nodded, adding the observation to his growing collection of thoughts about the familiarity of the structure's appearance, the Cutezarians, and the concepts they used. At the end of the tour, he stopped her at the door.

"Thanks. You make me feel like part of the company."

"You are," she said in a serious voice. "You help us all in ways you don't even know. And there's something to Forest's idea about talented amateurs. Besides, I have personal reasons," she teased.

"Anything you wish to share with the Chaplain?" he asked causally.

She laughed. "Only if it involved him."

Craig chuckled. "We can't have the poor man burdened with unnecessary expressions of feelings can we?"

"He might think he has the responsibility to do something about them when he should be concentrating on getting well," she reminded him lightly.

Putting his arms around her, he rested his face against her hair, grateful for her wisdom.
She stopped him when he started to speak. "Remember, no promises yet."

He could only nod and hold her. Feeling his struggle for control, 'Shonya stood quietly with her arms around his waist until he took a deep breath and slowly let it out.

"I'd forgotten the emotional turmoil of adolescence. I'm all feelings and no reason." He grinned suddenly, letting her go. "I promise I'll behave."

"You said that already," she observed dryly.

As they emerged into the daylight, 'Shonya noted the tired lines around Craig's eyes. "If you don't get some rest, Jeff won't let you attend your own reception tomorrow night. I'll skip dinner tonight, and see you tomorrow night."

"Will you go with me to the reception?" he asked.

"Of course," she smiled. "Now go."

He kissed her lightly and signaled the ship. Jeff was waiting. He took one look at Craig and ordered him to sickbay. A few minutes later, he looked down at his grim patient.

"The ulcer's bleeding again." Craig nodded. "You're not surprised?" Jeff asked.

"Pain's worse," Craig muttered.

"And you're mad."

"All I did was," Craig protested.

"All you did was tour the structure, walk, bend and stretch. And get all emotional over your guide," the doctor grimly finished for him.

"But..."

"Shonya called."

Craig suddenly relaxed. "I can't fight you both."

"Good!" Jeff said, "There's a time to fight, and a time to relax. Now's the time to relax." His hands were busy at the medication cart as he talked. He turned back to his patient with a grin. "End of sermon, Chaplain."

Craig closed his eyes and smiled. "Now I know how y'all feel when I say something that's difficult for you to hear."

"Every teacher should know how it feels," Jeff admonished.

"Pull your shirt out." As Craig obeyed, Jeff checked the scan results and explained his intentions. "I'm going to try the direct approach." Touching Craig's stomach at the most tender spot he asked, "That's it, right?"

Craig flinched and didn't answer.

The doctor held up a medication patch. "If drinking the medication won't seal the ulcer, maybe direct application will. The blood stream won't recognize the base I mixed the medication with so it will be absorbed directly into the stomach lining." After checking the exact location of the ulcer one more time, he applied the patch. "You'll know it's there, but it shouldn't irritate. Let me know if it burns."

Craig nodded obediently.

"Now drink this."

Craig drank the formula hesitantly.

"I insist you stay here until tomorrow afternoon. I'll release you in time for the reception." Craig nodded again. Jeff hesitated, and then confessed, "I need you to know I kept a private record of your conversation with 'Shonya on the day of Dr. Kobee's service."

Craig looked up, surprised. "What's so important about that?"

"The description of how you felt. When the medication didn't work at first I added that data to the medical information and asked the computer to compensate. The patch is altered for the current condition of your body. If it works, surgery may be unnecessary."

"Sounds good," Craig's voice sounded distant.

"I deleted everything else. I promise."

"Uh-huh." Craig smiled slightly then frowned. "I'm, I can't seem to concentrate."

"I also put a sedative in the formula," the doctor again confessed. "Every time I turn you lose, you do something dumb. Now you're going to sleep."

"You've made your point," Craig sighed.

"Goodnight, Craig," the doctor said firmly as he dimmed the lights and turned to leave.

"I bet I'm the most rested person at the reception." Craig grumbled.

"I heard that," the doctor's voice came out of the dimness. "Go to sleep. Now!" Returning to the tech's station with a smile, he met 'Shonya.

"Sheila said you're keeping him. But it can't be too bad if you can smile."

"He's not happy about me sedating him," Jeff grinned. "But he's bleeding again. If it weren't for the reception tomorrow, I'd go in and seal the ulcer tonight. He's strong enough now. But he might not be able to attend the reception."

"How long a recovery period does he need?" she asked.

"At least forty-eight hours. He might make a brief appearance at twenty-four hours. Remind me of tomorrow's schedule."

Their discussion was cut short by the med tech. "Dr. Keal!" Sheila Brown exclaimed, pointing across the room.

"Craig! What are you doing?" Jeff demanded his voice harsh with concern.

"Can't sleep." Craig's words slurred together as he sought support against one of the monitoring tables.

Afraid Craig would collapse before he could reach him, Jeff crossed the room in five giant strides and made him sit on the table. "Why are you up?" he scolded.

"Pain," Craig said shortly. "'Shonya's here?" Jeff nodded. "You're discussing surgery?" Jeff nodded again, without commitment. "I signed emergency consents, right?" Craig grunted as another spasm of pain came.

"Right," Jeff said neutrally gently forcing Craig to stretch out.

He immediately sat up again. "Jeff, do the surgery now and get it over with."

The doctor noted his eyes were clear and voice was strong. Craig was, for the moment, completely awake. "You might not make it for the reception tomorrow night," he warned.

"If I can't, I can't."

"Are you completely aware of what we're discussing?" the doctor asked. "It's not policy to discuss surgery with a sedated person."

With a nod Craig insisted, "Jeff, I know what I'm consenting to." His tone was positive, his eyes alert.

Jeff stalled by checking the medication patch.

"It burns," Craig complained, painfully stretching to see the wound.

Jeff shook his head. "You're not tolerating the patch. So much for that theory," he grumbled. He gently removed it and cleaned the area.

"I don't want to wake up with this same pain." Craig's voice became softer as he quit fighting the sedation. "Your pre-op's already done," His voice drifted away, but shaking his head he tried to sit up. Settling for leaning on one elbow, he willed himself awake. "'Shonya?"

"Here." She spoke from the other side of the bed.

Taking her hand, he implored, "Make him do it."

"He will," she assured him. "Relax. Everything will be over when you wake up. I'll pray and Jeff will operate."

"Good combination." The medication wiped out his smile.

Jeff eased him onto his back and looked up at 'Shonya. "I'll call the surgery techs." He smiled reassuringly. "Don't worry. He'll be okay. It's not a tough procedure. People with no other health problems normally recover in less than twenty-four hours. But with Craig's messed up system, it'll take longer. Most patients don't even need general anesthetic. But I'm glad he's sleeping."

"I'll tell Dorinda and Andez and they can pass the word along," 'Shonya said.

Dorinda Brodsky came to sickbay before preparations were complete.

"Dorinda, there's nothing you can do here," Jeff told her.

Andez Ronger followed close behind her. "Ensign, there's nothing you can do here," the doctor repeated.

Roger Lavera hurried in.

"Roger, there's nothing you can do here," he insisted, growing weary of repeating himself.

Next came Oliver and Forest.

"What is this, dinner break?" the doctor demanded in exasperation. "There's nothing you can do." The doors opened again and Captain Brodsky entered. Finally, Jeff saw the humor and chuckled. "Well at least I have you all here at once. The techs are administering the neuromuscular block now. We're going to bore a tiny hole into the stomach, insert the seal and attach it to the healthy stomach tissue with absorbable adhesive. Since Craig's body rejected the liquid seal, I'm using a synthesized human tissue seal. By the time the adhesive and seal are absorbed, the ulcer should be healed."

"Ready, Doctor." The med tech interrupted his lecture.

"Thanks." Jeff turned back to the group. "The best thing you can do is pray his body doesn't destroy the bubble. I don't want to resort to cauterization." Dismissing the group with a wave of his hand, he returned to surgery.

Craig was lying quietly, the sterile field device extending over his torso. Jeff put his hands into the sterile field's access membranes and they conformed to his fingers. He spoke to the field's computer: "Activate laser. Position on co-ordinates provided by scans."

The light wand moved to the spot. Slipping the small tube into the shaft of the light wand, the doctor ordered, "Activate beam and insert tube." The computer followed instructions, boring a small hole in Craig's stomach and inserting an access tube. Next Jeff inserted the folded seal attached to a minuscule biodegradable wire into the tube.

"Doctor," the med tech said, "I think the Chaplain's waking up."

"Get Dr. Reed in here to talk to him." After a small pause, he spoke to the computer: "Scope." The unit's microscope came up to eye level and the computer adjusted the field of vision until the inside of Craig's stomach came into view. The doctor saw the inflamed lining, then the ulcer. Shutting everything else out, he concentrated. "You've got yourself a nice ulcer there, Chaplain."

"Jeff?"

The doctor heard his name but didn't look up.

Something switched on in Craig's brain. He felt his head move, but couldn't locate any other part of his body. Forcing a deep breath, he decided it was easier to breath normally. Jeff's voice was somewhere near, and he tried to open his eyes. "Jeff?"

"Where's 'Shonya?" the doctor muttered.

Then Jeff heard her voice. "It's okay, Craig." She brushed Craig's hair back.

Craig opened his eyes, "'Shonya?"

"Everything's fine, Craig. It's the block so you wouldn't feel the surgery. Go back to sleep."

Smiling slightly, he closed his eyes. 'Shonya stayed, her hand against his face in case he woke again. Again, she wondered where they would end up when Craig was well. She pushed the thought away and concentrated on Jeff.

Jeff directed the computer-controlled device as it covered the ulcer with the membrane and attached the edges around it. Withdrawing the instrument, he looked up and spoke to the med tech. "While we're here, get the micro spray unit and fill it with the liquid seal. His stomach lining is inflamed." He looked up at 'Shonya with an unasked question.

"He's okay," she nodded.

They tried to relax until the tech returned. Craig moved his head against 'Shonya's hand but didn't open his eyes.

Sheila brought a tray. "It's ready and sterilized," she said, handing the cylinder into the sterile field.

The doctor attached it to the arm and guided it into the tube. "Activate, rotate and spray." The computer obeyed and discharged a coat of medication over the lining of Craig's stomach.

"Remove tube and sterilize wound," he instructed.

The computer's arm obeyed, and the procedure was over. Jeff covered the wound and removed the sterile field.

"Put him in the isolation room and watch his readings. Let me know when he starts moving.

## CHAPTER TWENTY

Craig opened his eyes and sighed as he looked around the familiar room. Yet he felt calm. Something inside him demanded this be the last time he spent the night in sickbay. "Please God, let it be so." He opened his eyes to find the med tech beside the bed.

"Need anything, Chaplain?" Bill asked.

"Water?" he asked.

"Not yet," was the answer. "Wait until your muscles are awake. How 'bout some ice?"

"Anything," Craig answered and tried to take the container Bill held. Nothing happened.

The look of surprise told Bill Chung what Craig was feeling. "It's okay, Chaplain. They blocked everything below your neck but the heart and lungs."

"Why?" Craig asked.

"Dr. Keal didn't want you to move in your sleep during the procedure," the tech answered.

"It's such a natural feeling. Like I'm just relaxing," Craig commented.

Bill nodded. "They used synthesized endorphins. It's like your body puts itself to sleep."

"How long?" Craig asked.

Bill fed him more ice chips and checked his watch. "In about an hour you should feel some sensation. Two or three before the effect is gone."

"And I lie here doing nothing?" Craig asked.

"Oh, you'll sleep. One of the side effects is that all the stuff in your blood system confuses the brain, and it responds by napping." He administered another helping of ice.

Craig let it melt in his mouth, then started to ask about 'Shonya, but yawned instead.

Bill grinned. "See I told you."

"Mind control," Craig grumbled. However, he couldn't fight off the desire to sleep and wasn't aware that Bill checked the panel of readouts, adjusted his pillows and lowered his head before returning to his station.

Jeff checked in. "Bill, how's the Chaplain?"

"Coherent when he's awake."

"Any signs of the block wearing off?"

"Not yet."

"But he's sleeping now?"

"Yes."

"Any other side effects?"

"Not that I can see."

"Good. I'll check in before I go to bed."

'Shonya called. "Bill, how's the Chaplain?"

"Resting."

"Everything ok?"

"He's fine."

"I'd like to come down and see him."

"Morning would be better. He's mostly sleeping and it's better if doesn't get worked up until the seal's been in place a while."

"What would I do to get him all worked up?" She asked.

She could hear the smile in his voice. "Doctor, I monitor the panels. I've seen what you do to his blood pressure, heart rate, and stomach secretions."

She laughed, surprised other people kept track of their relationship. "Please have Jeff call me when he comes in. I'd really like to come down tonight."

"I'll have him call you." He promised, smiling to himself. Those two could deny everything to the rest of the crew, but as far as Bill Chung was concerned, the Chaplain had very strong feelings for the Exec Science Officer.

He reported the Chaplain's condition to a couple dozen people over the next few hours. "We may have to start issuing medical bulletins over the ship's system," he mused.

"What's so funny?" Jeff stuck his head in.

"I keep repeating the same message to all these people who want to know how the Chaplain is."

"I know the feeling," he said with a grin. "How is he?"

"Sleeping."

"Any movement?" Bill shook his head. The Doctor frowned.

"Jeff?" Craig's voice came over the speaker.

Craig felt like he'd slept forever. The stretch he imagined he needed didn't materialize, but with effort, he could move his arms.

"There, he's moving his arms," Bill indicated the fluctuation of the readings.

"Good." The doctor touched the comm unit. "Be right there, Craig." He left orders on another patient then went to the isolation room. Craig was flexing his right hand. "Feels strange doesn't it?" Jeff remarked, taking the hand and rubbing it. "Feeling will return, but you'll be numb a while yet." He massaged Craig's arm, shoulders and ended with his other hand. "There, is that better?"

Craig nodded. "Thanks."

The doctor ran his hands down Craig's torso and legs. "Feel anything?

Craig shook his head. "Should I?"

"You will soon since feeling's returned in your body. How do you feel?"

"Like I've been here forever," Craig complained.

Jeff nodded. "When feeling begins to return, we usually begin massage to facilitate the process and minimize the patient's frustration." He said, checking the wound. It was merely a slightly warm, red spot. "Not bad. But you've already had enough frustration for a lifetime. After we get some nourishment in you, I'll give you a sedative. By the time you wake up in the morning normal sensation will have returned."

"I am tired." His patient agreed.

The doctor went to make the arrangements. A few minutes later, he returned from the med tech station with a slightly rumpled 'Shonya.

Craig was pleased to see her. "Hi. You didn't have to stay up," he said as he accepted the glass of formula she held out.

"I've napped a couple of hours. I'm fine." She waited until he handed the empty glass back, then took his hand and told him about her day.

While Craig's attention focused on her, Jeff prepared his arm for the IV. "Just talk to 'Shonya and don't move."

Craig looked at Jeff, then at 'Shonya, "I'm glad you came," he said.

"I wanted to be here," she said simply.

Craig felt a short sting as the IV device opened his vein.

"Steady," Jeff admonished in response to Craig's wince.

"We duplicated your experiment on the Chaplain's beads with the statues you asked about," 'Shonya followed the doctor's orders to distract him.

"Do they give off light?" Craig asked.

"They literally come alive," she smiled. "They're beautiful. We made a special recording for you."

Content to listen to her voice, Craig lay back until he began to taste something familiar. Frowning at Jeff, he accused, "You've done this before, haven't you?"

Jeff nodded. "Several times. You can taste it now, right?"

"Um-huh." Suddenly he felt a rush of warmth. Lightheaded, he closed his eyes. "Ummmmm."

"What is it?" 'Shonya asked in concern.

"The sedative, when given like this, simulates an adrenalin rush except it doesn't pump the body up," Jeff answered.

Craig's puzzled disorientation told Jeff he'd better hurry before Craig forgot his instructions. Motioning for 'Shonya to keep talking, he hurried to finish.

"Keep still, and don't fight it, Craig." She touched his face.

Opening his eyes, Craig smiled slightly. His voice was soft and fuzzy around the edges. "But you didn't finish about the statues." He took both of her hands, unaware of Jeff's hurried efforts to finish.

"I'll bring your computer tomorrow so you can see the video while you're still confined," she promised.

"I'll hold you to that," he murmured and fought off sleep another minute. "Jeff?"

"I'm still here." The doctor answered, stepping back into Craig's line of vision. "Did everything go ok?"

"Perfect," he answered. "Now go to sleep so my work can take effect and 'Shonya and I can get some rest."

As his eyes closed Craig let go of 'Shonya's hands and, with a final sigh, went to sleep.

\*\*

'Shonya arrived at the dig early in the next morning, hoping to complete the day's work quickly. Her goal for the day was to coordinate the presentations for the Cutezarians.

She met with Roger first. "Is your presentation ready?"

"It's done, but not yet linked," he answered.

"Shall we do that while I'm here?" she prompted.

Roger practiced his commentary for the presentation as they viewed his selected series of scans. "Link to all systems," he ordered and 'Shonya turned to go.

"Lnked," the computer announced.

"Roger," 'Shonya turned back to face him. "Good work. Daniel would have been impressed by your thoroughness and precision."

Surprised, Roger looked up from his computer. After a minute he said, "Thank you, 'Shonya, I appreciate that."

"Keep it up, but I think you've earned already earned the degree."

Then she met with Oliver.

"We are done, linked and ready to report." Oliver stretched his tall frame and smiled. "The students excelled in their analysis of the second structure. It will be interesting to watch the Cutezarians during the presentation."

Next was Forest.

"Work's done, and on line. Just finished." In contrast to his abrupt way of speaking, his big voice reflected pleasure in the student's work.

"Good," she answered. "I'll go back to the ship and consolidate it all." She smiled, pleased to have the rest of the day to organize the material. Back in her office on the ship, she reviewed the material and had an idea. "Computer, separate material on the Daniel K One from Daniel K Two."

She contacted Dr. Cabrailes. "Forest, do you have a particular student you'd like to have present the work on the second structure?"

"Sure do."

"I've separated the two sets of information and would like you to do the first presentation and your student the second."

"No problem," he answered.

"Would you have Oliver do the same?"

"Of course."

"And Forest, tell Paji I would like her to do the presentation of maps on the second structure, and I'll do the first," she added.

"Done," he answered with a chuckle.

"Thank you. Reed out." They disconnected.

In response to her question, the computer gave the time as 9:55AM. After reviewing both files again, she added modeling capabilities to everything and called sickbay.

## CHAPTER TWENTY-ONE

Craig thought the tingling in his legs woke him. However, when he opened his eyes he found Jeff lowering a scope over his legs, and realized the sound accompanying the shaft's movement was the culprit.

The doctor retracted the instrument. "It measures your nerve activity and circulation efficiency," he explained, following Craig's questioning gaze. "How do you feel?"

"Tingly," he said.

"Sit up," Jeff commanded with a frown.

Craig pushed himself up with some difficulty, the bed following him into sitting position. Taking a deep breath, he flexed his stiff muscles.

"Can you get up?" the doctor asked. They looked at each other, each remembering the recurring conversation.

Jeff shook his head. "Come on. Up. What'd they used to say about the third time being a charm?"

"What it meant I have no idea," Craig said. Swinging his legs over the side of the bed as it lowered, he accepted the robe Jeff held out.

Jeff watched Craig closely as he moved around the room, prepared for any signs of side effects. To his dismay, Craig suddenly bent over in pain.

It took Craig a minute to realize the pain wasn't coming from his stomach, but his leg.

Jeff reached for a container of ointment, pulled the chair up and gently guided Craig into it. Kneeling on one knee, Jeff applied the medication directly to the calf muscles

"Other than sleeping, muscle spasms are the only other side effect the anesthetic has. And not all patients experience them."

"I thought it was harmless."

"It's not the medication, but the complete inertness of the muscle it causes. I hoped you would escape it. The ointment relaxes the muscle, and then is absorbed locally to provide long lasting effects."

He kept talking, saying whatever came into his mind to keep Craig occupiedd.

When Craig's muscles finally relaxed, Jeff stood and instructed, "I want you to sit a while, walk, sit, then walk. When you feel ok, take a shower, and then lie down. I'll give you another IV after your nap and later we'll try the formula."

Craig nodded, still pale, but stood and walked around.

"You may be a little stiff," the doctor told him.

"A little?" Craig eased his shoulders back into the chair.

"Don't sit very long before you get up again. Sheila's on duty and she'll check on you every twenty minutes."

He lifted Craig's shirt. "Let me see the wound." The little round spot was very warm, but not hot. "Craig, I don't know about tonight. Can we wait until late this afternoon to make a decision?

Craig nodded, and then remembered. "'Shonya. We had a date."

"You may be able to keep a little of it," the doctor said cautiously. "If you have any more spasms, call Sheila. The system's name-activated."

"I didn't know that." Craig looked up.

"How do you think you got me yesterday?"

Craig grinned. "I only knew I woke up alone and felt strange."

"The isolation room's comm system responds to first and last names of all the doctors and med techs. That way the patient has some privacy, but can alert the station. The rest of sickbay is strictly voice activated. People in isolation tend to stay longer,"

"Why's he telling me all this?" Craig wondered as the doctor seemingly rambled on.

Jeff stopped mid-sentence and answered Craig's silent question. "Ok, move around some more before I go."

"Making conversation, giving me time to rest," Craig thought gratefully. With considerably less trouble, he obeyed.

The doctor seemed satisfied. "Better. Keep it up and I'll be back later." He patted Craig's shoulder and went on rounds.

Craig talked to Sheila, walked around, sent for his clothes and finally sat tiredly. He leaned back, shut his eyes and sat very still with no desire to move. When he stirred and opened his eyes Sheila was standing in the doorway.

She held out his clothes. "Dr. Reed just called and asked if you were ready for visitors. I told her to give you twenty minutes."

He took the clothes and headed to shower. "Thanks, Sheila."

'Shonya waited until Paji's material came up on screen and placed it in the file where she wanted it before going to sickbay.

As Craig came out of the shower area, he winced as he pulled his shirt over his still damp hair, but 'Shonya thought he looked better and moved less cautiously.

"Hi!" he greeted her, "Sheila said you'd be by." He hugged her, making a small sound of pain at the contact.

"Hurt?" she asked.

"The entry point is tender, but mostly I'm having muscle spasms. Jeff hoped I wouldn't have them, and he's unhappy that he didn't predict my reaction right."

The pain became worse and, finally letting her go, he said, "Sheila?"

"Yes, Chaplain?"

He drew a sharp breath with the new spasm. "Back."

She hurried in before he finished. "Dr. Reed, help him sit on the bed," she instructed.

'Shonya obeyed and helped Craig remove his shirt. Sheila knelt on the bed behind Craig and applied the ointment.

Folding and re-folding Craig's shirt, 'Shonya desperately wished she could do more. "How long? How much more does he have to endure?" she cried silently.

Craig took her hand. "It's okay. It's a different kind of pain and it doesn't last long."

"But it's vicious," Sheila added.

Craig grinned. "That's a fair description." After a while, he could breathe normally as the muscles relaxed. "That's better, thanks." He smiled at her as she climbed off the bed, but remained pale from the exertion of fighting the pain.

Jeff suddenly arrived as Craig took the shirt from 'Shonya. "You okay?" He asked, checking the wound.

"Little tender," Craig said as he gingerly shrugged back into his shirt.

"I'll get the IV ready," he said as he motioned Sheila to follow him. "I asked 'Shonya to give him the bad news." he told her as they walked back to the station.

"Craig," 'Shonya said as gently as she could. "Since you're experiencing the muscle problems, Jeff's afraid tonight's out."

The disappointment showed on his face. He rubbed his shoulder but said nothing. Finally, he looked up. "Jeff?"

"Yes, Craig?"

"Can we compromise?"

"We'll talk over an IV." The doctor chuckled. He returned to find 'Shonya massaging Craig's shoulders. "Hurt?"

"Not as bad," Craig answered.

Jeff nodded and motioned him to lie down. Craig flinched as he inserted the device. "I added antibiotics," the doctor said neutrally as he began the flow of medication.

Craig felt the rush of warmth. "You didn't." He groaned, closed his eyes, and let his head fall back onto the pillow.

"If you're going anywhere tonight, you're going to sleep all afternoon. I was wrong about you not experiencing the side effects, so I may be wrong in predicting the amount of strength you'll have."

Craig nodded, "Okay."

"What part of the reception do you want to attend?" 'Shonya asked.

Almost asleep, Craig answered, "The student's and Cutezarian's presentations."

"I'll send your uniform. I promise I'll come and get you before the students start."

Craig took her hand. "Sorry about the date," he murmured.

"It's okay," she assured him, but he didn't hear.

## CHAPTER TWENTY-TWO

Becoming aware of a presence in the room, Craig slowly turned his head, opened his eyes and looked around. Enough light filtered into the dark room to see no one was there.

"It's the sedative," he told himself. But the sense of presence persisted.

Suddenly praying, he poured out his grief over Dr. Kobee's death, his own frustrating recovery, and fears about his medical condition. Finally exhausted and unable to think any longer, he cried, "God, be with us!"

"I will never leave you nor forsake you."

Craig knew someone spoke the words. They were familiar. He'd read them. They were the ancient people's expression of God's assurance. But then, he may have just thought them. Yet they hung in the air, and Craig wasn't sure if he or someone else had spoken them. But it didn't matter. He knew he was in the presence of someone more powerful than he was. He lay still, surrounded by peace and finally slept.

When he woke, the calmness of the encounter remained. He had not dreamed it.

"Bill?" he spoke into the darkness, assuming a change of shift.

"Yes, Chaplain?"

"Where is everyone?" Craig sat up and activated the lights.

"Probably just leaving vespers and getting ready for the reception. Dr. Keal's on his way."

"Vespers? Is it that late?" It didn't occur to Craig to wonder if the congregation had prayed for him until he was washing his face. He put on the formal dress uniform 'Shonya had sent, and stretched out to wait for Jeff.

He sat up as the doctor entered. He couldn't remember seeing Jeff in evening clothes before. "Not bad, Doctor."

Red stripes down the outside seam of the legs decorated Jeff's two-piece black, high-collared suit. The doctor grinned self-consciously. "You don't look so bad yourself." He checked the panel of readouts and nodded. "Your counts indicate the infection's better. But I'll give you a couple more doses of antibiotics." He sat down. "The Captain wants me to be part of the greeting party along with himself, 'Shonya, and Andez. We're sorry, but I don't think you would last the evening if you started this early."

"It's okay." Craig waved the apology aside. "I'm glad for Andez. Have him come by and tell me about it."

"Alright." Jeff stood to go, and then hesitated. "You seem more relaxed, less," He searched for the word.

"Anxious? Frustrated?" Craig supplied.

He nodded. "Yeah. You finally look rested."

"More like renewed," Craig said. "I've been struggling to put things into perspective for a while."

"And you were able to do that?" the doctor asked.

"Umm-humm." He paused. "Evidently sometime during vespers."

Jeff smiled gently and laid his hand on Craig's shoulder. "That's exactly what we hoped."

Craig nodded.

"Jeff? Brodsky here." The comm button broke the comfortable silence.

"Yes, Captain."

"The Cutezarians are ready to come aboard. Transporter three."

"On my way," Jeff responded. "Time to go." He laid a hand on Craig's shoulder. "You are going to behave yourself tonight aren't you?"

"If I must," Craig allowed with a grin. He paused. "Thanks for the compromise."

"You're welcome. Rest. See you later." With a final reassuring pat, Jeff departed. In the corridor he met 'Shonya and they fell into step. "Craig seems to have conquered some of his impatience this evening."

She looked up, eyes sparkling. "What happened?"

Jeff shook his head. "He just said he finally put things into perspective."

As they were the last to arrive, Captain Brodsky looked around and asked, "Ready?"

The greeting party took their places in a semicircle facing the receiving platform.

"Commander Cooper, transport," the Captain ordered, and within seconds they stood face to face with the Cutezarian delegation. The Captain stepped forward.

"We welcome you to the ship, M. Curie, named for a great scientist of earth's history."

He stopped as the box translated. "We have anticipated this event a long time." The box translated. "Please allow me to introduce leaders of the ship's company." Captain Brodsky continued, stopping after each phrase so the translator could keep up. "Dr. LaShonya Reed, head of the science team."

'Shonya stepped forward and the visitors acknowledged her.

"Dr. Jeffery Keal, head of the medical staff."

Jeff stepped forward. The visitors acknowledged him.

"And Ensign Andez Ronger who is representing our spiritual leader, Chaplain Craig Lea."

The Ensign stepped forward and was acknowledged.

215

Jeff and 'Shonya exchanged frustrated looks, better understanding the tedious work of Captain Brodsky and his negotiating team.

The Chief Communicator stepped from the platform, holding his small personal translating box and spoke. Then his box spoke. "We are pleased to visit the place you inhabit." The Cutezarian also spoke in short phrases. "I am Dortec, the Chief Communicator."

The humans acknowledged the Cutezarian, and the slow process continued.

"This is Bartez, the chief of those who build," he said indicating one Cutezarian. "This is Rachax, the chief of those who." The box stopped and was silent and finally chose. "Govern."

Hiding their wonder at the word, the humans acknowledged the governor. The Cutezarian introduced the last of the party, "This is Ventez, the leader of those who meditate."

This time, the humans barely concealed their surprise as the box used the term for the second time, but they properly acknowledged the Cutezarian.

"We will now escort you. " The box translated, "to the reception area," Captain Brodsky led the way.

"And I thought archeology was exacting," 'Shonya whispered to Andez as they brought up the rear.

"Yeah, that's what I thought about Rev's required research," the Ensign whispered back as they followed the group into the reception room.

"Good job, Dorinda!" 'Shonya greeted Dorinda as they entered the reception hall.

The hall, located two decks above the living quarters, covered the entire front section of the deck, creating a huge half-moon shaped room. It was used only for formal occasions. Dorinda's decorations included golden, shimmering drapes fluttering against the walls as an accent to the viewing port, which covered the entire forward hull, effectively focusing attention on the magnificent view of the stars. The inside lights progressed through a cycle of one primary color, its secondary and complementary colors, then moved to the next color of the color wheel. The entire sequence repeated every twenty minutes, creating constant, subtle changes in the room's appearance.

Three long, white tables stood in the center of the room, two of which were filled with finger foods of all kinds. One table contained familiar food, but 'Shonya couldn't identify anything on the other. On each table were baskets of pita style bread made from the ancient grain. The third table connected the two food tables at one end, creating a u-shaped aisle. It held the drinks for both species.

'Shonya took it in slowly. "Now I know why you've been so busy the last two weeks," she told Dorinda. "It's perfect."

"I had some help keying the food information into the synthesizer, and hanging the drapes," she smiled. "It was fun. Especially the research and arranging the food."

Her husband caught her eye, motioning them to join him. "I intend to write about this." She continued as they made their way through the gathering crowd.

'Shonya nodded. "Craig told me you'd be the one who made sure the story got out."

"I studied archeological reporting. It's how I got hooked on the same hobby as Craig. Is he coming?"

"Later. Jeff insisted he choose which part he wanted to see. He can't eat, so you can guess what he decided." 'Shonya grinned mischievously.

"The Cutezarian's presentation," they said together laughing.

217

"What's so funny?" Captain Brodsky asked, taking Dorinda's hand.

"Craig's predictability," she said.

"What?"

"Never mind."

"As long as you understand." He'd long ago become used to their secrets and he shook his head. He turned to address the room. "May I have your attention?"

Conversation stopped.

"The Cutezarians have agreed to formal introductions, then we will allow you to introduce yourselves to them at a slower pace than a reception line allows. The large box you see is a translation device. You can hear its translation now." He spoke in phrases as the box translated. "Each Cutezarian also carries a smaller version to allow private conversation"

Walking to the end of the line, he began the introductions. "This is the Chief Communicator, Dortec; the Chief of those who study, Aratex; Chief of those who build, Bartez; the Chief of those who govern, Rachax; the Chief of those who meditate, Ventez."

He paused then introduced Dorinda. "Cutezarians, this is my mate. Her name is Dorinda. Some of you met her as she researched your culture in preparation for this event." He drew Dorinda close to him. "As you can see, she and I are about to become parents."

"Welcome and we hope you enjoy your stay. Please note the bread is made from your ancestor's grain. So enjoy the food and get to know each other." Dorinda gestured around the room, dismissing the formality of the introductions.

One by one, the Cutezarians greeted the Captain and Dorinda. Each one had their own way of questioning them about the pregnancy.

"Is this one to bear a live, young human?" Dortec, the Chief Communicator asked.

"How does the young one begin to grow?" asked Aratex, the Chief of those who Study.

"How long does it stay in the mother, and how does it get out?" Bartez, the builder asked.

"What does it mean to be parents?" Rachax, the governor asked.

The Captain Brodsky and Dorinda answered the questions as patiently and as truthfully as possible while the company around the room gradually began communicating. After a while

Dorinda and Captain Brodsky found themselves alone. Conversation flowed around them as they looked at each other with pleasure.

"Didn't I tell you life with me would be interesting?"

The Captain laughed. "I vaguely recall a conversation the night before we got married."

"You promised a partnership," she said.

"And if I remember correctly you promised to make my dull life infinitely more interesting."

"Well?" she prompted.

"It's not exactly what I envisioned, but I'd say we've done pretty well," he said with a smile.

"I'd say so," she agreed. She shifted her attention. "'Shonya's ready."

'Shonya moved forward and called for attention. The Chief Communicator moved the large translating box to the center of room, and the Cutezarians gathered within hearing distance.

Addressing the computer, 'Shonya continued; "Computer, prepare to display the presentation of all material on the tell Daniel K One." She addressed the group, her eyes betraying her excitement. "We have anticipated this meeting since the Cutezarians first contacted us."

She addressed the Cutezarians: "We who study the past often have sketchy information to compare our conclusions with," She spoke in phrases, following the Captain's example. "We understand your culture kept visual records of your history long before we began keeping track of time. It is our hope these records can be compared with our conclusions."

She then addressed the whole group again: "Let's get started." She spoke to the computer: "Computer, begin display with modeling." She paused until the image was complete. "We begin with my own specialty. The maps you now see were made before the structure was completely uncovered," She continued her commentary, describing the progression of mapping from that point to the final map showing the inner core and shafts running through it.

The Scientists, in turn, followed the same process as each presented their part of the data.
Roger added an explanation to the Cutezarians about Dr. Kobee's death.

At the conclusion of the presentation, 'Shonya again addressed the group. "We will take a break before viewing the second structure's analysis. Chaplain Lea will join us in a few minutes."

She left as humans and Cutezarians alike returned to the tables to enjoy food, drink and conversation. She couldn't help but notice the bread had become a point of mutual conversation. Every crumb was gone before she even got a taste.

'Shonya found Craig stretched out on the bed, eyes closed, breathing deeply. "It's a shame to wake him," she thought tenderly, then smiled to herself. "But he'd never forgive me."

She kissed him. "Craig," she said softly. He sighed and turned his head. She raised her voice. "Craig."

"'Shonya?" he asked without opening his eyes.

"The students are ready for their presentation. Of course, if you're going to behave yourself, do what Jeff wants and stay in bed."

He was awake now and grinned. "Why start at this late date?" However, he moved gingerly as he got to his feet.

"Full dress uniform." She nodded. "Looks good."

He turned her around and admired her teal, drape-style gown, that was gathered just above the waist and flowed to the floor. "Very nice," he said. "Are you ready for half a date?"

"Ready, Chaplain."

He leaned over to give her a brief kiss, but they both were breathless before he finally untangled himself and stepped back with a small grunt of pain.

Shaken by the depth of her emotion, 'Shonya didn't dare look into his face.

Putting his hands on her shoulders Craig shook his head and smiled self-consciously. "Jeff wouldn't approve of this." He braced his hand against his stomach and took a deep breath.

"Hurt?" she asked, touching his hand.

He nodded. "A little, but mostly it pulled."

"If you tore Jeff's seal, we're both in trouble."

"It's still there. I can feel the perimeter."

"Good, I'd hate to have to explain to Jeff. Let's go."

Leisurely they journeyed to the lift and up three decks to the reception room. All conversation ceased as the door opened and they stood hand in hand. The only voice they heard came from the translation box.

"Is this how you chose to honor your spiritual leader for his action that saved lives?" It was translating the Chief Communicator's question.

The Captain nodded.

"Great timing," 'Shonya muttered as she made him pause in the doorway.

He frowned, puzzled by her hesitation.

Captain Brodsky himself barked the order: "Attention!"

The military crew snapped to attention and 'Shonya announced, "Ladies and gentleman, Chaplain Craig Lea."

As the entire company broke into applause, Craig felt his face burning but experienced an unexpected thrill of pleasure at the same time. He stood still, not knowing what to say or do.

When the applause died, he managed, "I, ah, thank you." A twinge in his stomach brought him back to reality. "Go back to your conversations."

Jeff took note of the hand that sought to dispel the pain. Making his way to the drink table, he asked the steward for a glass of the formula he'd brought for Craig and returned to his place.

'Shonya pulled Craig toward the front of the room.

"Craig," Jeff stopped them and held out the glass.

Craig took it and sipped, then nodded. "Thanks." He took a couple of steps and looked back. "Jeff, please tell me there's nothing extra in it."

"That comes later. There's just something in it to slow down your adrenalin and stomach secretions," he promised.

'Shonya tugged his arm gently. At the front of the room, she turned and addressed the group. "The official reason for this honor is to show the Chaplain we appreciate his extra effort in the midst of his own ordeal. However, I think we all agree we've been looking for a way to thank him for his guidance, comfort and gentle reminders that God is always resent."

After the applause, she turned to Craig, who was inspecting the floor in embarrassed silence, and explained, "We have something for you."

Carolyn, the tech who had helped him in the lab, touched his arm and handed over a box. "It's from everyone," she said then added in whisper so only he could hear, "but the idea came from Roger."

Craig handed 'Shonya his glass, looked up and grinned. "I'm almost afraid to open it." He took in the scene of smiling faces. "I've spoken to most of this group often, yet I find myself without a thing to say," he paused as the group chuckled. "With God's help I merely did what had to be done. I only understood what was happening because of personal experience." He shook his head. "Even at that, God had to help me focus my thoughts."

Emotions threatened to overcome him as the memories came flooding back and he fought for composure. As he looked around the room, he encountered compassionate, friendly expressions. Just for a second he met Cooper's intense gaze, and the anger softened briefly before the mask fell back into place.

"How do I reach him?" The prayer returned instinctively.

And reaching toward God, Craig regained control. As Jeff watched, he saw the conflict of a thinking person fighting overwhelming emotion and understood why the ulcer had developed and perforated so quickly. "With such an emotional strain added to the physical irritation of the charge, it's a wonder he just has an ulcer," he reasoned.

"Whatever this is, it will mean a lot to me," Craig continued. Hearing 'Shonya say something, he shifted his attention. "What?"

"I said, open it," she said under her breath.

"Now?"

"Now." It was a command. Craig opened the container and burst into laughter. Meeting Roger's gaze he nodded. "It's perfect!" he said, holding up the gold plated hand laser. As the laughter died he asked, "Is it a working model?"

"We would advise you refrain from testing it in this place." Oliver delivered his solemn words with an affectionate smile.

To the Cutezarian's puzzlement, the company again broke into laughter.

"How will I ever explain this to them?" Captain Brodsky asked Dorinda, and only got an amused shrug.

"Well, what do you have to say for yourself, Chaplain?" Forest spoke for everyone.

Craig shook his head. "What can I say?" He implored, and then began an improvisational recitation: "I promise I will cherish it. I will never allow it to have a meltdown. I will never allow children to play with it. I will not improperly discharge it. I will..." He stopped, suddenly once again overcome with emotion in the middle of his humorous pledge. "It will always remind me of all of you. Thank you," he finally managed.

Deciding his stress level was high enough, 'Shonya took control. "Let's get on with the presentation of the second structure."

Craig gave her a grateful look and, giving into an impulse, suddenly leaned over to kiss her. "Thanks for the rescue," he whispered.

'Shonya didn't hear the expressions of approval from the group. Shocked by his public action, she looked up at him a few seconds, engaged in her own battle for control. "He's more sure than I am," she thought.

224

'Shonya's expression answered Dorinda's questions and she laughed to herself. Leaning over, she spoke to her husband. "That answers the speculation!"

Her husband took her hand and grinned. "Behave yourself."

Craig squeezed 'Shonya's hand, took his glass from her, and spoke softly, "You're on." And left her alone in front. Sitting with a twinge, he braced one hand against his stomach, and shrugged as a sharp pain tore across his shoulders. At the same time, he felt hands rubbing away the pain.

"Stay right where you are." Jeff's voice came as he unobtrusively massaged the contracting muscles.

'Shonya collected her thoughts and without comment spoke to the computer, "Begin display of the tell Daniel K Two." Then she turned to the company. "Paji Habib will narrate the mapping."

Paji stepped forward. "The first indication of a different type of structure did not become evident until the final stages of uncovering the structure. As you can see from the models, the first maps gave only the shape of the one huge room. As the display continues you can see the progression of clarity as the scans became fine-tuned and the structure was uncovered." The room, which started as a vague shape, became a very well defined picture and the benches became clear in their systematic placement.

For the benefit of the Cutezarians Paji began an in depth description of scan technology. "The computer uses sound and light waves to distinguish the open areas from the solid material, such as walls."

Craig's attention focused on the slowly turning model and he heard little of her description beyond this opening statement. He relaxed as he studied the suspended model.

'Shonya studied the faces in the room and got a glimpse of Craig's face. She thought he looked less tense but still too tired. When Paji finished, she had to refocus her attention to introduce Forest.

Forest introduced his student, Carol Madjer. The computer displayed a three dimensional map of the area with the all tells highlighted.

Carol's voice held only a touch of the nervousness all the students felt. Forest nodded encouragingly, and she finished with confidence. "From our preliminary scans, we identified five additional structures in the immediate area similar to Daniel K One. They seem to be the same type of multi-person dwellings as the first tells. As far as we can determine, the Daniel K Two is the only one of its kind in this area.

"This leads us to believe Daniel K Two served as the gathering place for the ancient Cutezarians who inhabited this village. There is another thing that supports this conclusion," She continued, pointing to the map. "Here is the tell Daniel K One, and here is Daniel K Two. We assumed Daniel K One was near the center of the complex. We were mistaken. Actually, Daniel K Two is at the center of six tells."

The group approved and talked among themselves before Oliver stood and took control. "My students and I agree. Due to the lateness of the hour, we will allow the computer to display our part of the report without narration since our procedure and process remains unchanged from the tell Daniel K One. It suffices to say my students were brilliant." That brought appreciative noises from his students and chuckles from the rest of the group. "When the display has finished, Roger Lavera may proceed with his report."

He sat down and the computer quickly displayed the series of images taken with the zero-light scan equipment, followed by the same images with the addition of light, then a series of images showing artifacts in-situ, and the process of lifting them from their place.

Roger began his narration when the computer displayed the artifacts in the lab after cleaning and marking for identification of their original site. "Daniel K Two brought us two surprises. First, we found statues made of the same stone as the Chaplain's beads. They even have the wavy lines carved on them like the beads which allow them to absorb energy and emit light."

For the benefit of the Cutezarians he explained, "Chaplain Lea first noticed the illuminating stones. Humans have a tradition of naming discoveries after the people who find them. Therefore, we call them the Chaplain's beads."

The guests indicated their understanding. The computer continued presenting pictures: statues with their small bodies and large heads, gold colored belts, large Chaplain's beads, shards of bowls and computer simulations of their probable original shape.

Suddenly the screen went black and Roger spoke into the darkness. "For the Chaplain's benefit, we repeated his experiment with the beads, using some of the statues we found. Since he was in sick bay, we want to show him this record of that experiment."

Out of the darkness, the computer projected a model of lab twelve and displayed Carolyn's reconstruction of Craig's experiment. The clock showed a time-lapse of an hour, then the power was turned off, the sides of the box removed, and Carolyn ordered the computer to create darkness. The statues came alive, and the lab lit up.

Craig drew a sharp breath at their beauty. The Cutezarians spoke to each other and the box said, "So this is what they looked like during the darkness ritual. Full of presence."

The humans did not understand, but were too engrossed in the gloriously alive statues to wonder what they meant.

Roger resumed his commentary in the semi-darkness. "The second surprise is the range of dates of these artifacts. Although some of the dates are the same dates as the artifacts from the Daniel K One, they range from one thousand to five thousand years before the Daniel K One."

He stopped, allowing his listeners time to digest the news. "This leads us to conclude this structure was finished before the construction of the rest of the community, but continued to be used long after its completion. "What's puzzling is the lack of daily living items. Cooking utensils, for example. There are still a lot of questions."

The computer finished its display, Dorinda's lighting scheme resumed, and Roger sat down. People shifted in their seats, some of them got up and walked around, talking among themselves. 'Shonya let them stretch but, catching sight of Craig's face, remembered the Cutezarian's presentation was what he anticipated most.

She escorted the Cutezarians to the center of the room, and called for quiet. "Settle down and we'll begin the last part of our presentation. The Chief Communicator will tell us how close to their understanding we came." She turned to the Cutezarian, "I understand you will give a verbal report, and then have a computer display for us." The box translated, and the Chief Communicator nodded. "Please address us," she invited.

After a short pause, the Cutezarian spoke, then the box translated. "We observed the construction of your ship and the compartments in which you live, and understand your conclusions. You have done well. You described this as a living area. It was not. It is preserved from early times. Our ancestors followed the example of their ancestors and traveled to spend time at a coming-away place like this, the meditation center for all the surrounding cities."

He stopped because of the conversation that buzzed through the room.

'Shonya motioned to the Chief Communicator to let them talk a minute and looked around for Craig. He was sitting forward in his chair, staring ahead with an unbelieving look on his face.

Craig's mind filled with questions. "Meditation about what? What kind of gods did they worship? Was it a spiritual worship or a cultic sacrificial worship? Were the statues supposed to represent the gods? What did the darkness ritual represent?" Hands on his shoulders interrupted his thoughts.

"You doing okay, Craig?" Jeff pulled up a chair.

Craig sat back with a wince. "So-so," he answered. "This is good stuff."

Dorinda came by and tousled his hair. "You look worn out. You okay?"

Grinning up at her, he combed his hair with his fingers the best his could. "I'm okay. How about you?"

"Exhausted. But no contractions." She sat beside Jeff and talked around him. "They're putting off the tour until Sunday because of the late night tonight. So I'll rest tomorrow if you will."

"Agreed, Sis."

Dorinda hugged him and turned to leave. "Love your new toy." She tossed the words over her shoulder.

"We can finish this discussion tomorrow." 'Shonya called the company back to order and indicated the Cutezarian speaker to continue.

"Ancient Cutezarians left their homes and came apart to spend a length of time at this center. This area continued to be visited by our ancestors even after they had moved into cities and learned to protect themselves from the storms.

"The structure with one large room served as the central gathering place. The large rooms in the other structures were group-gathering places. Your idea of the upper chambers being private chambers is correct. They are not resting places, but places for private meditation and study."

The speaker stopped and motioned to 'Shonya. She spoke to the computer: "Begin Cutezarian display."

She found a chair as the Chief Communicator took up the commentary. "You correctly concluded the purpose of the illumination stones. At first, the stones were used for light only. What you are seeing is a..." The box stopped to find a concept. It chose "Simulation."

"Simulation," the speaker repeated. "Of the development of their use."

The computer presented a model of a section of the tell Daniel K One, lit up like lab twelve. The next set of images resembled crude batteries with strands of metal wound around an illuminating stone leading to some a machine.

"There is a soft stone which can be pounded into very thin strands which helps the energy from the stones move from place to place," the narration stated.

"Electricity!" Everyone who recognized it uttered it in unison.

The computer continued, showing a series of machines, each one more sophisticated than the previous one. The humans did not recognize most of them, but all by energy for each came from the stones. Abruptly, a shift took place. The stones heated liquid, and the machines were steam

230

driven. Vehicles appeared, suspended above the ground instead of traveling on wheels. Then came images of air travel machines, and finally a large round space vehicle appeared. The display ended, and the room sprang alive with conversation.

"The stone does convert to energy." Roger voiced everyone's thoughts.

"That doesn't tell me how the buildings float," the Captain muttered.

"Maybe the liquid wasn't water, but produced a gas that became fuel." Someone else offered.

Craig didn't join the conversation, but sat forward again rehashing the information. He felt something even more important was ahead.

The speculation finally died down and the Chief Communicator continued. "We became a very private society since the time of shame. What you are about to see has never been seen beyond our cities. I received consent to show you this because of certain things we observed about you. The presence of one you call a spiritual leader, whom you call Chaplain, and your regard for him tells us the principles he represents are important to you. Your words for deities and well-defined abstract concepts also encourage us to share this with you.

"This is a re-creation of the darkness rituals held in the structure you call Daniel K Two. The Cutezarians in the reenactment are of my linage three generations ago. We are not certain the ritual is complete, for the actual ceremony was never allowed to be visually recorded."

He nodded to 'Shonya. She spoke to the computer: "Computer, Cutezarian file two, super model mode."

The inside of a structure much like the Daniel K Two appeared, the benches arranged in the same configuration. Presently figures entered the room. It wasn't a procession, but a gathering of beings with something in common. As the Cutezarians took their places, they seemed to speak to each other as friends would.

Jeff held out a second glass of formula as excitement flushed Craig's face. Unaware of his actions, Craig stood and reached for the glass in one motion. In fascination, he got as close to the display as he could without standing in front of anyone and leaned against the bulkhead.

His movement caught 'Shonya's attention and she remembered his remark in Daniel K Two about not being prepared. His expressions betrayed a mixture of feelings: disbelief, wonder, exhaustion, pain and excitement.

Her attention returned to the model as one Cutezarian entered alone and made his way through the maze to the center of the benches. The rest of the Cutezarians stood, moved into a close formation, arm's length apart, and placed their hands on the shoulders of the Cutezarian on each side of them. Lifting their oversized heads, they stood quietly for a long time.

The Captain joined Craig and Jeff moved over to make room. "Whatcha thinking, Craig?" he whispered.

"Alan, is it possible the box's choice of 'meditation' means to the Cutezarians what it means to us?" he whispered back, his voice ragged with emotion.

"Take it easy, Craig. It's too early to jump to any conclusions. Drink the formula." the doctor spoke up.

Craig nodded absently, drinking as ordered.

Everyone jumped as the box spoke into the long silence. "The single Cutezarian in the center is called the One who encourages. You would call the speaker the Encourager."

As the Encourager began, Craig tried to decide if the animated speaker was male or female. In either case, he/ she captured the audience. First, she/he spoke to one section, then another, looked up, then down with elegant gestures.

The humans found themselves leaning forward, drawn to the animated speaker, without even understanding the meaning of the speech.

Suddenly Craig realized he was holding his breath. Forcing a deep breath, he looked back at the Captain and found Forest and Oliver also leaning against the bulkhead.

Finally, the speaker released both the past Cutezarian and present human audiences.

The speaker raised his/her hands and the Cutezarians stood to repeat the touching part of the ritual.

With a deep collective breath, the humans sat back in their chairs, filled with wonder.

Craig sagged against the bulkhead and pushed back his hair.

Jeff laid a hand on his back. "Breathe deeply. Try to relax."

Craig nodded silently, grateful for Jeff's help. In a few minutes, his emotions and stomach settled enough that he felt under control. Looking up, he found 'Shonya regarding him with open concern and tenderness in her face. He smiled and motioned her he was okay.

His tired gesture made her realize the entire company must be nearing exhaustion. Collecting her thoughts, she moved back to the front of the room to address the Cutezarians.

"We are honored you chose to share this ritual with us. As you can see, we are overcome with emotion. We will be anxious to review this display and perhaps have a translation of the speaker's text?" She requested.

The Chief Communicator nodded, "It is perhaps a possibility."

She smiled and said to the group, "A firm commitment, don't you think?"

The company chuckled and broke into applause for the Cutezarians. Their visitors seemed surprised, but appeared to understand the expression of appreciation. They nodded, and Captain Brodsky escorted them to their quarters.

Craig sank into the chair someone brought and braced one hand against his stomach. Jeff's hands, firmly on his shoulders, urged him to remain quiet.

The room emptied slowly. Many of the crew and scientists came by to shake hands with Craig and make encouraging remarks before drifting by the drink and food tables one last time.

'Shonya deactivated the computer and gave orders for the food to be removed, then went to Craig. Her dress flowed around her as she pulled up a stool and sat in front of him. She felt exhilarated, but deeply concerned for him.

"Well, was it worth the effort?" she asked with a gentle smile, trying to mask her concern.

"Every single second," he assured her with a lopsided grin.

"Shall we call for a transport, or can you transport yourself?" she asked quietly, hoping not to sound patronizing.

He took stock and shook his head. "How about sending one down to meet us at the lift?"

"Good idea," Jeff said, and contacted sickbay with the orders.

They stood and Craig put his arms around her. She responded, gently avoiding the wound. He rested his head on hers a few minutes, and then stepped back with a grunt of pain.

"I'll shut things down here, and come down in a few minutes," she said.

Craig kissed her and nodded at the same time. They grinned at the awkward results.

Jeff took his arm and pulled him away as he tried it again.

"Now. Craig. You're about to crash."

And crash he did. At the turbo-lift, he sat on the waiting transport, shut his eyes, and let go of reality. Only the quick action on the part of both the med tech and the doctor prevented him from hitting the floor.

"Let's get him to sickbay and do some scans before he wakes up," the doctor said grimly.

Once there the med tech positioned the transport over the monitoring table. Jeff activated the panel and studied the results. When he looked down, he found Craig also studying the panel.

"Any damage?" he asked soberly.

"You still have an infection, but the seal's intact and keeping the ulcer from the acids in your stomach. However, the lining of your stomach is very inflamed. I think that's the source of your pain." Craig's quick recovery pleased him, but he delivered the lecture anyway. "The pulling you feel is the seal staying in place as the tissue around it moves. It means you're too active. When you feel it, stop whatever you're doing. Just quit!" A smile softened his words as he continued. "I think you're just exhausted. I meant an hour or so when I said a short appearance, not four hours."

"I know, Jeff. Thanks for letting me stay. I can't wait to get out of here and find out more about the Cutezarians."

"You'll do what I say," the doctor answered with a grin.

Recovering his humor, Craig returned the smile. "I'll do what you say, for now." He paused. "What do you say?"

"I'll give you another IV tonight with something for the lining of your stomach, antibiotics and a sedative. You'll stay here tomorrow and we'll talk Sunday morning."

He did a couple more scans then called the tech. "Move him to his room."

Craig raised his head. "My room?"

"You've spent more time there than anyone else," Bill chuckled. "It may always be your room like the stones may always be called the Chaplain's beads."

"Wonderful." Craig grumped. "I can walk."

"But you won't," the doctor insisted as he motioned for Bill to activate the transport and they moved him into the isolation room.

"You going to put me to sleep in full dress uniform?" Craig grumbled, moving to the bed.

"Complete with crossed arms and a daisy." Jeff grinned as he prepared the IV. "There's a robe in the bathroom."

Craig changed and reappeared in the long hospital robe, laying his uniform on the back of the chair.

Jeff patted the bed. "Come on, let's get this over with."

"'Shonya's coming down," Craig protested.

"It's okay, she'll be here soon."

Craig nodded, stretched out, allowed Jeff to insert the IV device, and waited for the warm rush of the sedative. 'Shonya arrived before it took effect and he reached for her carefully without disturbing the IV. "'Shonya."

She leaned over and kissed him. He responded with unexpected passion.

"Steady, Craig," Jeff warned.

Craig grinned. When the warmth suddenly spread throughout his body, he shook his head. "No."

"You ought to be used to this," Jeff said.

"It happens so fast and all at once," Craig murmured. Closing his eyes, he felt the weariness melt away.

"Feel better?" the doctor asked as he finished and shut down the air driven-device.

Craig nodded, his will to fight ebbing. "'Shonya?"

She sat on the bed, smiling slightly. "Just relax."

Ignoring her advice, he asked, "Will you see if the captain can set up a meeting with the Cutezarians early next week about the significance of what we saw tonight?"

"We'll talk tomorrow," she said, but he was already sleeping.

Jeff took 'Shonya's arm. "Come on, 'Shonya, you need rest too. You didn't exactly sit around doing nothing tonight." She hesitated. "He's okay. Just too much too soon." He drew her out of the room. "It won't be long before he'll be up and demanding to take control of his life again." He paused and added as they left sickbay, "and I suspect he'll want to settle some things with you."

Smiling, she considered for a minute, "I think I can handle that." She knew what she would tell Art. Her feelings for Craig remained nebulous, with the outcome still uncertain, but she had to stay and find out.

There! Her decision was been made.

And she found peace.

## CHAPTER TWENTY-THREE

Sunday morning found the off-duty crew members gathered in small groups, still discussing the implications of the events at the reception.

Captain Brodsky, after conducting staff meetings and planning sessions late into the night, chose to sleep in.

Dorinda kissed him as she got out of bed. "I get the shower first."

"Um-kay." He didn't open his eyes. "Late staff meeting last night." Listening to his wife's noises, he finally squinted at the computer's clock, which was reflecting 0600.

Commander Houng had agreed to man the conn until 0800, so he dozed as Dorinda moved around the quarters.

Before she left, she sat on the bed and tousled his hair to wake him. He turned toward her and put his arms around her the best he could. They giggled together as the baby's expanse prevented his hands from meeting.

"When does the shuttle leave?"

"Ten minutes." She smiled down at him.

"The tour includes breakfast and lunch?"

"Um-hmm. Breakfast on board the shuttle." She got up.

"Ok. I'll be on the bridge until the community meal and then back on until sixteen hundred. Please, please, call me if you have any contractions or need anything." He got out bed and reached for his robe.

"I promise. But I'll be fine." She took his hand and they walked to the door. "I'm sorry to miss the community meal. Yesterday Craig said he thought he would participate before he attends vespers to help Andez get used to being in charge with him there."

"Did Craig tell you when he's cleared for duty?" the Captain asked.

"Jeff won't tell him yet. He's afraid Craig will be frustrated when he can't go back full time from the beginning," she answered as she activated the door.

Captain Brodsky kissed her gently. They lingered for a moment, enjoying the tenderness. He leaned into the hall and called after her. "Take notes so you'll remember where to take me later."

"Yes, Sir!" She turned and saluted with a grin.

Passing officers, used to these domestic scenes on the officers' quarters' deck, reflected her smile as they also acknowledged the robe-clad captain.

The Captain went back inside, and considered breakfast, reflecting upon his pleasure of this posting. Assignment to the Curie was a relief after the tension of the military exploration ships. It was also his first command that allowed him and Dorinda to be together. He especially liked that part.

$**$

Based on her research and her husband's description of the buildings that floated, Dorinda had anticipated the tour for weeks. But she wasn't prepared for the grandeur of the city.

Dome-shaped coverings connected the buildings, creating spacious, open plazas between buildings and walkways that hovered above the ground the same level as the structures.

The Cutezarians' homes clustered in groups of three pyramids built around a huge covered plaza in the center. Clusters of homes surrounded the business area. Enclosed walkways led from each cluster into the heart of the city.

After the groups of four humans toured two residential clusters each, they all met in the main plaza of the city.

The translation box interpreted the guide's description of the buildings surrounding the plaza, beginning with the building on the tour's right.

"This is the ruling structure. The ruling body meets every light period to consider the petitions of the city's citizens. Across from it is the citizen's structure. This is set aside for public gatherings. The third structure is the storage structure for all public knowledge."

"A library?" someone in the group asked.

The box translated from English to the guide who conversed with the box for a minute, and then the box answered. "Not what you call books, but pictures that move," the guide spoke again and the box continued. "These are our oldest structures. Our citizens from other areas also visit them, so you will find guides available. You will be allowed to visit these structures as you wish. All citizens have received instructions to carry their translation devices while you are here so you can communicate easily. If you wish to continue to another area, please return to this place when you hear the first bell ring. If you wish to stay in this area, please come back to this place when you hear the second bell. You will return to the shuttle from here at the time of the second bell. "

Dorinda explored the ruling and the citizen's buildings quickly. They were magnificent, but the storage structure for public knowledge beckoned the archeologist in her. "I would like a tour of this structure," she told the box standing next to the attendant in the library. The box scrambled her words into Cutezarian, the attendant replied, and the box answered her request.

"Please be seated, a guide will be able to help you soon."

Dorinda smiled and the attendant mimicked her. Sitting on a marble textured bench, she leaned against the slanting wall and assessed the pyramid. The furniture on the open ground floor consisted of tables with viewing screens built into their tops. The second floor, built around the walls resembled a giant suspended shelf. The third floor, suspended from the tip of the pyramid, was a huge platform with a waist high wall partially enclosing it.

Tubes with doors that opened at each floor provided transportation. "Turbo tubes," Dorinda mused.

"What would you like?" The mechanical voice of the translation box interrupted her thoughts.

"I would like to see your public knowledge storage place, if I may," she requested formally, hearing Alan's admonition, 'Even if you're not official, you are, in effect, an ambassador.'

The guide began a description of the structure. "From this area we have the ability to view any picture in the history of our planet." The guide indicated the tables with viewing screens built into them and spoke into a speaker at the edge of one of the desks. The computer blinked and within seconds, Dorinda was watching computer-generated moving pictures of the Cutezarians. They seemed to be involved in a celebration.

"How long have Cutezarians been making moving pictures?" Dorinda asked.
After a moment of sounds from the Cutezarian, the box answered. "Long before the failed journey to the third planet from the sun of the third galaxy to which our early ancestors traveled."

"Have some of those pictures survived?" Dorinda asked instantly.

"A record of the journey was found long ago. Our computers re-created it. They are kept in the small high place above us, separated from the rest of the material. We do not wish to view the events of our time of shame."

"May we start there so I may better understand the development of your planet?" Dorinda liked watching the Cutezarians as they waited for the box's translation. It seemed to her they were studying the humans' voice inflections.

"I suppose it might be a good place to start. Come," The box finally answered. They stepped into a tube, the guide spoke and they were on the third level immediately.

As the guide seated Dorinda at a viewing screen, a bell rang in the distance. "I must leave you for a time."

The guide spoke into the speaker at the edge of the table. Dorinda heard one English word, "Stop."

The box spoke: "I have instructed the computer to show you the earliest pictures and continue until you say stop." And the guide left her.

The first few minutes Dorinda watched early Cutezarians prepare for a journey. Although they appeared larger than their descendants did, their heads were still out of proportion with their body size. Their larger size made them seem even more familiar.

She watched a round space ship take off and disappear. The next view was from an on-board camera, which quickly displayed three star systems. Dorinda recognized the second system as the Macron system. She came up with Qatari as the name of the next one, and was congratulating herself for remembering a name she hadn't used for years when a faintly familiar object appeared far away.

As the ship drew nearer, she caught her breath, recognizing the unmistakable shape of Earth's system. Inside the system, she named the passing planets: Pluto, Uranus, Saturn, Jupiter, and then just a glimpse of Mars before the screen suddenly went black.

It lasted only a second, and when the picture returned it focused on a close-up of ancient Earth. The haze shimmered bluer and purer than she ever remembered seeing it. As the shot tightened up so the shape of the landmasses could be identified, she stood and leaned on the table to get closer to the screen. The earth grew larger and larger.

"They're going to land!" she suddenly exclaimed in surprise. With growing excitement, she saw the planet take shape. "Stop!" She suddenly came to herself. The image froze.

Checking the time, she reasoned, "Twelve-thirty. The community meal should about be over." She touched her comm button.

"Captain Brodsky," her husband answered.

"Alan, I'm in a library. They call it the storage place for public knowledge. Do you know where it is?"

"The building across from the ruling structure, right?"

"Um-hum. Can you join me? I've found something exciting and important." She hesitated. "Is Craig there and doing okay?"

"He's sitting across the table, and other than being the only one, who's drinking instead of eating, seems okay." Dorinda heard Craig's chuckle in the background as the Captain continued. "If we can clear it with the doctor, I'll bring him along. "Good. Tell Jeff I'll not stress him out too much if he'll let Craig come out and play."

As she signed off, she imagined their amused and puzzled expressions.

Craig caught the doctor's arm as he walked by looking for a place to sit. "Jeff, join us I have a question."

Pulling up a chair, Jeff made himself comfortable with a smile. "I'd think you'd had enough of me by now."

"Jeff, how's the Chaplain?" Captain Brodsky asked as if Craig weren't there.

"The Chaplain's ulcer has quit bleeding. The seal is intact. His white count is better," Craig silently agreed. "But he'll still tire easily, and stress will do him in."

Feeling restless, Craig interrupted them. "Will you two quit talking about me like I was still in the isolation room?"

They grinned and the Captain explained. "Dorinda's on the planet and says she's found something interesting. The question is, will you release Craig for travel?"

"Physically, he should be okay if," He put his hand on Craig's shoulder and spoke directly to him, "If you'll restrain yourself physically, and avoid emotional situations."

"I can promise no physical activity, and the rest? I'll try," Craig assented.

"Ok, two or three hours, but no vespers tonight."

Craig hesitated. "I was looking forward to vespers."

"Go ahead and go," the doctor urged, "I probably wouldn't have let you attend tonight anyway. Still too emotional for you."

"All right. Thanks," Craig accepted the doctor's terms.

"Good." Captain Brodsky got up. "Transporter room three, ten minutes." He turned back. "Craig, why don't you bring that computer link translator thing you brought back from your last leave?"

"Sure." They parted and Craig went to get his pack together, wondering what had gotten Dorinda so excited.

"How exactly does this device work?" the Captain reached for the computer link as they met at the door of transporter room three.

"It's like the universal language translators. It looks for recognizable concepts and translates the whole program from those concepts into our computer's language. It was my father's last project before he retired."

The Captain nodded. "If Dorinda's find is something important, we'll try it out." He gave a signal to the transporter tech. "Now."

And they found themselves facing a somewhat startled guide.

"Is there information you wish to extract?" the mechanical voice of the box translated.

"My mate is here, and asked us to join her," Captain Brodsky said.

"Oh, the human female who wished to view the history of our planet." The guide sounded relieved. "There is not a problem. Come, I will take you to her."

"This is quite a place, Alan." Craig lagged behind as he took time to look up into the structure. "Everything is stone or metal."

"Come to think of it, I haven't seen any wood at all," the Captain replied. "Come on, Craig," he added.

Craig spotted Dorinda and lifted his hand in greeting. "Coming." Hurriedly, he stepped on the turbo pad, and gritted his teeth, hoping it didn't do the same thing to his stomach as the ship's lift.

It did. He groaned.

Seconds later Dorinda greeted them with enthusiasm, but slipped her arm around Craig as he sat on a nearby bench. "Are you okay?"

He shook his head. "Turbo lifts still bother me," Taking a deep breath he asked, "Now what's this marvelous thing you found?"

"I think I've found out why all this is so familiar to us," She replied, then turned to the guide. "Can we ask the computer to begin again with the first recorded pictures?"

"Do all of you wish to view them?" the guide asked. "Yes."

"Come, please." The guide led them to a small space in the corner of the pyramid, and spoke into a speaker in the wall. Panels parted and the pictures sprang to life on a giant viewing screen. "I will leave a translating device so you may speak to the computer." The guide stood off to one side to make sure the humans didn't need anything, but the screen claimed their full attention.

"Why are they so fascinated with our past?" the guide mused out loud. The translating box's super sensitivity picked it up and repeated the question in English.

The Captain, sitting closest to the box, heard the whispered question. Twisting around on the bench, he answered, "Because we are a scientific expedition."

"You are invited to stay as long as you wish," the box translated.

By the time the guide left, the passing scenes had switched to the on board cameras and familiar territory approached.

"The Milky Way!" Craig voiced their surprise.

"There go the planets." The Captain named them as they swept by. Suddenly, as the earth grew larger and larger he stood up and exclaimed, "They're going to land on earth."

As they talked, the box repeated everything they said in the Cutezarian's language. For some reason the useless repetition in a foreign language for someone who wasn't there struck them as funny.

Out of the laughter, Craig suddenly remembered the link device. "Dorinda, how do you make this computer freeze?"

"Ask it, I guess." She said, still laughing.

"Computer, freeze frame." Craig spoke to the box. It translated his request into Cutezarian and to their surprise, the picture stopped with a close up of earth.

"Alan, help me set up the computer link," Craig instructed.

"What's first?"

"This was Dad's first, crude model of the computer link. The probe attaches to the screen, the side marked T next to the screen." Craig handed it to him. "As a special favor to the Service, Dad has finished the infra-red device by now, so the filaments aren't necessary. But I got the first one." He grinned. "The only way they got Dad to retire early after the accident was to promise him special projects."

The Captain nodded, remembering Craig's father's vision had been impaired in the same accident at Quintana Military Base on Mars that had killed both of Dorinda's parents three weeks before their wedding. Thoughtfully he attached the probe to the surface of the viewing screen.

The probe looked like a paddle, six centimeters wide, implanted with computer chips in both sides of the black surface. One side contained the translator chips, the other the communication chips.

Craig touched the activator sensor and within seconds the probe was glowing and blinking as it went to work. It took only a few minutes for the link to search the Cutezarian's computer and find concepts with which to establish communication.

"It's ready to transmit," Craig said as the palm sized console lit up. He touched his comm button.

"Communications, Lt. Reecer," came the reply.

"Chaplain Lea here. I need access to the main computer core, please."

"Frequency open, Chaplain."

"Thanks Reecer."

Craig addressed the computer. "Computer, prepare to receive transmission."

"Ready. Please transmit," the computer answered.

Craig touched the transmit sensor and spoke to the translator box. "Computer, begin at beginning of file and resume program." After a brief pause, the file began again.

"Receiving," the M. Curie's computer confirmed Craig touched his comm button. "Computer, continue recording until receiving other instructions."

"Continuing."

Craig closed the channel so the computer wouldn't record the conversation in the room.

When the Captain was assured the link was complete, he excused himself. "I'll look at this later. If we're going to take information from the Cutezarian's computer banks, we'd best get permission to view it. I'll be across the plaza at the ruling structure."

"Good idea, Captain," Craig affirmed. "From what we're seeing, it'll be important to have a good relationship with the Cutezarians."

The Captain took one long last look at the ship landing on a familiar land mass. He wanted to dash next door, push down the door, rush into the chambers of the Ruling Body, announce the important discovery and demand use of the information.

However, he had managed to control the excitement by the time he'd crossed the plaza. Surprisingly calm, he prepared to go through the required channels.

In the library, Dorinda and Craig watched with growing fascination. The sphere sprouted three spindly legs with large padded feet for soft landings. The craft settled onto the earth, and long ramp descended to touch the ground.

From the craft emerged beings, larger than the contemporary Cutezarians, but obviously still related: oversized angular heads perched on top of tall, thin bodies.

"These must be the Cutezarians whose remains we found at the tell," Craig mused.

"Craig!"

He jumped and put his hand to his stomach as Dorinda suddenly grabbed his arm. "What?"

"Look! That's Africa. The pyramids. Why didn't we see it?"

Craig nodded. "So, if we're looking at Africa, are these the people who taught the ancient peoples the art of building? And what about all the legends of gods from the sky?"

Caught up in the excitement of her discovery, he suddenly asked, "Wonder what time period it is on earth?"

She looked back at the screen. She didn't answer him, but continued her own thoughts. "And speaking of ancient times, don't the Cutezarians getting off that ship look familiar?"

"They've always looked familiar." Craig repeated what they had already said to each other. Quickly he reviewed archeology classes, but the information kept hiding in the far corners of long-ago-filed-exam-answers in his mind.

"Computer, freeze," he said suddenly as the head of an ancient Cutezarian was shown face on. "Computer, enlarge," Craig ordered forgetting he wasn't addressing his own computer. However, the picture flickered and one face filled the entire screen. Craig studied the face, then closed his eyes and continued his mental search. Suddenly, like a picture flashed on the screen of his mind he saw an enormous statue of the face and remembered its origin. Rising slowly, he walked to the screen.

Dorinda couldn't stand the suspense. "What is it, Craig?"

"The Easter Island statues," he said quietly with awe as he gazed at the screen.

Dorinda shared his feeling. "If the original Easter Island people's ancestors came from Africa, they could have carved an ancient memory. It also could explain the pyramids in Egypt, South America, and Old Mexico. If they all had ancestors who were exposed to the Cutezarians, each set of descendants would pay homage in their own way after reached their final homeland."

Craig was silent a long time, thinking through some things he'd read as a child. "There was this anthropologist that came up with a theory about the Polynesians coming from Peru." He touched his comm button. "Computer, name anthropologist who proved the Polynesians came from Peru."

"Thor Heyerdahl, on the Kon-Tiki. There is a tradition of a great battle on the shores of Lake Titicaca, and the defeated people, led by Tiki, a man-god, disappeared. The legend grew from half-truth stories that have some factual proof. Theory says they made their way to the coast and made reed rafts commonly used on that lake."

"Computer, stop."

"So, if the Easter Island people came from Peru, that means they must have had ancestors from Africa." Dorinda took up his thoughts.

"If I remember correctly," Craig continued. "Heyerdahl took a second voyage on a replica of ancient raft-type boats. Ra, I think the second one was called. He sailed from Africa to the islands around South America. I'll have to look it all up." They fell silent, each reviewing what little they remembered about the seemingly insignificant voyages of a twentieth century anthropologist.

Craig suddenly grinned and shook his head. "We've got to get the scientists in on this." "If a couple of amateurs find answers to this age-old controversy, they'll be very upset."

"Nevertheless, Craig, it is an amateur's dream." Dorinda's eyes twinkled at the thought.

"Craig, this is the Captain." Craig's comm button interrupted them.

"Yes, Captain?"

"Permission is granted for full use of this file. If you will use the command 'stop video only', the computer will cease showing the video, but continue transmitting. It will transmit much faster that way. We'll call a meeting first thing in the morning and view the file together. Meanwhile, this is classified."

"Can Dorinda come?" Craig asked.

"Dorinda will be the guest of honor. I'll see you aboard," He answered affectionately.

"All right," Craig signed off, turned to the translation box and repeated the command.

The screen went blank and the speed of the blinking lights on the link doubled. When the link beeped, signaling end of file, Craig detached the probe and addressed the ship's computer. "End of file."

"Save with name Lea Special I. Do not link. Material is classified." Turning to Dorinda he asked, "When is the tour supposed to reassemble?"

Dorinda regarded him in shock. "I'm afraid they're long gone."

"It's okay," Craig laughed, touching his comm button.

"Yes, Chaplain?" Communications responded to his hail.

"Beam us aboard."

Dorinda hugged Craig as they parted at the transporter door and made him promise to go straight to his quarters and stay there for the rest of the day.

Detouring by sickbay, Craig leaned on the tech's workstation. "Can I get a glass of the formula? And don't tell Jeff I'm hurting."

"Craig - what have you done?" The doctor came around the corner.

"Jeff!" Craig dropped his head and ran his fingers through his hair. "It's classified. But it's the most important discovery we've made. And my stomach's working as hard as my mind."

Jeff nodded to the tech and the keyed in the code. He studied Craig a minute, then leaned over and keyed in two more codes. "A little more of this, and a lot more of that." He handed the glass to Craig and instructed, "Don't drink it till you get to your quarters."

"What did you put in it?" Craig asked wearily.

"Nothing you haven't had before," the doctor answered as he ushered Craig out. "Have a nice nap," he added.

'Shonya ran to catch the lift as Craig entered. "Hi, I was just coming to see you. They said you went to the surface with the Captain. What happened? You look exhausted."

Craig grinned. "It's classified so I can't tell you much about it." He rubbed his stomach. "I got excited, and now Jeff's mad because I'm hurting again. He added stuff to the formula, and I think I'm in trouble."

In his quarters, Craig sipped the formula and told her what he could. "Dorinda went on the tour this morning and wound up in the place we would call a library. She came across the Cutezarians' earliest preserved pictures. We discovered it's a record of a trip to ancient earth." He spoke quietly and it took her a minute to understand the importance of his words.

"It's what?" She left her chair and came to sit next to him on the sofa. "A journey to earth?" she repeated.

He leaned back and put his arm around her. "And that's all I can tell you. Tomorrow morning you can see the whole thing with the rest of us. Dorinda and I only saw part of it."

"You didn't see it all, and you're this excited? I'm surprised you're not jumping up and down."

"I promised Jeff I'd take it easy." He finished the drink and sat the glass down. "But I'm jumping up and down inside."

They sat in silence. After a few minutes, Craig took a deep breath and let it out slowly. "Now I know what Jeff put in the formula."

"Does your stomach feel better?" 'Shonya asked quietly.

"Yes, and the rest of me too." He leaned back and closed his eyes. "Jeff told me to have a nice nap. I should have known."

She watched him unwind. "You gonna be there tomorrow?"

"Wouldn't miss it for the life of me," he said with a yawn.

"I'll bring dinner tonight." Leaning over, she kissed him briefly and was gone before he could persuade her to stay.

Craig stretched out on the bed and addressed the air with a sardonic smile, "Jeff, who are you gonna put to sleep when I'm well?"

## CHAPTER TWENTY-FOUR

A grumbling assembly of students and scientists waited for Captain Brodsky the next morning. They were there, although reluctantly, in response to the Captain's specific orders.

"We already have so little time on the surface," Quantro complained.

"There's a lot to do," Roger added. "And I'm hoping the Cutezarians let us work on more pyramids."

"I can't figure out why they haven't dug up these sites. They're advanced enough." Dr. Cabrailes seemed more concerned about the Cutezarians than the delay.

"I think I have the answer to that riddle," Captain Brodsky said as he and Dorinda entered the room. The crew stood at attention, and Craig slipped into the empty chair next to 'Shonya when the "At ease" command was given.

"They have pictures. Motion pictures." Captain Brodsky explained, "In the past they used film of some sort, and then computerized it. While touring the city, Dorinda discovered a library of these pictures. I've called this assembly so you can view the ancient Cutezarian culture and a remarkable trip they took."

Walking to the front of the room, he addressed the computer: "Computer, activate classified file 5998546."

As the picture came to life, he added. "The Cutezarians have given us permission to transmit and study these records. There will be ample time for extensive study, but first let's just view it."

The room grew quiet as the journey began.

Suddenly someone exclaimed, "The Earth's system!"

Craig smiled to himself, remembering his and Dorinda's excitement at the discovery. The group verbalized the planets as they passed.

"Pluto, Uranus, Saturn, Jupiter, Mars."

"We are seeing a journey into our own solar system." "Shonya mused aloud.

"There's the moon," someone exclaimed.

The scientists began leaving their seats for a closer view. By the time earth came into view and became clear, they stood in a tight semi-circle around the screen. As the land separated from the oceans, they had all reached the same conclusion. There was awe in the voices that repeated in unison.

"They're landing."

"We're seeing our own history here," 'Shonya mused.

"Africa." The Captain stated the obvious.

A buzz of conversation went around the room as they watched the legs settle onto the soil and the ancient Cutezarians step out of the ship.

The picture went black for a split second then resumed, showing an encounter with primitive humans. Ancient man approached the foreign craft in many wary stages. The Cutezarians waited without moving. Ancient man moved closer, crouched, moved closer, and crouched again.

"These are our fearful ancestors," the Captain voiced everyone's thoughts.

The next Cutezarians out of the ship carried a large black box between them as they made their way down the ramp. They activated it and it held the attention of primitive man as it blinked, collecting data as the humans talked among themselves. After a while, the box slowly began producing the clicks and syllables of the ancient African speech.

"Obviously it's an early version of the translation boxes," someone said.

"Does anyone understand ancient African languages?" Craig asked the group.

With his typical sense of humor Oliver stretched to his full height and answered in his unique accent, "I am not that old."

When the chuckles died the Captain asked, "I assume that's a no, Oliver?"

"I am afraid so, sir," came the answer. "Not that ancient."

"Craig," the Captain turned to him. "Is the computer concept translator program overlaid on this file?"

He nodded. "It automatically becomes part of the file when it's transmitted."

"Computer, can you translate?" The Captain addressed the computer.

As the computer consulted its programs, the scientists watched and listened to the continuing conversation on earth.

"Insufficient data for detailed translation." The computer answered.

Craig commanded, "Compose a commentary from the action portrayed and concept comparison verbal clues."

The computer consulted again. "Composing."

"Reverse video." Craig ordered and waited. When the box first started speaking, he said, "Stop." Then, "Forward and begin translation."

"The Cutezarians descended from the ship, and the humans finally allowed them to approach. The Cutezarians bring a message. Humans are fearful. There is a spirit who creates all beings. Humans do not understand.

Cutezarians speak of the spirit who will help them. The humans shake their heads and do not understand."

The screen went black, and resumed the record with the Cutezarians building houses. They demonstrated stone cutting using water, sharp stones and hammers. Although fascinated, only a few humans were brave enough to try it. Most stood in clumps and watched.

Next, the picture showed the construction of a building. A foundation of huge rocks formed a large square, and each row of rock sloped up. Within several rows of stones, a pyramid shape became evident.

The Cutezarians moved the stones against each another while pouring water over them until they fit so tightly they didn't tilt even when the humans, no longer fearful, sat on them, and then jumped on them. This process was repeated as the picture faded, and refocused several layers later.

"It's magical seeing the process like this," Dorinda observed.

"How'd they move the stones?" Forest wondered.

No one had the answer, so they continued viewing. After the first couple of layers of stones, the Cutezarians began building a ramp consisting of loose stones and sand. The camera swung around and Forest's question was answered.

From the distance four Cutezarians came into view, moving a huge square stone with ropes tied around it, and from the distance the stone appeared suspended about ten inches off the ground. As they approached, the observers could see a small-motorized platform with a single track in the center. The Cutezarians' ropes merely acted as guides.

"There you go, Forest." The Captain pointed to the screen. "I suppose later, all the ancient people remembered were the ropes and improvised their own method to move the stones," he added.

"Or maybe imitated the track by using rocks or logs to roll them over?" Craig wondered.

"Could be," someone agreed.

Three completed large pyramids suddenly appeared in a triangular cluster, without any indication of time passage.

"I wonder how long this all took," Roger verbalized.

A few seconds later, the camera zoomed in on the plaza of the pyramids where the Cutezarians and humans were sharing a meal. It seemed a record of an intense conversation, with both sides talking and the translation box chattering into their silence.

"It's like listening to a three sided-conversation," Dorinda said.

"And not understanding any of it," 'Shonya laughed.

"Computer, provide commentary," the Captain ordered.

"Translating," the computer answered. "Cutezarians speak of the spirit which directed them to come to Earth and share knowledge with this planet. The humans want to know more. Cutezarians tell of one who created their world and all the space around them and wants to awaken the awareness of the spirit's presence in all beings. The Cutezarians were told to travel to this place and share their knowledge wherever they went." The computer was silent.

"Computer, freeze," 'Shonya suddenly commanded.

"Craig, are they spiritual ambassadors?" she added incredulously

"Impossible." Craig shook his head.

"There it is, right in front of you," Forest insisted.

"Now, let's not get carried away," Craig argued.

"Seems like I said the same thing to you a couple of nights ago," Jeff reminded him.

Craig could only grin. "See, I followed your advice."

"Sure you did."

"Craig's right, we shouldn't impose our spiritual concepts on this culture just because their terms translate into similar language." Oliver reasoned.

"Computer, continue," the Captain commanded.

A construction site of a fourth half-finished pyramid materialized as the display continued; ancient humans transported stones to the site. As the camera panned the site, a sudden cry of panic pierced the air. The Cutezarian recording the action spun around and the picture became a moving blur. It focused again in time to document the descent of the body of a Cutezarian worker as it fell from the top of the structure.

Aboard the M. Curie, the audience watched the ancient accident in horror.

"Oh, my God," someone said. "Sorry, Chaplain."

"My thoughts exactly," Craig replied.

The action held them spellbound as the ancient humans and Cutezarians reacted to the accident. The Cutezarians surrounded the unmoving body while the humans, poised for flight, hovered around the area.

The Cutezarians confirmed the death of a fellow traveler and knelt around the body as the picture faded.

A collective sigh escaped from the onlookers as the spell was broken.

Captain Brodsky recovered first. "Computer, freeze video," he commanded.

"It happened so long ago, but it's so real," 'Shonya said softly.

"Kind of makes you feel you should do something," Roger agreed.

"Shall we continue?" the Captain prompted, "or shall we suspend this and let you go back to work?"

The file had become their work.

"Computer, continue," Oliver gave their answer.

"A funeral?" Forest asked as the file continued.

The ancient Cutezarians gathered in a circle around their dead companion. Curious, the ancient humans crept toward the circle. Gently the leader of the party inserted a tube into the dead Cutezarian's arm, and attached the tube to a small hand-held pump then another tube ran to a large clear collection container. The pump drew liquid from the body.

"Are they embalming him?" the scientists asked themselves.

"Red blood!" Forest exclaimed as the first liquid reached the collection container.

When the blood finished dripping, the Cutezarian took the tube from the bottle, inserted in into another container, and activated the pump again. An unidentified liquid replaced the blood taken out.

"They are embalming," the Captain murmured in wonder.

The next series of pictures showed the Cutezarians moving the body, putting it into a box and transporting it to a prepared grave not far from the pyramids. Before they buried their companion, they drew close to each other and repeated the hands-on-shoulders part of the nightly ritual. Finally, they liberally anointed the box with drops of blood before putting it in the ground. It was then covered with earth.

A miniature pyramid about the height of a man was constructed over the gravesite.

The picture faded to the last encounter between the Cutezarians and humans. As the Cutezarians started up the ramp carrying the translation box, they turned around, and the humans fell to their knees in imitation of the Cutezarian's action at the funeral.

Carrying the translation box, the Cutezarians hurried back to the humans. The leader went to each of the humans and, repeating the same phrase, lifted each to their feet.

"Computer, translate," Captain Brodsky commanded.

"Translating," the computer spoke. "Cutezarian is speaking. Do not worship us, but the one who sent us."

However, the on-board camera recorded the ancient humans gazing longingly into the sky until the ship was out of range.

"End of file."

## CHAPTER TWENTY-FIVE

Deafening silence.

"Do you realize the implications of this?" When Oliver finally broke the spell, others found their voices.

"Will we have time to study this material?"

"Is there more?"

"This is an actual record of a journey to earth, not a simulation?"

"It was presented to me as a historical record," Dorinda answered the last question.

Craig sat quietly trying to ignore his uncomfortable stomach and restlessness, but finally gave in and paced to relieve his jangled nerves.

'Shonya, acutely aware of his presence, resisted the protective tenderness threatening to overwhelm her.

Unable to gain quiet, Captain Brodsky ceased his efforts and finally nodded to his aide. "Tenn-shun!" came the sharp bark from the lieutenant. The crew snapped to attention, and the scientists regarded him reproachfully.

"Pardon me," the Captain apologized to the civilians. "I needed your attention." They forgave him with chuckles and small laughs. "Look, it's almost lunch time. Let's break. I'm declassifying this file. You can access it under Lea Special I. This afternoon you can work on the planet or study the material. Tomorrow we'll meet back here for discussion. "This afternoon I'm going to the planet to request an interview with the High Counselor." As the Captain looked around the room, he saw excited, perplexed, thoughtful people. "Let's quit for now, okay?"

As if waking from sleep they adjourned, discussing the new information in light of their own discipline.

Craig, Jeff and 'Shonya shared lunch. The doctor had insisted Craig begin a carefully controlled diet to reestablish his body's acceptance of solid food. But Craig felt no real need to eat since the formula provided all the nutrition he needed. After a few bites, he felt full and finished the meal with a glass of formula.

"Don't worry, Craig, you'll be able to eat solid food again. Just take it slow," the Doctor assured it.

"Like everything else right now," 'Shonya added with a grin.

Catching her double meaning, Craig sat his glass down, leaned back with a grin and ran his fingers through his hair "Yes, Ma'am," he drawled in his best Forest Cabrailes imitation.

Jeff got up with a disgusted shake of his head at 'Shonya. "I should have called you earlier and let you lecture him before I released him from sick bay the first time."

"With Craig's stubborn streak, it wouldn't have done a bit of good," she replied.

Craig got up, echoing Jeff's disgusted shake of the head. "If you two insist on talking about me in the third person, I'll go away and let you do it." He added as he left he added, "I'll be in my quarters viewing the library file."

Returning to the table, he kissed 'Shonya with a grin. "Dinner?"

"Dinner."

\*\*

Craig pulled out his computer, stretched out on the bed and asked for the file, and watched the journey over and over, his wonder growing each time.

"God, what am I seeing? Help me control my emotions and think around my excitement. Give me wisdom and insight beyond my own abilities. Help me not insist it mean what I want it to."

263

Switching to his personal log, he spoke as long as he could think, trying out the plausibility of his conclusions. He heard his own voice drift, and realized how tired he was. He struggled to finish, but each time he started a thought his mind drifted. Finally, feeling betrayed by his own body, he gave up.

"Link to system," he instructed wearily and laid the computer aside.

"Linked," the computer answered. But Craig didn't hear.

**

'Shonya spent the afternoon with the teams, going from one conference room to the next. Her excitement level rose as she reviewed each team's ideas.

Craig didn't answer when she called, and she assumed he had taken Jeff's admonishment to take the comm button off and spend afternoons in silence. She gave him another hour and went to his quarters.

"Come," he responded when she touched the alert button.

She found him half-awake, lying on the bed frowning at the ceiling.

"What's wrong?"

Without comment, he handed her the computer and watched her face as she read.

She stood up in her excitement and read it. Then she read it again and finally sat on the bed, her eyes glowing.

He moved over to give her more room and said, "I'm apprehensive about it. The implications are scary. Have I simply superimposed my beliefs on their record so I'm seeing things that aren't there?"

"Your conclusions make sense to me. Let's see what the others say. If you're right, it'll change the way we look at God's work on earth."

"Not so much that as the way we look at God," he replied. "We've always said God uses things that go wrong to bring glory to the Deity. If I'm right about this, it could show how God used ancient human's misunderstanding to begin the revelation of the Godhead to humans. The Cutezarians planted a spark that turned into an awareness of a power beyond humanity. And it provided the means through which Christ showed his ultimate love—the blood sacrifice." Realizing he was rambling, he stopped and took a deep breath. "End of speech."

She smiled and they fell silent as they considered Craig's conclusions.

After a while, he sat forward, pulled his knees up and leaned his elbows on his knees. "I don't know. I've prayed about it and it seemed right as I worked. But I'm still human. I can't really get outside human history. I'll send the file to a couple of my Profs at seminary before I write anything official."

"Good plan, but are you going to share your conclusions with us tomorrow?" she asked.

"Yeah, but only as theories," he answered cautiously

"That's all any of us can do at this point," she agreed.

"The advantage the scientists have is they've got their teams. I've spent the afternoon going from group to group, and believe me, they're bouncing ideas around."

"You must be tired," he commented.

She nodded and got up. "And hungry."

Craig went to wash his face and she sighed tiredly, her unusually restless sleep since Dr. Kobee's death catching up with her. Suddenly she was a child again. She saw the explosion; the bodies fly out of the transport and heard the voices that accompanied the tragedy. Shutting her eyes, she willed the vision to go away, shook her head angrily, and went to the food synthesizer.

When Craig returned from the bathroom, he found her browsing through the menu program.

"I don't have the slightest idea what I want," she said wearily.

Stepping between her and the display, Craig looked intently into her face. "Are you alright?"

Something in her responded to the concern in his voice. "I haven't slept very well lately," she confessed, but checked the impulse to tell him about the accident.

It didn't seem like the time to probe. Instead, Craig took her hand and issued an invitation. "I have to go by sickbay for my daily scan and injection. Come with me and we'll go to the R & R deck when Jeff's done with me."

She nodded her assent and spoke to the synthesizer. "Georgia Peach Tea, iced." She turned to Craig and kissed him. "That ought to hold me."

They went into the hall as she sipped her tea. "What are the injections for?"

"To help the inflammation of my stomach lining. I still have a lot of discomfort. Jeff's afraid if it continues the seal might let go, or other ulcers develop. He's warned me I might always have a sensitive stomach." Craig rubbed his stomach as he spoke. "But if that's the worst I have to live with, I can handle it."

The doctor was waiting when they arrived. "Brought some moral support, I see," he greeted Craig then 'Shonya. "How are the discussions coming?"

"Interesting," she answered. "If you want, you're welcome to come by viewing room A tomorrow at eight."

"I'll be there. Thanks for the invitation." He refocused on Craig. "Let's get this over with, I have a dinner date."

"So do I," Craig grinned and stretched out on the nearest exam table.

Jeff activated the scan panel and studied the graphs. "Not better, but not worse," he said, dissatisfied, as he lifted Craig's shirt and checked the small wound. "Same here. It should be completely gone by now. You're still jumpy and stressed?" Craig nodded. "How would you feel if I injected the stomach directly?"

Craig groaned. "I'd feel hurt."

"It won't hurt much," the doctor grinned.

"How long will this take? My date's hungry."

Jeff patted his arm and went to the tech's station.

Craig sat up and asked, "You want to go alone?"

"I'll wait."

The doctor consulted his personal computer that contained all the medical information from the last five hundred years. He knew what he wanted, but needed the correct combinations of drugs to allow him to inject the anesthetic directly into Craig's stomach. He took his time referencing and cross-referencing each drug, his own stomach growling. Yet he made sure he had just the right amount of each drug and that they were completely compatible with each other and Craig's out-of-balance system. Finally satisfied, he keyed the formula into the medical synthesizer and returned to the treatment area.

Craig and 'Shonya were holding hands, deep in serious conversation. It struck him they were in love, friends, and colleagues all at the same time. He wondered if they had admitted what was so clear to him.

"Lie down," he ordered as he approached. Craig released 'Shonya's hand and obeyed. "You'll feel a sting like the IV device." He sterilized Craig's abdomen.

"Ready?"

Craig braced himself and nodded grimly.

"Don't tense your muscles like that." He massaged Craig's stomach. "Relax. It won't be that bad."

He relaxed, and the doctor laid the medication container against Craig's abdomen then activated the device.

With a grimace, he closed his eyes and endured the discomfort without moving. A cool sensation slowly replaced the dull ache, and his stomach felt strangely empty.

"I put your stomach to sleep," Jeff told him, then gave orders. "Lie still five minutes, and then take 'Shonya to dinner. But you can't eat anything. We'll try solid food again in a couple of days. Before you retire, call me and I'll meet you here for one of our famous IV sessions. Or better yet, I'll come to your quarters." He checked his watch. "Oops, I'm almost late. See you later. Bye."

And the Doctor was gone. 'Shonya and Craig exchanged grins and he closed his eyes.

'Shonya kept track of the time. Craig was nearly asleep when it was up. "How does it feel?" she asked, touching his hand.

He replied with a small smile without opening his eyes. "Strange, but calm. Finally calm." He opened his eyes with a sigh and sat up. "The constant ache gets to me," he admitted. He slid to his feet. "Are you ready?"

She nodded and he put his arms around her. "You've been patient through all this."

"It's worth it." Touching his face with both hands, she stretched up to kiss him. His response was immediate, complete, and passionate.

Craig knew he risked tearing the seal but he pulled her close, lifting her to her tiptoes. Only when he felt light headed did he reluctantly let her go. He leaned against the table with a sigh.

Emotion swept over 'Shonya, threatening to drown her. As he sat, she put her hands on his shoulders and struggled for control. When she got her breath back, she ran her fingers through his hair and down his jaw line. "You okay?"

Lifting his head, he nodded and smiled into her shinning eyes. "I don't think I've ever felt this way before," He said simply.

She laughed softly. "I'm not sure what it is, but I haven't either."

"Well, whatever it is, we'd better get out of here before it gets us in trouble." It wasn't time to push 'Shonya yet.

Craig slid off the table and, arm in arm, they left sickbay. They were alone in the lift.

"Now, do you want to tell me what's been keeping you awake nights?" It was time for that.

Retreating to the other side of the lift, 'Shonya shook her head. She didn't want to see the pictures again.

Craig hesitated, giving her a few seconds, and then followed. "Hold lift," he commanded, gently laying his hand on her back. "What is it?"

His touch broke her reserve. "Daniel's death brought back the memory of an accident I witnessed as a child," she began hesitantly. "Well, it really wasn't an accident. I saw my sister killed," And she told him everything.

He listened without comment until she ran out of words. Silently, he wrapped his arms around her and held her until the tears stopped. It wasn't a passionate embrace, but a healing touch.

As her emotions calmed, 'Shonya realized this was the comfort he offered Laura and Nathan Kobee as they faced Daniel's death.

Quietly he wiped the tears away. "You okay?"

Nodding, she smiled. "Thank you."

"It's one of the things I'm here for." He commanded the lift to continue. When they arrived at the R & R deck, he ceased being the Chaplain and took her hand as they exited.

The bottom deck, aft section, was the smallest deck on the ship and held the most unique feature of the M. Curie. A series of restaurants lined the deck, each preserving the art of cooking an ethnic food. A luxury the military personnel weren't used to, it had quickly become known as the "R & R" deck. For the scientists it was a touch of home. No one pretended the food actually tasted better than the food synthesizer, but the smells and atmosphere made it a refreshing experience.

"What looks good?" he asked, "Since I can't eat, it's your choice."

"Italian." She pulled him toward the sign proclaiming "Italiano." She already knew what she wanted, and was shortly addressing a plate of pasta.

"Give me a preview of tomorrow's discussions," he commanded his voice full of envy. "If I can't eat, at least give my mind something to chew on."

She grinned and shared what she could without giving it all away. As they talked, time slipped by.

Gradually they became aware everyone had discretely left the tables near them empty.

Craig looked around with a grin. "I think everyone decided we needed privacy."

"It's a precious commodity on this ship."

"Craig?" His comm button broke into their conversation. "Keal here."

"Jeff, what is it?" he answered.

"I don't suppose you know what time it is?"

Craig grinned. "No, tell me."

"Eleven o'clock and you should be resting. I'm on my way to your quarters. Be there."

"Walk slow, Jeff."

Nevertheless, the doctor was waiting for them when they strolled down the corridor.

"What happened to your date?" 'Shonya asked as Craig ushered them in.

"She turns into my wife when the nursery closes." The doctor laughed and pointed to the bed.

Craig obeyed the silent command, tossing his uniform jacket on the bed with a sigh. The doctor sterilized the vein and inserted the device.

"It still hurts," Craig muttered.

"Goodnight, Craig," the doctor said as he removed the device.

Craig felt the rush of the sedative and closed his eyes with a sigh. "Why do you keep doing this to me?" he groaned.

"Because it seems to me you can't avoid excitement," the doctor lectured. "And seriously, if I had my way I'd sedate you every night to completely relax you and speed the healing of your jangled nerves. But if I did that, I'd want you back in sickbay to monitor."

"I don't want to be in sickbay." Craig insisted, opening his eyes and frowning.

"I'm working on a milder tranquilizer for you to take the first few weeks you're back on duty," the doctor assured him.

"Give me a date," Craig demanded lazily, closing his eyes again.

"Not until your stomach lining's not inflamed," Jeff insisted.

"Not good enough," Craig muttered.

"Be quiet and go to sleep." 'Shonya reached down and affectionately brushed his hair back.

"Seems I have no choice," he grumbled, reaching for her hand. With a sigh, he relaxed. Gradually his breathing became regular and he let go of her hand.

"Don't worry." Jeff put his arm around her shoulders as they went into the hall. "He's doing fine. It'll just take time. Forcing him to stay quiet in his quarters would be just as stressful. We'll have to rely on him to restrict his own activities. The cycle of activity followed by tiredness and napping will be with him a while. This'll be the tough part."

"And long," 'Shonya added.

"What really worries me is I don't think his stomach will get better until the rest of his body is back in order."

They stopped at the turbo lift. "How's the relationship going?"

"Interesting. A little bit scary," she admitted. "And I've put off defining my own feelings until we're back on emotional equality." She faltered. "But I'm not sure Craig's the one who's in trouble emotionally. He knows what he's fighting. I see him struggle and feel with him. I see him awake, then sleeping and feel tenderness. And I wonder if it's his need that makes me feel that way. But the chemistry's there too." She shook her head, remembering his comforting arms and their last kiss. "Definitely there."

The doctor laughed. "You'll work it out. I think it's the real thing, but you're smart to wait until he doesn't rely on you so much."

"Thanks. Goodnight, Jeff." She hugged him and entered the lift.

## CHAPTER TWENTY-SIX

The atmosphere in viewing room A was already charged with the energy of excited chatter when Craig arrived. He wandered around the room, listening to the discussions.

The scientists disagreed about everything except the importance of the find. Apparently, everything else was open to debate. Discussion ended when the Captain and 'Shonya arrived.

Captain Brodsky took a mental roll. They were all there and eager. "Okay, 'Shonya, let's begin," he said with a small smile.

"We think the visit in the file took place long before our recorded history. If we accept the theory that the human race first lived in the general area of North Africa, the distribution of the ancient peoples would not be complete at the time of this visit. The descendants of the people we saw would have taken vague corporate memories with them as they dispersed.

"Craig has brought to our attention two voyages taken by an anthropologist named Thor Heyerdahl. He showed ancient peoples had the knowledge to construct rafts that became one with the sea and were capable of very long distance travel. His theories could explain the pyramids of Central and South America. He also theorized that the people who made the statues on Easter Island originally came from South America. You'll need to look up the results and controversy surrounding his work."

She stopped and motioned to Dr. Cabrailes. "Forest."

"Most ancient cultures used stone." He spoke in his straightforward, forceful manner. "The Egyptians, Thais, Chinese, whoever built the great lost city of Africa, the

Incas, Aztecs and other Indians of South and North America Indians. Some cultures lost it, some of it died when the civilization died, and some made stone: bricks, stucco, and terra cotta.

"Inventions usually don't just appear. One person has an idea. Another modifies it. Finally, something useful happens. So I ask. Is this the start of Earth's stone building? You can see the pyramids of Egypt, Mexico and Peru came from people's corporate memories.

"Did the pyramid tombs evolve by combining the memory of the large living pyramids with the small one built over the grave? How about cemeteries with stone markers and funeral services? Did they start here?"

Craig smiled as Forest stopped and abruptly sat down. "Maybe he realized he said more than two sentences all at once," he thought.

"Craig," 'Shonya prompted.

With a deep breath, he faced the group. "I have an idea we witnessed more than the origin of building. From the beginning of recorded history, humans have worshiped things or beings from the sky. In the beginning, this awareness found expression in myths, and later in Judeo-Christian tradition, by placing God's dwelling place in the heavens. The spirits lived there." A general buzz of conversation interrupted him.

"I see I don't need to elaborate on the implications of that." He grinned. "Every culture on earth tells myths about the gods or spirits, and usually the gods live in the sky - except the evil ones. Yet, the Cutezarians insisted they were not the ones to be worshiped, but rather the 'one who sent us.'"

He hesitated and ran his fingers through his hair, needing time to think.

"Go ahead, Craig," 'Shonya urged gently. "If we disagree, we'll pretend we're in vespers and dissect you later."

The laughter put Craig at ease and reminded him these people would think about what he said before accepting it as truth.

He pulled up a chair, turned it around, and leaned against the back of it as he faced the group. "Whether you're interested in this from a religious or historical perspective, let me throw out some questions. Were the Cutezarians acting as ambassadors of the 'One Who sent us?' Did the ancient humans misunderstand and worship the beings from the sky instead of the deity they came to share? Look at the file again when you have time to consider the implications. Are we seeing the beginnings of a tradition of blood sacrifice? If primitive man misunderstood the message, they could also have failed to comprehend the Cutezarians' use of the blood at the funeral."

Craig stopped, realizing he was pacing. He made himself sit again before continuing.

His excitement made 'Shonya smile. It was fun to see him full of enthusiasm.

"Yet in their misunderstanding, they set into motion the very thing God used eons later to demonstrate divine love for humanity. "The shedding of Christ's blood was the culmination of centuries of blood sacrifice. God used something humans already knew about to glorify the Godhead. However we feel about animal and human sacrifice we must understand this." He suddenly became aware of the amazed looks with which they were regarding him. He stood and held his hands out to them. "There it is. Do with it what you want."

As he sat beside 'Shonya, he sighed, leaned back and listened to the unrestrained vocal reaction. "Even if they shoot me down, I managed to get them as excited as I've been," he whispered with a grin.

"So parts of the theory about God being invented by humans because of space visitors are correct?" someone asked.

"Could it be that their facts were correct, but not their conclusions?" another wondered.

'Shonya finally stood and put her hand on Craig's shoulder. "We have proof of two things in this file," she said. "These beings did visit earth and the ancient humans misunderstood the message they brought. Everything else will be examined and re-examined. What we talked about today is only the beginning."

Dorinda Brodsky caught her eye. "Dorinda?"

"To change the subject just a bit," she spoke with a small smile, knowing their reaction in advance. "The black box that changes the words of the beings who ancient man took for  gods into understandable ideas could have been the beginning of the "oracle" idea—the place to go to find the word of God."

The room again erupted into spontaneous conversation:

"Impossible."

"Fantastic."

"God has always existed beyond man."

"My country's natives tried to worship the first white man they saw. Even Tiki himself was thought to be a god, and light-skinned." Andez Ronger voiced his thoughts.

"Was that because the Cutezarians were light skinned?" Forest asked.

"Could be. The Indians of Peru also had legends of light skinned men from the sky," Andez agreed. "And figures on some of the temples resemble space travelers."

No one questioned him. His mother came from a long line of Legend Keepers in his tribe.

However, Andez's remarks triggered Craig's next question, that stopped all speculation. "Is it possible the Cutezarians visited Earth more than once?"

"What?" 'Shonya spun around and looked down at him in amazement.

"Why?" Forest added.

"How else would they have known their message went wrong? That is, if we assume something on Earth initiated the national shame that caused them to withdraw from the mainstream of interplanetary life," Oliver replied.

"Some people think the earth drawings, especially in Peru, were markings from runways or marks to help returning beings find a place to land." Quantro, who grew up in Central America, also joined the conversation. "They've been explained, mythologized and de-mythologized. But I've studied those drawings, and it's possible."

The surprised looks turned toward him.

Captain Brodsky took control. "Let's ask the Cutezarians. We have a formal interview in three days with the entire High Council. Prepare your questions about their society in general. I've been given permission to submit them in advance of the interview to give the Cutezarians time to put together a historical presentation. The interview will start 0800 sharp." He looked around. "Need I say it? Be there!"

The laughter broke up the meeting but it took a long time for the room to clear.

Jeff caught Craig's arm before he could escape. "Craig, sick bay before lunch."

"Whose lunch?" Craig asked with a tired grin.

"My lunch, if you want to get technical," he answered with a small laugh. "You 8can have yours anytime you want after I get through with you." Noting Craig's flushed face, he changed his mind. "You're all worked up again. Scratch that - sickbay - now."

Craig shook his head. "Can't be helped. I'll spend the rest of the day in my quarters. How about vespers tonight?"

"Maybe, wait 'til I see the scans," came the cautious answer.

With a frown, Craig watched the doctor retreat and almost ran into 'Shonya waiting outside the door. "Where you going?" she asked, taking his hand.

"Sickbay," he groaned.

"You're getting tired of the routine and Jeff's enjoying having his own private patient. He started in the general medicine and surgery. He misses it. On board most of his work is administration and crises medicine. He's the Captain's personal physician and it looks like he's adopted you."

"Just what I always wanted. I bet he lies awake nights thinking up new ways to put me to sleep."

'Shonya laughed. "Can you come to my quarters for dinner tonight? Jeff and I've been working on some new things for you to drink."

"So I won't go on an eating binge?" he grinned.

She chuckled then voiced her concern. "No, so you won't lose your desire for the way foods taste before you can tolerate solid food again. I cleared it with Jeff this morning."

"Okay. A change of scenery would be good." He looked around to make sure the corridor was empty, and then kissed her quickly. "Bye."

"When you're back on duty, you can't get away with that kind of behavior," she called after him. Her smile faded as she entered her quarters and prepared to receive the pre-arranged communication from Art.

After restrained greetings, they briefed each other on the progress of their missions. Art's last question was "How's the Chaplain?"

Instantly on guard, she searched his good-looking, rugged face for clues to the question's motivation. "It's funny," she thought, "I've always been aware of Art's looks, but until I see Craig all dressed up, I'm scarcely aware of his."

"Improving," she answered aloud. "Why do you ask?"

He ignored the question. "You're not coming are you?"

With sudden relief, she realized he was going to make this easy if he could. With a small shake of her head she said, "No, Art. I'm not coming. I'm sorry. I really care for you, and will miss being with you." After a small pause she asked, "How did you know?"

"You, the funeral, and the Chaplain," he answered. "Your feelings were pretty obvious."

"I still don't know how it's going to turn out," she explained. "Craig's still too ill for either of us to know." She suddenly smiled. "But I've got to stay around and find out."

"I can see that," he allowed. "I hope it turns out like you want."

She wasn't sure what she wanted, or if he meant his good wishes, but was glad to have the interview over. "We'll keep in touch?"

"You bet," he promised a little glumly. "If this doesn't work out, you know what ship I'm on."

279

"I'll remember," she said softly.
With a small wave, he was gone.

## CHAPTER TWENTY-SEVEN

Frowning, Dr. Keal studied the panel above Craig. "Jeff, you can't make it change by glaring at it. Give me the bad news and let's get on with it." He was tired of lying on the table and watching Jeff's grim expression. Craig started to sit up, but the doctor pushed him back.

"Just relax, I'm not finished." He commanded, touching the computer's keypad. An entire unit separated from the panel and hovered over the bed.

"What?" Craig wondered, lifting his head to get a better view.

"I'm experimenting with a new unit. Lie still." Moving the unit close to Craig's abdomen, he looked through eyepieces on the side of the unit and addressed the computer. "Computer, enter results into Chaplain Lea's medical records." He unconsciously lectured as he studied Craig's stomach lining. "Just as scan technology replaced the old fashioned x-ray equipment, this will replace the conventional scan equipment. Without putting anything into your body, I can watch your organs function or not function, whichever the case may be, and..." He made some adjustments. "...And I don't like what I see." He ran the new unit over Craig's torso without further comment.

After what seemed hours, he retracted the unit, handed Craig his shirt and motioned him to get up. "Computer, cease." With a sigh, the doctor leaned against the table and faced his patient. "Here's what we've got. Your stomach lining's still very inflamed - not good. The seal's holding, the ulcer's healing slowly - that's okay. It's the lack of activity in your digestive system that concerns me. I don't know what I expected since you haven't tolerated solid food since the surgery. With the IV's and formula, your nutritional balance is fine. The problem is to find a way to reduce the inflammation before your digestive system completely atrophies."

Fighting his growing apprehension, Craig massaged his stomach and muttered. "I don't think I'm going to like this."

"How does it feel?"

"It burns, contracts sometimes, a constant dull ache," Craig answered with resignation.

"The way I saw your stomach throbbing, if it were your head, you would have an unmanageable migraine. I would have to sedate you."

"Which you're going to do anyway, aren't you?" Craig asked quietly.

The doctor paused. "In varying degrees," he finally admitted.

"No," Craig groaned through clenched teeth.

"Craig," the doctor responded quietly but firmly. "I've tried everything I know to help your system recover from the charge. You're better. Your emotions are under some control. You're thinking clearer. Yet any tiny bit of excitement stands every nerve in your body on end yelling at the top of its little electronic voice. The result is over stimulation of your entire system. Besides exhausting you, the result appears to be the inflammation of your stomach lining. Which brings us back to the problem at hand."

Craig looked up, met his doctor's concerned gaze, and came to a decision. "Okay, Jeff. Tell me exactly what you propose."

The doctor nodded and was silent a few minutes, working out his strategy. "Okay. I'll allow you mornings. Do whatever you want within reason. Breakfast and lunch will be the formula, and lunch will contain a mild sedative. You must spend the afternoon in your quarters, reading or napping. Dinner will be liquid also. I don't think you're ready to attend vespers yet. But I'll allow visitors after vespers, like before the surgery so isolation doesn't cause frustration. Then I'll bring you another formula, which will contain a somewhat stronger sedative, and you will sleep all night. I'll allow you to stay in your quarters, but you have to come every day for scans and injections, which will contain a specific treatment for the inflammation. We'll follow this routine for two full weeks, then re-evaluate. Understood?"

On the edge of being overwhelmed, Craig could barely manage a nod. To escape the doctor's sober gaze, he slid from the table. Head down, he measured the area with the length of his stride. Jeff perched on the table and watched him digest the routine.

"I suppose it's better than being restricted to quarters. Or never eating again," Craig thought. "And I'm getting tired of being exhausted all the time." He stopped and, turning to look at the doctor, asked, "If I stick to your routine, will I get better sooner?"

"That's a reasonable question," the doctor allowed. "If I can keep you quiet and away from stimulation for long periods of time, we can shorten your recovery time."

Craig nodded, but had one more question. "What about smaller doses of the drug you gave me the day of Daniel's funeral?"

"Also a good question. It's too addictive, even in small doses. I'd like to stay away from them."

Craig nodded again slowly. "Okay. I won't fight you," he said quietly.

Jeff crossed the room. "All right!" They stood eye to eye a few seconds, and then the doctor patted Craig's shoulder in encouragement. "It won't really be that bad. You're exhausted after a morning's activities anyway. If I sedate you, we'll avoid the two or three hours you spend just trying to calm down enough to rest. It's a matter of you giving up some control. And I know that's difficult now you're functioning better." He went toward the med tech's desk.

"Can I go to my office in the mornings?" Craig asked.

The doctor looked turned back in surprise. "And do what?"

"Just be there. See if Andez needs any help. Catch up on some paperwork," he answered vaguely. "I won't even go in uniform," he added.

The doctor considered, and then nodded. "If that's your only activity. The idea is to have a half-day of activity and a half-day rest, not a whole day's activity crammed into four hours before you rest."

"If I go to the surface, I'll do that instead of the office," Craig promised.

"Agreed," Jeff went into the med tech's station. "I'm altering the formula just a little. Since we're going to be doing specific treatments for your stomach, it doesn't need as much of the anesthetic," he explained as Craig followed him in. He finished the alterations, keyed in the final formula and handed the glass to Craig when it appeared. "Don't drink it until you get to your quarters. Dorinda has an appointment with Dr. Canady in a few minutes, and the Captain asked if I wanted to see the baby."

"Is everything okay?" Craig asked, turning back.

"Um-huh. Mostly routine. But as the time for delivery gets closer, Ruth wants to see her more often since she'll deliver early."

"Keep me posted."

"Will do. And Craig," he called after him. "Take off your comm button every afternoon. That's no longer a suggestion. It's an order."

Glass in hand, Craig walked slowly toward the lift. "What am I going to do?" he asked the floor as if it held the answer. "God, give me patience."

His next sensation was pain as he watched the glass fall from his hand, bounce against the wall, and send its contents into the air. Bracing one hand against his stomach, he closed his eyes and leaned against the wall with a groan.

A string of harsh words brought him back to reality. Amid dozens of scattered containers stood Cooper, cursing at the mess. His expression of concern was not for Craig, but the contents of the containers. Cooper swore again. "You should pay more attention to where you're going - Sir," his sharp voice accused.

"Cooper," Craig panted, "I was thinking about something else. I'm sorry."

"Well," Cooper conceded, bending to put the containers back into order. "I really couldn't see around the boxes."

Craig's breath returned slowly. "What's in them?"

"I'm experimenting with laser toys." It was a challenge.

Craig ignored the tone, trying to prolong contact. "How did you get interested in toys?"

"My brother owns a factory. An experimental model malfunctioned and killed his son. He asked me to do R&D for him so it wouldn't happen again." His delivery was short and unemotional.

"Will you show me some time?" Craig had time to ask before Jeff rushed out of sickbay.

"I heard noise. Craig?" He put his hand on Craig's shoulder.

Cooper hastily gathered the containers and moved away, saying over his shoulder, "Ah. Yeah. I guess. If you really want to see."

"Cooper needs to watch where he's going." Jeff said forcefully.

Cooper turned to protest. "No, Jeff. It was my fault. I wasn't paying attention." Craig looked up at Cooper as he spoke.

The angry expression didn't change, but Cooper's voice was less hostile. "Sorry, Chaplain. You okay?"

"I think so, Commander, Thanks."

Jeff took his arm, "Come on, we'll check the seal to make sure it's still intact and get you a refill."

'Shonya was waiting for him when he finally got back to his quarters with a fresh glass of formula. "Oooooh, you look grim."

"Jeff just laid down a strict new routine."

"Stomach's not better?"

"Not much. He's frustrated because all his technology and toys haven't given me the quick fix he's used to." With a sigh, he slouched on the couch and pulled her close. "So. He's allowing me mornings to do whatever I want, and then putting sedatives in my lunch formula so I'll rest all afternoon. If I behave myself he's allowing visitors after vespers, then more sedation at night." He grinned suddenly. "But he didn't restrict how much time I can spend with you."

"And you didn't bring it up?" she laughed.

"And risk being put off limits again? Uh-uh." He laughed, drinking the formula.

After her conversation with Art, 'Shonya felt more comfortable with Craig, but if he noticed any change in her, he didn't show it. She decided he wasn't yet ready for the subtle emotions. "Will he ever be?" she wondered.

They discussed the morning's meeting in detail. "Has anyone expressed a problem with my conclusions?" he finally asked what worried him the most.

"They were all too astonished, I think," she laughed. "Oliver thinks he's three meters tall now. He realizes his ancient ancestors played an even more important part in the scheme of things than he thought. But they're all anxious to talk to you about it."

Craig suddenly felt the effects of the sedation. Leaning his head back he shut his eyes and complained, "Jeff said a mild sedation with lunch."

"You are kind of worked up today," she reminded him.

"Yeah, I suppose," he said with a yawn. "Tell everyone we'll start visiting tomorrow. I don't think I'll be ready tonight."

"I'll bring dinner here late tonight instead of you coming to my quarters." She started to get up. "Oh, I forgot. Remember the questions everyone gave the Captain for the Cutezarians to illustrate?" He nodded.

"They sent word there was so much we wanted to know they need time to locate and put together all the information. The Captain set the interview back one week." She kissed him, but evaded his arms as he reached to pull her back. "No time to play right now. I just wanted to see what Jeff said."

Reluctantly Craig headed toward the sleeping area as 'Shonya activated the door sensor. "Make sure Alan schedules the interview in the morning. Jeff won't allow me to deviate from this routine."

"No problem. Good night."

"Bye." His last thought as he got into bed was a prayer: "God make this work, please."

**

So the routine began:

Andez learned to expect Craig to arrive unannounced some mornings, and visitors were allowed to return to Craig's quarters for discussion after vespers.

Craig felt more useful when Andez fell into the habit of discussing the day's plans and lesson for vespers with him.

Craig also returned to his routine of personal devotions and preparation of lessons, putting aside the knowledge that it would be some time before he would present them to an audience.

Between the time his morning activities ended and the sedative took over, he began drafting the presentation he hoped to give to the Cutezarians.

Although, at times, Craig still felt like a child being put to sleep, the routine made him more comfortable with the treatment.

Without official explanations, the scientists' routine also changed: public presentations began taking place in the morning, private or team exploration and experiments in the afternoon.

'Shonya and Craig returned to the routine of dinner in his quarters. Often she stayed after the discussions until Jeff brought the last glass of formula. Sometimes Craig made her stay and, sitting close until he was unable to stay awake, he would lay his head on her shoulder and give into the sedation.

'Shonya wondered how she could ever sort out her feelings for him: the tenderness from his need, the companionship from love, the intellectual sharing they both enjoyed from the joy of his presence, her emotional attachment from her physical desires. During this time as she observed him every different way: in the mornings, rested and animated, participating in discussion, at the tell, or with Andez in the office, and in the evenings giving into tiredness, then the sleep of medication.

In the middle of the routine, she realized how deeply she loved Craig. And it filled her with inexpressible joy.

## CHAPTER TWENTY-EIGHT

Craig finished the outline of his presentation and submitted it to the Captain for approval.
Monday night before the Wednesday interview Captain Brodsky was among Craig's post-vespers visitors and stayed after everyone but 'Shonya had gone.

"I'd like you to give your presentation, and then stay for consultation. It'll be stressful. I suppose we should take Jeff in case you get in trouble," the Captain proposed.

"You'll have to take care of that, I can't ask." Craig grinned. "I promised not to fight him."

"What if we tell him you'll stay in your quarters all day tomorrow?" the Captain suggested.

"I'll go crazy," Craig moaned, but agreed. "Jeff will be here in a few minutes and you'll hear his objections first hand."

"If you're correct in assuming the Cutezarians visited the Earth a second time and became secretive after that, your presentation could help the Cutezarians deal with this thing they call their shame." 'Shonya added, taking his hand.

Craig looked down at their intertwined fingers, a little confused by her growing public displays of affection. The door sensor beeped. "Come in," Craig invited.

The doctor hesitated in the doorway when he saw the reception committee. They all smiled, and the Captain acted as spokesman.

"We have a favor to ask of you."

"Oh no you don't," he said. "Craig has four more days on this routine. He's doing better, and I will not authorize longer hours away from his quarters." He shook his finger

290

at Craig. "And if you're not careful, I'll sedate you in the mornings too."

Craig grimaced. "I told you he wouldn't budge."

"I'm not really asking you to allow longer hours as much as a more stressful situation. I want you to clear Craig to go the surface with the scientists, present his theories, and remain for questions." The doctor started to protest, but the Captain continued. "Craig agrees to stay in his quarters all day tomorrow, under supervision and sedation if you insist. And you will accompany the team to the surface in case Craig needs you."

Jeff could only shake his head and capitulate. "Okay. I don't think it's necessary to sedate you in the morning if you'll stay quiet," he told Craig.

"Thanks, Jeff," they said in unison.

The doctor handed Craig the glass of formula and shook his head. "Good night," he said firmly.

Craig waited until he and 'Shonya were alone before drinking the formula so they would have a little time before the medication took effect. "It's as much of a relief as a frustration. At least I don't toss and turn until I can relax and sleep. But I don't want to sleep. I want to talk to you."

"That's one reason Jeff's making you take it. Even if you want to sit up and talk, you have to go the bed."

'Shonya got up and tugged him to his feet. "You might as well give in or you'll fall asleep right where you are. The sofa's not long enough for your legs." As they got up, he leaned over to kiss her, and she responded with the freedom of knowing exactly how she felt about him.

"Something's changed," he murmured. "You ready to talk about it?"

"Not yet." Feeling content, she settled into his arms.

He held her as long as he could before he knew he was falling asleep on his feet then kissed her again. His voice was soft and slightly slurred. "I've got to go the bed. Now."

She laughed. "The bed's that way, mister."

"Night, 'Shonya." He finally said and released her. "I'll find a way to get even with Jeff. Someday," he muttered in frustration.

Shonya's smile lingered as she entered her quarters.

True to his promise, Craig stayed in his quarters but studied the Cutezarian file. In nervous anticipation, he reviewed his own notes and was pacing when Jeff entered.

"I said rest," the doctor ordered as he took the computer.

"Sorry. I started out just reading the file and got excited." Craig sat and activated the chair's computer. "Recline." The chair elongated and he laid back, waiting for the Doctor's next move.

"I'm going tomorrow. If you get into trouble, I'll stop everything. You have to promise to mind me. You've come too far for a major setback." Jeff ran the life scanner over Craig's body. "When you're ready for lunch, call and I'll bring the portable scan along with the formula. I won't have you wandering the corridors."

"Yes, sir," Craig said.

"Don't sir me, just be quiet." Jeff handed the computer back. "Computer," he addressed the ship's unit. "Activate entertainment center." He turned back to Craig, "Watch a video or listen to music. That kind of rest." The large screen on the far wall activated and displayed its menu: environmental control, games, nature video with music, nature sounds background, music, video titles, record and display.

"Computer, list video titles," Craig said in resignation and swung the chair around to face the screen.

"Okay, now relax and pick something while I give you the injection." The doctor reached down and pulled up Craig's shirt. "It'd be quicker if you'd take it off," he said. Craig sat up and shrugged out of the shirt. "Ready?"

Craig grimaced, "Ready." He kept his eyes on the screen as he endured the slight discomfort, and felt the now familiar coolness of the medication as it coated the lining of his stomach.

"When the sensation wears off, you'll be ready for lunch," the doctor reminded him as he finished. He went toward the door and heard Craig's voice.

"Computer, display Survey of Ancient Religions."

"To each his own, I guess," the doctor grinned.

**

One of 'Shonya's proposals for the Cutezarians concerned obtaining permission to continue excavation of the area. Scanning the remaining sites of the area, she worked in total absorption.

Yet on another level, she was aware of a new dimension in the developing relationship with Craig. She hadn't intentionally neglected social contact. Art was proof of that. But the great distances separating personnel working in space had severed other developing friendships. Many of her friends had quit seeking close relationships, but she'd continued with her work, neither seeking nor completely denying them. She had friends and colleagues of both sexes scattered over the galaxy.

But Art and Craig were different. It amazed her she felt so deeply for both of them at the same time. She knew she often held people, especially men, at a distance for her own convenience. Somehow, they both broke through that barrier, and she wondered how.

The friendship between her and Craig might have continued for years before becoming anything else without the intervention of Craig's crises.

"Then again, something else may have triggered the transition from friendship to love," 'Shonya thought. Her thoughts strayed and Craig's words about God using even misunderstandings for the glory of the Godhead came to mind. "Us together would be something good coming out of something bad."

"It's possible," she mused aloud, enjoying the warmth of her feelings.

"Anything's possible, 'Shonya," Jeff said as he entered the lab.

She shook her head and refocused her thoughts. "Jeff! I didn't hear you come in." She got up and offered him a chair.

"What's possible?" he asked, noting her gentle smile.

"Something I'm trying to work out. How's Craig?"

"I left him viewing - what was that? Something about ancient religions." The doctor shook his head. "Someone needs to teach that man how to relax."

'Shonya grinned affectionately. "He is single minded."

"And stubborn," Jeff added. "That's why I finally put him on a forced routine. But tonight you can take his dinner and the final formula to him if you want. But watch out, by dinner time, he'll be overjoyed to see anyone."

'Shonya laughed. "I'll watch my step."

**

"'Shonya will bring your dinner and late night snack. The Captain, Dorinda, my wife, Dr. Canady, and I are out for a final fling before the baby comes." The doctor explained as he ran the sensor of the portable scan over Craig's torso.

"Computer, add to Chaplain Lea's record," he commanded then addressed Craig. "Drink this." He held out the glass. "I'll go over the results and let you know how you're doing Say hi to 'Shonya."

Craig drank and sighed in boredom. "If I watch one more video, I'll go nuts."

"Don't worry, you won't be bored this afternoon," the doctor promised. And he left Craig fighting the extra sedative in the formula and returned to sickbay feeling like a conspirator.

'Shonya spent the afternoon polishing the proposal drafts she received from the scientists. Finally satisfied, she consolidated them into one file. Her stomach reminded her of the late hour, and she went to sickbay.

The med tech gave her the formula and she continued to Craig's quarters.

Craig was up, but not fully awake. He gave her a tight, warm hug. "Hi. It's good to see you."

She looked up at him with a laugh. "Jeff warned me you'd be people starved. I'll order what I want to eat and we can have some dinner."

"Such as it is, but I've got to wake up first." He grinned and went to wash his face.

When he returned she had an omelet and toast for herself and a white paper coaster under his glass of formula. "Sorry, it's the best I could do with limited resources," she grinned.

"Well, at least it's pretty," he said and sat beside her. Craig drank his formula in silence then sat back to watch 'Shonya.

As she finished he took her hand. "About those promises," he started.

"What promises?" she asked, her emotions suddenly crowding out reason.

"The ones we weren't going to make," he said cautiously.

"Oh, those promises," she answered, trying to be equally cautious.

"How do you feel about them now?" he asked.

"I think we're getting closer." She smiled gently.

"Just checking," he said with a grin.

"Testing the waters so to speak?"

"Putting out fleeces, Biblically speaking of course," he chuckled.

"Well Chaplain, keep checking the fleeces," she encouraged with a mysterious smile.

Her response delighted him, but before he could speak her comm button interrupted. "'Shonya? Jeff, here."

"Yes, Jeff?"

"I didn't say you could stay all evening."

"Jeff, where are you? You're supposed to be on a date." She asked in exasperation. "And how did you know I'd still be here?"

"I'm taking a break. And I bet I could predict what you're talking about." They could hear the chuckle in his voice. "Anyway, how's Craig?"

Craig had closed his eyes and leaned his head back against the wall. 'Shonya got up and went into the sleeping area. "Jeff, what did you put in the formula?"

"Not enough to put him to sleep, but he won't want to talk much. Put a video on, make him lie on the couch and leave him alone."

"Oh all right," she whispered angrily. "But..."

"He needs rest," the doctor insisted. "Keal out."

Craig reached out and pulled her close as she returned to the couch. "He did it again, didn't he?" he said.

"Kind of, but just enough to make you stay put." She hugged him. "He said to put on a video, lie on the couch and don't strain a muscle."

"Ummm," He nodded. "Put something on." He stretched out and let her pick the video. "I'm getting tired of heavy thinking."

Without comment, she chose a comedy and started to leave.

He caught her hand as the computer projected the images into the room. "Stay?"

She sat on the arm of the couch and watched him relax. Soon they both were interested in the video, and she began squirming, as the arm got uncomfortable. He sat up and she slipped onto the couch, his head on her lap. In that position, they finished the video. Then she picked another comedy. 'Shonya could see the medication take effect, and wear off as the evening progressed.

The party broke up early and Jeff decided to deliver Craig's late night snack himself.

He went by sickbay before stopping at the corridor computer access terminal. "Computer, locate Dr. LaShonya Reed."

"Deck six, room 91E. Chaplain Craig Lea's quarters," came the answer.

"Doesn't anyone obey orders?" With a shake of his head, he resolutely marched to Craig's quarters.

The videos had suited Craig and Shonya's mood and sense of humor, and their earlier conversation was set aside in their laughter. For the moment, they were good friends enjoying being together. The door sensor beeped and reminded them of reality.

"I think we're in trouble," 'Shonya said. "Jeff said to leave you alone."

"Come," Craig said.

Jeff put on his stern expression and waited for the door to open. "I told you to go home," he began as it swished open. But he'd heard the laughter, and saw Craig's eyes were bright and clear. "Well, at least you're relaxed."

"Come in and sit down." Craig sat up and ran his fingers through his straight hair. "It's your fault I made her stay. Your stuff kicked in and I didn't want to be alone. Anyway we had a good time, and I'm fine."

"Okay. Sorry to break up the party, but drink." The doctor handed Craig the glass.

"I'm beginning to feel like a sedative depository," Craig complained.

"Just a few more days," the doctor encouraged.

Craig finished the drink. "I know. But I feel out of control."

"I'm sure I would too," the doctor conceded. He stayed until Craig showed signs of the medication taking effect.

"Okay, 'Shonya, go home," he said gently.

She nodded, got up, and Craig followed her slowly to the door. "We'll talk about the promises later," he said softly.

She smiled. "I'm sure the topic will come up again."

Craig leaned against the doorframe and touched her face.

Her feelings started tumbling again.

"Quit messing around. Give her a hug," Jeff commanded. "And hurry up. I want to check you out before you go to sleep."

'Shonya stepped into Craig's arms and he sighed. "This feels good. Can't you stay?"

"Say good night, 'Shonya," the doctor interrupted.

"Goodnight, 'Shonya. " She impishly obeyed.

"Not you, him," the doctor said shaking his head.

"Good night, 'Shonya," Craig said softly, dutifully following the old comedy routine.

She kissed him briefly and slipped out the door.

"Come on, Craig." The doctor pulled him to the bed area. "Undress. I need current readings so I can keep better track of you tomorrow."

The patient obeyed, and then stretched out on the bed. Jeff pulled out his life scanner and did a complete exam. Somewhere in the middle of it, Craig went to sleep.

"Rest, Craig," the doctor said pulling the thermal sheet over him.

**

Captain Brodsky got out of bed and into the shower first on Wednesday. It was his turn to be anxious to get to the planet's surface.

The night before 'Shonya, Oliver, Forest, and Roger had joined him in a late meeting to co-ordinate their presentations. They also viewed the final version of the file on earth's culture they had put together in response to the Cutezarian's presentation about their culture.

The schedule included a quick tour of the transportation system as the first order of business, followed by a video from the Cutezarians, then the presentations of the scientists and the Chaplain, allowing time for questions. The culture video was scheduled in the afternoon, also followed by a questions and answers period. They had agreed Craig's presentation would be the most important one of the morning.

Reviewing the meeting as he showered, Captain Brodsky prayed for strength and guidance for all involved, but specifically for Craig.

LaShonya Reed slept as late as she possibly could and still make the shuttle. She admitted to her image in the mirror as she hurriedly combed her hair how much she looked forward to watching Craig. But she also anticipated the opportunity to study the Cutezarians during his presentation. Would they believe him? Would they refuse to consider his conclusions? What had thousands of years of seclusion done to their culture? Putting these speculations aside, she ordered breakfast and reviewed her own presentation.

Jeff got up early, made rounds with his staff and still had time to share breakfast with his wife and play with his four daughters. Then he went back to sickbay and put his medical kit together. Praying for Craig, he asked God to clear his thoughts and touch him physically.

Oliver and Forest, both without family on board, met for breakfast in the public mess hall. At first, they merely nodded and lifted their hands in silent greeting as they got their first cup of coffee, squinting at each other through tired eyes.

"Morning, Oliver," Forest finally spoke.

"Morning, Forest," Oliver answered over their second cup of coffee. "Are we ready?"

"Soon as I wake up," Forest allowed with a wry smile.

At the conclusion of their meal, they prayed together for the entire interview, and all involved, both human and Cutezarian.

Craig felt as if he'd slept for days. It seemed like a long time since he'd even been out of his quarters. Excitement and apprehension fought for the upper hand when he considered the impending interview.

As he prepared, he prayed God would give each presenter the right words so the Cutezarians could at least understand their conclusions. After reviewing the Cutezarian files and his notes again, he went to sickbay, carrying his uniform jacket.

He met Jeff outside. "Morning, Craig. You look rested. I was coming to bring you breakfast and drag you in for the morning routine," He said handing over a glass of the formula.

"Beat ya'. Let's get this over with before I die of impatience." Craig finished the formula and laid his coat over a chair before stretching out on the exam table. Closing his eyes, he tried to relax during the scans and was startled when Jeff pulled his shirt out and laid the injection rod next to his skin.

"Come on, relax," the doctor said.

"Sorry," he muttered, preparing for the discomfort of the long injection. He closed his eyes again and prayed for strength.

With sudden, blinding clarity, he realized determination alone wouldn't get him through this if his body didn't tolerate the stress.

"Craig? What is it?" The doctor saw the anguish of that reality on his face. "Don't move," he added. Craig remained silent until the doctor finished. "What's bothering you?"

Craig got up gingerly, tucked in his shirt, and faced the doctor. "Jeff, I finally know what you've been trying to tell me for the last three months." He shook his head and reached for his coat. "It finally got through to me. Determination alone can't overcome the stress."

The doctor raised his hands in surprise and resignation sighed, and addressed the ceiling. "For months I have lectured, medicated, and tried to protect this man from stress. Then he comes up with his own answer."

Craig put his arm across the doctor's shoulders and led the way out of the room. "But I didn't find my own answer. What you've been saying finally sunk in, with some help from God hitting me over the head."

"Well, at least it came from a power greater than me," the doctor conceded.

Craig chuckled, and turned serious. "Spiritually, we're taught to listen more readily to God than to people, but sometimes God keeps trying to tell us something through a person and we can't see it." He shrugged. "In the last two weeks, I finally feel I've gained control. I'm thinking instead of just feeling. I guess I still don't have much tolerance for anything." He stopped and added, "Except sleep, that is."

"Progress at last." Jeff suddenly grinned. "You're not just saying this to make me feel better, are you?"

"Would I do that?" Craig asked innocently.

"If you thought you could talk me out of sedating you, yes," the doctor laughed. "But I do detect some good things happening. If we keep up this routine for another week,"

"Another week!" Craig stopped in the middle of the corridor.

The doctor tugged his arm. "Come on, we'll miss the shuttle." Then he stopped again and put his finger against Craig's chest. "If you get restless, start to hurt, or have any other symptoms, you'll tell me. Right?"

"Right. Maybe. Okay," Craig nodded.

They met 'Shonya in the lift and Craig took her hand but didn't say anything. They both looked at the doctor innocently.

He didn't comment.

"'Shonya, what's the schedule today?" Craig asked, and then watched her as she went through the plan.

"But, first we have a tour of the transportation system," she finished.

The lift slid to a stop and they entered shuttle bay number one. The Captain was already motioning them to hurry. They settled in and the Captain finished giving the pilot her orders. As the shuttle cleared the shuttle bay, he turned and surveyed the group. Oliver and Forest, in the two seats on the left were already deep into conversation. Roger and the two students who were handling the laser recorder clustered on the right. 'Shonya was talking to the pilot. Craig sat next to her empty seat, studying his computer and Jeff merely looked out the window.

Captain Brodsky got their attention and addressed the whole group. "After the tour of their transportation system, the first thing we have to do is get the Cutezarians' approval of the schedule. The proposed schedule is linked and you can pull it up under the file name 'C Interview One'." Everyone called up the file. "Take a few minutes and look it over Now's the time for questions."

After a while 'Shonya asked, "What if the Cutezarians have more to talk about than Craig has time?"

"If we can clear it with the doctor, we'll ask if we can return in the morning," the Captain answered.

Jeff remained cautious. "We'll see how it goes today."

The group chuckled at Craig's audible sigh.

"Will there be time for us to interact with each other if one of us comes up with an idea we would like to discuss? Oliver asked.

"I intentionally allowed time for it," 'Shonya answered. "Just keep it slow enough so that the translation box can keep up."

"The Cutezarians already have the tour of the system set up, right?" Roger asked.

"Yes," the Captain answered. "Anything else?"

They exchanged satisfied looks and shook their heads. 'Shonya took a seat next to Craig and took his hand. "Whatcha thinking?"

He looked at her in wonder. "My whole life has been dedicated to telling the Good News to people, but most of them have something in common with me. "This is one of the most important interviews I've ever had, and I'm not even sure I have the right conclusions." He turned in his seat to face her and continued, his intensity growing. "When I speak in vespers, or share my beliefs with someone, it's something I'm sure about. I'm sure that God loves us, God sent Christ to earth as a revelation of the Godhead, and Christ died to make it possible for our relationship with God to be made right. Even when we talk theology and things that are open to personal belief, it's still based on the things I know are true. "Now here we are, about to change the way a planet views its history, and I'm not even sure about the validity of my presuppositions."

He had started out speaking quietly to 'Shonya. But when he looked up, he saw his feelings echoed in the faces of everyone on the shuttle.

"Well put, Chaplain," the Captain's tone was quiet.

There was nothing else to say.

## CHAPTER TWENTY-NINE

A guide greeted them as they entered the city through an access porthole. "Welcome to Atex, the ruling center of the planet of Cutezar. If you will come with me, we will go immediately to the entrance of the transportation system."

The greeting was short and to the point. The guide led them past the ruling structure and down the covered walkway toward the first set of living structures. Stopping suddenly, the guide turned toward the covering and walked into a bubble protruding from the walkway.

Craig thought it looked like a viewing port, but was surprised when the guide motioned them inside. Everyone hesitated and finally the guide said, "We will go down."

Craig suddenly understood. "It's a turbo lift." He reached for 'Shonya's hand. "Let's go."

The guide nodded and motioned the rest of the group into the bubble, then spoke. A door slid into place, separating the bubble from the walkway and handrails slid up from the platform.

As it dropped through the tube, Craig sought support from rail hoping the sudden drop of the lift wouldn't bother him. When he opened his eyes, he was in the middle of an underground city. He waited until everyone exited.

'Shonya hesitated. "Jeff?" she called the doctor, worried about his sudden paleness.

Craig waved Jeff away, insisting, "I'm fine." Letting go of the rail, he followed the group and forgot his stomach as he looked around.

Cutezarians hurried everywhere in and out of doors clustered around a semi-circular wall of the huge circular cavern. Imagining they led to places of business, Craig speculated on the activities that took place beyond the openings.

To complete the circle, a tube came out of the wall opposite the doors and disappeared into the wall on the other side of the area.

Many Cutezarians stopped and looked at the visitors curiously but Craig could see they had been prepared for the humans' appearance. He nodded to the Cutezarians that approached him and continued his survey of the area.

Presently a car slid into the area, one side lifted and approximately thirty Cutezarians came out, looked at the humans, and went on their way.

Stones laid together in a tile-like manner covered the walls, floors, and ceilings. The colors were the same blues and reds in the layers of the stone mesas of the surface landscape.

Kneeling on one knee, Craig examined the pattern on the floor.

"Craig, are you coming?"

Craig didn't look up.

"Craig," 'Shonya repeated. There was no impatience in her voice because she realized his ability to shut out everything else and concentrate on the thing before him meant he was getting better. She smiled as he looked up in surprise and stood, dusting his hands and knee.

"Any time you're ready," Forest stuck his head out the door of the car.

Craig grinned and joined the group. The door slid into place and quiet descended.

"Roger, the designs on the floor are the same angular line designs as on the benches in Daniel K two," Craig broke the silence "But the color showing through is mostly red like the stone in the storage jars, with just a few blue like the illuminating stones."

"But the stones on every third row of the wall are blues," Roger replied.

"Quiet," 'Shonya ordered with a smile. "The guide is trying to talk."

The guide spoke. The metallic voice followed. "There are many such areas on the planet. All transportation is below the surface since travel above the surface is not possible after the darkness ritual. We have access to all areas of our planet through this system." They felt a sudden shift as they veered right. "Because of the storms on the surface nothing grows. We have developed ways to handle this problem. We would like you to see one of the places plants grow. Each city has an area like this. It provides our citizens with fabric for clothes and food as well as a place for diversion."

"A garden?" Forest asked.

"A place where things are cultivated, harvested and replanted," Oliver rephrased.

The Cutezarian spoke. The box hesitated then said, "Yes. Useful plants as well as those pleasing to the senses."

There were no more questions, and Craig listened to the pleasant hum of the car a few minutes, letting his mind wander. He was just considering the propulsion system when Roger asked about it.

"In the beginning, it was…" The box hesitated. "…Steam. Then, when our ancestors learned how to bypass the conversion and use the energy of the storm directly, implants in the cars and the passage way attract and repel each other to guide the car, while a unit pushes it forward."

"Magnetic polarization!" Forest exclaimed. "Extremely advanced magnetic polarization."

Silence returned.

"How fast are we traveling?" 'Shonya wondered aloud.

The box started to translate then faltered.

"How much space are we traveling through per time period?" Craig tried rephrasing the question.

The box translated that, but the guide remained puzzled. Finally, the guide spoke and the box translated a tentative question, "Speed?" The humans nodded. The guide hesitated then asked another question. "You measure speed?"

The group grinned and the Captain voiced their thoughts. "It's all right. For centuries, humans have been obsessed by speed. We think in terms of the question 'how fast?'"

The guide nodded. "When we must arrive quickly at our destination, we use the transporting beam."

"Rigid time schedules are not something the Cutezarians live by, I take it," Oliver noted.

"Time?" The guide asked through the metallic voice.

Craig laughed at 'Shonya's expression. "See what you started."

"Okay, who wants to tackle the human concept of time?" The Captain asked.

Oliver bravely volunteered. "Periods of light and dark cycles are divided into equal segments."

Craig took 'Shonya's hand, leaned his head back, and closed his eyes. Listening to the hum of the car and Oliver's musical voice, he relaxed. His mind wandered to the impending interview and the doubts returned. He frowned and felt his stomach churn uneasily.

"Don't think about it," 'Shonya urged.

Craig opened his eyes and turned his head. "What?"

"Whatever it was that made you frown and your stomach turn over." She said patting the hand rubbing his stomach.

"It's okay. As soon as we talk to the Cutezarians, I'll know if my conclusions are acceptable." He turned in the seat so he could see her better and told her what was worrying him and the reactions he anticipated. When they looked up everyone was standing in the open door of the car, waiting.

"At least you two can come walk in the garden," Captain Brodsky said with a grin.

Craig let go of 'Shonya's hand with a trace of self-consciousness, suddenly aware the Cutezarian guide might not understand their display of affection. However, the attention quickly shifted.

Carefully laid out in grids of about twenty meters square, the garden contained a great variety of plants. From front to back, each grid's plants were progressively taller, until the last rows of plants were taller than Oliver. Some appeared edible, some sported puffy flowers while others resembled weeds.

Despite the absence of brilliant colors, the smells and different shades of green blended with tans and browns delighted the human eye. The visitors wandered through the area examining the flowers and plants, guessing which plants provided food and which became textiles.

The guide allowed time to explore without offering further information about the plants. When they returned to the car, he explained as the box translated. "The filaments of the tall plants are refined and woven into stiff fabrics and the flowers of many plants are made into soft fabrics. The tubular roots of many of the plants are eaten and many of the leaves are edible. We have studied your eating habits, and will serve selected plants to you for the mid-day meal."

Jeff caught Craig's expression of interest, leaned over, and tapped him on the shoulder. "Uh-uh, Craig. Don't even look interested. Anything like salad would tear your system up. You're sticking to the routine: liquid on the ship and rest. You hear me?"

Craig grinned and made a face. "Ugh."

Captain Brodsky looked over his shoulder. "What's that Chaplain? I didn't quite understand your reply."

"Yes, sir, Doctor, sir," Craig replied in his best cadet style.

The group re-entered the car smiling, and as the door isolated them from outside sounds, their attention returned to the guide.

"Underground cultivation!" Oliver exclaimed. "How do they get enough light for photosynthesis?" he added.

"Light?" the box repeated; evidently the only concept it understood.

Forest laughed and tried his luck at explaining. "Yes, light, what is the source? We understand plants need light to grow tall and create colors."

The guide listened closely to the box, then nodded and replied. "Light is provided through the same system as the transportation system. The High Counselor will cover energy in the interview."

"How is the garden maintained?" 'Shonya asked.

"Those who find tending plants and growing things satisfying, choose to make it their existence's work. Some of the plants are harvested, others are allowed to grow out their cycle, and return to the soil to provide seed for the next cycle."

The train veered left, and before they could ask where they were going, the train slid to a stop. They had returned to their original destination. On surface, the guide prepared to leave them at the entrance of the ruling structure.

"We thank you," the Captain said formally. "Your information is appreciated."

310

After listening to the box's translation, the guide nodded. "We felt we could answer two of your questions at once by taking you to our source of food on the transportation system."

"Your tour raised many more questions," the Captain answered with a smile. "But we are a people who ask questions."

The guide's face lit up briefly, in what was the Cutezarian's expression of pleasure. "We knew that from the first time we contacted you. It attracted us to you." The guide stopped suddenly. "Now go to the council chambers, and the High Council will answer more of your questions." Nodding, the guide left them standing in the entrance of the ruling structure.

A bit dazed at how far they had traveled in a short time, the humans stared at each other a few seconds before finding their voices.

Craig shook his head and broke the silence with one final question. "How do the plants get water?"

"I haven't the slightest idea," 'Shonya responded with a smile, pushing him toward the entrance.

The interior of the structure had three levels like the library. Huge rooms lined the corridor of the shelf-like second floor. The tables in the second-level rooms were nearly as long as the room, with chairs along both sides and ends. They reminded Craig of the pictures he'd seen of old fashioned conference or boardrooms.

Oliver looked into one of the rooms and groaned.

"Oliver, what's wrong?" Captain Brodsky stopped and strained to see around the doctor's tall frame.

"The chairs, Alan, look at the chairs."

Following Oliver's gaze, the Captain burst into laughter.

"What's so funny?" Forest demanded.

"We forgot how small the Cutezarians are and how long Oliver's legs are in comparison," the Captain finally said.

"It's going to be a long morning." Oliver moved on shaking his head.

They were still smiling as they were ushered into the room where the High Council waited. Dortec, the Chief Communicator, greeted them.

"Welcome humans. You met some of us when we visited your ship: Bartez, chief of those who build, Rachax, the chief of those who govern, and Ventez, the chief of those who meditate." The box translated the words govern and meditate without its earlier hesitation.

"Please, be seated. We understand our time is limited. We hope you do not require a specific greeting ritual."

"We are pleased to be here. It will not offend us to set aside the usual diplomatic greetings," the Captain answered with a smile.

"Then we will begin." Dortec nodded and addressed the entire group. "What you will now see is compiled from the requests your captain relayed to us." He smiled and added. "You wish to know much, so the journey through our society will be abbreviated." The Chief Communicator motioned and an aide spoke to the computer. Panels from the front wall parted and a viewing screen appeared.

The meeting room had no table, and armless chairs sat randomly around the room so it resembled the viewing rooms on the ship. The group surveyed the short-legged chairs and grinned at each other as they took their seats.

Oliver sat in the front row so there would be room for his legs, and stretched out. The others stepped over him as they chose their seats. 'Shonya slid her chair as close to Craig as she dared. Resisting the urge to pull her closer, he settled for draping his arm against the back of her chair and stretched out his legs as the room came alive with images.

Forcing himself to put aside the almost overwhelming awareness of 'Shonya's distracting presence, he concentrated on the metallic voice providing the prerecorded narration.

"When our ancestors discovered the illuminating stones emitted energy, civilization as we know it began," the voice informed them. A room appeared, illuminated by the trays of stones. "However, as we evolved we needed illumination during the times between energy stone regeneration." The file showed huge craters of stones set in circles, exposed to the full effect of the storms. "We began creating ways to store the stone's energy. This is the result."

A compound resembling a generating plant appeared, ringed with huge boulders of the carved illuminating stones. Wires, wound around the stones, led from them into several pyramids. As they watched, the first plant was transformed into a series of updated versions.

In the last version, one set of rocks became the energy source and others were heated in liquid to produce a second source of power, steam, which provided power for a series of converters. The narration said these converters collected the storm's static and stored it for use.

But they were onto the next subject before Craig could figure out how the electricity was distributed.

"The illuminating stones are also used in all structures. The upper rows of each structure are made of these stones." The voice continued as the city appeared in a three-dimensional graph model. "And the same stones are placed below the city. During the great storms, the peaks of the structures interrupt the flow of the energy and force it under the walkway to the tones under the city. Both the stones in the peaks and under the city receive a charge so they push against each other enabling…" The graph showed the current flow around and under the city "…The city to reside above the ground."

"That takes care of Alan's question," 'Shonya whispered.

"Electromagnetic energy?" Craig whispered back. She nodded, and when they looked back to the screen, a familiar model had appeared.

And a new subject was introduced. The translation box resembled the one the ancient Cutezarians carried off the ship upon landing on ancient earth. The metallic voice continued. "The box that translates ideas was developed because of an ancient directive from the Spirit of All Things. This directive told our ancestors to travel and awaken in the inhabitants of other worlds the knowledge that the Spirit of All Things exists and reaches out to communicate with all beings."

The English translation was awkward, and Craig repeated it several times to himself. When he finally understood, he suddenly pulled his legs up and sat forward, resisting the sudden urge to jump up and demand the computer to freeze so he could ask questions.

But 'Shonya, having also worked through the translation, anticipated his reaction and patted his back. Relaxing, he sat back and grinned with a small disbelieving shake of his head.

Meanwhile, the box continued the narration. "Before the time of shame many journeys were taken. Our ancestors used this box to translate their words as they obeyed the Spirit of All Things. After the time of privacy began…"

While the voice continued, the computer displayed a series of changing boxes, ending with the small personal sized box the Cutezarians currently carried and the larger model for group participation. "…We continued developing the device, keeping up with any changes in Cutezarian dialects. Also, there has always been a group of Cutezarians working on the device. We knew we would eventually be discovered, or the Spirit of All Things would signal the time for following the ancient directive had returned."

A general stirring among the humans told Craig others had concluded their preliminary thoughts were correct, and the speaker was indeed referring to a spirit sending the Cutezarians on journeys. Earth had been but one of many stops.

Craig sighed, realizing if they were correct about the second journey to Earth, a great civilization had cut themselves off from interplanetary life because of something they witnessed on earth.

Suddenly restless, he unfolded himself from the short chair, went to the back of the room, leaned against the wall, and crossed his arms.

Jeff let him stand alone a while then joined him. "Craig?"

Craig lifted his head and smiled. "I'm okay. It's so much more than I hoped to learn, I've got to sort it out."

"And that's causing stress you don't need," the doctor grumbles as he fished the hypo rod out of his medical kit.

"No. It's too soon to resort to medication," Craig objected.

"I put together a series of very small doses to control your body's reaction to stress. Now relax," he commanded.

With a sigh of defeat, Craig slumped against the wall and allowed the doctor access to his neck vein. "I think I'll hate injections for the rest of my life," he muttered, moving his head from side to side to stretch the muscles and ease the sting.

"You'll get over it." Jeff's tone was more sympathetic than his words.

In a few minutes, Craig relaxed as the ache in his stomach eased.

The presentation ended with a model of the planet Cutezar. "There are thirty major living areas." The model rotated and the humans could see their locations. Most of them were located away from the area of the tells. "Each is connected to the others by the transportation system, grows its own food, has its own variation of language, its own ruling council, a building for community gatherings, and its own protection and cloaking devices.

"Only this city has the structure for holding of public information. Other cities access this information, or come here to study the public information. It is also in this city where disputes that are not solved in other cities are presented to the High Council. We believe the Human's word is capital, although we do not completely understand the concept." The computer screen went blank, and the metallic voice concluded, "Any further questions can be directed to those at this presentation."

Sudden, thoughtful silence filled the room.

Captain Brodsky finally spoke. "May we request a break, Chief Communicator?"

"That is acceptable," the box answered.

Oliver gratefully pushed himself to his feet and walked around the room, stopping to talk to Craig. "I am considering the possibility of rearranging our presentations. Perhaps they will affect the Cutezarians as much as their presentation did us."

Craig grinned at his choice of words. "It'd be a good idea to start slower." He reached for 'Shonya's arm as she went by. "Oliver and I think we need to change the order of our presentations."

She considered. "Like what?"

"Save Craig's presentation until last. Put mine first to give them an idea about the use of stone and ancient culture. Then yours to establish our home planet and let them get over that shock, then Craig's to show them what happened," Oliver explained. "Forest was going to discuss specific ancient sites of stone carving, techniques of cutting the stones, and cultic rites associated with those sites, but he feels we need to establish the link between the two planets first. He'll do his presentation this afternoon or tomorrow, depending on how things progress."

"Craig, can you handle this?" Shonya asked in concern.

"I think I'll be fine," he said cautiously. "I want to watch the Cutezarians put things together."

"Okay, let's tell the Captain and get on with it."

She stepped away, and it surprised Craig to find he had to let go of her hand. He didn't remember taking it, but was amused that it had become such a natural action for them both. She smiled gently and went to find the Captain.

The Cutezarians signaled they were ready to start again, and Captain Brodsky spoke first. "Because you have been so kind to let us view so much of your culture, we wish to present some conclusions we have drawn. In light of new ideas your presentations have given us, we wish to change the order in which our presentations are given."

He waited until the box finished translating then introduced Dr. Zamwashi.

Oliver stood and first addressed the computer. "Computer, Zamwashi file, five six nine." As the computer began the display, he addressed the Cutezarians. "The images you will see are from our ancestors. They are computer re-creations of ancient cities and structures."

Images of the Egyptian pyramids appeared in the room. The Cutezarians leaned forward, recognizing the familiar

317

shape. Oliver didn't comment directly on their interest, but started generically. "Most of Earth's truly ancient societies worked with stone. These are the pyramids of Africa, a place called Egypt."

The computer continued, switching to South American scenes.

"This Aztec temple, built by ancient inhabitants of Mexico, is half way around the world from Egypt," Oliver continued. "Workers of the ancient China's first ruler, Qin Shi Huang, constructed this tomb and magnificent statues. They are part of a huge multitude of warriors outside the tomb." Rows of life sized terra-cotta archers, infantrymen, cavalry troops, charioteers, and horses entered the room.

"This city was built by ancient Africans. Its design is different from the others, yet it is made of stone." A recreation of Zimbabwe sprang to life.

"And finally, this is a temple from a place we call Cambodia." The computer showed the ancient intricate carvings of the Angkor Wat, now a fully restored Buddhist monastery.

"You can see each place is different, yet we feel the ancient people may have gained the knowledge of working with stone from some common ancient experience. As societies matured, some learned to make bricks. Bricks are manufactured blocks of stone made of earth and straw or other material. Some people lost their ability to work in stone, and some continue to carve and build from stone much as the first builders did. Some didn't build at all from stone, but carved images instead. These are statues carved from stone which were found on an island known as Easter Island."

The computer displayed the statue and the Cutezarians gasped in surprise as they watched it revolve, displaying all sides of the magnificent carving.

Without further comment, Oliver ended his presentation, returned to his chair, and stretched his legs out in front of him.

Captain Brodsky let the Cutezarians study the last image, then got up, and commanded the computer to cease display. "We are aware of the nature of the information we are displaying and how it relates to your planet, but let us continue before we stop to discuss the material. Dr. LaShonya Reed will continue."

Still it took five minutes before the Cutezarians calmed down enough to listen. Craig felt compassion for them. He knew what was yet to come.

"Computer, display Reed, file systems one." 'Shonya waited until the computer projected a moving model of earth's solar system before continuing. "As you can see, all the planets in our system revolve around a huge star we call the sun, and at the same time they rotate on an imaginary axis." She let them study the model before continuing.

"Although we inhabit other planets in our star system, our home planet is this one." She pointed out Earth. "The third planet from the sun." The image showed a close up of Earth. "Unlike your planet with one land mass, ours has a major land mass on each side, with several smaller ones."

The computer switched to a simulation of ancient earth before the division of the land. After briefly showing the separating process, the display switched to a three dimensional display of the ancient Cutezarian's journey.

Unable to control his restlessness, Craig moved to the far left wall so he could watch the present day Cutezarians' reactions as they recognized their own record of their ancestors' last journey.

First, they showed disbelief. As the computer superimposed their record's close up of Earth over the one 'Shonya displayed, their facial expressions shifted between dismay and excitement. Leaving their chairs, they gathered around the image.

Forest joined Craig to check on him. "You holding up ok?"

Craig nodded and grinned as he whispered. "We must have looked like that when we discovered the Cutezarians landed on Earth."

"Yeah, and I know how they feel," he whispered back.

Captain Brodsky and Jeff joined Craig by the wall as the Cutezarians continued their silent inspection of the display.

As the images of the journey progressed, 'Shonya finished her narration. "If someone landed on this land mass and showed the people how to cut stone, the knowledge could have dispersed over our planet."

The computer superimposed a globe over the final approach of the ancient ship and marked the sites of pyramids or stone carvings from Oliver's presentation.

With a growing smile, Craig watched the Cutezarians' reactions. They pointed to Africa then thoughtfully traced a line across to Peru.

Roger twisted in is chair. "Craig, you're right, the Cutezarians visited Earth more than once!"

Realizing the implications, the Cutezarians' somber expressions reflected deep thoughts and questions. Their focus turned to 'Shonya, seemingly waiting for her to confirm their thoughts. 'Shonya looked over at the group gathered by the wall.

Captain Brodsky nodded and mouthed, "Tell them."

Returning her attention to the Cutezarians, she very deliberately said, "The beings your ancestors shared their message with on the third planet from the sun of the third galaxy from yours." She paused. "Were our ancestors."

The Cutezarians suddenly withdrew to a distant corner away from the translation box and intently discussed the information. The discussion lasted so long the humans became concerned the Cutezarians were going to reject the information and send them away before hearing the rest of the story.

"Craig, maybe you'd better see what you can do," Captain Brodsky quietly ordered.

Craig picked up one of the personal sized translation boxes and approached them, sensing their apprehension. Uncertainly he held the box out to Dortec for activation.

After a brief hesitation, Dortec spoke to the box then motioned Craig to speak. It was Craig's turn to hesitate. In the brief silence, he prayed, "Give me the right words, exactly the right words."

Slowly delivering his carefully chosen words, he began, "I know what your ancestors found when they returned and landed on the other side of the world from the first landing. I think they visited the ancestors of people we know as Aztecs and Incas. We assume this because of markings on the ground. Humans have speculated that they seemed to be landing sites to be observed from above. They are located on earth in the area you see marked on the map. On the second journey your ancestors found human sacrifice. They saw spiritual leaders, also known as witch doctors, tearing out the hearts of living beings. They found buildings of stone and ancient civilizations that worshiped animals and strange spirits from the sky. What they witnessed so horrified them they immediately came back here, never to leave their planet again, convinced of their failure." Craig stopped, holding his breath. He'd taken an awful chance.

After a long, suspense-filled minute, Dortec reluctantly nodded. "You are correct."

Encouraged, Craig quietly urged, "Come back. Sit down. Let me tell you the rest of it."

Warily the Cutezarians consented. Craig pulled up a chair, turned it around so the back was toward the Cutezarians, leaned his arms wearily on it and stretched out his legs, finding himself on the same level of the smaller Beings. Looking up, he found all eyes focused in his direction.

He stalled, running his fingers through his hair, praying for strength. His stomach hurt and massaging didn't help. Dr. Keal noted the symptoms. Silently he stepped over, tilted Craig's head slightly, and quickly injected the medication. Craig accepted the doctor's attention without comment, rubbing the entry point to ease the sting.

Taking a deep breath before starting, Craig repeated his prayer, "Give me the right words."

"Can I assume you all have studied the journey Dr. Reed spoke of?" he asked tentatively, not sure where to start.

After a short consultation, Dortec spoke and the box translated. "We have."

Craig nodded. "Okay. Let's go back to the beginning. We believe your ancestors visited ours at a time in our history before we possessed knowledge of traveling over the waters. When that knowledge was perfected, those who left their original homelands carried distant memories of the visit and knowledge of stone cutting. You'll notice the people who lived closest to the place your ancestors visited built structures most like those your ancestors built. The people farther away came up with new designs or modified the original shape.

"Even those who did not build remembered something and carved what they remembered best, the shape of your ancestors' heads and carved the huge statues of Easter Island." Craig finished his summary and took a deep breath to get ready for the rest. His tension eased a little and the ache in his stomach subsided as the medication took effect.

Jeff watched Craig relax, thinking, "I wish the small doses lasted longer, or that I could give him larger doses without interfering with his thinking or control. But then he'd have too much in his system, and I couldn't sedate him later, and he might really need it."

Craig continued. "But there was more than a building process left in the memories of my ancestors. They misunderstood your ancestors' message about the Spirit of All Things. They thought your ancestors were deities and worshiped them instead of your Spirit of All Things." He paused to let the box finish the translation. Then he let the silence grow as his listeners processed the idea. And he worried as they shook their heads in denial and consternation.

"Why?" the box finally asked.

"You may not realize the people were primitive. Your ancestors came from the sky where the sun resided. They were unlike anything like humans had ever seen before. What makes me think they erroneously worshiped your ancestors are many stories, we call them myths, refer to spirits from the sky. These stories occur in various forms throughout our planet. From the beginning of storytelling, the dwelling place of the mythical deities was the sky. Even as our understanding of the Creator grew, we tend to think of our final resting place as being in the sky."

That sent the Cutezarians into another discussion. "This is not what we meant," the box said, echoing their despair.

Craig plunged on. "But remember the goal of your ancestors was to awaken the awareness of the existence of the Spirit of All Things in the beings they visited. And on Earth, this was accomplished."

Another discussion erupted. "I'm never going to finish," Craig thought wearily.

Dortec again answered for the group. "This cannot be, for the record of the second journey shows things far from our understanding of the Spirit of All Things."

"Yes," Craig answered carefully, "I know. But if I understand what you said earlier, your ancestors defined their purpose as 'to prepare other beings to accept the revelation of the Spirit of All Things by awakening them to the existence of the Spirit of All Things.'" He stopped and waited until they agreed. "That implies the ability to know the Spirit of All Things existed in other beings besides yourselves. Either that knowledge had not yet become part of the conscious belief, or they had known the Spirit of All Things and that knowledge was forgotten or ignored." He stopped again.

After listening to the translation twice, his audience agreed.

"Although my ancestors did not follow the intended direction, your ancestors' mission was accomplished," he continued. "The existence of a spirit greater than themselves persists in all of forms of Earth's myths. In these stories, the spirits dwelt first in the sky then came to Earth, taking on many forms. What your ancestors witnessed on their second journey was the beginning."

Conversation interrupted him. Craig waited for quiet, then continued, "Let me change directions and tell you how your ancestors' mission was accomplished in the end.

"I'm going to go back to the first record. Remember the worker who fell and the funeral that followed?" The audience nodded. "They sprinkled some of the fallen one's blood on the grave. Why do you do that?"

Ventez answered. "It is our way of acknowledging the life force and shell are no longer together."

Craig accepted the explanation. "I think my ancestors misunderstood this action because, as civilizations began to form, it became a tradition to shed blood in the context of worship and sacrifice."

Craig suddenly felt his emotions rising, got up, and paced in his excitement, worried he wasn't presenting the concepts well. He took a deep breath and plunged on.

"For an unimaginable number of years, variations of blood sacrifice took place all over our world. Some cultures used merely the best and purest animals. Some sacrificed perfect children or young women untouched by a male, or a perfect male child. In some cultures blood of any living thing was believed to appease the deities, while others tore the hearts out of living beings."

Resuming his sitting position, Craig faced the Cutezarians.

"Our specific word for the Deity we worship is God. God used this tradition born of a misunderstanding and taught a race of people called the Israelites, to use the blood sacrifice as a way to express sorrow for not putting God above all other things and people in their life. In this way God made right the relationship between God and these ancient people." He stopped to let the Cutezarians digest the terminology and concept. Uncertain of how his presentation was being understood he became restless and got up to pace.

"You have quite a grasp of the theories of the development of religion," Captain Brodsky remarked as they met in the back of the room.

"How do you think I got interested in archeology except through history?" Craig grinned. "There are other theories and always will be. But none of them ever satisfied me. Too much left to chance."

"Like what?" Oliver, also walking to stretch his legs joined them.

Craig checked the Cutezarians before getting involved in the conversation. They were still consulting each other, asking the computer to repeat his last statements. "Well, the one with the longest life says the early people worshiped things that gave them the ability to exist: the earth, the sun, and the spirits who made things grow. And they began to do things to appease the spirits. These practices culminated in human or blood sacrifices, and that is what God used to introduce atonement for sins."

"Perhaps both theories are different parts of the same one," Oliver suggested. "If the ancient people had the blood ceremony in corporate memory, it could account for the escalation of rituals into blood sacrifices."

Craig nodded thoughtfully. "Maybe. That's a good idea. Now we get to the important part," he added, noting the Cutezarians were getting restless. He resumed his former position with a small sigh, beginning to feel the strain of responsibility. If he didn't get this message across, he feared the Cutezarians might withdraw even further from the universe around them. Taking a deep breath, he prepared his thoughts.

"Shall we continue, or do you want to discuss anything before we go on?" He stretched his legs as casually as possible to keep the Cutezarians from sensing his tension.

"Finish. Then we will discuss." Dortec spoke through the box. "But we wish you to explain 'chosen people'."

Craig studied Dortec as he spoke. He had a fleeting feeling the Chief Communicator's expression had changed from puzzlement to either understanding or excitement. He couldn't tell.

"Okay. God choose a certain people to be an example for all peoples and nations in order to show how the Deity would relate to those who followed God's commandments. But these particular people failed their part of the agreement, so in the end God used the blood sacrifice to show all humans God's love for them." Craig hesitated. "Do you have a concept for love?"

After translation, the Cutezarians nodded. "The action of putting the good of another above all else in one's thoughts, feelings and actions," the box answered.

"Now which direction do I go?" Craig asked himself. "Keep it basic," came the reply from somewhere inside. To the Cutezarians he said, "God very much wanted to make right the relationship that had gone wrong. God tried again. This time God chose an individual instead of a nation to illustrate this relationship. An offspring, we say son—a male child—was sent to live with and know human experiences and to show a living example of the right relationship with God. Humans understand how much a good father loves his children, and how much anguish it is when an offspring dies.

"To prove God's love to the stubborn creation, humans, he allowed the final blood sacrifice to be the blood of his offspring - the Son of God. He allowed the ancient people to put his son to death. By doing this, God opened the way for the relationship to be made right between God and people." Craig stopped, weary and afraid he hadn't said it well. He rubbed his forehead and ran his fingers through his hair.

After deactivating the translation box, the Cutezarians engaged in what appeared to be a heated debate. Finally, Dortec activated the box and, as if he knew the effect of what he was about to say would have on Craig, asked, "Are you speaking of what humans have called salvation?"

Craig grabbed the back of the chair and leaned back. His breath came out in gasps. At first, he had to concentrate just to breathe normally. Then he searched for the right words—any words. The whiteness of shock filled his mind. It refused to give him anything. He cleared his throat. He got a little air, but it didn't help him think.

'Shonya was afraid he was about to pass out as the blood drained from his face. Then as his knuckles turned white, she was afraid the back of the small chair would snap. Desperately she wanted to put her arms around him and tell everything was ok. She could only pray.

Jeff got to his feet and started forward with the injection rod, but Craig recovered, shook his head, and waved the doctor back.

"I'm okay, Jeff. Thanks," he managed, sounding strangled. He swallowed and turned back to the Cutezarians. "Does that word hold a concept for you, or did your computer translate it from our vocabulary?"

Dortec's expression was one of pleasure. "The night of the reception I requested permission from your Captain to study the history of your beliefs in the deities. You see, I too am—what was your word? Curious. But not knowing your ancestors were the beings our ancestors visited on their last journey, I missed the significance of the symbols. I was not sure until now you were speaking of the same people and a relationship with their God."

Not so surprised as before, Craig laughed shakily. "Well," he asked, "how did I do?"

Dortec got up and approached Craig. The translator's metallic voice said, "I think, Chaplain Craig Lea, you are a fine teacher. And we have much to discuss. Now let us refresh ourselves with nourishment."

But Jeff intervened. "The Chaplain, because of the damage done to his system during the electrical storm, is to follow a very strict diet, and must return to his living quarters to rest. We will let you know when he is able to return."

"Do you agree?" Dortec asked Craig.

Craig nodded wearily. "I see the wisdom of his instruction. May I return?"

"You are welcome," Dortec answered. "This afternoon we will speak with the scientists. Thank you for your information. It will be shared with all for consideration. We will be patient in waiting for your return."

Dortec turned to the doctor. "Will the rest of you join us in the public meeting place for nourishment?"

"Yes. Go ahead. I'll be there after the Chaplain has returned to the ship."

Craig crossed his arms on the back of the chair and laid his forehead on them with a sigh.

"And you, Craig, go to sickbay. Pick up the formula and go straight to your quarters. Maybe you can have visitors tonight and maybe not."

Craig nodded without lifting his head.

'Shonya laid a hand on his shoulder. "You okay?"

Lifting his head, Craig rested his chin on his arms and grinned tiredly. "I'm not sure. Exhausted, shaky, nervous inside. Jittery. My stomach hurts. But I think I'll live." He stood and looked at her a long time, wanting to hold her, but knowing he shouldn't. "I'd like to stay, but I'm going to collapse if I don't get some rest." Putting his hand on his physician's shoulder, he touched 'Shonya's hand briefly, and signaled the transporter tech to beam him aboard.

"He'll be all right in a few days if he rests." Jeff sought to relieve the distress in 'Shonya's eyes.

"I hope so," she replied with so much feeling, the doctor did a double take, realizing she'd solved the questions about her feelings for Craig. And he knew her answer.

## CHAPTER THIRTY

After the vegetarian lunch, Dr. Keal returned to the ship to make rounds with the staff and check on his private patient. The formula he'd ordered contained as much sedative as he dared give Craig at once.

Craig's gray complexion and the darkening circles under his eyes as the morning had progressed worried the doctor. It was same the look as - Jeff didn't want to think about the first crisis in sickbay. Notifying sickbay, he ordered a transport to the Chaplain's quarters.

At Craig's door, he spoke to the computer. "Computer, medical emergency. Override security code and open door."

Craig was lying on one side, curled up on the sofa, his back braced against the sofa's back. Jeff pulled up the small stool that did double duty as extra seating and footrest, and ran the life reader over Craig's torso. He got the same mismatched readings as immediately following the charge. Sighing, he muttered. "I shouldn't have allowed it."

"Allowed what?" He looked up and met Craig's gaze. "You shouldn't be awake."

Craig grinned slightly and closed his eyes. "I'm not."

"You put more effort into this morning than anything since the funeral, and the stress almost did you in," the doctor lectured. "I should have stopped you," he added.

Craig turned onto his back. "It's okay, Jeff," he said wearily.

The door opened to admit the tech with the transport. "I'm taking you to sickbay for a full battery of tests." Jeff explained the transport. "Craig?"

He stopped. Craig was no longer listening. Motioning to the tech he added, "Help me get him onto the transport."

In a way Craig's semi-awareness reassured him. At least they weren't completely back to square one. Craig slept until they moved him to the examining table and when the doctor looked down from the panel, he met Craig's sleepy gaze.

"You're just napping when you need to be sleeping." The doctor scolded unhappily.

"Only part of me wants to sleep," Craig murmured.

Studying the readouts, Jeff lectured, "No wonder you're only napping, your adrenaline level is twice the normal level. You are not returning to the surface soon. Get used to that idea." Craig nodded solemnly. "You simply have to relax, let the medication work, and give your nerves a chance to get untangled."

"How?" Craig asked.

"I don't know. I don't dare give you any more medication. Try some deep breathing exercises."

"You serious?"

"Yes. The readings indicate your pulmonary volume is also way down, like an asthma attack."

"I think I held my breath all morning," Craig confessed wearily.

"Ok. Ten deep breathes. I think that was the standard for relaxation exercises," the doctor commanded.

"Ready?" Craig nodded reluctantly. "Breathe."

By the fifth breath, Craig was beginning to drift, and by the last one, his eyes closed as he gradually let the medication take over.

Keeping close watch on the readings for a couple of hours, Jeff was pleased to note Craig's heart rate gradually slowed to match the pulmonary rate, and the chemical balance reestablished itself. By late afternoon, Craig's normal color began replacing the dark cast, and Jeff felt he could leave his patient alone.

Back in his office, he replayed the ancient Cutezarian's trip to earth and reviewed Craig's presentation. Then he watched it again.

"Remarkable," he said aloud. Humbled, his concept of God broadened, he re-examined his own relationship with God.

"Jeff?" 'Shonya hailed him.

"Yes, 'Shonya?"

"We're back. Where's Craig?" She sounded anxious.

"I took him to sickbay to run a full set of scans, and left him there with the med tech," he answered without letting her know his own concern.

"I was worried. He reminded me of," she trailed off, not wanting to put the crisis into words.

"Um-hum," the doctor answered. "Me too. The readings were like before. But he woke up fairly soon, and his systems seem back in sync. I'll keep him overnight and see how he is in the morning. You can go by tonight."

"Not till then?" she asked.

"No." He answered in a very firm tone.

"All right," she hesitated. He could hear the emotion in her voice as she added, "Thanks." She signed off abruptly, overcome by her own emotion.

"Yep, I was right. Our CSO is in love with our Chaplain," he thought. And he celebrated.

**

Craig was still sleeping when 'Shonya entered the isolation room. But he seemed restless. Hoping for some kind of reaction, she touched him, and it enchanted her when he grew quiet.

"Even while he's asleep, he responds to me," she thought.

She suddenly felt anxious as she realized the depth of relationship his response implied.

Willing away her doubts, she found a chair and unfolded her computer. She called up the record of the Cutezarian's trip to earth. Then she reviewed Craig's presentation. "God, help me grasp you are indeed the creator of all things, and put into action respect for all things and beings. Help me remove the boundaries I've created for you. Help me know you are always at work in my life."

As she reflected, she looked up and realized Craig was in trouble. Dampness glistened on his forehead as he became increasing restless. Suddenly pulling his pillow from under his head, he started to toss it across the room. 'Shonya quickly took his arm and touched his face.

"Craig!" she called. "Bill?" She activated the room's comm unit.

"Dr. Reed?" came the answer.

"Get Dr. Keal here as soon as possible. Craig's is having a recurrence of the dream."

"Right."

'Shonya pried Craig's fingers from hers and touched his face again. "It's okay, Craig, it's only a dream." She brushed his hair back. "Craig wake up!"

Craig turned his head toward her voice. In the dream, he stood in the middle of an electrical field, trying to explain why God existed. But every time he came to his conclusion, the field strengthened and threatened to choke him. Someone kept calling his name. When he located the direction of the sound, he turned and saw 'Shonya standing outside the electrical field, calling his name. He fought to free himself of the restraining field, but only got more entangled.

Jeff hurried into the room to find 'Shonya trying to keep Craig quiet. He helped her restrain Craig's arms.

"Craig! You must relax. It's a dream," he insisted, hoping to reach him.

Craig felt something restraining his arms, forcing him to relax.

"Craig, relax and it will be over," Jeff continued.

In the electrical field, Craig heard Jeff's voice and turned toward it.

Jeff felt Craig's efforts and repeated, "Craig, relax." He looked at 'Shonya. "'Shonya, hold both arms, I'll get his shoulders." She nodded. "Okay, shift position. Now." As they sifted positions, they could feel the tension in his body began to ebb. "That's it, Craig, relax," Jeff soothed.

In the dream, Craig thought, "If I do what they say, maybe the field will weaken." He felt the continued pressure on his shoulders and arms, and since he couldn't move, forced himself to relax.

"That's it, Craig, it's over, it's just the dream," Jeff kept talking.

Suddenly freed from the electrical field, Craig felt release. Yet 'Shonya and Jeff couldn't reach him. He could only hear their voices. He approached the meter high barrier that separated them. He knew had to get over it and gingerly stepped up on it. It held him. Suddenly freed, he stepped down to the ground.

And opened his eyes.

"Craig?" Jeff repeated his name.

It took Craig a few seconds to focus on their faces and realize they were restraining him.

"Jeff? 'Shon? What?" Then he took a deep breath and sighed. "It's okay. I'm awake."

Jeff removed his hands with a small pat of assurance and activated the panel. 'Shonya let go of his arms and took his hand. Craig wearily closed his eyes.

'Shonya broke the slightly embarrassed silence. "What was it about?" Craig frowned. "The dream."

He considered, reconstructing its strangeness. "I was trying to conduct a very important theological discussion." He started with a grin, and ended with a sigh. "But I was imprisoned in an electrical field that went from the floor to the ceiling, a column kind of thing. Every time I came to my conclusion, it tightened around me and I couldn't finish what I wanted to say. And I couldn't get out. Then I could hear you both, and feel the pressure holding me still," he stopped.

Jeff looked down from the panel. "We get the idea, don't get worked up again." He watched the panel as Craig nodded and took a deep breath. "That's better." He pulled up a stool. "The dream occurred as the medication's effects wore off; probably a result of this morning's stress."

Craig nodded again. They were all aware the electrical storm and Craig's presentation to the Cutezarians were mixed together in the dream.

"The good thing is your readings returned to what's normal for you right now much quicker than before. But you're not improving the condition of your stomach by getting all worked up." He stopped. "End of lecture. But if you're going to continue these talks, you have to find a way to stay calm."

"I don't think it will be such a strain next time. It'll just be application and theology now." Craig tried to assure himself as well as the doctor.

'Shonya laughed. "I don't even have to look at Jeff's readings to know every time you even think about it your blood pressure goes up."

335

"Okay, so I'm excited. I'll do my best to keep it under control."

"Well, right now, you're going to stay the night here, and in the morning I'll decide what you're going to do," the doctor interrupted. "Here. Drink. I left out the sedative." He handed Craig a glass of the formula. "You shouldn't sleep all the time."

"What do you suggest I do?"

"Anything but leave sickbay."

"Am I allowed to ask why I'm confined?" Craig asked softly, without challenge.

"First of all, when I came to your quarters, your color was gray; as bad as right after your first encounter with the storm. Second, although they corrected themselves quickly, your readings were jumbled like before. Besides that, in your dream you incorporated the two things that frustrate you most right now: the residual effects of the charge and the fact that it keeps you from presenting your thoughts as clearly as you would like. And I'm not sure how you'll react tonight or tomorrow. We're going to have scans, constant monitoring, extra injections into the lining of your stomach, and if you don't behave, isolation. Got it?"

"Yes, thank you," Craig said meekly with a grin, handing him the empty glass.

"Okay, now talk a few minutes, I'll be back."

"I think you scared him," 'Shonya commented, watching Jeff's retreating back.

Craig nodded. "When I woke up, I didn't know if he was mad at me or himself. He kept muttering something about 'shouldn't have allowed it.'" He drew her onto the bed. "Now tell me what new things you learned."

With shinning eyes, she sat facing him and smiled. "First of all, they admitted we looked familiar to them, but they weren't sure if it was because of the ancient records, or because our small round heads remind them of their children." Craig leaned forward in surprise. She gently pushed him back. "But then, their children outgrow the condition," she finished with a grin.

It caught him by surprise and he laughed aloud. "They outgrow the condition?"

"I don't know if they were serious or if they have a sense of humor." Her smile widened. "And sure enough, they brought their children to visit, and they all have round heads. Beautiful little beings with perfect round heads. The adults treat them with distant affection."

"What else?" Craig settled back to listen.

"Their space technology is indeed still in place. Two cities of the planet have kept the technology alive ever since the time of shame and even now continue developing new research.

"It seems after the time of great shame the Cutezarians were released from the commandment to travel to other places and prepare other beings for The Spirit of All Thing's revelation." Craig's eyes widened and his mouth opened. "But that's not all." She didn't give him time to say anything. "They've put all their energy into making sure all Cutezarians know the Spirit of All Things in a way that's unique to each individual."

"Hold it. You sound like you're talking about a personal relationship with God as we understand it." Craig interrupted.

"When I substitute 'God' for 'The Spirit of All Things,' I can't help it." She chuckled. "And that's not all. All these centuries they've been waiting for some event to act as a signal for them to resume the journeys of their ancestors."

"What?" was all Craig could get out.

"Stop that!" The command came from the door.

"Stop what?" 'Shonya asked, surprised.

"Whatever it is that's making the readings do that." Jeff pointed to the panels.

With a grin, Craig laid his head back and forced his body to relax.

The doctor smiled at Craig's instant obedience. "At least you're learning. Seriously, Craig..." he shook a finger for emphasis. "If you want to go back to the planet in the next week, you've simply got to relax."

Jeff escorted 'Shonya out of the room saying, "Say goodnight, 'Shonya. It's time for doctor things." All she could do was wave over her shoulder. However, as he pushed her out Jeff comforted, "You can come back after dinner and say goodnight properly."

Craig endured the tests and injections from his all too serious doctor. Finally, they both began to relax: Craig because the treatments always cooled the ache in his stomach, and Jeff because of Craig's rate of recovery from the encounter.

The last test finished, they settled down to talk. Craig sighed and leaned back against the bed.

"Did I wear you out?" Craig nodded. "Sorry." Jeff was quiet a minute, getting his words together. "Okay, Chaplain, here's what we've got—." He stopped at Craig's grimace.

"What?"

"You only call me 'Chaplain' when it's official, and I haven't liked that too much lately." Craig grinned.

"Well, this is official, but not that bad," the doctor responded. "Ready?"

"Ummmm," Craig still wasn't sure.

"The bad part is your extreme reaction to the stress. I was afraid you were in real trouble. The good part is that you've recovered fairly quickly. It's..." He checked his watch. "...Six-thirty and your readings are close to the ones this morning. But you didn't help the inflammation by the stress in between." He stopped.

"So," Craig prompted.

"So, because you recovered this quickly, I'll let you go back. But..."

"I'm not going to like this," Craig muttered.

The doctor ignored the interruption. "I'm going to try gradual addition of solids to your diet again starting next week. We'll keep the half-day schedule, but change the type of sedatives I prescribe. I'm getting nervous about the prolonged use of these drugs. And I have a problem with that because since I've forced you to actually sleep afternoons, your condition has gradually improved. So, we're going to continue that indefinitely with lighter sedation." Craig groaned. "We're setting the return visit back to Monday, for two reasons. You. And Dorinda's ready to deliver any day. The good news is, if you behave yourself, I may allow you to hold vespers Sunday." He laughed at Craig's delight. "Then I'm putting you on a schedule. Vespers once a week for a month, then twice a week for a month and so on at a pace I set when I see how you handle the stress. When you're planning with Ensign Ronger, let him know you'll be in the office in the mornings and in your quarters in the afternoon. Work out the vespers schedule according to however many services a week you're allowed at that time."

Craig nodded, contemplating the next six or seven months. "Andez has developed a ministry of his own. I think it might be good to have him conduct vespers once or twice a week on a permanent basis."

"You're taking this really well," Jeff said, surprised.

Craig shook his head. "No, I'm not." He looked away, struggling silently. Words wouldn't come.

"You need to know how close," he finally began. Talking about his emotions didn't come easy. But Jeff needed to know. "To disaster."

Even now, the morning's experience almost defied expression.

"I've," he faltered.

"What is it, Craig?" the doctor prompted.

"I came this close," he said, measuring a small space with his forefinger and thumb, "to losing control. It was like I...I was made of glass, and if anyone - even 'Shonya - had surprised me one more time, I would have just shattered. I was, and still am, so excited. So awed. Overcome. Thousands of hot needles were jabbing me. I don't know what it would've looked like, but I..." He sighed. "...About broke apart."

Jeff understood. "At the worst you'd probably passed out. But I hope I would have seen it coming and intervened," he comforted. "How do you feel now?"

"I ache, like I exercised too much, and my stomach hurts. But I'm not on the edge like this morning. I'll do anything to keep from having that feeling again." He shivered. "I didn't like it at all."

The doctor grinned and got up. "I'm sorry this seems like we're doing everything the old fashioned way. Technology hasn't seemed to do its thing this time. But, I'll take your answer as a 'yes' to following my orders?"

Craig nodded. "There won't be as much reason to push in the next session." He meant what he said. "I just had to get to a certain point this morning."

The doctor nodded and handed Craig a computer. "Okay. Here's your computer. Read something soothing. I'll check in later."

Instead of something soothing, Craig called up the word processor and set about clarifying what he wanted to ask the Cutezarians in the next session. Sometime later, the med tech brought a glass of the formula. Craig looked up briefly and acknowledged Bill, then looking down was instantly reabsorbed into his work.

Bill Chung returned to his station with a grin, now understanding what the doctor meant about Craig's ability to completely shut out everything but the job before him. It was a good sign, and Bill entered the observation into his nursing notes.

Craig drank the formula slowly as he worked, without stopping to wonder what was in it. Blurred vision surprised him, and the next thing he knew 'Shonya was taking the computer as it slipped from his hand.

"Computer, save," she instructed softly, assuming he had fallen asleep working.

Craig opened his eyes as she folded it. "Hi," he said softly.

"Hi. Jeff said I could come by and say goodnight."

He grinned at her tone and took her hand. "He's not your father, you know."

She chuckled. "No, but he's your doctor."

He stifled a yawn.

Picking up the computer, she turned toward the door. "I saved your work. I'll take this to your quarters."

"Thanks." Closing his eyes he asked, "'Shonya? Will you go with me to the next session?"

"I'd like that," she responded in surprise.

"Am I invited too?" Jeff entered the room.

Craig opened his eyes and smiled. "You can invite yourself. Tell Alan. He's in charge." His eyes closed again. "I think I'd feel better if you were there."

"Good night, Craig."

'Shonya kissed him. "'Night." She felt lighthearted, her worry released by his good humor.

341

He raised a hand in farewell, and they left him alone.

"God," He prayed one more time. "Give me your words. What is it you have for me to accomplish? I've proceeded on the assumption the Cutezarians also worship you. Help me find out if that's true. If it is, help me know how to convince them we worship the same Creator of the Universe."

## CHAPTER THIRTY-ONE

The enforced quiet that followed gave Craig time to review all the conversations and records of the first interview.

First thing Wednesday morning Jeff ordered Craig in for a new set of scans. Compiling his report, the doctor noted a slow healing of the existing protected ulcer in spite of increased inflammation of the stomach lining. He noted increased nerve activity, decreased ability to sustain concentrated effort, but an excellent attitude.

"Computer, add information to Chaplain Lea's medical record, and tell me his location."

"In his quarters," the computer responded.

The doctor nodded in satisfaction and headed that direction.

"Come," came the invitation in response to his beep.

Craig was stretched out in the lounge chair, reading his notes from the interview. "Jeff!" Craig looked up with pleasure.

"Stay put." The doctor found a seat. "It's just ten thirty, have you been to the office?"

"A couple of hours," Craig said defensively. "You said not to push it. I got restless with all the activity, so I came back here to study."

"At least you're being sensible. Maybe you won't be too upset when I tell you we're definitely not returning to the surface until Monday. You just can't handle it."

Craig didn't argue, but agreed with a solemn nod. He knew he couldn't keep going on will alone. "I can work on the paper I want to present to my seminary professors," he thought.

"Are you really the same patient? You know the one who fights me every time I try to sedate him for his own good?" Jeff interrupted his thoughts.

Craig grinned and set his computer aside. "I have to admit I'm a little shook up. I've always known God must exist for all beings, but for it to become such a reality has..." He gestured helplessly. "Well, at the least, I'll never view God quite the same. There's so much to study. To know. To write." He shook his head. "On Crytis III I was confined pretty much to base. It's Level 10 restricted. I served only the human community. This is my first interaction with beings who haven't had extended contact with us. And to have it be like this..." He trailed off.

"But you saw other beings on Crytis?" Jeff encouraged.

"Yeah, I watched the ships come and go every time I got a chance. And I read everything I could get my hands on. Translated myths and legends hint at the gods other species believe in, but it's hard to tell who or what beings worship when that's all you have."

Jeff let him talk, enjoying his renewed enthusiasm.

Friday the doctor located his patient sitting in the chapel looking up at the sculpture of the giant arms holding the universe together. Sitting on the step created by the platform, he issued a gentle ultimatum. "You've got to make a choice between going to the planet to the Darkness Ritual and conducting vespers Sunday. If you go tonight, you'll get all worked up and we'll have delay you leading vespers another week at the least."

Craig didn't answer. Although fascinated by the Cutezarian's mystery, he eagerly looked forward to speaking again.

"You've done your part. We're not sure what we'll see, but maybe you'd be more objective if we went without you and reported what we felt," Jeff encouraged.

Craig nodded.

The doctor took his silence for indecision. "We're going to be here a while, and the Captain promised he would get permission for you to attend the rituals as many times as you want."

"Can you return to the ship tonight after the ritual?" Craig finally asked.

"The Cutezarians say we can return tonight. It's the night of least electrical activity."

"You all have to come to my quarters for discussion just like you do after vespers." It was both a question and an order.

"Agreed."

"Okay. I'll stay on board tonight. I'm really looking forward to speaking at vespers again." Craig stood and gave Jeff a hand up from his low seat, and they shook hands at the chapel door.

"Enjoy," Craig said with envy.

"Rest," the doctor ordered.

Smiling, they parted.

Following his doctor's orders, Craig slept most of the afternoon, finished his "semisolid food stuff," and after pacing a while, made himself sit and study until his visitors arrived. Once he began he became absorbed his research, and was startled when they came bursting into his quarters like friends on their way home from a good party.

"And we have arrived at the studiously quiet quarters of the distinguished Chaplain Lea." Oliver was acting as guide.

Craig looked up and blinked a couple of times as he put aside his concentration. "I see you did nicely without me," he grinned, catching their mood.

'Shonya kissed him briefly, thinking, "He looks so content, more like himself."

"Sit," he invited deactivating the lounge chair. "Does anyone want anything to eat or drink?"

"Water."

"Ice cream."

"Italian freeze."

"Mixed tropical fruit."

"A cheese sandwich."

They all talked and laughed at the same time as they gathered around the food synthesizer.

"Well?" Craig demanded, remaining standing as they settled into seats. "Report."

Finally, clearing his throat for effect, Oliver started. "The building stands in the center of its own plaza instead of sharing the space with other buildings. It's simple, yet elegant. The structure has the three sets of windows like the ancient structures, but we were told they are mostly ornamental because now they have ways to create artificial illumination. Attached to each window stone was an ornamental metal woven rope, which hangs to the floor.

"That answers our question about how the ancient ones opened and closed the windows. The Captain asked how the metal ropes were installed, and they said they were attached to the stones before they are set in place, and the surrounding stones carved so the ropes fit into a groove They manipulated the stones with the cords." He stopped to breathe.

"The metal ropes we thought were belts are remnants of these cords from ancient times," Roger interrupted.

Oliver nodded and continued, "Although the structure is much larger than the ancient one, the stone benches are shorter than the original ones since the Cutezarians themselves are smaller. They are, however, arranged in the same circular pattern. The encourager still stands in the center of the room."

"Encouraging in the round, so to speak," Forest added with a grin, and took up the narration. "The Cutezarians came in all at once. They touch each other on the shoulders. Like we shake hands. When they all got there, they stood up and touched each other's shoulders. Like in the video."

"The gathering was simple," Captain Brodsky spoke up. "Chanting of some sort, and the encourager."

"The encourager was female." 'Shonya carried on the report.

"Wait," Craig interrupted. "How did you know?"

"The females wear a cowl over their heads or around their neck in addition to the white robe," 'Shonya explained patiently, then continued. "She was exciting to watch. The translator box could hardly keep up with her. From what we gathered, she spoke of the principals and directives of the Spirit of All Things, a very complex concept of individualism, community, and planet-wide following of the directives for the individual which in turn complements the directives for the community and planet."

"What is it? A civil gathering? Some kind of worship?" Craig asked in great anticipation.

"We're divided. You're the one who insists we can't impose any of our belief system on the Cutezarians," Jeff reminded him.

"Okay," Craig conceded. "You're right. Tell me everything again."

The discussion ran later than Jeff liked. Finally he slipped out, went to sickbay, and concocted a rather strong formula. When he got back a weary, but intense Craig was still seeking information.

"Okay, everybody out!" He commanded, and received reluctant obedience.

347

"Would you consider the Scarlatti concert tomorrow?" Craig asked 'Shonya as Jeff shooed her out. "I know classical isn't your thing,"

"She would love it." Jeff insisted. "Say yes, kiss him and leave."

"Yes," She laughed. The kiss was short.

Alone with his patient, Jeff faced him grimly. "Drink this, go to bed, and stay in your quarters tomorrow all day."

Properly chastised, Craig drank the formula, noting its stronger taste. "You put more of something in this," he accused.

"Don't worry about it, just relax."

Sleep came. And so did the regularly occurring dreams with which Craig struggled. But this was different. He became the encourager. Humans and Cutezarians alike listened to everything he had to say. Yet when he ran out of words and energy, they expected more. Words deserted him when he needed them most. Finally, 'Shonya left her seat, took his hand and led him outside, assuring him it didn't matter if he didn't have all the answers.

And he rested.

Sunday morning Craig woke earlier than he had for a long time but lay in bed, remembering. He could see 'Shonya's face at lunch with the directors as they laughed over the formula and soft food Jeff prescribed while she devoured her favorite spicy Italian foods.

Forest had presented a sample of his latest experiment with the ancient Cutezarians' grain. 'Shonya had loved the chewy texture. "Goes perfect with Italian," She'd declared.

He saw her as they walked to the music hall for the chamber music concert. The feel of her hand in his as the last strains of Scarlatti lingered. And he still felt the reluctance of letting her return to her quarters, and savored their embrace. He puzzled over the mysterious strength of the long, unhurried kiss, after which she just left. There wasn't anything left to say.

Closing his eyes, he felt content, and napped until he was in danger of being late for the community meal.

'Shonya and Andez insisted he join them at their table. Craig greeted the others at the table then sat down to listen to the conversation. It wasn't anything special: kids, family, work, laughter and sharing of friendships.

It occurred to Craig how much he had missed this. "You look like someone who's been away a very long time and finally found his way back home," 'Shonya whispered, touching his hand.

"It just occurred to me. That's exactly how I feel," he whispered back.

Near the end of the meal, Andez Ronger rose. This was the time for announcements and sharing of special needs. After dispensing with the normal stuff, he looked down at Craig and smiled. "It is my pleasure to tell you Doctor Keal has set up a schedule that will allow Chaplain Lea to return to duty. I would like him to greet you and tell you about it." He sat and motioned Craig to stand.

Getting slowly to his feet, Craig suddenly became aware of the affection he felt for the people he served. He looked up, pushed his hair back and said, "Greetings."

Amid the laughter came applause indicating they shared the affection.

Enduring the embarrassment, he continued after regaining control of his own emotions. "Doctor Keal set my schedule for returning to full duty as follows: mornings I will be in the office, afternoons I will be resting in my quarters. Starting this evening, I will be allowed to conduct vespers once a week for a month, then twice a week for a month, then three times, and so on. Ensign Ronger will continue his duties as he has been in my absence. He's done an excellent job. I'm asking him to continue holding vespers twice a week even after I've returned to full-time duty."

The group approved and applauded the announcement. Craig looked over the group and tried to finish his speech. "I want to express my gratitude to all of you for your concern and prayers, and I'd better quit before I get all worked up again. If I do, my doctor might confine me to quarters and I'll miss my chance to speak this evening." He gave a small wave and sat amid the chuckles.

Andez dismissed the group.

'Shonya accompanied Craig to his quarters. They walked slowly, each knowing he needed to be alone, but not wanting to part. They lingered at the door.

"Are you ready for tonight?" she asked quietly, without looking at him. There was so much more she wanted to say, but knew he needed to get through vespers first.

"Yes," he answered. "What is it?" he asked as he bent to look into her face.

But at that moment, Jeff came by and handed Craig a glass of the formula. "I noticed you didn't eat much. Drink, then go rest." He took a few steps then retraced them. "Craig, I'm looking forward to hearing you speak again."

"Thanks, Jeff," Craig said in surprise.

The doctor took 'Shonya's arm. "Get it over with and - let him rest."

"Later—when my guardian isn't around." Craig whispered as he leaned over to kiss her.

'Shonya laughed at Craig's little-boy conspirator's expression, and allowed Jeff to pull her away.

"Have you told Craig about Art?" he asked as they entered the lift.

Shaking her head, she confessed, "I'm not sure how to, or when."

"On a ship this size, someone will let it slip. For the sake of your relationship, you need to be the one to tell him," he reminded her gently.

"I know."

## CHAPTER THIRTY-TWO

Craig hoped Jeff hadn't gotten carried away with the sedative. He drank the formula and stretched out on the bed to review his notes one more time. However, he experienced a slight dizziness, and by the time he realized what it was, he barely had time to mark his place before he felt the computer slip out of his hand.

Waking up, he felt sensation begin in his lower back and move up his spinal cord into his neck and brain: a strange feeling, like someone pulling consciousness up over his head.

Still feeling strange, he found his way to the shower then, seemingly in slow motion, wandered around as he dressed for vespers.

The habits of preparation returned. Checking the computer's time, he realized he had just enough time follow the familiar routine of going to the chapel office during the dinner hour as he prepared for the service.

The office showed signs that Andez expected him. He took off his uniform coat and smiled as he moved about the office. There was the pitcher of cold water, a schedule of events on the desk, and his favorite chair had been moved from his own office to the Chaplain's room. He poured a glass of water and made himself comfortable.

"Andez is welcoming me back," he thought with gratitude and turned his thoughts to the service. "God, you are," he prayed, "I know I can't make anyone believe that you are, yet I have an opportunity to widen horizons. Help us let you out of our boxes of personal experience. Help us broaden our limited view of you. You are the giver of all life, all knowledge, all insight, the source of all things," He let his mind wander as he meditated upon the spiritual needs of humankind.

A sound brought his thoughts back. The sound came again.

"Rev?" Andes knocked again quietly.

"Yes, Andez?" Already they had returned to the routine of Andez calling him a few minutes before vespers. It felt comfortable.

The ensign stuck his head in. "Five minutes, Rev," he said with a grin. "Welcome back."

"Thanks, Andez." He got up, put on his coat and paced nervously until Andez entered, and together they stepped through the door that led to the Chapel. They took their places on the platform before Craig looked around.

The room was full.

Andez laughed at Craig's surprise. "The Captain cleared everyone's schedule, canceled all tests and put the ship on computer control until after vespers," He said with a grin.

'Shonya didn't fight her feelings when she saw Craig's expression. She watched him sing and give his attention to Andez as he conducted the opening — things she'd witnessed many times before, but she was aware of a joy she hadn't felt before.

When Craig moved to the podium he sought her out and their eyes met briefly before he ceased being the one with whom she had a developing relationship and became the Chaplain.

Craig also felt it. He had a fleeting urge to leave the platform, take her hand and tell these wonderful people he loved her, but as began speaking, all else fell away.

With a prayerful heart he continued. "I'm reading from Exodus, chapter 3, verses 10 through 14."...So now, go. I am sending you to Pharaoh to bring my people the Israelites out of Egypt." But Moses said to God, "Who am

I that I should go to Pharaoh and bring the Israelites out of Egypt?" And God said, "I will be with you. And this is will be a sign to you that it is I who have sent you: When you have brought the people out of Egypt, you will worship God on this mountain. Moses said to God, "Suppose I go to the Israelites and say to them, 'The God of your fathers has sent me to you,' and they ask me 'What is his name?' Then what shall I say to them?" God said to Moses, "I am who I am." This is what you are to say the Israelites: 'I am has sent me to you.'"

Craig looked up, addressing the group. "These words come from the commissioning of Moses. "When God called him, he had three objections to God's proposed plan. The first one concerned his personal inadequacies. 'God, I can't do this.' How many times have I said that in the last three months?" He grinned, and the congregation smiled with him.

"The second was a little more complicated: 'The people will want to know who sent me.' Moses didn't come out and ask 'What is your name?' It was asked, approaching the issue of the authority of the one who sent him. "Need I remind you of the importance of the connection between the name and the character in that society?" He paused. "Moses is asking for more than mere information here, he's seeking the significance of the one who sends him. The third question has to do with how he would convince the people to believe. God gave him a miracle to help. But let's deal mainly with the second.

"The answer about authority came in a cryptic way. 'I am who I am.' Compare those words with chapter 33:19, 'I will have mercy on whom I will have mercy, and I will have compassion on whom I will have compassion.' This is not a rejection or a none-of-your-business answer, but a statement of the actuality of the existence of the I Am.

"Twentieth century writers said 'I think, therefore I am.' And that has been our test for animals, androids and beings we have met in space. 'Are they aware that they are?' Many things can alter reality. Dr. Keal has made me well aware of that lately." His smile was self-conscious. "But to be aware of one's own existence is the test of whether or not there is a thought process present.

"However, this goes beyond the simple awareness of one's own existence. It's a statement showing the divine freedom of God, the majesty and mystery of God. It's a statement of the significance of the speaker. 'I Am who I am'—I am real—I am here—and will be anywhere you are—we said it to each other the first night on the planet—God is with us here—wherever here may be. 'I really am here and there.' "

Craig felt movement in the congregation and looked around the room. The Captain and Dorinda got up and made their way out. Although momentarily concerned, the topic at hand recaptured his full attention.

"This significant statement became the authority of Moses. 'Say the I Am sent you.' The One beyond all else - the One who is able to be all places at all times, the One who chooses to be with you." He stopped, as his own memories of God's presence, strength and help in the last months threatened to overcome him. He looked at his notes, struggling for control.

"Help him," 'Shonya prayed.

After a deep breath he continued. "The Spirit of all Things. Whatever that means to them, I think the Cutezarians have given us a pretty good description of the I Am." He thought, "Well, I've said it out loud."

To the congregation he concluded. "I Am who I Am. With the confirmation of the actuality of God, and the reassurance we have received in the last months, we affirm that actuality in ourselves." Looking around the room, he finished with a question. "What better time is there to believe?"

"A little more emotional than I'd planned," he thought, returning to his seat. However, the faces of his listeners reassured him and he relaxed.

Andez waited a minute before moving to the next part of the service. Then he left the platform and placed a chair in front of the congregation saying, "I don't know about you, but it's a pleasure to have the Chaplain back."

The audience agreed, and applauded as Craig came down from the platform. Turning the chair around so the back faced them, he sat, stretched his legs, and, crossing his arms, rested wearily against the chair. With a deep breath, he brushed his hair back. "Okay, let the discussion begin." He fleetingly remembered Dorinda and the Captain's departure, but the questions had already begun.

"Chaplain, what were the steps you went through that convinced you the Cutezarians have a worship system?" an ensign asked.

Looking back, Craig replied. "There are certain general questions we routinely ask when we..." 'Shonya smiled at his use of the word 'we.' "...Approach an archeological site. But the first hint came when 'Shon - Dr. Reed reported the Cutezarian's application of the word 'meditation' in describing the upper chambers of the Daniel K One. We told each other it wasn't possible and went on. When we toured the Daniel K Two, I had this feeling I wasn't prepared because I didn't have a lesson ready. But what really triggered it was the video the
Cutezarians showed the night of the reception. Then little by little, the Cutezarians themselves confirmed it."

The ensign nodded then grinned. "And how did you rate a private tour of Daniel K Two before it was officially opened?" He added "Sir," for effect more than referring to rank. Craig was their pastor in this setting. Rank had no meaning here.

Craig felt himself blush. "I never used to do this," he thought. However, he answered the question with a grin. "I, ah, know someone with authority."

They acted like they didn't believe him.

"Sure."

"Uh-huh."

"Yeah."

"Who would that be?"

'Shonya kept a straight face, but felt her own face change colors. Suddenly aware of the crew's affection for Craig, she realized their relationship was going to be very public.

"Hey, now, don't be so hard on the Chaplain his first time back," Forest chided.

"Thank you, Forest," Craig replied, and the group again became serious. Looking up, he encountered Commander Cooper's challenging, half-interested and half-antagonistic gaze coming from the door where he often stood during the discussion part of vespers. "God, show me. How do I reach Cooper?" He wasn't even aware the thought became a prayer.

"Chaplain," Oliver interrupted his thoughts. "Is it possible the writer of this scripture was giving us, not the exact spoken words, but a reaction to Moses' report of the encounter? And the writer put it into theological language?"

"Hey, don't be so hard on the Chaplain his first time back," Forest repeated.

They laughed, but still expected an answer. Craig allowed silence to return before attempting an answer. The mood had turned thoughtful, and Craig answered quietly.

"Oliver, we're back to the old discussion of where the ancient culture stopped and God's words began. We all must discover the actuality of God for ourselves. Let's say the writer accepted Moses' report of his discovery of God's actuality and put it into theological terms. Does it take away from the validity of its expression and encouragement Moses' experience give us?"

"Don't we find courage to search for ourselves by the fact that others have found what we seek?" 'Shonya asked.

"The more people who find the answer from different directions help us know we're looking for the right thing, or help us know our experience is one we can believe in," Andez spoke up.

"Maybe it's not so important to know if God said the words or put them into Moses' mind. Moses knew he had encountered God. The people accepted it." Forest joined the conversation.

Craig listened to the discussion and again understood the strength he drew from the people he served. A med tech stepped in and tapped Jeff on the shoulder.

Lt. Reecer didn't give Craig time to wonder what the news the med tech brought. "What prompted your statement about the Cutezarians and The Spirit of All Things expressing the I Am?"

Craig laughed. "I knew that would come back to haunt me. It may just be the way their term translates into English, but the "Spirit of All Things" made sense to me."

Jeff came back in and motioned to Craig. "Excuse me a minute," Craig apologized and went to the door.

"Dorinda's in labor, and asking for you."

Craig's eyes lit up and he immediately turned to the congregation, speaking from the back of the room. "Dorinda's in labor. Andez will finish."

He and Jeff started down the hall and Craig found 'Shonya beside him. He took her hand.

"Jeff, is everything okay?" She asked.

"Everything's fine," he answered. "How you doing?" he asked Craig.

"Shaky and tired." He knew it wouldn't do any good to fake it.

"I'll get a glass of the formula to help your stomach settle down," the doctor promised.

Craig nodded. They finished the journey in silence.

Dr. Canady met them and took Craig's arm. "You don't have much time."

Dorinda looked tired, but smiled as Craig kissed her. "Hi, Sis. With the first baby you're supposed to be in labor for hours, and here you're ready to deliver."

"I always do things my own way." She reminded him, and then panted through another contraction.

Dr. Canady came in and began preparations to convert the room into a delivery room. "Out!" she shooed Craig.

"I'll be right outside," he promised.

Jeff brought a large glass of formula as 'Shonya and Craig settled down to share the wait.

An hour later, Jeff took advantage of his patient's presence in sickbay and insisted on an examination. He finally handed Craig's shirt back and nodded.

"You're going to be fine, but it'll take time. I'm not taking you off the formula quite yet, although we'll keep trying the soft diet. I'll sedate you occasionally when I see stress signs. You'll recover, but you can expect to have occasional stomach distress."

Craig accepted it, and returned to the OB waiting room with a smile.

"Good report?" 'Shonya asked.

Craig nodded. "He says the worst is over, and I'll be fine, but experience some queasiness."

They sat, paced, shared refreshments, held hands and sat together some more, then talked and paced some more. Finally, exhausted, they sat on a couch and leaned against each other.

"How's your proposal coming?" he asked after a few minutes of silence.

"I finished today. It looks like we'll get to uncover all the structures in the community." She said. He nodded and they fell quiet. "It was a good devotion." She said after a few more minutes. "A good thing for us to think about right now." And they were silent again.

"I'm glad. I hoped I wasn't speaking just out of my own interest," Craig commented thoughtfully. After a while, he sighed. "'Shonya, I still don't know if I can do this. If I'm this tired every time I speak, I can only hope it'll get better like Jeff promised."

"It probably depends on what you do in between active times doesn't it?" She was gentle in her reminder to follow doctor's orders.

"You mean if I allow Jeff to continue giving me stuff to make me sleep afternoons instead of going to my quarters and studying?" he chuckled.

"I didn't know that was an ongoing argument between you and Jeff, but if that's what it takes," she said softly. "The last time I talked to him he said it wouldn't last much longer." She did a quick mental calculation of Jeff's proposed schedule for Craig's return to full duty. "It's not that long. I estimate it'll take almost that long to finish this project. Meanwhile you'll have time to be part of the dig." She paused again and added as casually as possible. "And time for us." She felt his immediate response.

At first he wasn't sure he heard her right. He sat up, surprised at her invitation, quickly trying to stuff his rising emotions back where he struggled to keep them. But he failed. Pulling 'Shonya close to him, he rested his chin on her head.

She listened to his heart beat and felt his struggle.

"Then we are us?" he asked and stated hopefully at the same time.

She leaned back in his arms to look into his face. "We were brought together in a rather unique way and I think we're both under control enough."

"Chaplain?"

The voice belonged to a med tech. "The Captain's wife would like to see you."

Craig kissed 'Shonya briefly. "We will get back to this," he said firmly.

She watched him disappear into the room with a gentle smile. It was time, and they both knew it. She felt relief and excitement. The uncertainty was over, and a real relationship was about to begin! "Thank you," she prayed silently. "Help our relationship grow. We want to love each other and you. Help us keep them in the right order. And help me know when to tell him about Art."

Craig grinned at the tech's look of unexpressed envy, but didn't invite comments as he quietly followed the tech into Dorinda's room. She drew him to a seat on her bed as he took her hand. Dr. Canady nodded as he silently asked permission to sit.

Craig turned his attention to Dorinda. "Hi."

"Hi."

"Was it hard?" he asked.

"Ruth made it as easy as possible," she said with a tired smile.

"Everything all right?" he asked.

"Perfect," she said. "A perfect baby boy. Alan took him." They smiled together. "They're with the pediatrician weighing and cleaning him now." She suddenly yawned. "I'm sorry, I just got an injection. I wanted to see you before I went to sleep. How does Craig Alan strike you for a name?"

"You don't have to do that," Craig objected mildly.

"We want to. It's so good to be with you again. I feel like I have my family with me." She smiled and paused. "I loved your devotion, what I heard of it. My water broke in the middle of it."

Craig laughed. "I don't think that's ever happened to me before. But then you've always been known for your firsts. It's in the computer system so you can view it later."

"As soon as I can. And I'm starting a series of articles on Cutezar," she said.

"But right now, you need rest," Craig said then grinned. "Somehow those words seem familiar."

"You did sound like Jeff," she agreed. "You look exhausted yourself." She closed her eyes. "At the risk of repeating myself, I'll rest if you will." She reiterated her words from the night of the reception. "It's over. Go home."

He stood and kissed her forehead. "It's a deal. I'll check back in the morning." He held door for the Captain as he left, and met his namesake for the first time.

"Craig, meet the new Brodsky family member."

"Alright!" Craig touched the soft head and skin, and was amazed at this miracle of life.

"Are you ready for your new duties?" the Captain asked.

"Ah," Craig stuttered.

"You're the designated uncle, you know," the Captain grinned.

"As long as I don't have to change diapers," Craig agreed.

He found 'Shonya sitting where he left her and sank onto the couch with a sigh. "Now where were we?" he asked leaning his head back and closing his eyes.

"Not now, you might go to sleep on me," she laughed but they sat few minutes, enjoying each other's presence.

"You have this habit of keeping me on track," he grinned. "The night you all went to the darkness ritual, I dreamed about the ritual. Only I was the encourager. I spoke about the paper I'm drafting. I've been wondering how our history might have been different if our ancestors had understood the Cutezarian's message. Anyway, I spoke until I couldn't think of another thing to say. But everyone sat there, waiting for more. I was done, and didn't know what to do. Finally you got up, took my arm, and led me outside. You made me understand it was okay if didn't know all the answers." He smiled and took her hand. "Lately you've been rescuing me from my emotional attacks," he finished.

"I'm glad I was part of the answer." She smiled.

He grinned. "Definitely not part of the problem."

Eyes closed, he was comfortably drifting when he felt a small hand on his knee. He opened his eyes and sat up in delight. "Nathan, what are you doing here?" he asked picking the child up and giving him a hug.

"To see the baby," Nathan said seriously in his small voice.

Craig looked up at Laura Kobee. "He insisted." She smiled indulgently. "He's such a good kid and very seldom defies me. I just had to let him come. But I think he wanted to see you too."

Craig stood Nathan on the seat beside him, got up and held out his arms. Nathan responded in the way the game went and jumped into his arms, landing with such force Craig staggered a little. "Oomph," he grunted.

'Shonya and Laura were instantly beside him. "You didn't tear the seal?" 'Shonya asked, afraid to finish the question.

"I'm fine, I think," he said breathlessly. He caught his breath, carried Nathan to the room and stuck his head in. "Captain?"

The Captain came to the door. "I have a visitor who insists there's a baby here he wants to see," Craig said.

The Captain opened the door and invited them in. "Nathan, this is Craig Alan Brodsky." He held up the newborn and Nathan gently repeated Craig's touching actions.

The little boy giggled in delight and the baby waved his arms. "I like the baby," Nathan declared.

"We can visit the baby again, can't we?" Craig asked.

The Captain nodded and Craig carried Nathan back to his mother. "He likes the baby," Craig told her as he put the boy down. He took Nathan's hand and turned to 'Shonya. "I'll be right back." Putting put his arm around Laura, he led them out of sickbay. "How are you? Anything I can do?"

"Some days are better than others," she confessed. "And Nathan keeps me busy." She paused then continued with a half- smile. "I'm returning full-time to the bio-tech lab next week. You did all you needed to at the funeral."

'Shonya followed them to the door. At the turbo lift, Craig leaned down, hugged Nathan, and turned him over to Laura. She embraced Craig, took Nathan's hand, and entered the lift.

"If our relationship continues, he'll always be leaving me. It's the way it'll be." 'Shonya thought as she returned to her chair.

Jeff came out of the OB area and crossed to the med tech's desk. By the time he entered the code for Craig's formula and returned to the waiting room, Craig was back.

Handing him the glass, Jeff instructed, "The first one was for dinner, this is your midnight snack. Get some rest or I won't let you out of your quarters tomorrow." Craig hesitated. "Go ahead, Dorinda's okay. She's sleeping. The baby's fine. The Captain's napping."

"You didn't put anything in it? I..." Craig started.

"I did, and I will until you don't look so exhausted after you've spoken," the doctor defended his action, then smiled, "It won't be long. Bear with me. Now, it's late. Goodnight." He turned to leave, but turned back. "Good devotion. Very timely." And he was gone.

'Shonya put her arm around Craig and they went slowly toward the lift.

"I haven't ever asked why you chose cartography," he said the first thing he thought about, wanting to hear her talk.

"When we returned to the United States, my parents managed an agricommunity. We mapped and made computer models of the land before we planted crops. We determined what type of soil we had, where the water was and where we needed to irrigate. After we planted, we made models to analyze the root systems of the plants to see what grew best in what conditions."

She smiled. "My parents actually worked together in peace a while before they drifted apart and my mother finally returned to Europe. My Dad and I continued working, and he let me do more and more." She paused. "I haven't talked about that for a long time. It was fun. Then as I got older, it was a challenge, and finally my life's work." She looked up at his tired face. "Why do you ask now?"

"Seemed like it was time to know," he said vaguely, with a casual grin.

"Okay." She drew the word out to keep from jumping up and down. "What made you become a chaplain?"

"That's easy." He paused. "I was military born and bred. I knew no other way. My father you know about: a military expert in computer linguistics. He put the cap on artificial intelligence by writing the final program that taught computers to think in language instead of translating language into numbers first.

"But you might not know my mother's a military chaplain. I was raised in the chapels of the bases on Mars and Earth, and became aware of God as the source of my spirituality in my late teens. Mother taught me and Dorinda - her parents' beliefs centered on the goodness of the human spirit until later - anyway, Mother taught us about God and my father taught me about the military and computers. When I felt I should enter my mother's profession, I'd already been accepted into the academy, so it felt right to be a military chaplain." He spoke simply, without embellishment.

In silence, they entered the turbo lift. Craig braced himself against the wall.

"The drop still bothers you?" 'Shonya asked.

"Yeah," he said shortly.

They didn't speak again until they stood at the door of his quarters. "Come in for a minute?" he asked, knowing what he needed to say.

Sensing his suppressed emotions, she agreed. They stood in silence for a minute as he drank the formula. He sat the glass down and put his arms around her. "How long did you say we'd be here?" he asked.

"Approximately a year."

"That ought to be long enough," he said.

"Long enough for what?"

"To discuss those promises."

She smiled deeply. "What promises?"

"The promises we should talk about." He held his breath, hoping for the best.

She disengaged herself and, taking his hand, led him to the sofa. "First, I need to tell you about someone," and she told him about Art, including how hard it had been to choose between them.

Listening closely, Craig analyzed every expression and inflection of her voice, hoping to find reassurance that she was sure of her choice. He saw certainty and was relieved. "I was afraid of something like that when I heard about your visitor. I didn't play fair by being sick, and didn't even know it." He smiled. "But I can't say that I'm sorry either."

She chuckled. "I did accuse you of unethical use of illness."

He smiled, and after a small silence added, "I'm glad you decided to stay."

They sat close together, each feeling the depth of the moment. Leaning over, Craig broke the spell with a kiss. She felt his emotion and returned it.

"Now, about those promises," she said gently.

"'Shonya, there's so much to say," he paused, half expecting her to stop him, but for the first time she didn't interrupt. "But," He suddenly leaned his head back and shut his eyes as he felt the tingling that signaled his body's reaction to the medication.

She understood what was happening and touched his face.

He opened his eyes and grinned slightly. "Since something keeps interrupting us, I suppose I'll start with I love you."

She smiled, "I love you."

They looked at each other for a moment. Craig didn't know if it was the sedative or emotion that made him feel the room slowly revolve as he kissed her. An electrical charge started in 'Shonya's head and moved down her spinal cord to her toes.

Finally! They expressed the long suppressed emotions. But her thoughts were swept aside by tender feelings and the awareness of his physical presence. When they again became aware of reality Craig was half lying, his head resting on the arm of the sofa, and she was leaning against his chest. Each took a deep breath and regarded the other with wonder and love.

Craig smiled up at her then closed his eyes, giving into the medication's action. "I love you."

"Dr. Reed?" Shonya's comm button startled them both.

"Reed here," she answered after a brief hesitation, her voice still ragged and breathless with emotion. "This is Paji. I know it's late, but I just was going over some scans of the next structure and found something I want to ask you about. Can you come by the lab?"

'Shonya smiled down at Craig, who was shaking his head. "I'll be there in a few minutes, Paji."

"Thanks."

"Reed out." She touched Craig's face. "When I was watching you with Laura and Nathan this evening I couldn't help but think. If our relationship continues, it's always going to be like that."

"Like what?" he asked a bit drowsily.

"Full of people." She smiled. "I have my students, but one or two at a time." Craig laughed softly. "I act on the basis of the logical rules of science and intuitive creativity. The people I'm responsible for are perfectly capable of doing the same job I do. They just choose not to, and I like administrative work. But people depend on you for a lot more than just information." She stopped at his quizzical look then laughed. "You can't imagine it any other way can you?"

He shook his head slightly. "Can you imagine leaving your logical rules of science?" She shook her head. "Neither can I," he said ambiguously.

Causally he traced little patterns on her forearm. "Could you handle it if some of the people in my life spilled over into yours?" He asked softly, his voice slightly fuzzy around the edges.

She kissed him and when he finally held her away from him to catch his breath, she smiled down at him. "I think I can manage."

Craig closed his eyes and smiled.

## CHAPTER THIRTY-THREE

Hovering between sleep and awareness, Craig resisted the need to relinquish the comfortable drifting. Suddenly the expectancy of the day overwhelmed him and he sat up in bed, anxious to get started.

"'Morning," he greeted the assembled group who awaited him aboard the shuttle.

"You doing okay?" Dr. Keal asked causally.

"Well rested, thank you," he replied with a grin.

The Captain signaled the pilot and, amid clearing procedures, Craig slid into the empty seat next to 'Shonya giving her a quick kiss. No one commented, and that set the tone for the quiet trip.

Contentment settled over 'Shonya. It was all right. She let herself enjoy being near Craig.

As the guide led them into a first floor room, in which every seat was filled, Dortec greeted them. "We welcome you." Following Craig's surprised gaze, he explained. "You have met Ventez, and the rest are the leaders of those who meditate from many of our cities. We reviewed the information you presented, and decided to come together because we wish to know more. And you may also ask of us what you please."

The crew settled into the same seats the negotiating team had occupied when talks with the Cutezarians had first begun. The sheer number of Cutezarians intimidated Craig. He met Jeff's eyes and his look challenged Craig.

"You promised." The doctor reminded, shaking a finger at him.

"A bit more than I expected," Craig admitted with a grin.

The Captain took charge. "We would be honored if you would begin," he addressed Dortec.

"Is the young one safely born?" Dortec asked formally.

"Yes, my mate has delivered a male child. Both she and the child are doing well," the captain answered.

"Excellent," Dortec answered. "There are many questions we would like to ask, but we prefer to allow the Chaplain to begin."

Captain Brodsky agreed and nodded to Craig. He unfolded his legs from the low chair and paced the room, putting his thoughts in order.

From 'Shonya's description he could now tell the males and females apart. He noted the equal distribution of males and females in the leaders of those who meditate.

"I don't know exactly where to start," he began, determined to find out what or whom the Cutezarians worshiped. "So I'll ask a question: how do you communicate with the Spirit of All Things?"

"Upon creation, the Spirit of All Things puts something in all beings that responds to the Spirit of All Things. If each of us acknowledges the Spirit of All Things as guide and provider of all life and strength, that which is in us directly touches the Spirit of All Things as the Spirit seeks to speak with us."

Dortec's manner made Craig feel the Cutezarians had anticipated his question. He remembered Dortec's stunning revelation about studying the ship's religious material. It gave him confidence to continue.

"From this belief came the ancient directive to travel to other places and awaken this response in other beings?" Craig asked.

"That is so but not complete," came the answer.

"Explain, please," Craig prompted.

"Our ancestors believed they were to awaken in other beings the awareness of the existence of The Spirit of All Things, and through that, prepare them for the messages of The Spirit of All Things." He continued after a short silence, and it seemed to Craig he spoke very gently so not to insult his guests. "It is not simple. We do not expect you to understand."

Craig smiled. "We can understand. In our own history, a man named John had a specific job. It was to prepare the listeners for God's message. "The Spirit of All Things, God as we say, is aware of the creation's limitations. I sometimes wonder how many times God has to prepare humans for the message. We haven't learned very well."

The Cutezarians discussed this remark and finally found the humor in it.

Ventez, the leader of those who meditate spoke: "We have individuals who have that problem. We call them," The translator searched for the proper concept. "-Unconscious," it finally said.

Surprised, Craig chuckled. "I've often thought a person has to be physically unconscious not to see God's presence in the universe. But then I spend much of my time studying God's presence." He became serious. "But you mean unconscious as spiritually unaware, not a physical condition."

The Cutezarians nodded. "The awakening of the spiritual awareness has been the focus of our efforts," Ventez answered with the remains of her smile.

Craig paced a moment. "Now, may I change the subject?" They nodded again. "Did your ancestors always return to a place to see how the message was received?"

"No. Some of our ancestors recorded they counseled the second journey should not take place. Those who took part in the journey acknowledged they did so out of their own directive, not following the Spirit of All Things. The price we paid was isolation. When humans follow their own directives, is that not sometimes called a transgression?" Ventez answered.

"It is," was all Craig could think of to say. He was quickly coming to the point of having his hopes confirmed. When he recovered he asked, "What did your ancestors do when they realized they had transgressed?"

"It is recorded the leaders separated themselves from all other Cutezarians, retreating to the meditation place, the structure you uncovered and named Daniel K Two. There in isolation, they communicated with the Spirit of All Things. We continue that practice to the present time." The box answered for Dortec.

*"Ventez and Dortec are taking turns answering my questions. Like I'm a student and they are professors,"* Craig thought. However, he didn't let his amusement show as he continued. "Why do you think the Spirit did not direct your ancestors to go back to see how things turned out?"

"You have helped us understand we do not know how or why the Spirit of All Things allows events to proceed," was Dortec's cautious answer.

"Humans still often have trouble with that concept." Craig smiled, then again changed the subject. "How does the belief in the Spirit of All Things enter into your daily existence?"

"The Spirit of All Things guides all parts of our society. All young Cutezarians are instructed in the Spirit's ways and teachings. There are many things about which each of us decides what we accept as truth, but the Spirit of All Things guides this society," Ventez answered.

Suddenly inspired, Craig asked, "Is there any other record of the society transgressing from the Spirit of All Things' directives?"

"Each Cutezarian is responsible for following that which they receive as personal directives. However, because of the price the society paid for our ancestors' transgression, the society has not again transgressed the Spirit of All Things' directives." Dortec was equally cautious in his choice of phrases.

Craig stalled for thinking time. He pushed his hair back from where it always fell, walked around the room and finally addressed his fellow humans in amazement. "I can't believe I'm hearing this. Is it possible the Cutezarians really do worship the same God of the universe and have broken fellowship with God only once? Could they have repented, restoring the first agreement with the Spirit of All Things and never again broke that relationship?"

They regarded him with amazement as he continued.

"They're living in time equivalent to our Old Testament times, but they haven't continuously rebelled or allowed other things to take the place of God in their society. Is this how our ancestors were meant to live?"

Jeff put his hand on Craig's arm. "Calm down."

Craig took a deep breath and nodded, then turned to the Cutezarians. "Do I understand each Cutezarian is responsible for their own relationship with the Spirit of All Things but at the same time is also responsible to keep the society in the right relationship with the Spirit of All Things?" He took his time, making sure he didn't rush the translating box.

Startled, the Cutezarians asked the box to repeat his statement.

Finally Ventez voiced their answer. "We do not use the same concept but we agree with it. It is only as each Cutezarian remains in communication with the Spirit of All Things that the society remains in communication with the

Spirit of All Things. We did not expect you to understand this."

"Let me begin at the beginning of our recorded saga. I jumped around a little the last time we spoke." Craig started hopefully.

Jeff saw the signs of fatigue in Craig's face and motioned the Captain to call a short rest period, but Craig intercepted the message with a shake of his head. "If I keep starting and stopping, I'll never get through it."

He turned back to the Cutezarians. "When the human race did not follow God's – our name for the Spirit of All Things," he paused, and getting no reaction from his friends about using the two terms synonymously, continued. "God's directives." He paused again, choosing the word the Cutezarians had used, "they transgressed, and communication between the people and God was broken. But God, wishing to commune with humans, set in motion a way to reestablish the relationship.

"God spoke to a man named Abraham; called him from the multi-spirit worship of that day, and gave him directives. Abraham followed them. The One God showed him and his descendants how to worship the One God. He taught them how to make the relationship right again. When they transgressed by using forms of the blood sacrifice we spoke of yesterday. The ritual expressed their sorrow when they transgressed.

"From Abraham descended a nation God wanted to be an example so all peoples of our world could see a good example of the relationship between the One God and creation. But these people, whom we spoke of yesterday also, called the Chosen people, lost the concept of personal responsibility and commitment to the One God. The nation's focus shifted away from the relationship with God.

Other things took God's place in their lives." Craig paused and took a deep breath.

He was tired and tense, afraid once again he could not speak clearly enough to get across the vital idea. 'Shonya's expression and the orders he overheard Jeff giving to the med tech told him the tiredness showed. He was too tired to try to hide it.

"I'm in for another night in sick bay," he thought wearily.

As he paused, the Cutezarians began speaking among themselves. Without the aid of the translator Craig could only speculate on what they were saying, however he sensed their surprise had turned to reassurance, as if he had confirmed something they had been considering.

"Stand still." Jeff brought him back to reality as he laid the injection rod against Craig's neck.

Craig obediently allowed the administration of the medication, trusting Jeff not to give him anything that would interfere with his ability to function.

"Now sit a couple of minutes," the doctor instructed.

With a sigh, Craig slid into the chair next to 'Shonya. As she scooted her chair closer, he put his arm across the back of her chair and shoulders, too tired to wonder what the Cutezarians thought.

"I'm almost done. You all can help me answer their questions. I never realized how complicated it sounds to someone with a different concept of God." He paused. "But I'm convinced," He paused again, his hesitancy contradicting the strong words. "They worship the same God we humans often think exists just for us."

To his surprise, she agreed without echoing his uncertainty.

Encouraged, he continued. "It makes me wonder if God had a pattern for the universe and that pattern developed or is developing according to the nature of the beings of that planet."

"Then, what you're saying," The Captain spoke in phrases, formulating his ideas as he went. "Is the way each being approaches God will be unique to that planet, but God seeks the same thing from all beings."

"Do we assume all beings must experience a fall as did humans and our world?" Craig asked when the Captain paused.

"Is it possible for any created being not to fall?" Captain Brodsky asked.

"That's beyond me." Craig grinned. "I suspect not. We need help outside ourselves to keep from transgressing. And when it does happen, I assume a way of redemption is provided." He relaxed as the medication eased the stomachache.

"A Christ figure?" 'Shonya smiled fondly at him.

"Possibly." Craig didn't commit himself.

"I think that's where I was going. Is there a Christ figure here?"

"I don't know yet. I don't think so," Craig said honestly, and returned to the Captain's original statement. "What is it God wishes?"

"Response, worship, acknowledgment of God's presence as supreme in one's life, repentance upon transgression, love." Forest joined the conversation for the first time.

'Shonya took up the discussion. "And as the being lives in God's presence, the Godhead provides ability or strength to live according to God's directives, as the Cutezarians put it. I assume from these talks that, although the society as a whole has not broken the covenant, the Cutezarians do transgress on an individual level. Did I understand they still remove themselves from society if they 'transgress'?"

"That's what I believe I heard," Oliver answered.

"But can individuals sin without the society breaking the covenant?"

"Our own ancient people had rituals for redemption of sin, didn't they?" Jeff asked.

Listening to the discussion Craig took several deep breaths and began to feel he could continue. The Cutezarians finished their discussion and turned their attention back to Craig.

Getting up, he whispered to 'Shonya, "I think this is my cue."

"Please continue," Ventez requested.

With a quick prayer for wisdom, Craig picked up the narrative. "When the example of how a relationship with God could be if humans did not turn from God failed, the Godhead chose to demonstrate a continuing interest in a relationship with humans.

"Let me go back and give you some background. Your ancestors saw early humans sacrificing the hearts and blood of others to please the deities they thought ruled the world. The One God taught us that was not acceptable.

"I'm going to use the pronoun 'he'. It solves some problems. We don't really believe God is a male being. God is a spirit, neither male nor female." He paused. "I'm sorry. Our language is sometimes difficult. We insist on assigning gender to almost everything."

His listeners smiled at him as if they had already discovered the difficulties of the language. He returned the smile and continued. "God taught the chosen people to sacrifice animals instead of people. That practice continued many years. Abraham and his offspring, the chosen people, sacrificed animals.

"Then God sent a special representative who was his own offspring to become part of the human experience.

378

We spoke of this yesterday, but let me expand. God's son came as a human baby and was, in an incomprehensible way, both God and human: God reaching out to humans.

"But the desire to transgress and go our own way had grown strong in us. Although many believed the special messenger was from God, many also rejected him and sought to destroy the person we refer to as Jesus the Christ.

"Jesus was the human name of God's Son, and the Christ was a title denoting the part of the God-man who revealed God to humanity. Jesus Christ allowed his enemies to put him to death. The shedding of his blood ended the requirement for each person to make a blood sacrifice.

"In order to make right our relationship with God, each individual must first accept that Christ was sent of God. We accept the blood Christ shed and the sacrifice it stands for is the instrument God chooses to use to mend our relationship when we transgress.

"We begin to understand the depth of love that prompted God to want to make our relationship with him work. Finally, we must admit we need the sacrifice in our lives because we have transgressed. This is often the hardest part. It means giving up our own image of ourselves as our own final authority."

"When we express regret for transgressing, God applies Christ's sacrificed blood to our acts, and makes right our relationship with him. This is one of the great mysteries of our relationship with God."

He paused as his listeners discussed. When finished, he continued.

"Our relationship with God is one of the heart instead of regulations and laws. The way we live is very similar to the way the people who followed God's directives when they were required to give individual sacrifices lived. But the motivation comes from the love God has put inside us instead of having to follow prescribed laws applied from the outside."

He stopped, suddenly aware of how long he'd been speaking. Sitting on the end of the table with a sigh, he realized how very tired he was. But watching the Cutezarians spurred him on.

"Please, just a little while longer," he prayed.

Turning their attention from Craig, the Cutezarians held a private conference. Finally, Dortec activated his translator and spoke. "The Human experience is different from that of the Cutezarians. When the individual transgresses, withdrawing from daily life shows regret. This follows the Ancient Ones' ritual of isolation. The isolation continues until the one who transgressed has repented, to use your concept, and reestablished the relationship with the Spirit of All Things. There are times the isolation lasts many time periods and, because of the loss of daily productivity, is done at great cost to the one who transgresses. The times it does not last as long, the cost is not as great. In either case, the transgressor must withdraw."

The speaker stopped to allow the humans time to understand the translation. Then he added, "Yet we have come to the conclusion the one you call God is the same Spirit of All Things whose directives we follow."

Craig looked up in surprise, and then smiled at 'Shonya and the Captain. "We had also come to the conclusion you worship the same One God we worship."

Humans and Cutezarians exchanged looks of mutual respect. It was as if every being in the room had been holding their breath, and all at once let it out in one big corporate sigh of relief.

Craig's suspicion that the Cutezarian's reactions also reflected some humor was confirmed when the box interpreted Dortec's next words. "It is so like each being to see the other as worshiping their own deity instead of each worshiping the One deity of the universe."

"My I ask how the Spirit of All Things was revealed to your ancestors?" Craig asked with a smile.

Another conference. Ventez answered with some hesitancy. "It is recorded. There were those who went apart and spoke to the Spirit of All Things. Very little is known of these mysterious ones. The structures you uncovered were inspired by the stories of those who first withdrew from society and listened to the Spirit of All Things. The Ones-Who-Went-Apart taught others to communicate with The Spirit. Sometime in our history, we accepted it was possible for all Cutezarians to communicate with The Spirit of All Things. It was no longer just Ones-Who-Went-Apart who could communicate with the Spirit."

"Thank you for your answers." Craig bowed slightly.

Captain Brodsky watched Craig sink gratefully into his chair, stretch his legs and drape his arm across the back of 'Shonya's chair. She patted his leg and smiled encouragingly.

The Captain took the floor. "Are there questions you wish to ask about the Chaplain's presentation?" Hearing Craig's tired chuckle, he turned with a frown.

"Sorry, Captain," Craig said with a grin. "But I simplified and compacted it so much, there have to be lots of questions."

Dortec agreed. "There are many questions, but we think it wise to review all the information. We also request permission to use your computer information on your worship of God to further our knowledge."

"Permission granted," the Captain quickly answered.

"We'll establish a link as soon as we return to the ship."

"Good," Dortec answered. "The Chaplain's presentation was complete enough to satisfy us for now. Are there any question you wish to ask of us?"

'Shonya spoke immediately. "You showed us an enactment of an ancient ritual. We attended a Darkness Ritual. Has the purpose of the ritual changed, and what does it mean to you?"

Ventez, the leader of those who meditate, listened to the translator's words twice before she rose and answered. Her reply sent Craig scrambling to his feet. "Do not you also have a Darkness Ritual?"

"Vespers?" he asked incredulously. "Are you telling us your Darkness Rituals are worship services?"

"I do not understand the worship service concept," the metallic voice answered for Ventez. "But this part of the light/dark cycle is put aside for Cutezarians to focus all attention upon the reality of the Spirit of All things and the place the spirit has in each Cutezarian's life. The custom did not originate as a directive from the Spirit of All Things, but began when our ancestors changed from living in the protective holes in the stone wall..."

Craig frowned.

"Caves?" Jeff supplied.

"Okay." Craig nodded.

Ventez didn't finish the original thought, but explained. "Many Cutezarians were damaged beyond survival before they knew the danger of the darkness. Finally they learned to use the illuminating stones in the living structures to interrupt the flow of the storms around the structures for protection during the darkness storms."

'Shonya and Craig exchanged triumphant smiles and the speaker stopped. "We decided your ancestors must have used the stones in this manner," She explained.

The box translated the Cutezarian's sound of approval.

"I'm sorry," Craig apologized. "We didn't mean to interrupt your description of the darkness ritual."

Ventez continued. "Each group who shared a living structure retreated inside at darkness and gathered in the large room on the bottom floor to communicate with the Spirit of All Things.

"As Cutezarians began building living places in clusters of three structures, those who shared the area began meeting in one of the group's structure and began holding it just before darkness so they could return to their own structures in safety. Then they began building the clusters closer together. Finally, they built one structure just for the ritual. We now have protective coverings over our walkways, and we have the gatherings after the darkness. Our large cities have several ritual structures like the one your scientists visited. It was after the time Cutezarians began living in what you call communities the meditation area you uncovered was built."

"Our scientists could not understand enough of what was said during the ritual they attended to understand its purpose." Craig said thoughtfully. "But what they described makes more sense now. Thank you for trusting us enough to tell us this." He paused and asked cautiously. "Was there ever a time recorded when your ancestors worshiped anything or anyone but the Spirit of All Things?"

Ventez answered with another question, as Craig's had no meaning for her. "What else is worthy?"

'Shonya joined Craig and spoke to him and the Cutezarians at the same time. "If they couldn't - you - can't imagine anything else worthy of worship, imagine the horror and extreme reaction your ancestors had when they returned to earth to find the Indians of South America sacrificing other humans and worshiping strange gods of the air, of the earth and animals?"

The Cutezarians listened, thought, and then asked the box to repeat her statement. Suddenly Ventez seemed to understand. She also addressed both humans and Cutezarians.

"We have often wondered what was so bad that would make them forever cease their directed activity. It could have been a combination of what they saw and the knowledge they had acted contrary to the directives of The Spirit of All Things."

"This may have been the beginning of the promise they made to The Spirit of All Things," Dortec mused.

"Which was?" the Captain prompted.

Dortec hesitated. "I believe we can tell all," Ventez encouraged.

Dortec nodded. "It is recorded they promised the Spirit of All Things if they were released from going to other places, they would make sure all Cutezarians knew of the Spirit's existence. It is recorded the Spirit of All Things granted them a release from the directive. However, it was not permanent. Our ancestors were directed to maintain and improve the ability for interplanetary travel. They did that. And so has all generations including the present. The Spirit of All Things promised a sign would appear. At that time, the Cutezarians will resume travel and awaken in other beings the awareness of the existence of the Spirit of All Things."

The humans responded according to their own anxiety reactions: Craig paced massaging his stomach, 'Shonya stood very still, concentrating, and the rest of the group rose to their feet in anticipation.

Ventez left her seat, stood on the stairs, and addressed the humans in front of her. The lower pitch of the translator's metallic voice reflected her earnestness. "We, after much study and discussion, have come to realize the

Spirit of All Things has led you here. The interaction between us has convinced us you are the sign. We are beginning preparation to resume the journeys of our ancestors. We already have a course plotted for the far reaches of our universe."

The room was silent. Everyone remained frozen in place.

Captain Brodsky found words first. "We are the sign? Why?"

Ventez spoke slowly, thoughtfully. "You are descendants of the last beings our ancestors contacted. Your home is the place of our ancestors' failure. We have also learned from you that the Spirit of All Things follows a plan that is not ours. Our mission will be to awaken the knowledge and prepare other beings for the Spirit of All Things' revelation. We will no longer be afraid of what follows our visit. We will leave all that follows to the Spirit of All Things."

'Shonya was suddenly filled with excitement. "Will you allow us to view your preparations?"

"We would be honored," Dortec answered.

After wandering across the room, Craig leaned against the far wall, arms crossed on his chest. Overwhelmed, he lowered his head. "God, am I hearing correctly? We are the instrument?"

"Craig?" Jeff laid a hand on his crossed arms. "You doing okay?" Craig was perspiring, pale and exhausted.

"You can answer that for yourself, can't you?" Craig looked up and brushed his hair back with a tired grin. "But don't you dare make me leave yet."

"Sorry I asked. I'll call in orders. You finish here, and don't argue with me about spending the night..."

"I know, in sickbay. If you won't rush me now I'll gladly trade this for one more night in sickbay." Without waiting for an answer, he pushed away from the wall. "And can we see if I can do this without medication."

He indicated the injection rod the doctor held. "I'm starting to feel fuzzy around the edges."

'Shonya and the Captain made arrangements to observe the space travel preparations and returned to their seats as Craig returned to address the Cutezarians.

"As you said earlier," he started. "There are many questions but, also like you, we need time to understand your revelations before proper questions can be asked." He stopped. "We, I, am overwhelmed to be the sign from the Spirit of All Things. We do not consider ourselves worthy of being the instrument of God. Yet we know, just as God is using you to draw us closer to him, the Spirit of All Things can use us in a beneficial way to you. Still, we are, humbled. Does that translate?"

He was suddenly dizzy, unable to think. Brushing his hair back, he leaned against the short, stone wall between him and the Cutezarians.

Worried, 'Shonya left her seat and laid a hand on his back as she joined him.

"It translates."

Craig heard the answer from Dortec in the distance.

"Transport, beam Chaplain Lea directly to sick bay. Now!" Dr. Keal's voice also seemed far away.

"Wait!" Craig suddenly reached for 'Shonya, addressing the Cutezarians, "Did I get it right? You are resuming the journeys of your ancestors?"

"The leaders from the city that kept our technology updated submitted a plan after our last meeting,"

Ventez answered. "What we debated about was whether or not to tell you."

Craig leaned against the wall and took 'Shonya's hand. "I had to make sure I got that right before I left. Dortec, the people of earth invite you to visit us again if ever the Cutezarians return to that part of the galaxy."

"That work has been finished long ago," Dortec smiled. "I doubt we will be asked to the visit you again. But as our ancestor's visit to your planet changed your history, so has your visit here changed ours."

"We are pleased," Craig answered for them all.

"Craig, quit stalling," Jeff insisted.

"Oh, all right," he grumbled. And gathering 'Shonya into his arms, he touched his comm button. "Cooper, two for sickbay."

## *Read the second adventure of the M. Curie Discoveries*
## The Twins of Zae

By Jo Bower

*M. Cur*ie's presence is requested by the Monarch of Zaetheria because she intercepts Craig Lea's digital copy of Dorinda Brodsky's novel as it is being transmitted to him.

Dorinda's novel, Monarch of Zaetheria, tells the story of the Zaes. This is a society dominated by male twins. But Vantheria knows she is the female half of mixed twins. Her twin is male. Yet, mixed twins aren't supposed to exist. She and her twin are the only mixed twins on Zaetheria. As she searches for answers, she discovers layer upon layer of ancient secrets, deceptions, and beliefs.

The first half of The Twins of Zae is a novel within a novel. The reader experiences the Zaes as Chaplain Lea reads Dorinda's book. However, he keeps getting distracted by daily life aboard the USS M. Curie, a marriage, computer glitches, and graduation of the students aboard the ship.

The action of the book changes as the Curie arrives at Zaetheria and interaction with the Monarch Vantheria, her twin and people, and the humans changes how they all view belief the God of the Universe.